For the nans who do it all over again.

THREE PART HARMONY

HOLLEY TRENT

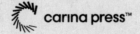

carina press™

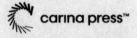

carina press™

ISBN-13: 978-1-335-21585-7

Three Part Harmony

Copyright © 2019 by Holley Trent

Recycling programs
for this product may
not exist in your area.

www.CarinaPress.com

Printed in U.S.A.

THREE PART HARMONY

Chapter One

As the youngest son of a media-hogging firebrand senator, Raleigh McKean had been stepping out of vehicles straight into bullshit for more than thirty years. With his father's distinctive forehead, red hair, and conspicuous height, it was impossible for him to blend in. Even when people didn't recognize him for his association with the man who'd introduced the controversial Barnes-Wilkins bill, Raleigh could rarely go anywhere and expect that he could kick his feet up and relax. Travel hadn't been enjoyable for him since the first time his mother had pushed him and his siblings onto a rally stage on the first stop of the stump tour. He'd been eight and his parents had threatened unspecified punishments later on if he didn't smile.

He didn't have to smile anymore, which was a good thing. There was nothing amusing about the unforeseen mission that had him scrambling to LaGuardia on a weekday morning to catch a flight to LA. After all, it wasn't every day a man learned that his best friend had lost her mind and started shacking up with a married man.

And his wife.

Or maybe Raleigh had gotten that wrong. Maybe

Stacia was shacking up with the married *woman* and the man was a bonus prize.

Either way, the shit had the potential to be as bad for Stacia's career as it was for Raleigh's health, and he didn't know if he'd be able to mitigate the fallout. He hadn't been able to eat more than soup for days. He hadn't been so stressed since that time his father decided he ought to run for president.

"Woman's gonna make me stroke out," he murmured to the driver as he squeezed into a ride-share sedan outside LAX.

There was another rider in the vehicle, headed the same way, and there he was, raving like a loon.

Typical.

Fortunately, the rider was not a woman, and therefore did *not* take offense to Raleigh's disordered prattling.

The driver dropped him off in front of the modest Hollywood estate Adrien and Dara Valliere had recently rented.

After double-checking the address, Raleigh hauled his bag up to his hip and marched toward the gate, squaring his shoulders as if he were headed into battle. He could never guess what he was going to get out of a confrontation with Stacia. She was a thin-skinned author who didn't court opinions, but he was special and he offered them whether she wanted them or not. He was not only the publicist Athena Publishing had assigned to her more than six books ago, but the vicious wretch's closest friend.

Or so he'd thought.

She hadn't said one word to him about her scandalous goings-on with the Vallieres, and he'd slept under the same roof with all three of them more than once.

Suddenly, standing there on that yellow brick driveway shaded by so many towering palms, it dawned on him that their cagey behavior around him in recent weeks wasn't due to mercury being in retrograde. All along, the trio had been trying to disguise their nascent romance, and for good reason. Even the slightest whiff of impropriety would get the Internet hate machine cranked into full frenzy mode.

"Well played, Stacia," he murmured as he stabbed the call button from the sidewalk. Then he grunted with appreciation, running his hand along the cast-iron rails of the gate. "At least the place is secure."

He had to give her credit for that. It'd taken a small miracle to get the woman to build a fence around her property back in Richmond. Whether Stacia wanted to be or not, she'd earned a respectable degree of fame. She wrote mystery books women wanted to read, and her series was at that very moment being adapted into a television version.

Unfortunately, the man playing the charming hero happened to live on the other side of that gate. With his wife.

Raleigh stabbed the button again and peered at the camera. "I know you see me. I heard the speaker click and the little light turned on thirty seconds ago."

A very Stacia-sounding sigh emanated from the speaker box. "What are you doing here, Raleigh? I didn't know any of your other authors were in the area. Athena normally sends out emails when there are official signings."

"No one's here. I'm in LA on my own dime." Around four thousand dimes, actually—and that price was for a one-way ticket. He wasn't made of money, especially since his rent check had just cleared.

"Oh? Why's that?" she asked.

Grinding his teeth, he took a deep breath in through his nose and moved closer to the camera. "Open the gate, sweetie, so I don't have to make a scene in front of Adrien Valliere's driveway. The last thing you need is for a ranting redhead to show up in living color in a center spread in one of those trashy gossip magazines with a so-called reporter speculating wildly on why he's there."

"And for that ranting redhead to be identified as one of the McKean spawn."

"Oh, so you *do* understand how this shit works, then."

"I'm going to pretend that sarcasm wasn't for me and that you're just cranky because you haven't eaten."

"You know I'm right, Stacia."

The paparazzi loved Adrien Valliere. They'd been swarming him since the earliest peeps had gotten out about his involvement in the adaptation. He was a gen-uinely nice guy and people were fascinated by him be-cause he'd been on the covers of so many of Stacia's books. They were finally getting a chance to see him move and talk. But the problem with that was that he had an extraordinarily private wife who was just try-ing her hardest not to get entangled in his fame. That was why they'd moved to the gated property in the first place. People had been starting to stalk that poor woman and, unlike Stacia, she didn't have the heart to shame them into knocking it off.

There was a buzz and the pedestrian gate gave an inward lurch.

Raleigh scurried through and hit the button to reverse the swing in case there were any cameras following him. Because he'd been lying low and having a relatively boring, unproblematic existence, he hadn't been splashed in a tabloid for a few years and he wanted to continue that trend.

Stacia appeared from the north side of the property, picking her way barefoot up the stone path. Her unbound, wiry hair was more nest than style and her eyes were covered with dark shades.

"Late night?" he quipped.

She cleared her throat and canted her head in the direction she'd come from. Without moving her lips, she said, "I'm staying in the pool house. Remember?"

"Yes, that's the lie you told me. It was a lie, right?"

"Shut up and keep walking."

"Fine."

He kept his mouth shut until they were safely ensconced in the cute little guesthouse and had the door closed. Then he cast his gaze about and scoffed. There was no furniture, except for a single sofa and a couple of bar stools at the kitchenette counter. The place had the sort of stale smell that usually permeated unlived-in domiciles. Of dust and unflushed drains.

Stacia drew the curtains shut. "So…"

"Yes. *So.* Given the close nature of our relationship, I won't beat around any bushes. What the hell are you doing?"

Turning to face him, she took off the sunglasses and blinked. She had deadline bags under her dark brown eyes, and he was glad. She deserved them for giving him the stomach ulcer he could feel forming.

"Don't play that innocent ingénue role with me," he snarled when she did that Bambi blink again. "I know better. Spit it out. My job is to keep your name on people's minds so you sell more books, but it seems you've found *another* way to make people think about you."

She rolled her eyes. "Fine. I'm sleeping with the Vallieres."

"Such a quaint way of putting it." He dropped his bag at his feet and emitted an impassioned snort. "You're doing a little more than sleeping with them, in my estimation."

She sucked her teeth. Shrugged. That was the Stacia he knew—the one he kept on a short leash at public events. She was much more sociable in text than in person, but he'd found that that was typical of Athena's authors. They weren't people-people.

"Okay. Yeah. So. How'd you figure it out? What'd I miss?"

"Oh, just little things, like how sometimes you or Dara will forget to log out from the other's email account before sending me something. Only takes me thirty seconds to figure out the writer's style doesn't match their name, by the way. People who aren't intimate don't let other people mess around on their computers." Grimacing, he amended, "Actually, it's probably an A-plus plan not to let people you're banging have access to your computer, either. Remember? I learned that lesson with Allison."

Allison had been the closing bookend in Raleigh's long period of serial monogamy. She'd been the complete package—gorgeous, intelligent, and socially conscious.

She'd also been a political operative who thought he wouldn't mind her passing on tidbits about Raleigh's estrangement from his father to her boss.

Raleigh had been at work staring down a nasty deadline and his phone had buzzed to inform him that he'd backed up his computer to the cloud.

He most certainly had not.

The worst part was that she'd played dumb about it. She'd reminded him that he shouldn't give away his trust so easily. He'd needed that lesson and he'd been wallowing miserably in it for two years.

"Dara is the singular most trustworthy person on the planet so I don't worry about her having access," Stacia said, "but look. This is complicated."

"Yes, polyamory tends to be by design."

"We didn't plan on this happening," she said with a weary sigh. "You see, one thing led to another, and I didn't tell you about those things because I didn't want you going full Raleigh on me."

It was his turn to stare and blink.

She smiled in that Stacia way with pressed-together lips and mouth twitching at the corners. For her, it was practically a grin.

He could almost trust that she knew what she was doing when she smiled like that, but that wasn't going to stop him from worrying. People were going to judge her and the Vallieres harshly if they found out, and her career wasn't even his utmost concern. Her well-being was. She was his friend, and he loved her in spite of her being ridiculous.

"Oh, hell, you're making that face like someone poured you the wrong wine." She manually uncurled his upper lip with a few indelicate pokes of her fingers. "It's *fine*, Raleigh. I appreciate you worrying about me, but we're very discreet. Those people out there…" She waved her arm demonstrably toward the street, most likely toward the people with cameras waiting for Adrien to return. "They're never going to figure this out because they can't possibly imagine that anything would happen under Dara's nose. She's the sweet one, right? They're always going to make her out to be the wounded party, and she's right here. Obviously, she's not going to miss anything. They all believe that I'm the Vallieres' very good friend, and that makes sense to them. I write the books. Adrien stars in the TV show. I live in their guesthouse when I'm in LA and tell them all the secrets of the upcoming stories."

"You're a side chick to two people."

She let out the tiniest titter of amusement, put her hands on his shoulders, and gave him a silly little shake. "No, babe, I'm a primary source of entertainment around here. And come on. The only reason you figured out the scheme was because you have unprecedented access to all three of us. No one else does. Honestly, you should be flattered."

He was. A little.

Raleigh may have been the head-down, walk-fast type, but Stacia had a knack for making her fans think they knew everything about her when in truth, she only fed them chaff. She was intensely private.

"Who all knows?" he asked.

Stacia was going to do what she wanted, but Raleigh needed to settle his nerves about the situation. If the circle of knowledge was small, they might be able to keep the truth sheltered.

"My parents and Adrien's parents."

"You told your *parents* and not me?" he asked with more than a little indignation. She rarely even answered the phone when her parents called. She answered for Raleigh by the third ring.

"I was going to tell you, but I hadn't figured out how yet. With our parents, it was sort of a necessity because they like to know where their babies are at any given time. Obviously, with Dara being estranged from her family, there was no need to tell them anything. My parents honestly don't care because they thought I was going to die a spinster, and this is…" She snorted and gave her red eyes vigorous rubs with the heels of her palms. "Well, this is *far* from that. Adrien's parents are crunchy hippie Cajuns. They're fine with the arrangement as long as our relationship is a closed one. Even they have their limits."

"Huh." He still couldn't believe it. The little Grinch he couldn't get out of her house for a signing, without resorting to savage deceit, had played nice enough to worm her way into a ménage.

The Good Lord was almost certainly humbling Raleigh in that moment by teaching him the limits of his intelligence. The shit didn't make sense.

"Yeah. So." She gave him another little shake. "Any other questions? Hate to rush you, but I was supposed to send feedback out on a script for the TV show today, and it looks like it's going to be a doozy. The screenwriter took some liberties. Normally I try to be hands off with the show, but they can't rewrite my characters' traits without me noticing."

"So, you're dismissing me?"

"No, silly!" She bumped his thigh with her hip and rubbed her eyes again. "Of course not. Stick around. Adrien's working, but Dara's here. She's working, too, though. Trying to get my inbox down to zero. If you can entertain yourself until dinnertime, we can promise to be much more interesting after that."

Raleigh drummed his fingertips against the sides of his arms. His goal hadn't been to bust in on the threesome and be the bad guy. He'd only wanted Stacia to know that she wasn't being as discreet as she thought she was, but that wasn't true. She was perfectly discreet, but Raleigh's tuning was calibrated a bit differently than the general public's. Stacia was the one person on a planet of billions who'd seen his foundation and all the bare wood studs that held up the roof that was his personality, and yet she still loved him anyway.

Of course he'd notice if something was off, even if no one else would.

He raked a hand through his travel-flattened hair and shook his head. "Okay. I'll leave you to work. I'll catch up with you later, I suppose. I booked a one-way ticket not knowing how long I'd be here. I need to try to get a ticket back to New York for tomorrow, and I suppose I can find some other way to entertain myself in LA for a few hours, right?"

"If you can't find something to do here, then where can you?"

"Exactly."

"Use Dara's car, if you want." Stacia was already shuffling toward the door. "She won't care."

"Thanks, but I can just call for a ride. I hate driving in LA."

She shrugged and passed through the open doorway. "Suit yourself. Keep me updated. My cell's on."

Stacia left him to his own devices with no further pleasantries.

Raleigh jammed his hands into the pockets of his slacks and stared at the spot where she'd been standing.

Typical.

He'd flown three thousand miles to save someone who hadn't needed saving.

It could have been worse, though. He could have crossed the country to support someone who'd never return the favor for him. He'd been systematically pruning people like that out of his life for more than a decade. He was used to people trying to use him for access to more powerful or more important individuals. His father, mainly, and that said a lot about them.

Stacia had been the only person he'd met in recent years who'd not only recognized him on sight—"Oh, God. You're that polka-dot-tie guy's son."—but who hadn't interrogated him about his past privileges. In fact, when she'd been formally assigned to his author roster, he hadn't even been able to get her to respond to his emails.

That'd been the basis of an honest friendship, to him—him doing the chasing for a change, and her knowing whom he had access to but tuning out any mention of it, just like he did.

Groaning, he headed to the bathroom with his bag in tow. He needed a shower and shave to feel like himself again, and then he'd deal with travel plans and figure out what he'd do with himself for a day. He was in the land of sunshine and excess. The sun, he avoided by virtue of being a natural ginger. The excess, though— that, he could appreciate.

For a day, anyway.

Then it was back to business as usual. Books didn't sell themselves, after all.

Chapter Two

Plopping into his purchased seat at the Hollywood Bowl, Raleigh peered into his wallet at his credit card for hints of imminent melting, but the plastic remained structurally sound. He was going to have to transfer funds from savings to cover that whopper of a bill when it came, but it'd be worth it. He'd been wanting to see Rock Paper Sinsters live since college, but senators' sons didn't let themselves get seen watching bands who had famous proclivities for stripping down to their underwear between songs. It was their shtick. Everyone knew that, but supposedly, there was such thing as propriety.

At thirty-eight, Raleigh was nearing a stage where he was giving far fewer fucks about propriety. The band was still amazing after so many years, and he didn't know when he'd ever have a chance to see them again. Their touring future was up in the air, and Raleigh had bought a seat close to the stage. It'd been spendy, but it was either that or a slice of bench up in the nosebleeds.

Intermission came far too quickly and Raleigh mourned that the halfway point had already arrived. Still, as concertgoers hovered around him, he took a moment to check his messages and send a text to Stacia that he was going to miss dinner. He also scrolled through emails from work. There was nothing urgent happening. No major book launches imminent, or even any minor ones. Athena had recently merged with another house and they'd put a moratorium on August releases so they could streamline their processes. He was ahead of the game on everything else he needed to do and had left some work for his assistant to finish up.

He hated leaving the office, even when there weren't a million fires to put out. If he wasn't there to answer questions, instead of emailing him, people would go looking for the *other* fiction publicist, Everley, as though they were interchangeable.

They weren't, and it was obvious to him that the scheming witch had been trying to absorb some of his list since her first day. She'd come by her job without having a single qualification for it, and likely assumed she could collect a few of his bigger authors with the same ease.

There was no doubt that the moment he gave her an inroad, she'd snatch what was his and run. He worked his ass off for the authors on his list and like hell if he was going to let a woman who'd landed a rare publishing job via nepotism reap the perks of his decade of effort.

"Phones are a cancer," the man seated at his right said.

Curious, Raleigh shifted his gaze toward him.

He wasn't even looking at Raleigh. He had his forearms propped atop his knees and was staring ahead at the empty stage.

Certainly, he'd been sitting there all along, but before that moment, Raleigh hadn't paid any attention to him. He'd been in such a hurry to find his seat before the warm-up band took the stage.

Raleigh couldn't see his face. A sheet of limp inky hair curtained the side. Hadn't been washed in days, probably. Some people claimed their hair styled better a day or two after shampooing, but Raleigh wasn't one of those people. Black soap and a hot blow dryer were two of his dearest friends.

"A cancer," the man repeated.

He was wearing a long tweed coat that hadn't been in style since the midsixties, and even then, only with certain Madison Avenue types. The cuffs were frayed, and there were buttons missing. The temperatures may have been falling at night, but they wouldn't be cold enough to justify the tent he was wearing. His build was too slim for the coat. Perhaps it'd been a thrift store find and he'd really loved that plaid pattern.

Raleigh grimaced. People who dropped nearly a thousand bucks on VIP-section concert tickets tended to prefer bespoke.

And they brushed their hair.

The man rotated one of the many rings piled on his left fingers and turned his head toward Raleigh. Dark sunglasses. No visible eyes.

Gorgeous tan skin, though, despite the distraction of his uneven shave.

Wide mouth. Full lips.

Raleigh's gaze lingered there for longer than was polite, but his fascination couldn't be helped. Lips were his weakness, and had been since high school when a lacrosse player named Devin Williker had cornered him and informed him at extremely close range that Raleigh would be taking Devin's sister to the fall formal. Devin had the lips his little sister *should* have been born with, and perhaps he knew it. He wouldn't have licked them when he realized Raleigh was staring if he didn't. He wouldn't have laughed and leaned in even further to whisper, "Sorry, McKean, I'm already taken," before walking away.

Raleigh had never seen a more beautiful mouth on a man until that very moment.

"They should bring back pay phones," the stranger in the coat said. "I'll call you when I fuckin' feel like it, you know?"

His voice had the kind of growly quality to it that reminded Raleigh of past nights of consensual depravity and the rough mornings that followed.

It'd been ages. Depravity was easier when the actors were anonymous, and Raleigh couldn't feel completely anonymous anymore. He'd been burned too many times.

But the visceral memories of those old wounds inflicted by Allison and the mistakes before her didn't quell the desire to chase and win and claim. To touch those lips with the pads of his thumbs and hold them there until they parted and moans escaped from between them.

Fuck, I'm hard up.

Swallowing a self-deprecating laugh, Raleigh forced his stare downward toward his phone, because he couldn't risk his imagination running any wilder than it already was. Respectability was his shield. The media ignored him when he was boring.

But he was only human, and humans hadn't yet evolved to completely overcome their harmful temptations. He looked at the stranger again, gaze immediately tracking to that sumptuous bottom lip.

"You don't carry a phone?" Raleigh asked, struggling to keep his tone level and normal in spite of his heart's sudden racing. "What if someone needs you?"

The odd man didn't immediately respond. He just kept staring at Raleigh, or at least, Raleigh thought he was. It was difficult to tell with the dark shades. After a minute, and a jostle from his other neighbor returning to her seat, he said, "I guess I have a phone."

"You guess?"

"I didn't buy it."

"Oh. I see." Raleigh chuckled, somehow managing to keep his focus on the opaque dark lenses. He needed to be able to see through them. Eyes said everything. Mouths lied. "You're a Luddite. I don't see how it's possible for anyone to be one nowadays."

"Don't get me wrong. I like tech. Wireless this and that. Guitars and televisions. I just don't like phones. I don't like being at people's becks and calls."

"You could just not answer."

The man snorted, turned forward, and fidgeted his rings some more.

Raleigh would have been content to let the conversation peter out so he could get back to his phone and ignore his wicked urges to do reckless things like flirt or touch. He *was* at a number of people's beck and call, even during the hours when he wasn't contractually obligated to be. Adulting was a scam.

"What do you do?" Raleigh's new friend asked.

"What? For a living?"

The man grunted.

"I work in publishing." Raleigh had never been able to easily explain his job in a compact sentence. His job was one of the sorts that he had to give a brief overview for, before launching into a few more sentences of detailed explanation. He wasn't in the mood, though. "I get books in front of the readers who want to read them."

If the guy was enticed at all by the revelation, he didn't show it. He didn't move a millimeter.

"Pay's okay," Raleigh murmured, gaze falling to that mouth yet again. He closed his eyes against the sight.

Get a grip, McKean.

It hadn't even been that long since he'd last kissed anyone. He'd had a fling during his most recent vacation. Nothing serious. No sparks, but he'd scratched the itch.

Or so he'd thought.

"And I get to stay behind the scenes for the most part," Raleigh muttered.

"How does one get into a job like that?"

"If you're asking if I went to college thinking I'd get a job in the publishing industry, no."

The honest truth was that Raleigh had gone to college doing anything that wouldn't make people immediately think he was going to follow in his father's footsteps. He avoided classes on law and policy, and even the interesting sociology ones that called to him. He'd heavily stacked his schedule with coursework in the sciences until he learned that science was political, too. By junior year, he'd switched to history. History wasn't always honest, but it taught him when to ask questions. He'd been a skeptic before. His degree only legitimized his curiosity about truth.

"I got into publishing kind of sideways," Raleigh said, opening his eyes and turning his attention to the stage, the venue, the sky—anywhere but at his companion. "Picked up some fact-checking work at a small press. One thing led to another."

"Nice."

"What do you do?"

Again, the guy didn't immediately answer.

Raleigh hated that shit. He hated having his personal business probed and then for people to not expect that turnabout was fair play.

"You're not from here," the man said, sidestepping the question.

Facing forward, Raleigh gritted his teeth. The guitar techs were scurrying about on stage. The show was due to begin again soon.

Thank God.

Any excuse to discontinue the disquieting chat would be a welcome one.

"What gave it away?" Raleigh asked.

"Accent."

"Which one? People who know me say I have at least three."

"Maybe that's what it is. Can't figure it out."

"Living in New York for any period of time does interesting things to speech patterns."

The guy nodded. "Aye. I've heard that."

And there were some interesting things happening with the stranger's speech patterns. Raleigh had always thought he had a pretty good ear but the sounds the guy made didn't fit into any neat accent box. Not quite American or any kind of English, really.

"I do lots of things. Sometimes in New York."

Raleigh raised a brow. "Yeah? What does that mean? People as evasive as you are usually make their money via illicit means."

"Do I look like I have money?"

Suspecting he'd regret it, Raleigh gave him a look

from head to toes. That coat was awful and his ripped black jeans had evidently been through some traumatizing things, but his boots were high end. Burgundy crocodile. Metal-wrapped heels.

He'd seen those boots in a magazine spread during one of his recent bouts of insomnia. When he couldn't sleep, he flipped through magazine pages and let his eyes blear on the pictures until he could no longer keep them open. Those boots had been memorable because they'd evidently been hand cobbled by a retiring Italian elf and built on a magical golden last that was stored in unicorn tears.

That elf had made three pairs.

Raleigh cut the guy a look and hoped he could read the suspicion in it.

"What?"

"You have money or you have a rich patron," Raleigh said.

"Sugar daddy?" His lips quirked.

"Or momma. You're pretty enough, I guess, from what I can see of your face."

The man turned his hands over in concession, but shrugged. "My own money. Can't say I made all of it, though."

"Why's that? Are you so rich that your money makes its own money?"

"Aye."

Raleigh sucked in some air through his teeth and let it out. He avoided the rich ones usually. They were always so demanding. "All righty then."

Raleigh understood wealth. He'd grown up a prep schooler in a neighborhood populated by old money and start-up geniuses. Naturally, he'd never considered *himself* wealthy. His parents were wealthy. He was simply privileged. His financial safety net had been cut off sometime around his junior year of college. Generally, in childhood, he'd been left to his own devices. The press in his university town in Connecticut had afforded him privacy. But eventually, the gloves had to come off. A reporter had identified him outside a bar and had asked him if he shared his father's politics.

He'd told the reporter to go fuck himself.

Truly, he understood that the guy was just trying to do his job, but Raleigh had felt a bit put upon at the moment. He was standing outside a popular gay venue and hadn't exactly been out at the time.

He still didn't know if his father cut him off for being queer or because he hadn't spouted the perfect sound bite for the press. Apparently, Raleigh's response had been a big deal. His father had to issue a press release about it and about how Raleigh was simply "a kid" and that he "didn't think" and that people should "ignore the sensationalism and concentrate on things that really mattered." Raleigh had taken a picture of that statement, and for the longest time, it'd been the screensaver on his phone.

The guy canted his head toward the stage. "You like this band?"

"I should think so, given what I paid for the ticket."

"You can never tell. Some people go where they want to be seen, not where they want to be."

Raleigh was going to argue that point but, ridiculous as it was, there wasn't anything dishonest about it.

"Maybe you're right," he murmured.

At the buzz of his phone, he looked down at the screen and immediately rolled his eyes. There was an email notification from his work account flagged as important.

The sender was his department rival Everley Shannon. The subject line read: Would you like me to take care of this?

Immediately, Raleigh's mind spun myriad possibilities. That she was at his work computer, scrolling through his notes. That she'd taken some calls for him and was trying to take point. That she was, again, discovering new "opportunities" for her authors and asking if he wanted her to include his.

The woman couldn't keep her eyes on her own paper even if she had on blinders and her head bracketed in place.

He opened the message and quickly scanned the tightly written note.

I saw you were out. Crate of early review copies came in for that tie-in book. I can get them mailed out before the weekend if you need me to. Let me know.

-ES

"Need me to," he mocked, tucking the phone away.

"Cancer," his neighbor said.

"I'm starting to agree with you."

"Sometimes people do."

"Just sometimes?"

The man shrugged. "You know how it goes. People don't talk to learn anything. They talk because it makes them feel seen. They don't try to absorb or remember."

"I think that's a hugely overreaching statement."

"My experience." He shrugged again. "People don't

like hearing about it. Look." Suddenly he grabbed Raleigh's arm and leaned forward, pointing at the stage. "That guy right there? See him? In the skateboarding shorts checking the mics?"

"Mm." Raleigh stared down at the hand clenched around his arm, half repulsed by the stolen familiarity in the gesture, and half satisfied. Delighted, even, and he tried to force that thought out of his brain. His hunger for intimate touch was fucking with his common sense. "What about him?"

"Can't hold down a damn job. He's worked for at least six different bands in a year."

"How do you know that?"

"Subscriber. I see a lot of shows. I remember faces."

"Oh?"

He sat back and spun his rings again. "Yeah. Call it a curse."

"Fine. It's a curse."

The corners of his mouth inched up again and Raleigh's gaze followed. "Sometimes people agree with me."

Raleigh filled his lungs and held his breath until his pulse slowed. "I'm starting to see why."

Chapter Three

Raleigh.

That was his name.

He had a face Bruce Engle hadn't been able to forget, and by virtue of his career, Bruce encountered a lot of faces.

Whenever he got a new idea and decided to start a new venture, he did deep dives into research, only taking a break when his body demanded he feed or rest it. He needed to know who all the movers and shakers were. He didn't like waiting around. Bruce had emailed him, he thought. He couldn't remember what publishing house he worked for, but he'd certainly contacted him. He hadn't responded, but apparently, that was the norm. No response meant no.

Raleigh, he mused as the band retook the stage.

Bruce didn't recall the picture on his staff bio page being so flattering, but perhaps that was because the man had been head down at his desk with a phone pressed between his ear and shoulder and was semi-glowering at the camera.

They ought to redo it.

Or maybe it didn't matter to them.

Mattered to Bruce, though. He could take a better picture.

He patted his pockets for his phone and remembered he didn't have it. He actually didn't know when he'd last seen the thing.

Was it silver or black this time?

He couldn't remember. He couldn't even remember the brand, only the configuration. The thumb thing seemed farther from the edge than it'd been on the last phone.

He gave Raleigh a nudge.

Raleigh's brows snapped together as he turned to him.

He had one of those looks—like one of those stuffy and starched dukes on romance book covers, but Bruce didn't see redheads on book covers very often. Red hair perfectly brushed back. Moss-colored eyes. Aristocratic nose. Extremely white teeth. Chiseled chin.

He was starting to suspect that whoever had taken that picture had wanted it to be as unflattering as possible.

How gauche.

"What brand is the phone with the thumb thing? The circle?"

Raleigh's eyes narrowed.

Bruce tended to evoke that response a lot.

"The thumb thing?" Raleigh asked.

"Yeah, you tap it." Bruce demonstrated on his wrist. "Like this."

"I think they pretty much all do that now."

"Oh." He slumped. That was going to bother him—not knowing what it was.

He'd figure it out later, though. He wouldn't be able to sleep if he didn't.

"Let me have yours."

"My phone?" Raleigh asked.

Bruce extended his hand.

"What for?"

"Want to take a picture. I don't have my phone."

Raleigh reached slowly for the phone, casting a speculative look in Bruce's direction.

Bruce got that a lot, too. He couldn't say he was used to it. It was just the way things were.

He worked out how to open and focus the camera and pointed it toward Raleigh.

"What are you doing?"

Bruce took the picture, tapped the shot to view it, and nodded appreciatively.

Much better.

He handed Raleigh back his phone, and for some reason, the man seemed to deflate with relief. That was *not* a common reaction. Usually, people didn't breathe easily until Bruce had walked away. He was a lot. That was what his sister always told him.

"You should use that one," Bruce told him.

"For what?"

"Everything from now on. I like your face."

Raleigh laughed. "Oh?"

"Yeah, it's a good face. I'll remember it."

"Like all the others."

"No. Not like them." Bruce hadn't been interested in them.

The band was cranking a familiar baseline that had the crowd whooping and leaning into the act once more, Raleigh included.

Bruce had already been in that audience countless times. Same band. Different venues. They were reliable, but predictable. He already knew what they were going to do.

Raleigh was new.

He was catching the rhythm in his body and letting it back out through his tapping foot.

Bruce peered down at it.

Brogues. He was wearing brogues.

Bruce supposed those were respectable, but he'd always been a poor judge of that. Being in the business he was, he didn't have much experience with respectable. The music industry was full of talented people scrambling to make a buck any way they could and too many people in it lost their souls.

He wasn't going to lose any more of his. Refused to.

Some people thought he never had one to start with—the guys in his own band, for instance. He'd screwed them over, they said.

He didn't understand that.

All he'd done was asked for a little air.

By the time Bruce looked up again, the amphitheater was clearing out around him. Raleigh stood at his side, arms folded over his pressed blue shirt. He was looking at Bruce like he was a vagrant who'd decided to lie down for the night just behind his car.

"I'm not asleep," Bruce said preemptively. "Or drunk or stoned or whatever. I was just thinking."

"For forty-five minutes? In a place this loud?"

"I'm good at that. Lots to think about. Chord progressions and such. I think they mixed up a few. Rhythm guitarist is new."

"I see."

He may have said that he did, but he didn't sound like he did.

Bruce was used to that, too.

Raleigh was starting to leave.

That got Bruce to his feet. He was reaching without thought, grabbing Raleigh's hand and shaking it as though the introductions had already gotten started. "Theo." He nudged his sunglasses up. His eyes were clear and white. He was sure they were. He wanted Raleigh to see. There was nothing wrong with him.

Raleigh was slow to return the shake. His gaze was fixed on Bruce's, lips pressed into a tight line.

Sober as a saint. See?

He never touched that shit. No one ever believed him.

"Raleigh," Raleigh finally said. He extricated his hand from Bruce's, though the gesture seemed to be more out of self-preservation than disgust. Sometimes Bruce came on a little strong. He couldn't help it. When he had ideas, he had to act on them or they'd run away.

Bruce tilted his head toward the nearest exit. "May as well wait a minute. You'll get to your destination at exactly the same time. No use running into the crowd."

"I take it you spend a lot of time watching theaters empty."

It was more fun than waiting in a parking lot with a silent chauffeur. Gary didn't talk to him anymore, beyond good morning, good evening, yes sir, and no sir. Not that he'd ever said much in the first place. He'd gotten weary just like everyone else. They said Bruce talked in circles. That was what his manager told him, anyway. All the bullshit streamed through him before making its way to Bruce.

"Where are you going after this?" Bruce asked.

"Staying with a friend. Gotta head home tomorrow. Need to be back at work by Friday. I've got projects to see to. Packages to ship." Raleigh's lips tightened at that statement.

Bruce was curious about those projects. He wanted to know what they involved and maybe if his name had ever come up, but that wasn't important at that moment. What was important was Bruce wheedling a few more words out of the redhead about anything at all substantive.

He was dead curious about the buttoned-up executive who snarled at his phone and wore brogues to a rock concert.

"Hey. Did you know that it's illegal to lick a toad in Los Angeles?"

Raleigh's brow creased.

Bruce nodded. "Strange but true. Don't go licking any toads. Bad for your criminal record and probably your health. Hey. You know Mel Blanc?"

He couldn't tell how old Raleigh was, but he would have been pleasantly surprised if he recognized the old Looney Toons icon's name. Most people looked forward to the next thing. The future didn't have facts yet. The past had plenty.

"Yeah," Raleigh said. "What of him?"

"He's buried in LA. His tombstone says 'That's All Folks.'"

Raleigh cracked a smile. The creases at the outside corners of his eyes deepened.

Thirty-five. Forty.

Old enough for brogues and belts and tucked-in shirts.

Bruce couldn't remember the last time he'd tucked

his in. His nan's funeral, maybe, and that hadn't lasted for long. He tended to gravitate toward chaos whether he was trying to or not.

There was something irresistibly compelling about Raleigh's brand of orderliness. The erect posture, his careful phrasing, his...*discipline*, perhaps. He was enviably finished in a way Bruce wasn't and likely never would be.

He'd never liked that sort of polish before, but maybe that was because everyone else he knew who bothered to shine their shoes and iron their collars didn't have voices so velvety.

"Does it really say that?"

"Ayeee*eyes*." Bruce cringed. He always lost track of what country he was in. If he devolved to his natural speech patterns, no one would ever understand a word that came out of his mouth. That was what his mother said, anyway. She tried to be kind, but her idea of kindness had been to ship him off to a tiny village in remote Scotland so his grandmother could deal with him.

Patient saint that she was, his nan hadn't dealt with Bruce so much as let him run amok, which was exactly what he'd needed at the time. He'd been sad when that had ended.

His parents had been sad, too, because Bruce hadn't been reformed into the biddable schoolboy they'd hoped for.

No, he'd been messy at four and he was still messy at fourteen when they showed up in their posh car to pick him up. For some reason, their disappointment had pleased his nan. She'd always been enigmatic. She hadn't said one word when they'd returned him right back where he was at fifteen—back to the wild place with all its ewes and geriatric widows who wore tan orthopedics.

"Rest in peace," he murmured, making a hasty sign of the cross.

Raleigh's brows crept together again. Even that act was elegant. He could probably make a thing as crude as spitting look like fine art.

"Hey," Bruce blurted anxiously. "Beverly Hills used to be a farm."

"Really?"

"Mm-hmm. Beans."

"Interesting. Anything else?"

"No. Just lima beans."

Raleigh *almost* smiled. Bruce could tell he wanted to, but he was probably afraid Bruce would keep talking if he did.

Bruce was used to people scurrying away. He never got to the conclusion fast enough. Perhaps, for a change, he'd said something right enough, or short enough.

Or perhaps, Raleigh was simply a more patient sort.

Bruce didn't know many of those. Sometimes, he forgot that those existed.

He shifted his weight, pondering, and slid his sunglasses back up his nose. The past hour with Raleigh was the closest thing to a real date Bruce had been on in ten years, and Raleigh didn't even know he was on it.

Could change that, maybe?

He snapped his fingers, but when no genie appeared to make his wish come true, he opted to take matters into his own hands. Magic was unreliable, anyway.

"Hey."

Raleigh straightened his already-straight belt and glanced Bruce's way.

He had hazel eyes, or something like it. Gray that gradated to brown near the pupils. Enchanting.

"You got more about lima beans to tell me?" Raleigh asked.

"If you want. I could talk all night."

Raleigh really did smile then.

Bruce changed his mind about the picture. He needed a newer new one. A better one with the smile. Bruce liked the smile because it felt personal. Tailored for him, in a way.

"Talk all night. Is that a euphemism?"

"No, unless you want it to be. I'm open either way." Bruce was out of practice with flirtation, if that was even what he was doing. He couldn't tell. Usually, if he wanted someone to go home with him, his name was enough. But Bruce hadn't given Raleigh his name. He'd given him a lie because sometimes lies were more honest.

"Do you sleep with men?" Bruce asked. "Since we're on the subject."

Raleigh's smile vanished.

Shit. I broke him already.

It was hardly a record. Still, Bruce was optimistic that he could turn things around. Raleigh was standing there with his head cocked and brow furrowed. That probably meant he was thinking. Thinking was more positive than fleeing.

Bruce checked his watch. Normally, that amphitheater cleared out in a predictable amount of time. Sometimes, he liked to guess how long it would take and see how close to accurate he was. About eighty percent of the concertgoers had filed out already.

"I like to know upfront," Bruce explained, shifting

his weight. "Saves me angst. Attraction is an energy sucker."

"You're attracted to me?"

It sounded more like a rhetorical statement than a question so Bruce didn't respond.

He didn't know how to explain himself, anyway. Bruce could certainly get a stiff cock just from having the man look at him in a certain way long enough, but at the moment he was more stimulated by the discussion, the reactions, the responses.

Just by having him stand there that long.

Fucking would be perfectly fine, and the more Bruce thought about it, the more he wanted it. Brogues or not, Raleigh looked like he'd be good at it. A man that haughty had to have the pipe-laying skills to back up the attitude. But it wasn't Raleigh's attractiveness that was compelling Bruce, really. It was his attentiveness.

"Don't misunderstand me," Raleigh said. "I'm always flattered when someone shows interest, but people aren't generally so forward."

"Like I said—"

"Yeah. Saves you angst." Raleigh snorted and turned his focus to the stagehands dismantling equipment and set pieces. "I know a little about angst."

"Shifty exes?"

"Those, too."

"You don't pick well."

"You really do speak your mind, don't you?"

"Whether I want to or not."

Raleigh's gaze pivoted back to Bruce. "Yes."

"So, you…"

Raleigh performed a shrug. A graceful one, of course. "Yes."

"Oh."

Oh oh oh oh.

Bruce clapped his hands with triumph and gestured excitedly toward the exit.

It was as though the pesky little id imp in his brain had shouted *"Green means go!"* into his skull to get Bruce moving, and he did. "Shall we?"

"Shall we *what*?"

"Can get a car. I've got a place."

Raleigh laughed then—an honest, genuine laugh, not like one of those dry ones people who were just being polite tended to do. "I think you've skipped some steps. Generally, introductions are made, there's some song and dance meant to assess compatibility, some will-he-won't-he, and *then* we're supposed to pretend we're doing anything but heading out to fuck. You're supposed to ask me if I'd like to go someplace for a drink so we can continue our conversation about the band or something."

Bruce didn't drink, and he didn't see the point of pretending he wanted anything except what he'd stated. He didn't know how to do that. That wasn't a lesson his nan had taught him. Mostly, she'd just taught him when to back off. Usually, he got that right.

"I did say talk, aye? We can talk about the band if you want," Bruce said. "But if you'd prefer, we could just get down to it and come back 'round to critiquing the performance later. It's unavoidable, in my experience."

"This is highly unusual."

Bruce shifted his weight again. Some people could picture how the scales of probability balanced, but he'd never developed that ability. That part of his brain simply wasn't flexible enough. So, he panicked. "Is that a yes or a no?"

"I don't know. I need more information. You could be some sort of predator. How do I know you're well intentioned?"

Bruce scratched his chin. He didn't know if he'd ever call wanting to be forcefully topped well intentioned. That didn't sound right in his head, but he suspected he was getting caught up on nuances that didn't matter. "Are you asking me if I'm harmless?"

"You don't look harmless. You look like you'd drag me into an alley to exsanguinate me."

Bruce grinned. That was a good one. He hadn't heard that one before.

Unfortunately, Raleigh looked like he'd meant it. "How about this? Get out your cancer box and text a friend where you're going. If you don't turn up, they can send in the SWAT team."

"Give me the address."

"Really?"

Raleigh nodded and, as Bruce had instructed, took out his phone.

Bruce rattled off the address and watched him tap it into an open text dialogue. He didn't wait around for him to send the message. He was already headed toward the stairs and motioning for Raleigh to follow.

He usually didn't like going home. He hated being there, where the only noise was noise that he made and nothing talked back.

Solitude was demoralizing, but he didn't have a choice. He could surround himself with people whose sole interest was in squeezing the joy out of him and calling it art, or people who wanted him to write checks for this thing or that thing, or people who wanted to fix him.

Nobody wanted to just talk to him or hold him or fuck him just for the fun of it.

Why would anyone want to go home to nothing night after night?

Chapter Four

"He never responds. Drives me freakin' insane," Everley murmured into her bourbon and cola.

Across the bar booth, her friend Lisa gave her one of those slow nods like she'd heard it all time and time again and she was bored with the complaints.

"Okay." Everley set down her glass and straightened her spine. "I'll stop complaining about him."

"Thank you."

"It's just that—"

"Nope, nope, nope." Lisa wagged a finger in front of Everley's face and then pressed it to Everley's lips. "Shhh. Peace. Be still."

"But—"

"Find a new obsession."

Everley nudged her hand away and harrumphed. "I'm not obsessed."

"You're obsessed."

Okay, maybe a little.

Everley liked what she liked. Unfortunately, with all the fish in the metaphorical sea that was New York City, she'd developed a thirst for the one who always showed up for work meetings a minute after she did so she couldn't sit near him.

She didn't think that slight was entirely in her head. She knew how things must have looked for him. Her father was a major stockholder of the media company that owned Athena and also a vice president of the publishing house. His grandfather had discovered early bestsellers for the house, and so he'd gone into the business with gusto, the same as his father before him. Everley's parents expected the same enthusiasm from her.

Unfortunately, she didn't possess it. She'd tried, but couldn't muster it up.

She'd dropped plenty of clues as a teenager and college student, or at least thought she had. She'd thrown herself into mathematics because that was as far away from publishing and media as she could get.

But despite her noble intentions, she'd still landed there.

One night over dinner with her parents, she'd had a moment of weakness and said too much. *"No one's hiring. I need to work."* The following Tuesday, her father had escorted her into an office at Athena that already had her permanent name placard on the door.

She'd told herself it was temporary and that she wouldn't get comfortable.

Only the first part was a lie.

At some point, she'd have to tell them that she wouldn't be trying to advance through the ranks. She didn't want to be a publisher. No one had ever really asked her what she wanted to be, except Lisa. They'd all just assumed that she wanted to have a part in that legacy.

Selfish or not, she didn't. She still wanted to play with numbers, and troubleshoot why small businesses didn't thrive. That was her dream, but Shannons didn't deviate from the plan, even if the plan was someone else's. *"You were raised for this,"* her father always said.

It was too late to wish for a sibling. Maybe they would have been born with the right heart for being a cog in a big, expensive machine.

"I get it," Lisa said, waving for the waitress.

Jalapeño poppers and two-for-one cocktails were their Wednesday-night tradition. It was the day Lisa emerged from her off-the-grid western New York retreat and rejoined civilization for a while.

"I mean, he's easy on the eyes, I guess."

"You *guess*," Everley said, deadpan.

Lisa shrugged. "Not really my type. And I think you need to learn to develop crushes on men who aren't mean to you."

"He's not mean to me. He ignores me. You know why. Everyone at Athena does that unless they absolutely have to talk to me. They don't trust me."

"All the more reason for you to move on, in my estimation."

Sighing, Everley grabbed the bill before Lisa could attempt to pay it. Lisa's start-up business was in its infancy. She rarely even paid herself yet. For the time being, Everley could certainly afford drinks and appetizers. Eventually, the well would run dry, but still, there were some perks to being a trust fund baby.

"I just think we could click. That's all. We could bond over our pushy fathers."

"Maybe. I think he's too old for you, though, so maybe it's a good thing he treats you like Casper."

"I'm nearly thirty." Everley grimaced. That meant she'd been working at the company for seven years, and a year of that had been in the mainstream fiction imprint. Seven *years* going through the motions. Seven years wasted.

She hated herself for it, more and more by the day.

"How old is too old for nearly thirty?"

Lisa shrugged. "For all I know, he could be thirty-one, but he'd be an old thirty-one."

"That makes no sense whatsoever. How is someone old for their age?"

"I can't explain to you what I can't even explain to myself. He just is. I can sense it."

"You've only met him once—at that company cocktail party last year."

"Once was enough. At first, I thought he just had a stick shoved too far up his ass. That may still be true, but that's not his only issue."

"Conversations with you are always so enlightening."

Lisa flicked the ends of her dreads and gave Everley the same dark-eyed "Oh, sweetie" stare she'd been giving her since their freshman year at Columbia. From the very start, Lisa had been helping her unscrew her head from her ass.

"Fine," Everley huffed. "I won't bring him up again."

"I believe you."

The waitress swooped over and grabbed Everley's credit card.

"You won't bring him up, but I'm sure I'll have to because you'll be sad, and I'll have to ask you why."

"I'm not sad!" Everley huffed. "Just frustrated."

"I know. I know. You're used to having people pay attention to you without having to work so hard for it." Lisa counted off on her fingers. "You're pretty, you're smart, you're rich, and you can crochet the hell out of a poncho."

"Making fluffy things out of acrylic yarn isn't really much of a draw. It's therapy. My therapist told me to either take up yarn work or exercise to shut down my self-deprecating thoughts. I chose to get back into exercise, but I broke my ankle getting out of the cab right in front of the gym. Remember that?"

Lisa nodded. "Signs are all around us."

"Yeah. Spare me the bougie fairy wisdom. I'm not that drunk."

Everley scribbled her signature on the credit card receipt and pushed away the cash Lisa attempted to foist on her. "I'll get back on that dating app and find a glacial redhead to go out with. Maybe that'll turn me off once and for all."

"Solid thinking, Ev." Lisa bumped her with her hip as they started through the packed bar and toward the exit. "Maybe, if you're lucky, you'll find someone you actually like. Maybe a nice foreign guy who'll sweep you off your feet and insist that you have to move to the Seychelles with him. Certainly, your father could understand you quitting the Shannon publishing dynasty for true love."

"If you truly believe that, you must have missed all that coursework about European aristocracy in college. Money and power are always going to trump love for some people."

"You think you could fall in love with Raleigh?" Lisa asked, chuckling.

"I'm not looking for love," Everley said. "My life is a mess and I'm perpetually unhappy with myself. I just want to be liked."

And possibly be adored while naked, but she didn't think that needed to be said aloud.

Raleigh was never going to see her naked.

He did a damn good job of not seeing her when she was fully dressed.

If only things could be different, she wouldn't have to try so hard to make her coworkers believe she was operating in good faith. If she were them, she'd feel the same exact way.

Her therapist had told her to just pick a time to leave and make a plan.

She wasn't ready yet, but every cynical response from her coworkers—or lack of response, in the case of one in particular—pushed her closer.

She wasn't a failure. She'd never been meant for the work.

For whatever reason, she never seemed to remember that when she needed to.

Chapter Five

Like hell was Raleigh going to broadcast his where-abouts to Stacia. He pretended he'd reached out to some-one just to keep Theo honest, but he didn't really want to have to explain to his friend of so many years that he was late because he had a particular kind of itch to scratch.

He was getting more and more curious about the person he'd be scratching that itch with as their taxi crawled into an exclusive, upscale neighborhood.

Theo peered out his window and fidgeted with his coat buttons.

Raleigh watched the meter. "Sorry to ask, but, are we going the right way?"

"Yeah."

"Okay. I see, and…" He glanced at the expensive abodes they passed and wondered how *anyone* could afford to live there. Those houses made Buckingham Palace look like a kid's school project. Theo claimed to be wealthy, and certainly had the footwear as evi-dence, but Raleigh knew how easy it was to make peo-ple believe what they already wanted to. Politics had taught him that.

"You somehow have access to this place," he murmured, choosing his words carefully.

"Yeah. Still haven't decided if I'll keep it."

"The access?"

Theo turned to Raleigh in a hurry, black brows shooting up over the rims of his sunglasses. "No, the house. You think I should keep it? You know anything about investments?"

Raleigh made a concerted effort to correct the sudden rictus on his face. Just that morning, he'd been pondering the splurge of getting his shoes polished. The man beside him apparently didn't care about such trifling expenses. He had unicorn boots and disposable houses.

"Investments?" Raleigh scoffed. "In general, I let someone else handle those for me, not that my assets are all that astounding. I've got a bit of spare change put away for retirement and a couple of stocks that I watch. That's pretty much it." He could probably do better if he got a roommate to split living expenses with, but the idea of sharing a shower with a person he wasn't sleeping with made him shudder.

"Is it fun?"

"Is *what* fun?"

"Tinkering with it. The money, I mean. Making everything work. Trying to grow it."

Raleigh crossed his legs toward Theo and gave his chin a considering rub. "Such an odd question. I've honestly never given that any thought."

Theo leaned closer, forearms to knees, dark lenses obscuring his complete expression.

Raleigh needed to see it. He wanted to slide the frames off Theo's face and see all of its respective components in one composition. Eyes and cheekbones and lips. Not enough to ask, though. In a way, he was enjoying the mystique. The mystery was fun without being dangerous.

"I've never had to worry about it," Theo said. "Tinkering, I mean."

"Lucky you. Most people are one missing paycheck away from disaster."

"I know. I don't forget. I've seen it."

"Where? On some film you've watched on your home theater's jumbo screen?"

"No. In life. Grew up in a quiet place. That was how my nan phrased it. Quiet, not poor. Nan didn't have money."

"But you do."

"I get it from the other side."

"I see."

"She wouldn't take my money until I told her it was her pay. She deserved it."

"What'd she do for you?"

Yet again, Raleigh didn't think he was going to answer. Theo had leaned away from him and pointed his stare out his window. He twirled his rings around his long fingers. Bobbed his knee. Rhythmically clucked his tongue for an age.

His posture was tense, jaw tight.

Raleigh reached for Theo's wrist in apology. He knew that at times, he was too blunt, too frank. He didn't know this man, Theo, and hadn't wanted to offend him—especially not when he was already so invested in figuring him out. He wasn't like anyone Raleigh had ever met, and that was refreshing. He was too used to people being predictable.

And *terrible*.

He was sick of terrible people.

"What *didn't* she?" Theo finally said, not looking away from the glass.

Raleigh retracted his hand and slid it into the pocket of his slacks. Theo didn't seem like he would have minded if Raleigh left it there, but he was still a stranger. There were proprieties to be observed.

"She's why I can fool most people into thinking I'm all right." Theo grimaced. "At least for a bit. Do you think I'm all right?"

Another odd question, and there was no simple way to answer it. It seemed important that he try, though. Theo had asked from what seemed like a place of genuine need, and Raleigh did have a heart. People just took him for granted too often for him to reward them anymore.

"So far, you have me intrigued," he said carefully. "That's nearly an impossible feat."

Theo grinned, but still didn't turn. Raleigh could see the sides of his cheeks bunching up.

"It is?" Theo asked.

"I'm quite discriminating lately."

"And I won. I got you to go."

Coming from anyone else, the words might have sounded boastful and cocksure. From Theo, though, there was a glimmer of awe as though he were stunned he'd managed it.

It was a refreshing change from Raleigh's usual interactions with men.

"Just up here," Theo told the driver. "Drop us at the gate, yeah? No need to pull in."

"If you say so."

Theo flung some cash at the guy without counting it and pulled Raleigh out of the car. "Come on."

He was inputting the gate code before the cab had even driven off.

Raleigh noticed that the guy was taking great efforts to lean and watch Theo interact with the box, so Raleigh put his body between them to block the sight. "You could be a little more careful," Raleigh said with a laugh.

"Hmm?"

"He was watching you."

"Yeah, they do that."

"Who's *they*?"

The lock clicked. Theo pushed the gate open and nudged Raleigh through. After it'd closed, he tugged him along at a speed Raleigh hadn't tried to approach since that time he'd thought he'd left his phone in a Yellow Cab. He'd been wearing better shoes on that day.

"Christ," he panted. "What's the hurry?"

"Want you to see it. I got you to come out here, so you may as well see it."

"See what?"

"I've got keys somewhere."

"To…the house?" Raleigh had to detach from him and double over to catch his breath. He didn't pretend to be in shape. The reason his clothes fit as well as they did had more to do with his forget-to-eat diet than mindfulness or exercise. He was trying to do better, but finding the time to get to the gym was difficult.

"Yeah, I think I… Oh!" Theo grabbed his arm and got him moving again. "I know where they are this time. Couldn't put them in my pants."

"No, I imagine you couldn't." Raleigh couldn't be

certain how Theo had even gotten his legs into those slim-fitted pants. It was a look Raleigh had never tried to pull off, but it suited Theo's lean build extraordinarily well. He wore his clothes; they didn't wear him—not even that grungy coat.

Finally reaching the side door of the massive stucco estate, Theo shoved his hand into the backside of what was, apparently, a hollow statue of Venus. Out of the goddess's ass came a duo of keys.

Theo picked one and attempted to slide it into the lock.

"Nope."

The other fit.

"Success!" he trilled.

"Your surprise worries me," Raleigh said, even as a laugh escaped him.

"Worries most people." Theo tossed the little key ring on the counter and moved Raleigh along. "I know a place."

"A place to—"

"Not up here. Too open. Too many windows. Can't stand the windows. Makes me feel like they can all see."

Raleigh didn't have a chance to see the windows or much of anything, really. Theo had led him to a carpeted stairway leading downward. Normally, he might have thought, *danger, dungeon down there!* but his overactive curiosity had diluted whatever sense of self-preservation he might have had. He was spawning more and more questions about Theo by the minute. He'd never been so curious about anyone—not even the mysterious authors he worked for without ever meeting in the flesh.

"I did this one myself," Theo said.

"Did what?"

"The room. They wouldn't let me do the others, but I did this one. They didn't care because no one could see it."

"Hell, *I* can't see it."

Raleigh fell over what must have been a sofa arm because he landed on soft cushions with pillows tilted on his face.

Suddenly, a lamp clicked on nearby. "Better? I got that lampshade in Marrakesh. Held it on my lap the whole flight home. They wanted me to stow it, but after all I went through to get…" Letting the story trail off, Theo perched on the coffee table in front of Raleigh and carelessly wriggled off his boots.

Raleigh winced, worrying far more than Theo did, apparently, about the new scuffs being added to the material. They weren't even his style, but he would rescue them and provide them with a better home if need be. He could be generous at times.

As he tried to sit up—he suspected he was sinking even deeper into the plush cushions—he scanned the objects on the tables. There was a lot of loose paper scribbled with notes and symbols he couldn't make out from where he was, various electronics cords, takeout food cartons, and what he thought were guitar picks.

Theo tossed his coat aside and his sunglasses after it.

"I hope those didn't cost you as much as your boots," Raleigh murmured.

Theo looked toward the castoffs as though he hadn't considered the possibility that objects might have values. Then he shrugged. "Soft landing. They'll be all right. So, the lamp. You like it?"

Theo's smile might have been stunning, but compared to what he'd been hiding behind those dark glasses, it may as well have been dishwater.

Shit, his eyes.

Raleigh thought his travel-addled brain had been playing tricks on him back at the amphitheater during that brief moment Theo had lifted his sunglasses. He'd thought the setting sun had been angled in just the right way to make his irises appear to be that yellowish color. They were probably close enough to brown to count as that, but that word wasn't right. He'd probably had a green-eyed parent and a parent with something darker.

With that mane of hair about his face and the silkiness of his movements, he looked like some sort of dangerous cat. Panther, probably.

Raleigh was pretty sure panthers were predators, but he couldn't remember if that meant he was supposed to run or be very still.

"Maids...get here at seven." Theo's gaze tracked to the ceiling. His eyes narrowed in contemplation. "If you're here then, just ignore them. They always have opinions."

"About what?" Raleigh asked, still dazed.

Theo pulled his arms out of his shirtsleeves and then lifted the garment over his head. That golden coloring of his face continued all the way down, apparently. There wasn't a mar or blemish anywhere on him. He was perfectly smooth except for the trail of hair between navel and waistband.

Raleigh wanted to touch him and see if he were as solid as he looked, but he was still trying to remember if one should run from panthers.

"Everything," Theo said, looking at him again. "I didn't hire them. They come anyway."

"Who hired them?"

Theo shrugged. "Mother. Father. I don't know. Maybe someone else. I fire them and then others show up. Can't get rid of them. I don't know why they come if they hate me so much."

"Why do they hate you?"

"Because I make it easy."

If Theo felt any particular angst about the subject, he didn't show it. In fact, he was whistling a jaunty little tune as he unbuttoned his pants and wriggled the snug denim past his hips.

"Efficient, aren't you?"

Theo's smile somehow managed to be both shy and boastful at the same time. How anyone could walk away from him, much less *look* away, Raleigh couldn't fathom. If Theo were a flame, Raleigh would most certainly be a moth. It'd been so long since he'd felt that kind of pull toward anyone that he almost didn't recognize the nerves for what they were: exhilaration.

"Nudity's a natural state, aye? I'm comfortable in it."

Raleigh imagined he would be, too, if he were built like Theo. He'd walk around all the damned time with his shirt open and pants hanging low on his hips.

"You can stay just like that if you want."

"Oh?" Raleigh intoned.

"You mind?"

"I don't know yet. What are we doing?"

Of course Theo wasn't wearing anything under those pants. He tossed them toward his discarded coat and sunglasses and raked his hair out of his eyes.

Raleigh couldn't imagine anyone being able to manage eye contact in such circumstances. There was a beautiful man standing nude in front of him, watching him as though he were waiting for him to recite a particular line, but Raleigh didn't have the script.

He was also still trying to figure out the panther thing.

Theo's smile may have been borderline shy before, but there was nothing tentative about his posture or where he put his hands. He glided his palms up his belly, trailed his blunt fingertips up his chest, and scored around the edges of his nipples.

Raleigh still didn't know what to say or if there was even a point to saying anything. He was fully dressed—buttoned up as tight as he could be—and suffocating in all that fabric.

And he ached. Needed to be let out, but if he did, he'd be giving himself away. He'd be showing how quickly that odd man had affected him and how desperately he needed to do something about it.

"I'm open," Theo said. "Whatever you want."

An incredulous scoff fell out of Raleigh's mouth.

Whatever he wanted would most certainly end with Theo tied to some substantial piece of furniture and Raleigh's spend dripping down his thighs. Obviously, that wasn't a getting-to-know-you sort of happy ending.

"I think," Raleigh said, swallowing thickly. Somehow, he managed to sit up straight in that cloud-soft sofa. "You should be a bit more specific. I can be very creative."

"I invite you to."

God.

Raleigh dragged his hand down his face. He didn't know any man who'd refuse a blank-check invitation when it was so freely given—especially not when they knew they'd probably never see that partner again.

There'd be no morning-after shame. They wouldn't be socializing in the same circles or running into each other at the nearby coffee shop. Raleigh lived on the other edge of the country.

That didn't mean he wouldn't exercise an abundance of caution. They both deserved that.

"Come here," Raleigh murmured.

Theo dropped his hands from his chest and made himself space between Raleigh's feet. "I'm here."

"Closer."

Theo's lips quirked at one corner. "How much closer?"

"Lean in."

Putting a hand at either side of Raleigh's head at the sofa back, Theo folded himself down and met Raleigh's gaze. "Here?"

"Closer."

"Which parts of me?"

"Pick one."

"Is it up to me?"

"Right now, it is."

Theo pulled his lower lip between his teeth and looked askance. Thinking, perhaps.

Raleigh waited. He kept his hands to himself even though his palms were itching and cock was aching to the point of distraction.

With him nude and so near, the musky undertones of Theo's cologne seemed suddenly abloom, enticing and goading, and telling Raleigh that one should be still when a panther was close enough to bite.

Or be bitten.

"Anything I'd like, then?" Theo asked.

"For now."

"Even this?" Theo set one knee on the sofa beside

Raleigh and then the other. He inched forward, glacially slow, wearing a smile that was full of sin.

What kind of sins do you know, panther?

Not desiring to conduct his movements in any way, Raleigh just waited to see where Theo would stop.

He didn't stop until the tip of his cock nudged the placket of Raleigh's still-fastened shirt.

"I like red," Theo said.

"Oh?"

"When I had my own money for the first time, I bought a guitar that was red. Still have it somewhere."

"So, you play?"

Theo didn't respond. He eased onto Raleigh's lap and tilted forward. Their bellies touched. Their lips almost did.

Raleigh notched his fingertips into the corduroy of the sofa. It'd be so easy for him to put his hands on Theo and satisfy his urgent need to touch, but he wasn't entirely certain that was what Theo needed. He seemed too eager to please Raleigh and that sort of generosity often came with attachments.

It wasn't that Raleigh was so averse to attachments. He just never managed to connect with people who wanted the same sorts of attachments as him, and for the same reasons.

If he and Stacia hadn't been so constitutionally similar, he might have pursued her. She was unquestionably trustworthy, but he'd known that the two of them coming together would likely end in some sort of destructive disruption to the space-time continuum. He tried to be a responsible world citizen as much as he could be, and he refused to be responsible for the demise of humankind.

"Sometimes, I like red, too," Raleigh murmured.

"It's my favorite."

"I don't have favorites, but I agree that red has a certain allure at times." Like right then. "Your lips are red."

Theo had been pressing them together. Licking them. "You like them?"

"Yes."

"You want to touch them, then?"

"Yes."

"If you do, will you touch other things, too?" Theo was already tilting his head for the perfect angle for kissing and Raleigh was trying desperately not to roll his hips.

"I don't know. Should I?"

"I don't know about should, but I want you to. I don't care where. Just touch me."

"And then what?"

"Fuck me if you want. You came here. I thought you wanted to."

"I never said I didn't."

"Then why are you so slow?"

"Why are you in such a hurry?"

"I'm always in a hurry. Things change. People change. Minds change. *Please* touch me once before you change your mind."

Raleigh hadn't intended to make him beg, but he'd be a liar if he said the sound didn't incite him. It had his blood heating, his breath shuddering, his cock throbbing.

His lips on Theo's.

And then his hands were kneading his lower back and inching toward his ass.

Theo's mouth was hot and tasted of mint, and briefly,

Raleigh let his thoughts escalate to the fantasy of the wet heat of Theo's mouth on his cock, swirling candy around him. Making him sticky. Licking off the sugar.

The possibilities multiplied in his mind. Sitting. Standing. Laying down. With Theo on his knees. With Raleigh on his.

Delving his tongue deeper into Theo's mouth, he groaned. Theo may have been the one begging, but Raleigh was just as affected. He ached just as much. His body was already seeking release, hips thrusting upwards, hands tightening into Theo's flesh.

Too fast.

He didn't even know the man. He'd always had a rule that he'd at least know a person's last name before they were intimate, but the rules somehow seemed suspended away from home.

Or perhaps he just didn't care anymore. Theo could admit that he was needy and starved for touch. Raleigh could, too.

With a grunt of effort, Raleigh shifted Theo to his back atop the sofa and gave his head a clearing shake. He needed to make himself care. Human beings had evolved to possess higher forms of logic and the ability to rationalize, and those had been meant to ensure their safety.

"Puts your hands behind you," he croaked. "Under your hips."

"Here?" Theo complied with a smirk, sliding his hands beneath the small of his back, arching his body forward more than necessary.

Yes, yes, I saw you.

Raleigh put his head back and closed his eyes.

That didn't make the picture in his head go away.

Those leanly muscled lines, the bent knee, the brazenly jutting cock.

Can't do this.

Not in the way he wanted. Not with a stranger.

He'd live. He'd take home the memories and perhaps do something about all that frustration later.

Putting his eyes on the bold creature before him, he pulled his fingers into his mouth and sucked each one. Crude, but he'd make it work.

Too much friction when he wrapped a fist around Theo's cock, but the instant moan he let out said that didn't matter. He didn't care if the tugging was slick. The knowledge of the touch probably did more for him than the actual sensation.

Raleigh wished he could compartmentalize that way. He thought too much.

Skimming the fingers of one hand teasingly along Theo's crease, he slid his other hand along the meat of Theo's shaft until slickness oozed at the tip and his belly started to strain.

"Look at me," Theo whispered. "Don't close your eyes."

Raleigh hadn't realized he'd shut them, but of course he had. His thoughts were on his own dick and how he was ignoring it—on how easy it would be to find a condom and breach that resistant pucker he kept brushing the pad of his thumb against.

Theo wouldn't care so much if Raleigh was looking at him then. He wouldn't be able to say anything.

"Watch me come."

Raleigh gritted his teeth and tried to lock his focus on where his hand was and not how Theo had dug his heels into the cushion beneath to bolster his balance.

He wasn't just being tugged off. He was bucking into Raleigh's hand, and the flesh was no longer dry. The friction was gone. Theo made his own lubrication.

"Squeeze it tighter," he rasped. "You won't hurt me."

Raleigh didn't, though. He knew his grip. He knew he would leave a bruise.

"*Please*," came Theo's breathy appeal.

"Next time."

That answer seemed to excite Theo enough—as much as hearing it come out of his own mouth excited Raleigh. He was shouting out, his wet heat spilling over Raleigh's fingers, his panther eyes obediently attached to Raleigh's face.

He'd barely recovered before he sat up and reached for Raleigh's belt buckle. Maybe he liked that feeling of crashing down rather than being still while he caught his breath. He was practically panting and Raleigh could see his pulse thrumming in his temples.

"What are you doing?" Raleigh asked him.

"Let me. Please."

"Let you what?"

Theo's fingers paused behind the button of Raleigh's slacks. Confusion creased his forehead. "You want to come, don't you? You're not one of those…uptight types? You need to be in control that way?"

Raleigh forced a labored swallow down his throat. "No."

He'd simply been in no position to ask.

"I like it. Let me do it," Theo said.

Raleigh found himself nodding.

He heard a little voice echoing in his head, *"Let him do it."*

Theo's fingers were quick and nimble. He had Raleigh free of pants and briefs in seconds, had Raleigh's tip on his tongue without much of a look.

Christ.

Raleigh couldn't look at him, either. Not with the way his stare was so focused and pleading for feedback.

The best Raleigh could do in response was lace his fingers behind his head, close his eyes, and try not to push his cock too far down Theo's throat.

Theo had done that on his own. He wasn't a tentative dick kisser. He didn't waste time coddling the end and plying the underside with gentle strokes. Some people might have liked and needed that, but Raleigh didn't. His foreplay had come when Theo had peeled off those skintight pants and stalked toward Raleigh with that hungry gleam in his eyes. He'd sucked Raleigh in halfway and then more without hesitation, minding his teeth, closing his lips, slicking the curved sides with his tongue.

He swallowed around him and worked his head back and forth. Theo may have been fearless, but that meant Raleigh had to be even more careful. Theo was putting his well-being in the hands of a stranger, which was foolish, but Raleigh wasn't going to punish him for it.

Theo needed a minder. Someone to back him away from risks.

Raleigh was a bit sad to realize it couldn't be him. He'd certainly never been bored, and by necessity, he'd become increasingly predictable in recent years.

"Okay," he whispered, pressing his thumb into the corner of Theo's mouth to throttle his sucks. "Not like that."

Not in his mouth.

Confusion played across Theo's features as Raleigh slipped out of the man's mouth and took himself in hand.

A stroke was enough, and he was adding the product of his own eruption to the mess already on his hand.

"God," he intoned.

As he sat back, Theo still had that look of eagerness on his face. His breathing was still a bit fast and pulse still visible in his temples and neck.

Raleigh dragged his tongue across his dry lips and sat back.

With his profession being what it was, Raleigh was almost never at a lack of words. He knew how to negotiate. He knew how to wheedle a bit more out of unyielding decision makers. He knew how to advance his interests.

Most importantly, he knew how to end a conversation.

He'd been learning that skill since he was eight and his father had decided to pursue political ambitions. People had always expected Raleigh to mind his father's business. He'd had to learn to change subjects. He'd developed a precocious mastery of tact.

With all those useful skills to boast, he couldn't figure out which one of them would help transition his drama with Theo into…something *else*.

Probably because he didn't know what he wanted.

"Oh, I'm a bad host. Shit. Never think about the right stuff." Theo scrambled to his feet and darted into a neighboring room. An attached restroom, perhaps. He returned with wet paper towels.

He handed them to Raleigh and then fixed Raleigh's pants for him.

"I like these pants," Theo mused.

Raleigh raised a brow and worked paper towel between his fingers. "Do you?"

"Yeah, they go with the shoes."

"You like my shoes?"

Theo didn't respond. He seemed to have drifted into another world again, kneeling on the sofa, staring toward the bathroom.

Curious, Raleigh just watched him and tried to understand.

After a couple of minutes, Theo seemed to snap out of the daze.

"You want a pillow? Blanket? You're going to spend the night, right? Until the maids come?"

After his brain had churned into overdrive to make sense of the rapid-fire torrent of words, Raleigh laughed. "You want me out by seven, you mean."

"No. You can stay. Stay forever if you want. I just figured you'd want to be gone."

Raleigh didn't try to make sense of the statement. Something wasn't quite right about it, but he didn't have the bandwidth to figure it out at the moment. The day had been too long—too eventful. Mostly good, though. Theo was good. *Different.*

"Let's just play things by ear, hmm?"

Raleigh wouldn't have to break any promises if he didn't make any, but for the moment, he was content to be in the odd stranger's company.

"Playing by ear," Theo murmured, taking on that thousand-yard stare again. "Yeah, I'm good at that."

Chapter Six

Everley was almost always at the office early. She liked to beat the morning public transportation crush, plus, she could think better before the parade of people past her office door began.

Of course she had to leave it open. She couldn't be the daughter of a VP and close herself away. She needed to be accessible, according to her father.

She scoffed, even thinking it.

Her father rarely ever made it into his office before eleven. "Off-site meetings," he claimed. "Networking," he said.

"Bullshit," she muttered.

Seven fifteen.

She drummed her fingertips on her wrist cushion and stared at the message Raleigh hadn't responded to. She had plenty to do without doing his work for him, but she could take thirty minutes to organize those packages.

But she wouldn't overstep. She knew better.

She'd learned that lesson from other coworkers, from the receptionist down on the first floor to the lady in HR who still hadn't corrected the spelling of Everley's name on her pay stubs.

They hated her. She got it.

She just wished she could do something to earn that derision for a change.

"It won't matter, Everley," she mimed her father as she opened the day's checklist. "They can hate you all they want to but you're going to be their boss someday. Hur hur hur."

She rolled her eyes and pushed back from her desk. Somewhere in that byzantine maze of a building was the box of tree ornament samples she'd ordered for a holiday anthology's promo. She needed to pick a ball, lock in the tagline, and somehow get that expense signed off on by five or else she was going to miss a placement opportunity at a major convention.

She was experiencing death by a million little bureaucratic paper cuts.

It'd all seem so much less miserable if there was one person in that building she could shoot the shit with. One person who could make her laugh and feel joy without guilt.

One person who'd defend her.

She didn't care if that made her weak. She was only human.

Chapter Seven

Raleigh wasn't sleeping.

That was evident to Bruce by his frequent sighs and his restless movements.

Bruce didn't do anything to alert him to the fact that he knew he was awake, though. He was garnering far too much enjoyment from Raleigh's idle fondling of his hair and his occasional cock shifts.

He'd shift himself *just so* beneath Bruce to eliminate some of the pressure, and ever so slowly, Bruce would nestle himself exactly where he had been before. He didn't mind the squish. Enjoyed it, actually. He didn't mind being hard half the night. The stimulation was pleasant and so was the company.

He was content to lay there on top of Raleigh indefinitely, if he'd let him, but the sun had come up and Raleigh had given up any pretense of trying to sleep.

His hands roved beneath the blanket Bruce had tugged down from the sofa back.

Bruce was excited at the prospect that he might probe lower, but Raleigh's touch stopped at the small of his back.

"Theo."

It was so odd hearing that name coming out of Raleigh's mouth, but of course, that was the one Bruce had given him. It wasn't a *false* name, exactly. Just one that no one used. It was a distancing name—it delineated the man he was from the man the public wanted him to be. "Act like a rock star," the label had said.

When Bruce hadn't been able to figure out what that meant, they'd banned him from speaking in public. No interviews. He couldn't even speak for himself during the VIP backstage shit.

Fans had thought that shit was great. They thought he was mysterious.

He wasn't mysterious, though. According to his mother, he was "Inscrutable." That was her "nice" English way of telling him he was off the rails.

"Theo," Raleigh repeated.

Bruce pushed himself up on his palms and stared down at the rumpled redhead. "Hmm?"

"Fuck, you even look good first thing in the morning."

"Do I?"

"You really are like a cat. Just roll off your cushion, give yourself a good stretch, and move on with your day."

Bruce didn't want to move on with his day. And he liked his human cushion, even the rigid bits.

Or *especially* the rigid bits.

"I need my phone," Raleigh said. "It's on the floor somewhere."

"You calling a car?"

"I should."

Bruce grimaced, but he got off and gave Raleigh room to search for his distracting little bauble.

Raleigh got moving after rubbing the sleep out of his eyes. "Tell me something."

"Something."

Raleigh's laugh was full of chest sounds. "Cute, but I didn't just want to hear the sound of your voice."

"What, then?"

"The accent. Where's it from?"

Oh.

Bruce frowned.

Raleigh didn't see. He was patting the floor beside the sofa. There was no way of knowing where he'd lost contact with his phone. Bruce certainly hadn't been minding it.

"Don't want to tell me?" Raleigh asked.

"I get asked a lot."

"So do I, but it's obvious I'm American, I think. Not so with you."

Bruce had worked very hard to flatten his accent. His father had said he'd get further in life. After all, he'd managed to drop all of his foreign inflections, and English hadn't been his first language.

"It's...complicated," Bruce said. "I grew up in Scotland. My mother is Scottish, but she fled to London as a teen and stayed. My father was born in South Africa. A bastard, to be honest with you. Mostly ignored by my grandfather until after apartheid ended both for legal reasons and other ones. He's Dutch and Indian, amongst other things. Definitely some Chinese and Malagasy in there somewhere, not that you could tell from looking at him. Extraordinary impact of colonialism, I suppose."

Raleigh paused his search and whistled low. "That's...quite a mélange."

"Yes. Quite interesting." Bruce shrugged. His mother had liked it. That was all he could say about it. He didn't particularly enjoy talking about things that were beyond his control, and most other people didn't enjoy him doing so, either. The eureka moment he'd had the day he'd realized that had been an uncomfortable mix of joyous and mortifying. He'd been careful ever since to try to offer silence until his input was requested. Often, he failed.

"And how'd you end up in LA?" Raleigh asked.

Bruce fidgeted with a sofa seam and shifted his gaze toward the curious redhead. "Doesn't everyone end up in LA at some point?"

"If only that were true. Tell me."

Bruce sighed. The story was boring for him. He hated telling it. "I ended up in a lot of places. This is one lily pad of many for me. Not my favorite one, but a crucial one, I suppose."

"Tell me what you mean by that."

Inscrutable Bruce. Get it together or he's going to leave.

He twisted the meat of his palms against his temples and tried to sort his thoughts through the series of custom filters in his brain: *Needless. Irrelevant. Boring. Useful.* "I… I worked here. Or maybe I still do. I don't know. Haven't decided. Put out some records…a while back. With a band."

"Oh? A band I've heard of?"

A triple-platinum band whose drum-heavy singles about bullshit were the background anthems for all sorts of commercials. Pickup trucks. Wrestling events. Vampire shows on cable.

Bruce tugged off a bit of string from the chair fabric and cringed at the little hole he'd pulled.

Shit. He didn't always notice minor things. He should have been minding his hands.

His nan might have hurried over with a little pair of scissors to snip off the line and gently nudge his fingers away. She'd always found him other things to fidget with—to *destroy,* he'd once thought, but no. To find productiveness in other ways even if they didn't all last.

His nan was dead, though. Had been dead for years.

"Theo."

The name didn't immediately pull him.

That'd been a mistake, giving Raleigh that name.

It'd *seemed* like a good idea at the time.

"I…" Bruce swallowed. Nodded. "Yeah. Probably. Band called Outward Reaction."

No one was neutral about the band. They either loved them or hated them, so he was afraid to look at Raleigh's face, but he needed to.

He needed to have catalogued those subtle changes in his expression and the increased set of perplexity when the statement didn't quite add up the way he needed it to. "You're…"

He'd found his phone. He was tapping the screen. Scowling at it.

"That's not your name. Theo."

Bruce shrugged jerkily. "It's mine. Just not what people call me."

"Who calls you Theo?"

"No one," he admitted. "It was easier than telling you I'm called Bruce. You didn't seem to know me. I liked that."

"Oh." Raleigh's expression smoothed. "I can certainly understand that."

"Because of your father."

Just that quickly, his expression reverted to that wary one Bruce didn't like as much. He was moving with purpose, now, fixing his shirt in his waistband. Smoothing his collar. "It seems you have me at a disadvantage."

"Did I recognize you?" Bruce admitted. "Yes. Pretty much immediately, but not because of the father thing. That memory came a bit later. I matched your name and face to what I saw on the website."

"What website?"

"Athena's. It's Athena, right? I get them all mixed up."

If Raleigh's brows had drawn together more slowly, Bruce would have added that sight to his list of things deserving further scrutiny—paint drying, water boiling, grass growing, Raleigh's scrunch of disapproval.

"You submitted. Widely," Raleigh said, pounding his fist against his thigh. "Bruce Engle. Three hundred thousand words of, what you described as 'pre-apocalyptic political horror centered on the individual.' Did I get that right?"

Not quite, but Bruce didn't see the point of correcting him. And it'd been four hundred thousand. He'd been in some sort of mania. He wasn't entirely certain he'd reached the end, either. In fact, he'd closed the book with a comma rather than a period to hint that there was more story to come.

He had so many things to say.

Bruce shrugged. "Postage is a bitch but email is free. I contacted everyone I thought who might be able to send it on up. I think it's an important book."

"Is that what you were thinking when you brought me here?"

Jarred, Bruce gaped. Raleigh couldn't have hurt him more if he'd slapped him. Contrary to what his bandmates thought, he wasn't so devious as all that. "I assure you, that was entirely at the back of my mind and I don't appreciate the insinuation."

"And I don't appreciate being manipulated for my position. *Fuck.* I should have known better. I—" Whatever Raleigh was going to append to his statement was snipped, dropped, and abandoned.

Bruce was still waiting for those words when Raleigh disappeared up the stairs.

When he realized he wasn't coming back, he scrambled to his feet and shouted, "It wasn't supposed to go like that. We were getting along so nicely. You're supposed to promise to stay in touch."

He was at the top of the stairs, peering into the dark kitchen. Raleigh lingered for a moment in an open doorway at the side of the room, lips parted as if to speak, but then another door opened, and there was the familiar chatter of reluctant staff.

They hated starting their day at Bruce's. They never knew what they were going to see.

Well, he wasn't going to give them a spectacle. Some other day, maybe.

"I won't be keeping in touch," Raleigh said, dangerously soft before departing.

"Fuck."

Bruce retreated into the basement, closing the door behind him before the cleaners could see that he was piqued and naked and start muttering again about how they didn't get paid enough for it.

He'd send them away just so he could be alone and they could be happy.

But the truth was that they were paid disgustingly well for their discretion, and he needed the noise.

Silence was such a cruel reminder for what he already knew—that there was no one for him. No one was patient enough. No one waited around for him to get to the point.

He didn't want to have to accept that, but he didn't see where he had a choice. Giving up was easier than constantly rebounding from one rejection to the next.

Chapter Eight

"Remind me why I'm here again," Lisa whispered several weeks later behind the antebellum-style paper fan she'd been recirculating hot air with for much of the past hour.

Everley cleared her throat and raised her own fan to obscure her lips. The fans were part of the party theme of 100 Years of Athena. The publishing house's first blockbuster had been a rambling Southern saga about a too-stupid-to-live family who were constantly stumbling into good luck. The book was beloved. Everley tended to just smile and nod whenever people found out where she worked and brought up that rank monstrosity.

"You're here," she said through gritted teeth, "so I look like less of a social pariah."

"Oh," Lisa whispered back. "Aren't you supposed to be schmoozing?"

Everley blew a raspberry and grabbed a few canapés when a cater waiter strolled past with the tray. "With whom? I've got pride. I'm not going to smile in these assholes' faces and pretend they don't despise me."

"They can't *all* hate you."

"You're right." Everley nodded sardonically. "My parents are around here somewhere. They don't hate me. They might regret not putting sterner restrictions on my trust fund, but they don't have any actual avarice of me."

"I feel bad for you. You know that, right?"

Once upon a time, Everley would have insisted that no one pity her. She was a big girl, after all. She could handle her business just fine.

With Lisa, though, that disingenuousness would be pointless. She recognized Everley's misery better than anyone.

Unfortunately, Everley was a person who needed people.

"I won't shame you into leaving this table," Lisa said.

"Thanks."

"But I will ask if you knew that you-know-who is seated with his back turned two tables away."

Everley peered into her wine glass. It was empty. She regretted that pact she'd made with herself to endure the event while sober. Her head had been in the right place, and yet somehow, so wrong.

"Is he?" she murmured.

"Nice suit," Lisa said. "*Very* nice."

Everley studied her nails. Light pink because they were in the gloom of late autumn and she'd wanted to remind herself that seasons changed. "He wears a suit well, I suppose."

Lisa snorted. "Right. You *suppose*. Is Stacia with him?"

Lisa leaned back and discreetly peered through the bodies at the table immediately behind them. "Oh. Yeah. I guess she is. Didn't see her at first. There's a lady with her. Dark hair. Blushing a lot."

"Her assistant probably. I don't think Stacia dates. If

she does, she never brings the person to these things. She does a good job of keeping her private life private."

"Good for her. People need to learn to mind their own business, anyway."

"So true."

Someone at the front of the ballroom clinked a crystal glass with a fork. "I promised a surprise for this year's anniversary, and I always make it a good one, don't I?" he said into the mic.

"Ugh." Everley put her forehead down on the table and thumped it softly a few times. When her father started talking, people always started looking at her.

She wanted a hole to open up in the floor so she could fall straight into the Sapphire Grand Hotel's laundry room. If she were lucky, she'd have a gentle landing atop some soiled linens. She'd fight her way to the top of the pile of towels, get rid of her bunion-inducing stilettos, and haul her ass to the wilderness.

After all, Lisa had joined the bandwagon with Everley's therapist and had been intensifying her encouragement to just *leave*. In down moments, Everley had found herself pondering. She had a little money. She'd be okay. The problem would be what would happen when the money ran out. That would take a few years, assuming she was frugal. There'd be no safety net for her if she hadn't established a steady cash flow by then. Her parents weren't going to offer funds *or* sympathy. They'd tell her she'd done it to herself, and what were *they* supposed to do?

"No one's looking at you yet," Lisa whispered. "They're all leaning forward trying to figure out who the sea of bodies approaching the stage is."

Everley picked up her head.

Sure enough, her father had invited a group of ten or so people onto the stage. Mostly men. And then there were more, quickly carrying out microphone stands and stools and a full drum kit.

Things started making sense when she looked at the slick graphics on the bass drum's head. "Outward Reaction," she read in awe.

"Wow. They're kind of a big deal," Lisa said.

"Well, they *were*." Everley leaned up and scanned the cluster of men for Bruce Engle. He had to be there. There was no Outward Reaction without him.

She found him in the back of the cluster, hair slicked back into a ponytail, beautiful mouth curved into a dour frown.

The frown went away, though, when her father draped his arm around his shoulders and laughed into the mic. "This guy right here is something of a legend at Athena."

Bruce leaned in and said into the mic, "You're too kind. You mean something of a joke, but I'm cool with that."

The crowd laughed.

"Well, he certainly got my attention after a while," her father said with a greasy chuckle.

She rolled her eyes.

"It hasn't been announced yet, but Athena has acquired all rights to Outward Reaction's final tour book."

The room breathed a collective gasp, even Everley. She hated to admit it, but that grab was a big deal. There was a documentary attached to that tour that was due to premiere at a major film festival, and all of Everley's contacts in the industry had said that the footage was explosive and captivating. People were going to want to learn everything they could about the band, and especially about why they'd broken up.

No one knew that. That secret was held tighter than Everley's generous ass in a new pair of shaping briefs.

"You'll see it in all the trade periodicals soon," her father said. "Just before we were going to battle it out at auction, my assistant reminded me that we had an in." He gave Bruce's shoulder a playful punch. "It's all about who you know."

Bruce looked like he was about to say something, but Outward Reaction's drummer, a bald brawler named Aaron Westhouse, took the mic. It dawned on her that he always did that. Every single interview she'd ever seen the band in, he talked over Bruce, if he and the others let Bruce talk at all.

That was strange. Common knowledge was that the pretty front man did the talking.

Maybe that's why they broke up?

"We're excited to be partnering with Athena," Aaron growled into the mic. "We're going to do a live acoustic set for you here tonight. Just so you know, it's being recorded. Hence those cameras you might not have noticed." He gestured to the camera operators and then swiveled a drumstick between his fingers. "And in case you were going to shout out the question, the answer is no. We're not getting back together."

He'd glared at Bruce for that last bit, which seemed a bit mean spirited, but Bruce had shown up. That said something, even if Bruce's expression didn't.

As the band finished setting up and staff made their way to their seats, Everley actually abandoned hers. Her view of the band was pretty good, but there was a column between her and the stool Bruce had carried his guitar to. The others were okay, she supposed, as far as looks went, but they weren't compelling. They hadn't written ninety-three twisty-turny *alarming* chapters in first person present tense, all of which had a stylistic lack of capitalization and no congealed plot.

His wordplay was interesting and often remarkably cutting.

He simply wasn't a good storyteller in that medium, and the entire point of a novel was the story.

She leaned against the wall near the door, hands across her chest, trying to affect a casual stance in spite of the fact that a quarter of the room had eyes on her. She did her best to ignore them. That was made somewhat easier by Lisa's approach. She carried with her two glasses of wine and immediately thrust one at Everley.

"At least try to look like you know how to work a room," Lisa murmured.

"I *am* trying. That just makes it worse."

Lisa brought her glass to her mouth and said behind the rim, "Saw Raleigh squeezing through the crowd after you. I thought he was following, but he went out the other door. Had a stank-ass look on his face."

"Because he was looking at me?"

Lisa snorted. "Stop that. But no. I don't think it had anything to do with you."

"Hm."

Fortunately, Everley didn't have time to fixate on the possible snub. Outward Reaction started their set, and no one could keep Bruce quiet during those. He *was* the voice. There was no band without him.

Their handlers tried to whisk them all out of the room immediately following the fourth song but, in a rush of rare courage, Everley handed her wine back to Lisa and took off for the stage.

"Ev?"

"Give me a sec."

Everyone at Athena accused her of abusing her clout and relationships simply for being there. For a change, she was going to salve her wounded soul and take advantage of the supposed perks of being a talentless daddy's girl.

Bruce handed her a guitar pick as she approached.

Confused, she stared at the gray plastic chip on her palm.

He did the same for the others who'd drifted up and explained, "I don't have a pen. Can't sign them. Sorry."

Someone produced a permanent marker.

A lingering member of the band grumbled under his breath.

Everley cut the bassist a scathing look. She didn't give a damn who he was or care about his feelings at the moment. As far as she could tell, Bruce hadn't done anything except be mobbed.

She was part of that mob.

Realizing that, she took a few steps back and just watched.

He graciously took pictures with various editors and VIP authors. Signed some programs.

But she noticed that every time he was asked a question, no matter how benign, one of those handlers answered for him.

By the fourth time, Bruce's lips had flattened into a thin line and his stare had gone vacant.

Shit.

Everley knew that look. It was the don't-want-to-be-here look. It was the same expression she'd had in her staff photo, but she'd had more of a smile in hers. That was mask enough for most people. Only Lisa could tell how bogus the picture was.

She eased through the gaggle and handed Bruce back his pick. "Hey. Thanks, but I don't collect those."

That seemed to fluster him. He stared at the little triangle of plastic in his palm and then at her, and she wondered if he was sensitive and if she'd made a huge gaffe.

"They told me to escort you to the, uh…" Everley racked her brain for a convincing-enough name for a high-end suite. She'd never been good at lying on the spot. "The… Silver Deluxe Lounge?"

Cringing, she hoped he didn't notice the question mark in her tone.

"They?"

"Mm-hmm." She put on her best fake-it-until-you-make-it smile and gestured toward the closed double doors behind him. "It's that way. If you're ready to go, just grab whatever you need."

"I didn't bring any of it. That's not even my guitar."

"It's not?"

"Doesn't play right. Plucky sounding. Cheap wood."

"You sounded good to me, but I admit I was paying more attention to your voice than to what your fingers were doing."

"Usually goes the other way around."

"What?" Everley asked, wondering what she'd just missed.

He didn't clarify. He grimaced. "You said there's a room?"

She gestured toward the doors again, deciding not to chase an answer from him. It didn't matter, and they needed to hurry before Bruce's entourage caught up to him.

Technically there was a room. She'd booked a couple of singles for the night so she and Lisa wouldn't have to fight traffic while tired, and possibly inebriated, to get home.

He abandoned the stage and made ground-eating strides to the door. He held it open for her.

She found Lisa's face in the crowd and held up her phone as an instruction. Lisa nodded.

Everley got her bearings. The hotel was massive and difficult to navigate, but she was pretty sure there was an elevator bank around the corner at her right.

"I'm Everley, by the way," she said, getting around him. "Everley Shannon. My father is Tom. Try not to hold it against me."

"Ah. Right. Yes. *Tom.*" He snorted. "Well, you can't help who we're related to. Trust me. My grandfather owned a diamond mine. He was repugnant. Treated people like shit. Only cared about my father because he came out good looking. Something for him to brag about. I smiled when I'd heard he died. Do you know what a blood diamond is?"

Overcome by his stream of candor, Everley tripped over a bit of misplaced air on the carpet but quickly caught herself. She swiped her keycard in front of the elevator reader and called up the car. "Um. Yes. I'm aware of what those are."

Bruce rubbed his chin and shifted his weight staring at the intricately painted ceiling. "It's a sour feeling having money that came from bad shit. I try to get rid of it but it keeps coming back. I suppose I should try to make some bad investments. That's not the only thing, the diamonds."

"I guess it never is," she said weakly.

Blessedly, the elevator was empty when it opened.

Noting that they were being followed by band entourage and publishing figureheads, Everley rushed Bruce into the car, stabbed the door closing button several times, and held her breath until the door had closed.

He leaned against the corner and stared at the door seam. "My grandfather left all of us money. I was a teenager. Wasn't in a position to refuse it."

She didn't know what to say in response to that. She didn't think there *was* a good thing to say, but she tried, anyway. "I don't think the money in my family is as old as yours, but I'm sure some of it was ill gotten. Unfortunately, living in New York, I occasionally have to spend it. I don't invest any, except for what I've put into my friend's business, but I do try to offload cash to causes I care about."

"Like what?"

"Various women's issues. Literacy causes. Voting rights. Environmental things. Depends on what's depressing me the most when I'm balancing my checkbook."

"I'm not so organized as that. I just give money to the places my nan told me to, but she made that list years ago and it doesn't seem like enough now."

The elevator stopped on the thirtieth floor.

If Bruce had realized how far from ground level they'd gone, he didn't comment on it. He boldly stepped out and looked around.

"I fibbed," she said, pausing in front of the closing doors. "You looked stressed and I had a room, so…"

Shockingly, he pulled her into his arms, laid his cheek atop her head, and hugged her tight. "Thank you," he sighed.

He held her like that for what seemed like an age, and she held her breath—not because she was appalled by his audaciousness but because she was afraid he'd notice what he was doing and pull away. "My hero," he whispered.

No one ever hugged Everley. She wasn't sure why. She was perfectly built for hugs, in her opinion, and she loved them.

"I…like being the hero for a change," she said pitifully.

"You're not supposed to wear white after Labor Day."

Everley frowned against Bruce's chest. "What?"

"You're in white."

"Because I look good in white?" It set off the hue of her rapidly fading tan. Soon enough, she'd transition to her winter ensemble of all gray, all the time.

"Tradition of the last century," he murmured. "Started by the wealthy, of course. They could afford to wear white and have it laundered, and also to limit their wearing of the garments to the warmer months. Most people couldn't be so picky."

"Huh. Didn't know that."

"You do look stunning in white." He was still holding her.

She had no desire to complain. The embrace somehow managed to be thoroughly chaste, and yet still soothed a ferocious, deep-seated hunger in her. There was a genuineness in it, or perhaps a kind of acknowledgment she'd been craving. He was good at it. She wondered if he knew.

"Neckline's a bit low, though."

"Yeah, so my tits'll distract people from my mean mug."

"Solid plan."

"I come up with a good one every now and then."

Bruce smelled of leather, musk, and perspiration, but it wasn't an unpleasant scent. She'd encountered far worse being crammed between businessmen in standing-room-only subway cars. She'd become a champion breath holder—a skill she hoped would up her value if draft time ever came for the apocalypse survival teams.

The elevators behind them opened. People stepped out. Bruce didn't let go.

"So…" she started.

"You're soft."

She cringed. "Been skipping workouts lately. My trainer stresses me out and I'm afraid I'll screw up my ankle again."

"Finer women in the nineteenth century were discouraged from partaking in strenuous exercise. They were thought to be too delicate and so much activity was thought to be harmful to pregnancy."

"You're just full of trivia, aren't you?"

"Can't get rid of it."

"Can't get rid of what?"

"Random facts. They stick to me like lint on wool."

"Interesting. Tell me a fact about…" Everley searched her brain for any random subject that might be able to stump him. She was enjoying the game. "Tell me a fact about this hotel."

"Placard out front said that the original structure built here had an unspecified infestation the owners couldn't be rid of. They set it afire and moved on."

"Jesus."

"Not his actual name. The Hebrew name Yeshua was more likely."

"Why do you know that?"

"I'm observant and curious because learning gives me something to do when I can't figure out how to be charming. Also, my nan had books."

She laughed. She couldn't tell if he was being funny on purpose, but his smile in response hinted that he didn't mind if she thought he was.

He was easy.

She needed easy.

"So did mine, but they were mostly there for decoration. She didn't want to crack the spines. So fancy, my grandmother. She used to wear shorts with pantyhose."

He didn't say anything for a long while and didn't move when his phone—wherever it was on his person—began to ring incessantly.

He rubbed her back, sighed into her hair. Still so chaste, when he could have easily taken advantage. She didn't know what it said about her that she'd come to expect that.

"You have somewhere to be," she said with reluctance. He was nice, and he *was* charming, despite what he thought. She didn't feel any urgent need to perform for him. For a change, she could just be herself, even if she couldn't quite remember who that was. "Where do you want me to take you?"

"Haven't eaten. They rushed me straight here from the airport. Don't even know where my bags are or if I have any."

"Why'd you let them do that?"

"It was so fast. I just…said yes and here I am."

That was exactly how Everley had ended up at Athena for seven years. She'd said yes, and there she still was.

"All right. So. You want food. I'll find you something that isn't an hors d'oeurve."

"Can I sit?"

"Of *course* you can sit." She guided him to her room, quickly hid away her preshower clothes in her overnight bag, and handed him the spare keycard.

"Give me twenty minutes," she said when he'd settled on the loveseat beneath the window. "I'll sort this out. Who's going to be looking for you?"

"No one I want to find me."

She pressed her lips together to keep laughter from seeping out.

"I mean it," he said. "They all hate me. I return the favor."

"Why do they hate you?"

"Because they put up with me for so long, and I decided that I was tired of being put up with. It fucks with their money, us not being an act anymore. I probably shouldn't have told you that, but when I'm tired I stop caring."

Her mouth opened, but whatever light, frothy thing about to fall out of her mouth got choked at the back of her throat.

What he'd said deserved heavy words—significant words—in return, but she didn't have any.

And because he was easy, he'd already moved on from the subject. He'd picked up the eyeshadow palette she'd left on the table and squinted at the backside of it. She would have bet her last dime he knew a little trivia about eyeshadow.

She still wanted to come up with some significant words for him, but those would have to wait. Brilliance wasn't easy to come by.

She left him to his reading and returned to the elevator bank. While waiting for a car to open, she texted Lisa.

Unexpected problem. Hungry rock star in my room. I'm looking for his stuff. Is there a shitshow down there?

Lisa returned: Yes and appended a side-eye smiley.

Cringing, Everley stepped into the elevator. She could do her best to buffer him. It was the least she could do to repay him for making her feel important to someone for five minutes. Well. I'm on the way down, sans rock star.

Lisa sent: I think I know which of these greasy assholes is supposed to be his shadow. Let me pull him out into the hall.

Everley: You're a blessing.

Lisa: No, I'm an instigator. Frustrating these screaming jerks is probably the most fun I'll have all year.

Everley: Blessing. Instigator. Same thing in my book.

And Bruce was the most stimulating conversationalist Everley had been in the company of all year. She could almost forget that her department peers hadn't sat with her at the dinner and that one in particular had walked right past her without saying a word when they'd checked in.

She was moving on.

The distraction was exactly the medicine she needed.

Chapter Nine

"You all right?" came Stacia's husky whisper behind Raleigh.

"Fine, why?"

"Because you're sitting at a fancy hotel bar tearing little napkins into smithereens and you've got two empty glasses in front of you."

"I'm not driving."

"Not my point."

"I needed some air."

"Raleigh. This bar is a hermetically sealed germ factory. The only air here has probably been pumped in from a musty alleyway. You walked out of that ballroom like you'd seen a ghost. Dara thought she'd said something to offend you. You stood up so fast and she was in the middle of a story."

He grimaced and pushed all the paper bits into a pile. "Shit. Sorry. Apologize to her for me, will you?"

"No. Apologize yourself."

"Okay. I will."

"*Now*," Stacia snapped.

"Okay. *Shit*." He tossed cash on the bar for the keeper and swiveled his stool around. Although he may have been a risk taker at times, he knew better than to poke at Stacia when she was in angry bear mode. She was sensitive about Dara. He imagined anyone would be. Dara was one of those gentle souls who went out of her way not to hurt people.

As they walked back toward the ballroom, Stacia murmured, "Tell me."

"Long story short, one-night stand turned bad."

"And that person is here?"

"Yes."

"Where?"

"With the band."

With the fucking band, and he'd been sitting right beside Raleigh for the entirety of a concert back in LA without Raleigh ever knowing who he was. He'd given him a bogus name because he'd known exactly who Raleigh was and what he might be able to do for him.

Raleigh should have been used to situations like that happening to him, but he stupidly kept hoping people would surprise him in better ways.

"For real? I didn't think musicians were your type."

"Only cellists, generally," Raleigh grumbled. "They sit so provocatively, and they tend to know it."

"Think you know a guy..." Stacia murmured, shaking her head with something akin to awe.

"You know everything of importance. That's more than literally everyone else on the planet."

"Is that good or bad?"

"You tell me."

Raleigh had intended to stay out of the ballroom for as long as the band was there, but he had no way of knowing how long they would linger. He figured they'd go in through the backside of the ballroom where the stage was arranged. The curtains behind the stage setup would be shrouding the doors and he'd be able to discreetly reenter and return to his table.

He didn't get so far as the door. The view of a certain nepotism-embracing employee caught him up short by the Perseus statue.

Every time he saw the woman, he pulsated with fury. That job she was in should have been someone else's— like that well-qualified single mom who'd rearranged the heavens to even make it into the city to interview. Or the guy whose marketing portfolio was a master class in social media engagement and who was prepared to spend his life savings to relocate from West Virginia.

But they'd hired Everley. She hadn't even had an interview.

Stacia tugged on his arm. "Come on. Let's get it over with and then you can scurry back beneath the log you live under."

He gritted his teeth and said quietly through them, "Everley Shannon."

Stacia got him moving, anyway, but returned under her breath, "Smile and nod, Ral. You do that so prettily. You don't even have to listen."

"Am I a friend or a bobblehead?"

Stacia chose not to respond.

Unfortunately, they couldn't do the busy-professional thing and just nod at the congregation in the hallway as they reentered the ballroom. Raleigh's direct supervisor was with them, and he'd called over, "Hey, Ral— you didn't happen to see Bruce Engle slipping out of the hotel, did you?"

Bruce.

Raleigh had tried not to see him from the moment he realized who was heading up to perform. But there he was. Mussed, but gathered, radiating with primality even from across a ballroom.

Of course he saw him. That was why Raleigh left. He didn't want to get spun around in that maelstrom of regret again, like he'd been in after fleeing from Theo's mansion.

Bruce's mansion.

He'd very nearly convinced himself that Bruce was just another rich prick user whose only redeeming quality was beautiful lips.

Stacia gave his arm a bolstering grip, and he needed it.

His gaze tracked briefly to Everley. She had her hands clasped in front of her belly and was standing in one of those debutante postures with shoulders back and hip thrust outward, meant to show off everything and nothing. He somehow suppressed the compulsion to roll his eyes. If she and Bruce joined forces under the same roof, Raleigh's head would likely explode. "No. I didn't see him."

"You know which one he is, right?" Joey asked. "Not sure how well you follow popular music."

"Yes," he spat. "I know and I didn't see him."

"Let's just leave a note with reception and with the concierge letting Bruce know where his belongings are. Maybe he went outside to get some air."

Ah, the air excuse.

Raleigh snorted. He'd know better than to use it the next time.

Everley cut him a startled look.

Stacia gave his ribs a discreet jab with her elbow.

"Like. Whatever," the other guy in the gaggle said. He was obviously with the band, judging by his heav-

ily patched world tour jacket and the tablet cover em-
blazoned with "Outward Reaction Staff." He shook his
head. "That guy is slippery as an eel. Used to be someone else's job to keep track of him whenever the band
traveled, but that guy wasn't available. I left Bruce's
manager a voicemail to see how I should handle this,
but he's in Aruba or something."

"He's a grown man," Everley said. "He doesn't need
to be babysat."

"Maybe not outside of working hours in general, but
I'm supposed to get all of those assholes together for an
AM photocall tomorrow. I guess if Bruce doesn't show,
the photographer can still grab headshots for the rest of
the guys' profiles."

"I think that sounds like a solid plan," Joey said.
"You can always catch up with Bruce later, even if
he's not in the group shot. Honestly, our publicity folks
would probably love to have a complete shot so we can
do our thing with them, but we're creative sorts. Aren't
we, Raleigh?"

Raleigh managed to nod and smile in the way he'd
learned when he was eight and his mother threatened
to pinch the stars out of him if he didn't.

"People are watching, Raleigh," she'd whispered.
"Act like you love it."

He'd wanted to go home, or anywhere but there.

Apparently, not much had changed in thirty-some
years.

The handler shrugged and waved at them as he
started away. "Hopefully he'll swing by the desk if he
doesn't make it back to the party. I doubt he'll come
back."

No one said anything else until the guy was gone.

Raleigh was about to excuse himself and Stacia when Joey knelt down to Stacia's gnomish level and said, "Hey, vampire. Did we get you in any shots tonight or are you still avoiding flash photography?"

"So help me God," she said flatly, "If you photograph me, I'm writing you into my next book as a serial killer bus driver with a snot fetish."

Joey laughed.

Stacia didn't.

Raleigh dragged a hand down his face and suppressed a groan. He'd been trying to get Stacia to play nice for years. Generally, she did, but she wasn't the kind of lady who liked to do the above-and-beyond thing when it came to having her face spammed around. She'd only showed up at the party in the first place because Dara talked her into it. Stacia simply didn't like being anyone's prop. Raleigh could understand that all too well. After all, he'd spent a large chunk of his life pretending to be a senator's perfect son.

Everley thrust her hand out to Stacia and spread on a toothless smile.

"I can't believe we haven't met before. I chat so much with you and your assistant in email. I'm Everley."

Stacia was gracious enough to shake the woman's hand. "You don't match the picture of you I had in my head."

"Oh?" Everley adjusted her clutch beneath her arm and refastened her hands in front of her belly. "What'd you think I looked like?"

"Like the kind of industrious worker bee who wears creased slacks and cashmere sweaters tied around her neck. Your style of written communication evoked a certain picture."

That was certainly not the picture Everley Shannon painted. She was less prepster, more casual vixen. She was more likely to wear dark turtlenecks with cigarette pants and body con dresses with schlubby boots than polo shirts and expensive flats. And prepsters didn't cut their hair so aggressively short and wear see-me-orange lipstick.

He saw her, all right. He regretted that. She was so much easier to ignore when he didn't have to look at her, and now he was going to walk away pondering just what, exactly, was holding up that unstructured satiny frock she was wearing beyond a healthier-than-fair endowment of T and A. It didn't have straps or even a zipper, as far as he could tell. In other circumstances, he would have enjoyed exploring the construction of such a garment, at least until it landed on the floor. Raleigh wasn't one to dwell on the past. Of course he'd move on to other interesting bits after that.

"I was a math major," Everley said. "I think the way I had to engage with the peers in my department might have impacted my communication style a bit."

"Huh," Stacia said, and she said it in that now-I'm-curious tone she tended to only use on people she wouldn't mind having a second conversation with.

Traitor.

Apparently, Raleigh would have to have a chat with her later to remind her of who their mutual enemies were.

"Everley's great, huh?" Joey said through one of his slick smiles.

Raleigh wouldn't have bet on it, but he was reasonably certain he saw Everley complete half an eye roll before catching herself.

He found himself wondering what she might have

been thinking, and that was regrettable. He didn't need Everley Shannon taking up any more rent-free real estate in his brain than she already was.

Unfortunately, at that moment, her father traipsed through the ballroom doors and perked up when he saw the cluster. "Stacia Leonard! Haven't seen you all night. Why's that?"

"Because !…" Stacia emitted a nervous laugh. "It's been great chatting. I need to get back in there. I told a caterer I needed Alka-Seltzer and she's probably standing by my table confused. Poor thing." Stacia dropped Raleigh's arm like a hot potato and hightailed it back into the ballroom. Apparently, she'd smelled a conversation on the wind and decided to flee to safety.

He wished he could. His stomach lurched.

"Glad to see you all in one place," Tom Shannon said to the remaining assemblage.

"Yeah, we do tend to clump by department at these things," Joey said.

Everley rolled her eyes for *sure* then. Raleigh knew that, again unfortunately, because he was brazenly staring at her.

It seemed to be due to some sort of spontaneous illness on his part. He couldn't stop looking because she was pretty with those dark-lashed brown eyes and high, sculpted cheekbones. He'd always known that she was attractive, but it was her expressions that were making him take notice. She wasn't as good at tamping them down as he was. The moment her father had stepped into the hall, she'd gone into panic mode. Huge eyes. Red cheeks.

Mortified.

He usually enjoyed drama when he wasn't a direct recipient of it, but not like that.

Parents could shatter egos with mere breaths, and he wouldn't wish that public shame on his worst enemy.

Not even Everley.

"So, what'd you think of our big news?" Tom asked.

Raleigh had seen peacocks with less pride than Tom had at that moment.

"It's certainly a big win for Athena," Raleigh said.

"Gotta get to work right away priming the publicity pump, so to speak."

"The team loves a challenge," Joey said. "We'll come up with something new and fresh to get it out there."

"Oh, I know you will. I think with Raleigh on your team, you'll rock this outreach." He gave Raleigh a collegial nudge. "Pun intended."

Raleigh swallowed a scoff. "I...don't do nonfiction."

Surely, he knew that. Raleigh had been working exclusively on commercial fiction for more than five years. He did good work there and everyone knew it. That was why he was left to his own devices, generally.

Tom waved off the complaint. "Work with Everley on it. Take her under your wing and get her up to speed. She'll be competent someday."

"That's...*really* not necessary," Everley said at the same time Raleigh said, "You'll have to find someone else."

While Tom seemed to be untangling the muddle of words in his head, Joey interceded with, "I know you want this to go well, given the status of the subjects featured in the book. Trust me to get the right team on it."

"Everley needs to be working on this," Tom said.

"Why?" she asked. "I already have a full list."

Raleigh didn't buy that. If she were so busy, she wouldn't be hovering around *his* authors. He held his tongue, though. If Everley Shannon wasn't truly the whimpering daddy's girl Raleigh had always assumed, he could extend a bit of grace.

For the moment. He knew from experience that impressions changed rapidly.

"You need to make bigger connections," Tom said.

"I thought my job was to give my *authors* bigger connections."

"Some don't need it. You've got to leverage that clout, kiddo. It'll get you further in life. I'm trying to help you out here."

Everley's lips pinched together so tight that not even a sliver of the burnt orange coloring could be seen.

Her father wasn't paying attention to her, though. He'd moved on to Joey, and they were talking about getting cracking first thing Monday morning.

Fuck that.

Raleigh planned to call out. Knowing the higher-ups in publicity, they'd get impatient and assign the workload to some other sucker. By Wednesday, Raleigh would be in the clear. Some other senior publicist could take Little Miss Nepotism under their wing.

She turned to Raleigh, brow furrowed and mouth opening, but he didn't give her a chance to speak whatever platitudes she had on mind for him. He was all out of grace.

"If you'll pardon me," he said, already turning.

The ballroom door was nearly closed when he heard Tom muse, "Hey. Where'd Raleigh go?"

Chapter Ten

"I'm sorry that took so much longer than I said," Everley gushed as she spilled into the room.

Bruce hurried into the little corridor and took the takeout bags off her wrists. "I was starting to worry."

He'd taken his shoes off and then panicked when she hadn't quickly returned. The fact she was gone so long made seeds of doubt bloom in his mind—that she'd found someone from the band to come fetch him. That she was setting him up and being a user after all.

"I got lassoed into an impromptu conference about your book's publicity. Was nearly impossible to get out of."

"It's not *my* book," Bruce said. "It's Aaron's book, and the rest of those guys. I didn't want to write anything for it, ended up putting in a few columns at my manager's insistence. I doubt they like anything I have to say."

He opened the first of the takeout containers and bent to inhale the aroma of beautifully seasoned rice.

"Why did you say yes? Why are you here?"

Her query was so quiet that he wondered if he were really meant to answer it at all.

He didn't, at first. He concentrated on dishing out

rice and vegetables. He hadn't eaten meat in years, but she couldn't have known that. There was enough in that assortment of packages for him to dine well on, even without premium protein.

A reasonable enough answer floated into his mind. He tried the best he could to articulate it. "When Daryl called, he said I had to do it because I left the band in such a lurch and this was the least I could do."

"And by lurch, you mean what?"

"I walked out of the strategizing session for the next album. We'd completed the agreed-upon number of records for the label and fulfilled all our touring obligations. I was prepared to go forward with them, but..." He shrugged and carried his plate to the sofa.

Everley, leaning against the dresser and staring down at seemingly nothing in particular, looked pensive.

He didn't really expect her to understand. Most of the time, *he* didn't even understand. He didn't generally tell people so much, though. Information was too powerful a thing. He'd just had to tell someone—anyone—come what may, and she'd been nice.

"Lots of musicians move on after their big bands split," Everley said. "Why was yours an exception?"

"Honestly, we weren't really a band. They were freelancers brought in to support me because the label wouldn't sign me on my own. They thought I was too erratic."

"Erratic?" Her brow creased.

He wasn't surprised. People always did that when he used words like *erratic* and *unpredictable* or *impulsive*. They brushed aside their concerns at first, because rock stars were supposed to be those ways.

But not like Bruce was, they quickly decided. Everley probably would, too.

He hoped she didn't, though. She'd rescued him, after all. If he couldn't rely on his savior, who could he trust?

"Unpredictable. They thought I needed a buffer so they gathered up some studio musicians and turned us into a band."

Bruce wasn't hostile about that part. The part he was hostile about was how they Columbused his music—*his* sound. They'd packaged it as a group effort, but it wasn't.

"Other thing is that I own the catalog because I wrote the music and lyrics. The label just…chopped my stuff down into digestible bits, is all. My nan fought for that. Said she didn't want me to be strung up high and dry like other artists had been. Said I needed to hold on to what belonged to me from the very start."

After a few more seconds of that pensive staring, Everley's brow smoothed and she nodded. "I think I like your nan."

"Yeah?"

She looked up at him and performed another of those earnest nods. "Really. Sounds like she was trying to set you up for success, even if no one else expected you to have it."

"That, she did."

"It's different for me. No one really cares if I succeed or fail. It doesn't make a difference."

"Of course it makes a difference."

She tilted her head toward the door. "Not to them, it doesn't."

He didn't want to believe her, but she'd said it, which meant she'd probably felt it.

He was angry for her, if she couldn't be. She didn't seem to be, anyway. She seemed resigned. He hadn't known her for long, but he thought a woman as kind as she'd been deserved better than resignation.

Make her laugh again, maybe?

He wasn't sure how to do that, but she'd found his storytelling amusing before. He could try that again.

"Hey. My nan did a lot of my thinking for me when I was busy thinking of stupid shit, like whether or not adding an ocarina to a score would give an earthier sound than a flute. I still have that ocarina, by the way. It's on my nightstand."

Everley smiled, but it didn't reach her eyes.

"Bothers you, doesn't it? Why don't you just say so?"

"I'm fine. It's not *them*." She gestured toward the door and scoffed. "Not exactly. I was just thinking that I wish I could have had someone advocating for me like your nan did for you. I wouldn't be in this place right now."

Which meant that they might never have met, and Bruce didn't like that idea, either. Now that he'd met her, he wanted to see how long she stayed in his orbit. He didn't feel so clumsy with her.

"She didn't see where she had a choice," he said. "She was a very proud grandmother. She wanted me to be happy."

"Sometimes, I don't think anyone on this planet wants me to be happy."

"Oh, that's bullshit. I want you to be happy."

She looked up then with an adorably crinkled nose and upturned lips. "You don't even know me. You might change your mind once you do."

"I doubt it. Also, I was just thinking the same thing."

He patted the seat on the sofa beside him. "Come tell me all about you. I'm comfortable around you. I promise not to go hunting for useless trivia while you speak."

"Hard to do while eating."

"You have me there."

She watched him watch her for a few moments, and he wondered what she was thinking when she looked at him like that. Usually, he assumed people were pondering some flaw in him, but she'd been kind. There was always a risk that she was very good at pretending, but Bruce was so weary of cruelness that even if she were pretending, he'd accept it. After the comedy of errors that had been Raleigh's parting from him, Bruce was going to play it straight. No obfuscation. No lies. He was what he was, and she could take it or leave it.

He wondered if Raleigh had been in that confab downstairs. Bruce hadn't wanted to look for him in the crowd, even if reflexes were pushing him to do so. He hadn't wanted to look at him and know that he'd thought Bruce was despicable.

After Raleigh had left, Bruce had wondered if he was, and if what he'd done had really been so wrong.

Everley sat beside him, curled her legs beneath her, and set the plate on her lap.

"You're going to stain all that pristine white."

"I know. I should change, but I'll be careful."

"I don't worry so much about stains. People expect me to be disheveled."

"Do you always do what people expect?"

"No. Sometimes I actually do what they want."

Judging by the slow dawning of understanding on her face, she'd needed a few seconds to process that. "I see." She played with her food, mixing together bits of this and that without actually eating it. "You want to know about me, but I don't know what to tell you. Nothing seems interesting enough."

"Beginnings are always interesting. Start there."

"Okay." She nodded slowly and finally shoveled some rice into her mouth. "But you have to do the same."

He snorted. "I have few secrets. Most of my life is laid bare for me on the Internet."

She grinned. "Humor me. That way I won't feel like I'm monopolizing the conversation."

"We have a deal."

"I was born on Long Island."

"London."

"My father went into his father and father's father's business."

"Same."

"My mother is a career socialite."

"Mine works in commerce. That's how she met my father."

"Are they still together?" Everley asked, breaking the call-and-response rhythm.

Darn.

He'd just gotten comfortable with it. Every so often, predictable things made him happy.

He crossed his legs in the opposite direction and turned to face her more. He liked having her so tidily in his field of vision, because she *was* a vision. Her staff photo hadn't done her much justice, either. Unlike in Raleigh's, she was actually aware of the camera, but she hadn't *really* smiled. She'd done one of those corporate glares Bruce saw so often on people who had respectable jobs.

Maybe they were all miserable.

"Yes, they're still together," he said. "They share a massive house with my siblings. They get on like wildfire, the four of them."

At six, when Bruce had learned that his mother would be having another child, he'd asked his nan if they were going to live in Scotland, too. All Nan had said was, "We'll see."

In the end, his parents had been perfectly content to raise Frances, and later Arnold, themselves.

Nan hadn't explained, but Bruce had figured it out eventually. He wasn't like them, and they didn't know how to make him be that way.

Everley did that stare at him again, lips parted as though she had words to share, but didn't let them slip.

Maybe he'd said too much or not enough.

Typical.

He speared a tender wedge of zucchini with his fork. "You'll have to tell me what you want to hear," he told her. "I alternately say too little or too much, and rarely settle into the in-between. I was rather poorly socialized as a child. Just me and Nan and all the other widows in rural Scotland, but she did the best she could."

"I'm sorry. If I'm slow to respond, it's because I can't tell if you want my pity or even if you think you deserve any."

"Deserve is a funny word, isn't it? Who gets to decide that? Who sets the bars?"

"I don't know, Bruce," she said softly.

He shrugged. "You can pity me if you'd like. I don't know if pity makes a difference in anything, but at least it's honest, hmm?"

"Who made the choice?"

"Which?"

"You with your grandmother. I think I have a very vague recollection of someone asking you about growing up in Scotland in an interview, but you didn't manage to say much."

"Yes. I have a tendency to go off track when I'm being questioned. I get nervous and I ramble and I lose my grasp on what the fucking question was in the first place, and so I figure at that point, I may as well keep prattling on until I get back around and hit the right notes. The band had an agreement, I suppose. Kept me from saying too much so I didn't embarrass us all." He gave her a sidelong look. "Poor working memory, is what it's called. I like to think I've figured out strategies for that, but old habits die hard when I'm with those guys."

"I'm sorry they're assholes."

He shrugged again. "And the choice was my parents'. By the time I turned two, they'd decided I wasn't the sort of child they could get away from long enough."

Her brows shot up and her body went rigid in the way of people who suddenly realized they left home without taking the kettle off the burner.

"Ah." He brushed off her concern. "You know how it goes. Drop off at nursery in the morning and pick up later in the day. They couldn't manage me well enough in the hours I was awake. I was everywhere at once. Prone to histrionics, they said. Etcetera, etcetera."

"You were *two*."

"I suppose even then, my personality had asserted itself thoroughly. Sending me to my nan spared them the stigma of actually having to get me diagnosed for things."

She made that appalled face again. She couldn't possibly jerk herself any more upright, however.

"I try not to judge. They were concerned about how people would perceive them for their failure to produce a proper little poppet, and I suppose they simply didn't have time to be bothered. Their careers were, and are, very demanding. They do love me, I imagine. You're giving me a strange look. Why?"

Everley gave her head one of those clearing shakes and muttered something under her breath.

"Say it aloud. I don't mind." Whatever she had in her mind to say, he'd bet that he'd heard worse things before.

"Unfortunately, I'm too polite, and I've always been told I'm not allowed to judge people's parenting decisions until I become a parent myself," she said.

"Do you judge your parents?"

"Absolutely."

He grinned. "So, that's an exception?"

"Seeing as how I'm the one they parented, I think special dispensation is called for."

"I give you special dispensation to judge mine. Go on. I'm curious."

"No. If I say what's really on my mind, you'll get upset with me, and I think we're too early in our friendship for hard truths."

"Is that what this is? A friendship?"

He didn't have friends. Not really, except for the old ladies in Scotland, what few of them were left. He didn't like to think about what he'd do when they were all gone.

"I—" She closed her mouth on the retort, but he wasn't going to let her get away with that.

"*Say* it." He needed someone to be honest with him, and he'd thought she would give him that. "Please."

"I'll…be your friend, Bruce, if you want." She groaned and tipped her head back on the sofa. "That sounds so pitiful. What is this, fifth grade?"

"I don't recall fifth grade being so interesting, and there was definitely a shortage of pretty girls about me then." He furrowed his brow. "Hold on. Is that something that's done? Am I allowed to tell friends they're pretty, or does that cross a line?"

"There are different kinds of friendships."

"Fascinating. What kind shall we have?"

She snickered and set her attention back on her food.

He was happy that she was loosening up again and that her features had relaxed to their normal state of prettiness.

"We'll figure things out as we go along, hmm?"

"Fine with me."

Bruce enjoyed being in someone's company, for a change, without having any expectations of performance. He didn't feel obligated to interact or entertain.

Or to impress, like he had with Raleigh. He didn't know what the difference was, but when Raleigh had sat down beside him at that concert, Bruce's brain had immediately churned into overdrive. It was as though a loud siren had gone off in his head calling him up for a battle and he hadn't been able to sit still or keep his mouth shut.

It was different with Everley. She didn't unintentionally stoke his excitement and leave him reeling. With her, he could turn it on at will and control the intensity.

Maybe her energy was just quieter. Easier to digest.

She took his plate from him when he'd finished and

put everything away. Food cartons were tucked into the tiny refrigerator. Trash set outside the room door so as not to befoul the air.

Everley stood in front of the wide window, hands clasped at her back, and watched the night.

He remained quiet, and stared. He had no way of knowing for how long. Sometimes he lost track of time, but usually when he was in the process of creating. Right then, he wasn't creating anything but simply admiring what had already been made.

"Can I tell you something?" she asked softly. "Something honest?"

"About my parents? You refused me that."

She shook her head. "Still not going there. I meant about your writing."

"Oh, well, *fuck*." Shame was barking at the back of his head, but he wasn't going to throw it any scraps. He breathed. "Why don't you...tell me about my writing, goddess."

"You're not going to want to call me that for long," she said with a solemn smile, "but...listen. I think you should stick to songs."

He waited for those shame-dogs to jump the fence in his brain and attack his calm, but they were confused. He hadn't been expecting her to say that. His thoughts refused to congeal on the matter, but his stomach weighed in. As though it'd been twisted into a ropy knot, it ached.

That meant that he'd cared. He'd known that, of course. No one spent so much time on a piece of art and then decided not to care once people had seen it.

"Would it make a difference if I changed my name on it?" he asked wretchedly.

She didn't respond, but she didn't have to. Silence said a lot, sometimes.

"No one cares about the songs," he said. "I say the same thing in some of them but no one notices. I thought if I wrote a story, people would get it."

"I noticed," she said. "If you were to print out every song and put a cover on them, no one would be able to guess they weren't poetry. But the moment you put a full drum kit and a bass guitar beneath them, the lyrics lose their significance for so many. They don't matter as much as the sound."

"I've got bigger things to say. How am I supposed to say them?"

"If it were only up to me, I'd have you go back to your music. Just you. No band. Just one voice. Or write musicals." She turned to him, brows lifted in interest. "You could turn that book you wrote into something else. Go back to the music. You understand it. You have *instincts* for it."

"Because no one tried to teach it to me. I figured out what I needed to. I can't get back out there, though, on my own. Remember, when I tried, they wouldn't let me do it without a group."

"So you do it without a label if you have to. You have enough money that you could set it on fire, if you wanted to. Create your own spheres."

"I don't know how to do that." In fact, the idea seemed too wide and bottomless for him. He didn't know how to even begin to illuminate it.

"I'll help you figure it out, if you want, but it might take some time. Is there a rush?"

He'd opened his mouth to say yes, because there was *always* a rush to get art out, but he realized that it wasn't art if it was rushed. It was just a product—something he'd packaged to satisfy other people. At some point, he'd stopped satisfying himself and hadn't even realized it. "There isn't, but I might need reminding."

"I'll remind you."

"Why are you so nice to me?" he asked, genuinely perplexed.

"Doesn't cost me anything."

Raleigh hadn't been so kind in the end, but that was completely Bruce's fault. Raleigh had thought there was a cost for Bruce being in his company, but they'd gotten wires crossed. He'd mangled things. If he'd had it all to do over, he would have said from the start that he recognized Raleigh from the publisher. Maybe he would have still gone home with him. Maybe not.

It was pointless to worry about, but he would probably rehash the disaster in his mind until the day he died. Raleigh was the sort of man Bruce had always thought he should grow up to be, but he didn't, and he wouldn't. He wasn't wired right and they would never view the world the same way, but for a while, Bruce had thought that they'd forged a bridge. That they could meet halfway and enjoy what the other had to offer.

The bridge had been a shaky one, as it turned out, because he hadn't been the right kind of honest.

Everley's phone vibrated on top of the dresser. She snatched it up and answered with barely a glance. "Hey, Lisa."

Rubbing his chin, Bruce wondered where his newest phone had gone. There was probably a way to check his messages remotely if he needed to, but he didn't *want* to. He understood that was irresponsible of him—what if there was an emergency?—but he'd found that people rarely bothered him with emergencies. They only bothered him when they needed his signature or his money. Never his company.

"We can meet downstairs for breakfast in the morning before you head out." She chuckled and fidgeted with the zipper pull at the side of her dress. "Quite fascinating, actually. We were just discussing lyrics. Uh-huh. Yeah. Eight o'clock. See you then."

She slid the pad of her thumb across the screen and set the device atop her makeup kit. "My friend Lisa." She pointed to the wall behind her. "She's over there. Checking on me. We'll meet for breakfast."

"So, I can be your friend until breakfast?" He figured he may as well ask. She'd hinted that he was fascinating. He liked that word.

She laughed. "Friendships don't have arbitrary expiration times." Still laughing, she headed into the bathroom.

"Yes, well." He popped the cap off a cold bottle of water. "We'll see."

Chapter Eleven

"Okay. I'm trying not to think about how humiliating this is, but could you help me?"

Everley stood in the bathroom doorway, gesturing to the snug zipper at the side of her dress. She didn't mind Bruce hanging out. In fact, she was developing a minor obsession with his particular brand of irreverent repartee, but if she didn't get out of her support garments soon, she worried she was going to pop blood vessels.

Unfolding his long body from the sofa, he set down the baubles of costume jewelry she'd piled on the coffee table earlier. He'd been commenting on how real they'd looked. "What'd you do to it?"

She groaned. "I might have been a little negligent when I zipped it. I think the zipper is caught in the fabric of my shaper."

"What's a shaper?"

"A torture device designed to make people look like they have an artist's ideal of a waist."

"Why do you wear it?"

"Because." She pointed to the zipper again. "Please. The elastic in the fabric is starting to chafe me."

"Nan always told me that because wasn't an answer. It's a conjunction."

"Ugh. Foiled by grammar. I wear it because I'm vain enough that I want to. Is that a good answer?"

He shrugged. "Suits me."

She lifted her arm.

He squatted a bit and pinched the tiny zipper between thumb and forefinger. Careful as a surgeon, he held down the fabric at either side while he wriggled the little piece of metal. "The last time I was this intimate with a woman, I had a paternity scare."

She wasn't sure if she should laugh, so she turned her head, coughed to let her amusement out on whatever sound she could, and then asked in a warbling tone, "I take it the child wasn't yours."

"Oh, there was no child. Ah!" He managed to unstick the zipper bottom from whatever it'd caught on. "Happens a lot in the business, unfortunately, but that was my first time. There should be some kind of bingo card of all the ways people try to use you. Did you know that the earliest known versions of bingo originated in around the sixteenth century in Europe? I learned that while following Nan around. She liked playing with her friends."

Imagining the scene, Everley couldn't suppress her giggle. "The Scottish gray-hairs."

"Aye." He smiled warmly. "They liked chatting with me. If their grandkids hadn't come see them in a while, I'd get all the special attention. They didn't care if I was a little precocious in some ways. I think that made them feel less bad about prattling on." He tapped the bottom of her zipper and stood back, hands on hips, wearing a triumphant look. "Mastered that."

"If you ever give up music, you can lend yourself out as a zipper knight."

"But then I'd have to touch people I might not like as much." He shrugged. "One damsel in genuine distress is all I have room for in my life right now."

She barked with laughter as she stepped into the bathroom. "Is that what I am? A princess in need of rescue?" The pictures he painted with his words could have endeared a grizzly bear, and she wasn't nearly as fierce as that. She was absolutely charmed.

"That doesn't sound quite right, does it? You rescued me first tonight, and perhaps the zipper was step one of me repaying the favor."

"You're repaying the favor just by keeping me company. Lisa has already heard all my complaints. It's nice to tell them to someone new. Feels like less of a burden that way."

Everley breathed out a hearty halleluiah as she rolled down her girdling undergarments and let them hit the floor. Hose next. She kicked it all out into the corridor toward her bag and reached for the bathrobe on the hook. "I just need a few more minutes." One false eyelash unit peeled, then the other. "I'm reverting to my larval state."

"What do you use to facilitate such a miracle?"

"Petroleum jelly and store-brand micellar water. Don't tell anyone. I can imagine the scolding looks they'd give me. My mother uses thirty-dollar cold cream that could probably strip off a layer of fur if left on too long. Lisa uses this Korean stuff she special orders. I just can't justify spending that kind of cash."

"I can get you the really good stuff for cheap. I've got cousins who work in the import biz."

He didn't sound like he was joking. Still, she laughed,

because no man she knew would readily admit such a thing.

"Are you going to be my dealer? Do I have to make furtive calls to you and whisper about that special under-eye cream that no other guy can get for me?"

He leaned in the doorway, smiling. "You can call me if you want. I usually don't know where my phone is."

"How the hell do you entertain yourself when you're waiting or bored or commercials are playing between television shows?"

"Really not an issue. I don't do boredom the way most people do."

"You must be some kind of demigod."

"If only. That would explain so much, wouldn't it?" He skated the pad of his thumb gently beneath the sensitive lobe of her ear. "You missed a spot."

The unexpected touch sent a shudder of awareness through her, as though his hand had been someplace else. Someplace lower.

His proximity alone was enough to set her body on edge. It wasn't just the way he was built—elegant leanness and beautiful movements—but the way he stared. Staring might have been rude to some, but in that moment, it meant she was being noticed. Regarded. Assessed.

Bruce didn't make assumptions. He asked questions. That was refreshing.

Maybe she'd been barking up the wrong sorts of trees all along. She'd set her sights on slick buttoned-up types like Raleigh because she was *supposed* to want men like him, but she was coming to understand that many of the things she was supposed to do simply weren't for her. She was limiting herself to the expectations other people had established for her, and she was *miserable*.

She grabbed a pristine white washcloth out of the basket on the counter, wet it, and dabbed at the bit of foundation left behind her ear.

"There. Now you have it." He nodded in approval.

She turned her head this way and that, showing him all her angles. "Any more?"

"No. You're perfect."

"Whatever. Instead of being a zipper knight, you can hire yourself out giving compliments to vulnerable women. You'd make a killing, especially if you wear your shirt like that."

He looked down at the rumpled gray-striped button-up. "Like what?"

"Half unbuttoned. Rock star chest is an aphrodisiac."

Playfully, he pulled back the plackets and lasciviously massaged his sternum. "Really? That's doing it for you?"

"No. Silly." She stuck her tongue out at him as she passed.

His humor did far more for her than his body did.

"I used to button all the way up to the collar," he said, following her back into the greater room. "My nan told me I looked like a square."

"Your *nan* did?" she asked with shock. Everley's grandmothers were the sorts who'd reach for smelling salts if she dared to so much as wear skinny jeans.

He shrugged again. "She was better at those things than I was. She knew what was what. Helped me loosen up my style a bit. Steered me away from the matchy-matchy stuff my parents tried to put me in." He plopped on the foot of her bed and lay back like a reclining sultan.

She found herself joining him. The space he'd left in front of him was the perfect shape for a conversation.

"What do your parents think of your style now?"

"Don't know. Don't care. My mother doesn't mail me cardigans anymore, though."

"I can't imagine you in a cardigan."

"I can imagine you in one and nothing else."

It took a few extra seconds for that quip to completely land in Everley's head. He'd gone from bell pepper to scotch bonnet in five seconds flat, and his inflections hadn't changed one bit.

"Too bold?" he asked cheerily.

"N-no," she stammered. "Just unexpected."

"My conversational skills are unenviable. I know this."

In her estimation, he was doing just fine, but she knew she wasn't typical. She tended to listen for the things people weren't saying rather than what they were.

"Not a hard stretch. You in that robe. You in a sweater. Belted, maybe." He danced his fingertip down her arm from her shoulder, pausing at her waist. "Not white, though. Brown like your eyes. Sultry. Reminds me of warm things."

No one had ever made brown sound sexy before. She almost believed him.

"Size too small," he mused, hand drifting down to her wrist and toying with the bones there. "So you have to pull it tighter at the front, and so there's no chance your bottom is covered."

Everley suspected that the expression she wore was trite. Her eyes felt wide. Her face felt unhealthily hot. Her nostrils had flared.

Being a New Yorker, she'd thought she'd known what

candor was. She got it in heaps every day passing construction sites, but apparently she really hadn't gotten such raw opinions before.

"And…who exactly would be enjoying that particular spectacle?" she croaked.

"I certainly would."

He'd sounded like he meant it. His gentle, but possessive, grip on her wrist felt like he did, too.

"Ah," she said weakly. "There you go, building up that CV for your rock star compliments business. You don't need to convince me. I already know you can put words together prettily when you want to."

"I mean it. I don't lie to my friends." He toyed with the ends of her robe belt, tawny gaze slowly dragging up her body and landing finally on her mouth. "You said we could be friends."

"My friends don't generally want to see my ass."

"Shame." He shifted up to his elbow, eying her body again with what seemed to be resolute consideration.

In Everley's experience, that wasn't good attention. That was the kind of stare her trainer had given her when she'd signed up for a six-month package before breaking her ankle.

She was about to sit up and move to discourage Bruce's assessment, but something about the way his teeth notched into his lower lip gave her pause. That was a hungry look, not a I-could-fix-you look.

That wasn't a look she was ready to chase away so soon.

"We agreed there's a spectrum of friendships, hmm?" he murmured. "Can I not plant myself firmly in the zone where I could appreciate what your cardigan doesn't cover?"

Please do.

"What sort of appreciation?" she asked with scrounged confidence. "Are you going to send me cards or write songs about it?"

"No, I'd touch it. That's how I appreciate pianos and guitars. I put my hands on them and make beautiful sounds come out."

She sucked in a startled breath put her hand over her suddenly thrashing heart.

Dear Lord.

"I…suppose friendship affords those sorts of benefits at times," she said in a creaky rasp.

"How about now?"

"*Now?*"

He gave her one of those long "Is your head working?" blinks. "When else?"

"What are you suggesting?"

"Can I see?" He nodded toward her, but pointed more specifically to the tie of her robe.

"I'm naked beneath this."

"You could put on some clothes, but that would certainly defeat the point."

"I just wanted to be sure we both understood."

"I appreciate that. No misconceptions, hmm? Tired of those." He picked up her hand and placed it over the topmost fastened button of his shirt. "Look at me, too. Tell me what you think."

"Are you serious?"

"I like attention." Bruce shrugged in that Bruce way that was becoming so familiar.

Oh.

Simple. Reasonable. Human.

She sat up cross-legged and unfastened his shirt as

he'd invited. As she nudged the sleeves down his arms, he played with the tie of her robe. Not tugging or un-knotting. Just teasing it.

"You can unwrap me, if you want," she told him. He was honest about his need for attention. She could be open about her need for affection.

"Yeah?"

She nodded.

He gave the tie an enthusiastic tug then, baring her chest and belly in one deft movement. He drew in some air between his teeth and let it back out on a whispered "Fuck."

Instincts had her reaching for the edges of the robe so she could cover up, but his were quicker. "Stop," he said, fast and soft. Still staring. "Let me."

She let him, but she couldn't look. Not at his face. Not at where his hands were. Not at herself.

She looked at the ceiling and awaited some clue that he'd finished.

"Look at you," he said. "Striped red from the seams. Runnels dug into your flesh."

"They'll go away within an hour or two."

"Can I trace them?"

She looked down then, too curious to ignore the things his expressions might have told her.

He was staring with that same interest as before, but with parted lips and fast breath escaping.

"You can touch me," she said simply. The permission seemed to cover all necessary bases for the moment, but she was coming to understand a bit the way Bruce thought so she appended, "Go ahead. I'll tell you if I don't like something. I'm not shy about that."

"So I can touch you here?" He dragged his index finger along the red welts beneath her breasts where the top of her shapewear had rested.

Those marks seemed to have forged direct pathways to her diaphragm. As his calloused touch alighted from one red streak to the next, her lungs seized, chest tightened, breath waned.

"Yes," she choked out.

"And here?" Nudging aside the edge of the robe, he followed the line around her waist to her side and then down to midthigh where the next ridge tattled on her vanity.

That ridge was connected to her toes. They curled as he traced.

"Yes," she whimpered.

"Where else?" His tone was full of awe and reverence—a sound she was unaccustomed to, though she hadn't really been listening before. From Bruce, it was as unmistakable as the color of his eyes or the opening chords of his band's debut. It couldn't be anything *but* that.

I deserve it. I do.

Gone was the confident voice of the woman who'd fought to make a department of mathematicians respect her. In its place was a half-murmured warble of need. "Anywhere you want as long as you tell me you like it."

"I do." Palms covered more territory than fingertips, and he was using both to massage away the streaks and also experimentally press to witness how gravity affected flesh. "All of you."

He said all the right things, and had the audacity to seem like he didn't know.

She'd never encountered a man before so in awe of the way a heavy breast reshaped in his hand.

"I never get to touch," he murmured, pushing her breasts together and tracing along the edges of her areola with his thumbs. "I never get to look and touch. Just fuck and then everyone moves on." He put his face between her breasts suddenly, and as lips and tongue tickled along the center path, her head fell back and a moan escaped.

She swallowed thickly and forced much-needed air into her chest. "I…guess it's a good thing you have me as a friend."

She threaded her fingers into his hair, which he must have loosened during her dinner run, and urged his face—his mouth—toward one tender peak. "Be creative," she whispered. "Hands touch. So do mouths and other things."

"I could touch all of you with all of me?" he asked before drawing her into his hot mouth and flicking his powerful tongue against her nipple.

She bit down hard into her lip to hold in the whimper of stimulation. She nodded, though, so he wouldn't stop licking, touching.

His focus drifted from one breast then the other, working both nipples to stiff peaks before moving on to explore other swathes of her body.

The bends of her neck. Her cleavage again. Down her quivering belly to her navel. He paused just beneath there, rolling his gaze up to her as his lips caressed and hands slid down her bare hips in the slowest of signals.

She closed her eyes and put her head back once more. She wasn't going to let herself think about angles and whether the one he was viewing her from was unflattering. If he were going to act like it didn't matter, she could be confident in the shapes she carried around.

He went lower, his stubbled chin pausing at the crease of her bikini line and hot tongue searing a teasing line across the tender skin of her belly. And then his thumbs found her, lightly touching the most responsive of her flesh and making goosebumps all over her stand at alert.

In spite of all the encouragements she might have given him, deep down she knew that what they were doing wasn't a thing friends did—not even the strangest of friends. They didn't stick their thumbs into their mouths and use that acquired wetness to greet clits. They didn't bend low and experimentally tease the tips of their tongues around those tender buds, trying to unlock certain sounds in their partner.

Bruce must have heard the one he sought, because suddenly there was more of his mouth on her and fingers teasing into her, and her body was going tense. Not because she was frightened, but because she needed the release so badly.

It didn't make sense to her—his worship of her—but she was trying to allow it.

She deserved reverence, rather than being aggressively ignored, for a change. More, she to be wanted the way she was without conditions.

Connections like that didn't last, though. Those men always went off exploring the next shiny, better thing, and of course Bruce would, too. He was an artist. His head was in the clouds where it belonged and where, if he were smart, he would choose to let it stay. He'd drift.

She'd remain.

It was what it was.

Still, in that moment, she wrapped her legs around his back to keep him in place. She shoved her fingers into his hair and guided him lower, not that he needed the help.

In that moment, she just needed a little control.

She needed to lie to herself that having someone stay would be a possibility. She'd lost her agility in making wishes as an adolescent, but she thought she remembered how they worked.

Lie to me and tell me someone wants this with me.

He slid more fingers into her and sat up on his shins, dividing his attention between her face and the fingers he was thrusting into her. There was something like wonderment in his expression.

She couldn't guess why.

She could feel the grimace of overwhelm on her face and see the way her body was contorting away from, and then toward, his probing fingers.

"Your whole body blushes," he said in a low rasp as he settled low again. There were no timid licks and shy kisses. He devoured her. Spreading, tasting, supping, and working her with fingers and thumb until she moaned in that frequency he liked.

"God, your hands." She hadn't meant to say it aloud, but he had to have known, anyway.

"You like them?"

She couldn't speak. He was rocking those long fingers into her and tapping her self-destruct button. Words were out of the question. Groans were possible, and also squeaks, apparently when he pressed the meat of his palm against her clit.

"I've always been a quick study when it came to instruments," he murmured against her thigh.

He was certainly playing her like one. If he'd told her

he hadn't meant to make her whole body tremble and teeth chatter, she wouldn't have believed him.

"You have a place?" Bruce asked after he'd brought her to a hard crest and pulled his body up atop of hers.

She closed her eyes. Swallowed. Tried to coordinate brain with body so she could drape an arm around his waist and keep him there. So lovely after being so unwanted.

His face was nuzzled in her hair, his hard cock a rigid distraction against her leg. He didn't seem to be looking for gratification at the moment, though.

"Do I have an apartment, you mean?" she managed to exhale.

"Or a house. I always wonder how people live."

"You wonder how people live right after you've had your tongue in them?"

"Sometimes during. Do you have a brownstone? Or an apartment in a high-rise where a doorman watches your comings and goings?"

"The latter."

"Ah."

He didn't say anything else. He nested himself half atop her, hooking his leg over hers and slinging an arm across her neck.

Apparently, she wasn't going anywhere.

Apparently, some wishes came true.

In the morning, he was still there, half on her, reluctant to move even when her phone started to continuously ring.

"Bruce," she whispered, snaking a hand down his bare back.

"Don't run away from me now," he said in a tone of false petulance.

She laughed, because the idea that she would hurry away from the first person in ages to seed joy in her was patently ridiculous. "I'm in no condition to run, but that's probably Lisa asking about breakfast. I can't see the time."

He sighed. "I suppose you must be responsible."

"I should be, yes, but you can come if you like?" She hadn't meant for the invitation to come out sounding like a question, but her confidence got tangled up somewhere between her brain and mouth. "If you don't mind being seen," she added in a hurry.

"Seen? Huh." He swirled his fingertips in the short hair over her ear. The sweet touch made her whole body tingle.

She hoped that feeling never went away.

"You'd hold my hand?" he asked. "Prance me about?"

She snorted. "I do all my prancing in private, and I'll only hold your hand if you want me to."

"No one ever shows me off."

The statement was gut-wrenchingly matter-of-fact, but she remembered what he'd said about people fucking and going home. About never connecting. She could make a safe inference from that—that he *wanted* to be showed off. For the life of her, she couldn't understand why no one had. He was a gem.

"I find that hard to believe that no one would parade you around," she said.

"It's true."

"Then they must not have known what they were missing."

"Think so?"

"Yes. And if you want a miniature spectacle—with me, I mean, I'll see what I can arrange."

"Not necessary. Just hold my hand. Act like you want me for something other than my money."

"I have my own money."

"The fame, then."

"I'd rather crawl into a hole and die than be famous. I'd prefer to be a flawed human being in anonymity where the stakes are lower."

He went quiet again. He kept fondling her short hair. His breathing was slow, body supple against hers rather than tense.

And then, after a minute, he said, "I'd very much like an omelet."

Apparently, they were going to have a little parade. A smile crept across her face in spite of her effort to subdue it. It was as though the universe had finally decided to cut her some slack and give her something good to counterbalance all the years of mistrust and micro-aggression.

And perhaps the universe was telling her to stop barking up certain trees, in spite of how alluring those trees were. Sometimes, nature made its creations becoming as a warning that they were too toxic to touch.

Warning accepted, Mother Nature.

She didn't need to chase after Raleighs when there were Bruces, and the Bruces gave her so much joy simply for *being*.

"Omelet it is, then," she said, smiling even bigger. "And maybe you can figure out where your luggage ended up. Can't help you with that."

"Because people would know you spirited me away last night."

"Exactly."

"You'd lose your job?"

"Oh." Her smile fell away and she pushed herself erect. "I wouldn't get fired. It's not that simple. I'm Everley Shannon. I'm supposed to be the one doing the firing one day."

There was a twisted irony in the fact that she might one day be tasked with letting people go from Athena when she was the one who most wanted to be gone.

Chapter Twelve

"I feel like I haven't really had a decent conversation with you in weeks," Stacia said. "What have you been up to since that ridiculous party? And why'd you lock down your social media again?"

She opened her napkin on her lap and let the restaurant host push her chair up to the table. She let out a little yelp when her sternum touched the edge.

Somehow, Raleigh managed to suppress his laughter.

They always did that. Short woman. Big chair. Aggressive scooting.

Stacia glowered at the host's back as he departed.

When he was out of earshot, Raleigh said, "I set my social media accounts to private because I needed to cull some followers. I had a little spike recently and took it in stride, figuring it was people who'd followed me over from your account, but then I realized it was something else. Political staff, not just from my father's camp, but his associates' and his opponents. He must be gearing up for some kind of party leadership shit again."

Stacia cringed. "Sorry."

He shrugged. "Nothing to be done for it. I'll keep my head down like I always do and let my brothers run interference."

"Your brothers?" Stacia's voice took on an elevated pitch of befuddlement. "I thought you guys only talk about sports and weather."

"That's generally the case, but I think they're being proactive." All of the McKean spawn had made a pact a decade prior to support each other's continued existences by keeping the fighting words out of their mouths. They didn't discuss religion, politics, or sexuality, and they most certainly no longer encouraged Raleigh to call their father and "patch things up."

There wasn't a patch big enough to repair that rift, and they all knew it.

"Anyhow, they're going to do what they can to make themselves a little more newsworthy than usual, so I get relegated to the boring category."

"Good for them. I'd always hoped they'd lighten up some day. I'm sure your nieces and nephews would love to see more of you."

"I know. I feel like shit that I have to avoid them as much as I do. Anyhow, besides that, I've been busy. You know how it is in publishing when we get near the holidays. Place turns into a zoo and everything is go-go-go. Did I ever tell you that Tom Shannon tried to attach that Outward Reaction book to me?"

Stacia raised a brow over the top of her thick-rimmed glasses. "And you said no?"

"Not quite. I've been at Athena long enough that I've learned how to duck and dodge commitments when necessary. Because Tom tried to buck the system with this particular book, procedures haven't caught up with it. No one knows what to do or when."

"But…wouldn't Everley know?" Stacia's voice had

relaxed down, back into its usual timbre of husky cynicism.

Everley.

He scoffed.

Little Miss Two Can Play That Game.

He avoided her. She went out of her way to ignore him.

Moving around each other in the office's so-called Publicity Row upstairs had turned into a comedy of errors. If they happened to be heading toward the break room at the same time, she'd about-face and mutter something about "Better things to do."

Hell had no fury like a publicist scorned, it seemed, and he found himself surprisingly offended.

"I mean, hasn't… *Everley* been there long enough that she would know how to put together a marketing plan, even if it's for something outside her usual comfort zone?"

Raleigh ground his teeth. "You don't need to whisper her name as though it might activate a curse that would unhinge one of the layers of hell. I'm not *that* sensitive. And I don't know if she would or wouldn't, to be honest with you, Stacia. She may mind other people's business but I tend to mind my own."

"She's still at it?"

"Well, no," he admitted reluctantly. "She'd been in the office, obviously, but she's pulled back on the team-player help-me-help-you bullshit. Has she contacted you or Dara again to ask if you needed anything?"

Stacia shook her head. "Nope. Maybe she learned her lesson."

"Or maybe she's super swamped with rock stars," he said acidly.

The assholes showed up whenever they wanted to and completely disregarded normal business operations. They all had ideas on ways to showcase the book—DJs Athena could send it to, and talk show hosts who'd certainly like to have them on.

When they showed up, everyone from reception all the way up to executive staff humored the disruptions.

Raleigh didn't. He stayed in his office, put on his noise-cancelling headphones, and whispered pleas to the god of petty prayers that Bruce wouldn't turn up.

He hadn't yet, but certainly, it was only a matter of time. He'd want his piece of the fame pie just like the rest of them, and he'd already proven that he wasn't above using whoever he had to get it.

"You could always pitch in," Stacia said. "Get the project out of everyone's hair that much faster."

"Fortunately, the English language hasn't yet shifted in such a way that the definitions of could and must overlap."

They went quiet again when the waiter came over to fill their water glasses and inform them of the soups. Raleigh chose egg drop. Stacia chose hot and sour.

"I want no involvement with it," Raleigh said.

"Is New York an at-will employment state?"

"Hush."

"You can't just pick and choose which books to work on."

"Tell that to Everley."

"Why are you so hung up on her?"

"I'm not."

"You *are*. You literally just said that she's minding her business now." Stacia twined her fingers beneath her chin and gave him a speaking glare.

"Don't start."

There are few people who could get into his head well enough to psychoanalyze him, and the one who was best at it was right in front of him.

Maybe he was a little hung up on Everley. It wouldn't be so strange if he was. He'd always gravitated to lovers who were bad for him. Lovers with unusual quirks and who had fresh things to say.

"You hold a grudge like no one I've ever known before," Stacia said.

"It's not so much grudges but having a long memory for the sake of self-preservation. Growing up the way I did, I had to develop a talent for making quick judgments about people. Obviously, I didn't always get it right. I made poor calls with people and invited them into my confidences and my bed, but for the most part, I think I manage to avoid a hell of a lot of drama."

Stacia's dark eyes slitted rightward and her smooth brow creased. "I suppose we'll be testing out that theory."

"What are you talking about?" He started to turn but she kicked his shin under the table.

"*Don't.*"

"Who is it? One of my father's aides?" He groaned. "That'd be just my fucking luck that I'd manage to avoid them online only to run into them on the streets. A few of his old ones work in local politics here or at the UN."

"I wouldn't recognize any of them. Honestly, I probably wouldn't even recognize your father if I saw him in person. Everyone says you boys look like him, but I don't see more than a passing resemblance. Maybe I know you too well."

"Someone from Athena, then? Staff from the publishing house swarms this place."

The Golden Duck was, in fact, situated in the ground floor of the building Athena and other major publishing institutions had offices in. By no stretch of the imagination could the fare be defined as exquisite, but the restaurant could get away with charging what they did because of their location. Publishing reps held working lunches and dinners there because it was so convenient.

Stacia probably wouldn't have minded going elsewhere, but Raleigh happened to like the soup.

"Yeah." Stacia pushed her glasses up her nose and studied her menu. "Someone from Athena. And they're headed this way. Brace yourself. Be nice."

"Hello, Stacia," Everley purred, extending a hand across the table for her to shake.

Fuck.

Because Stacia actually did have some home training, she shook it. She should have known better than to expect Raleigh to put on a cheerful face, though.

"Ms. Shannon. How are you?"

"I'm doing well. I just wanted to tell you that I got a sneak peek of your next book and I thought it was amazing."

"Thanks!" Stacia said in a bright tone.

Raleigh rolled his eyes. She'd evidently forgotten yet again that the two of them were supposed to be a team.

He wouldn't forget.

"I never get tired of hearing that," Stacia said.

I see how it is.

Raleigh sipped his tea. He told her that all the time and she waved off the compliments.

"I'm sure it'll do very well. I was at ninety-seven

percent before I guessed who the murderer was. I didn't see that coming, but it made so much sense."

"Hopefully no one will leak any spoilers about the ending like last time."

"I know, right? I was so annoyed about that! I'm pretty sure Raleigh did a hard cull of the reviewer list right after that, though, and whoever's left should know better."

"I burned the list into nothingness and salted the earth it'd sprung from, actually," he murmured.

Stacia snickered and raised her water glass to her lips. "Raleigh holds a grudge better than anyone I know."

He narrowed his eyes at her and pondered if their little team needed some adjusting.

"Well," Everley said. "I won't take up any more of your time. I just wanted to tell you that. Oh! And that I saw the first of the television show tie-in covers, too."

"Yeah?" Stacia smirked.

Raleigh had pretty good idea of why. She slept with that why.

"Adrien Valliere was born to be that character. He looks amazing."

"Yes, he does."

"Well. Best of luck with it, not that you need to hear that from me."

Raleigh finally looked at her in time to see her wave at them both and turn on her heel.

She was in a dark gray dress that hugged every curve, dark hose with seams up the backs, and studded stilettos that seemed as much a fashion statement as a warning. Who the warning was meant for, he didn't want to guess.

"It's so unfortunate that she's likable," Stacia said. "I don't want to like her, because that's what friends do for their friends, but I gotta tell you, Ral, I don't get the impression that she's the snake you think she is."

"Oh, you don't, hmm?" Raleigh liked to lie to himself that he hadn't inherited that famous McKean temper, but the truth was that he was simply better at avoiding the sorts of confrontations that could ignite it. Suppressing outbursts had become second nature for him, though sometimes, he had to slow his tongue and shave the spikes from his words before he spoke them.

Stacia was his dearest friend. She meant no harm. That didn't stop her assertion from chafing him.

"You're only saying that," he said in a controlled, quiet voice, "because she complimented your book and your boyfriend's picture."

"I'm not going to take offense to that coldness in your tone right now because I've obviously touched on a sore spot, but no, I'm saying that because of how weary she looks around her eyes and how her smile doesn't go all the way to it. I'm not an expert in body language and have never pretended to be, but I like to think I'm pretty good at what I do because I've got a knack for observation. And also..." She leaned back so the waiter could set down her soup and then accept her entree order.

Raleigh put in his as well.

"And also *what*?" Raleigh goaded when the server had moved on.

"And I hate to even suggest it, but I'd eat my shoe if that woman isn't attracted to you."

Stacia's words didn't land right. They were English. He was certain of that. In some way, she'd used them to mean things they typically didn't. She did that all the time in her books and people never figured out what she was getting at until the next chapter. Everything became all too clear, and then someone would get abducted and stuffed into a car trunk or something else equally awful.

"You don't believe me?" she asked solemnly.

"No, because I like for things to make sense, and that certainly doesn't."

Raleigh assumed that he spent about as much time thinking about his appearance as the next man, but he didn't gas himself up to believe that people enjoyed looking at him. He groomed for himself, dressed for himself. His intention was rarely to illicit attention, and he was content with being the instigator in new connections rather than the other way around.

Had things been different—much different—he might have thought, *Well, that's a beautiful woman. Drinks might be nice and we'll see what happens.*

But because Everley was who she was, her attractiveness was a deficit in his book. It made her more dangerous, and her supposed interest in him made her a live wire he wasn't going anywhere near.

One wrong move on his part, and she could go whisper to her father, and suddenly Raleigh would be out of a job. He'd worked too damn hard to get to where he was, and on his own merits, to tangle with her. Walking on eggshells around her while trying to assertively maintain his independence in the department was exhausting. One day, he'd slip up. He knew it.

He dreaded it.

"I'd actually guarantee she thinks so but would never come on to you directly," Stacia said. "You're not the most approachable of individuals. You've got that blue-blooded-coldness thing going on. Obviously, I can see right through it, but that's because like attracts like. I know your history makes it damn near impossible, but try not to assume that interest means ill intent. I'm guilty of doing that, too."

"I don't know if I can." He wished he could, though. He grew weary of his own cynicism at times and wished connecting with people wasn't always fraught with red flags—real and imaginary. Like when he'd gone home with Bruce. That had been easy, and *lovely*, until Raleigh was reminded of why he knew better.

He wished he didn't have to know better.

Raleigh sneaked a peek over his shoulder in the direction Everley had gone. He could just barely make out the gray of her dress. She was sitting with her back to the aisle. Whomever she was lunching with was obscured by the half wall between their table and the ramp down to the lower level. As a matter of course, he didn't pay much attention to her work schedule, so he couldn't possibly guess who was sitting across from her. Perhaps it was her father, whispering encouragements about industry domination.

There you go again, assuming the worst.

He took a breath and refilled his teacup. He needed distraction.

"Where are you going from here?" Raleigh asked Stacia, hoping to redirect both his malicious thoughts and the conversation.

The slow blink she gave him revealed she knew the game, but was going to play it anyway. She spooned up soup. Slurped it. "Richmond for at least a couple of weeks, I hope. I miss my house. Obviously, Adrien's doing stuff for the TV show and he's too tied up to visit.

Dara said she was going to split the difference between here and there. She's going to hang out in LA for a week and then head east. The travel burden isn't ideal. We're all sort of getting short shrift right now, but that's the life you lead as a public figure. As soon as Adrien goes on hiatus, we're going to bunker down somewhere and not leave the house unless we have to."

"Sounds disgustingly domestic."

"Jealous?"

"No."

"You're a lying-ass liar."

"So what if I am?" he groused. He wanted off the subject. On the best of days, he was sensitive about his dearth of romantic prospects, and Stacia knew that. What she didn't know was about his encounter with Bruce and how he still reeled from it.

Why couldn't he have found someone exactly that intense and passionate who *didn't* come with a chaser of deceit?

"If you get lonely," Raleigh said dispassionately, "I'm sure you'll start a new book series or something."

"Nah. I'm taking a break from writing."

That lie shook him out of his funk for the moment. Raleigh pushed his chair back from the table to give the heavenly lightning bolt sufficient striking clearance. When no electric singe immediately occurred, he scooted warily back up and dropped crispy noodles into his soup. "Huh."

"I mean it, Raleigh. My contract obligations are fulfilled for the moment. I can do nonwriting stuff like renovating my cellar, because it's creepy as shit, and maybe getting the roof replaced before winter."

"I heard your agent was shopping your next book around elsewhere."

"I'm sure that's what she wants you to think. You know the game."

He grunted. He knew it all too well. Loyalty had a cost. Athena had been paying handsomely for Stacia's, but they all had to know that one day, some other house was going to take a chance and offer her something she couldn't say no to.

They sat in a comfortable silence until the entrees arrived. As always, they each immediately scooped healthy portions off their friend's plate without comment.

Raleigh had just stabbed his fork into a particularly succulent piece of beef when a shadow fell over the table. A sideward glance gave him dark gray wool. Everley again.

He didn't look up.

"Sorry to interrupt again, Stacia. We're heading out and he wanted to say hello."

For some damned reason, Stacia stood, so Raleigh had to look.

She was shaking the hand attached to Bruce Engle, who was wearing one of those sheepish grins that managed to be half smug.

What. The. Fuck.

With the band coming and going from the office so much, Raleigh knew that Bruce would probably turn up. But not there. Not with *her*.

Raleigh took several deep breaths and set down his fork. As a redhead, he couldn't afford to show his passion in his skin. He looked like a spotted leper when he got piqued, and he was most certainly piqued. After all, he'd just been thinking about him, and there he was—a massive taunt bound into six feet of rock star costuming.

Apparently, Raleigh had just been shoved into one of Stacia's metaphorical car trunks.

Should I bang the roof for help?

Raleigh glanced stealthily around him in search of an easy exit.

There were none.

Fuck.

"Your books are trippy as shit," Bruce said with a chuckle.

"Yeah, just like their author," Stacia said. "I come by it naturally, though."

"Hey, me, too. I read them when I'm flying. I can always find them in the airports, except the third one for some reason. That's the only one I don't have."

"Yeah, that one has been in between print runs for a while. They were going to do it a couple of months ago, but with the television show starting, Athena figured they'd wait until closer to launch so they can sync the branding."

Raleigh caught the shift of the rocker's weight in his periphery.

Nervous? Him?

Raleigh didn't buy it. Men who took risks and exploited people the way Bruce Engle did wouldn't be made nervous by five-foot-nothing Stacia Leonard.

"You...wouldn't happen to have a copy I could buy off you, would you?" Bruce asked. "I don't like used if I'm going to keep 'em and I can't read on screens. Need to be able to follow along with my thumb."

"Oh, I've got *heaps.* Here." Stacia retook her seat, hauled her giant purse up to her lap, and rooted through the bag until she found a mangled sticky-note pad and a pen. "Just tell me where to mail it. I'm pretty sure I know where that box is." She added in a mumble, "Dara would know better, though."

"Hey. That's right decent of you. Thanks."

"Sure. It's really no trouble."

While Bruce scribbled, Raleigh waited for Stacia to catch his gaze.

He was going to have to come clean soon, or he'd be tripping into one humiliating scenario after another. The industry was too damned small and it seemed he wasn't going to be able to avoid Bruce.

"What?" she mouthed.

He cut his gaze toward Bruce in a silent warning.

Subtly, she turned her hands over in a "Huh?" gesture. Obviously, she didn't get it, and Raleigh couldn't be more direct just yet.

She shrugged and turned to Bruce. "Are you recording any new music soon, Bruce?"

He shifted his weight again and twirled a thick black band around his middle finger. He had on all the same rings as before, Raleigh realized.

He couldn't forget. Images of Theo's—*Bruce's*—libidinous hands wandering across his tan flesh and of them closing around Raleigh's cock would probably be seared into his brain until his dying day. He'd practically given himself away wholesale to Raleigh.

And for what? To get a stupid fucking book acquired?

Passion like that always had strings attached.

"I'm thinking about it," Bruce said. "Not sure how to do it. Want to do it a different way. Not the rock band stuff. That's over, you know?"

"Why? I thought audiences responded really well

to you. And you racked up so many awards. Don't you want that?"

"That's all well and good, I suppose, but I'm not a rock star. They don't make them like me."

It was a curious statement, and given the deep furrow of concern in her brow, Stacia thought so, too. She didn't probe it, though.

Nor would Raleigh. He couldn't let Bruce be his concern.

"My nan used to help me research things, but she's gone, so I'm kind of out on a limb sometimes." He crooked his thumb toward Everley. "Ev's helping a lot."

Everley's eyes widened at the sudden attention. "Um. Well, I don't know nearly as much about the industry as his grandmother did. She was very meticulous and would call around finding out who was who. All I do is help Bruce brainstorm. He does all the figuring out on his own, given enough time to think."

"Must be quite busy," Raleigh said blithely as his gaze fixed on the catch of her index finger around Bruce's belt loop. That grasp, with her knuckles grazing his hip, and the marked lack of distance between the two of them, exploded any suggestion that their relationship was strictly business.

Apparently, Bruce had found himself another sucker.

And apparently, Stacia had been wrong. That hadn't been attraction in Everley's gaze, but trepidation she was going to get caught.

Raleigh couldn't possibly get any lower.

"Doing that and working on the Outward Reaction book at the same time," Raleigh said through clenched teeth, "Well. Must have been a rare treat for you to come out for some air during your lunch break."

Stacia kicked his shin under the table.

He swallowed his grunt of pain.

"I'm...actually not planning on doing any work on that," Everley said. Her cheeks had turned a conspicuous shade of penitent purple. "I've been to a couple of strategy meetings but I suspect someone else will be doing the busywork."

"Must be nice to pick and choose," Raleigh said.

"Like you don't?"

Raleigh was so stunned by the retort that he was rendered speechless. Granted, he had walked right into that one.

Letting go of Bruce's loop, Everley shook out her hands, then took a deep breath and let it out. "I'm trying not to take on any major projects right now."

Raleigh really did try to hold his tongue, but he couldn't look at that lying face and pretend everything was fucking fine. "Big promotion coming?"

Stacia kicked the other shin.

He gripped the table edge hard and tried to tell himself that Bruce's arm snaked in such a possessive fashion around Everley's waist didn't mean anything. Bruce was handsy. He probably touched everyone that way. After all, there was nothing special about the way he'd been with Raleigh. He'd only been a means to an end. Certainly, Everley could expect the same from Bruce. Maybe she'd deserve it.

"I wouldn't know," Everley said. "Anyhow, we'll let you get back to your meal. Nice talking to you again, Stacia." She nodded vaguely in Raleigh's direction, and then left.

Bruce didn't leave. In fact, his feline gaze tracked

pointedly to Raleigh and he practically vibrated with annoyance.

"Don't," Raleigh preempted.

"You're kind of a jerk, you know that?"

"Only when I have to be."

"You didn't have to be."

"Then or now, *Theo*?"

"I—" Bruce bit off the words that should have come next. He raised both middle fingers at Raleigh, spit out an emphatic, "Fuck you," and then scrambled after Everley.

"Don't. Say. *Anything*," Raleigh snapped at Stacia.

She stared at him without blinking for so long that he wondered if he'd pissed her off enough that she'd gone into a trance state. Then, she said, "Fine," and shoveled kung pao chicken into her mouth.

Raleigh sat back, arms folded over his chest, fuming.

Things weren't fine. Nothing was fine. The person he'd foolishly let his guard down for was probably screwing the woman who made his blood pressure spike every time he looked at her. It was like the universe was having a laugh at his expense. Raleigh would be alone by necessity, and the two people he trusted the least would flaunt their newfound connection.

"Just fucking say it, Stacia."

"You told me not to speak."

"But you're going to anyway, so let's go ahead and kill the suspense. Say what you have to so I can do the same."

"If you say so. Don't get pissed if you don't like where the line of questioning goes, though." She angled her fork across the top of her plate and twined her fingers. "Bruce is the band guy you diddled with, I take it.

I didn't think to ask at the party because I was in such a hurry to get back to Dara. I should have asked. Maybe we could have talked it out then so that you'd be over whatever it is that's setting you off now."

"He lied."

"About what?"

"He knew who I was. I met him at a concert. He recognized me as an employee of Athena. He sent his manuscript to every active email account at the company. The guy was hungry for a publishing contract. The night we met, he told me his name was Theo. I didn't recognize him."

"What?" Stacia's pitch was practically in the stratosphere again. "How can anyone who hasn't been living under a rock for the past ten years *not* recognize Bruce Engle?"

"He was incognito." Raleigh pushed his noodles around his plate with his fork. "And maybe I was distracted. It was the night I arrived in LA to check on you."

Stacia sat back, and after a moment of introspective silence, made one of those little conciliatory *oh* sounds.

He didn't deserve the pity. He waved it away like he always did. "Anyhow, you know how I have to be. If I know people are trying to leverage me for some other goal, I immediately cut ties."

She nodded. "Did you give him a chance to explain?"

"His explanation didn't meet my standard."

"Damn," she murmured, and leaned back into the table. In a quiet voice, she said, "He looked like he was into her."

"Of course he is. Birds of a feather."

"I don't know about that, but I can say that they're

two incredibly attractive people who seem to be simpatico. If they crash and burn, it's not your business."

"No, it isn't my business until that fiery burnout leaches into daily business at Athena. And it will."

"Listen. I'm going to give you the same advice you gave me after Oren dumped me and I was in a salty, bitter funk."

Raleigh was certainly in one of those. He hated that feeling that he'd lost control over something, and there wasn't anything he could do to fix it except *wait*. Waiting was hard when it stung so much. "I don't remember saying anything particularly reflective."

"You told me to go out and buy myself something frivolous, so I bought myself a robo-vacuum. I call him Zippy. Way better than a cat."

"A…robo-vacuum," Raleigh confirmed in a flat tone.

Only Stacia could try to treat heartbreak with a trendy gadget. The strategy hadn't immediately worked, the best he could remember, but her floors were certainly clean.

"Made me a little bit happy," she said, "and after a while, I realized that you were right. I deserved to have something nice. Go do something nice for yourself and forget about…" She flicked her hand in the general direction of the exit. "That. Mind over matter. You've been a master at that forever. Don't let all that practice go to waste now."

"You're right." He straightened his spine and gave a determined nod that was all lie.

He wasn't some flimsy naif who crumbled at the slightest hint of trouble, but his life had gotten a bit messier than he could typically ignore. He couldn't let it stay that way, or he'd become bitter and hostile to the people who really did care about him, and he never wanted to do that.

He wasn't going to let Everley distract him any more than she already had. Eggshells or not, he was still going to get shit done at Athena because he loved his job.

And he certainly wasn't going to moon over the tragedy that was Bruce Engle. Everley could have him.

Raleigh would buy himself something frivolous. He wasn't sure what it'd be yet, but neither books nor concert tickets were anywhere on the list of potentials.

Maybe a nice sweater.

Chapter Thirteen

Bruce shambled into Everley's apartment and pulled her into his arms. He didn't know what to say, but she never seemed to mind.

She got him. He didn't understand it, but she got him.

"You should have told me you were heading back to New York," she murmured against his chest.

He wasn't ready to let go of her quite yet, even if it meant hearing her better. It'd been a fucking miserable flight and before that, two days of interactions that had left him confused and reeling. He wanted to go into the dark for a while to decompress, but he couldn't.

There was too much to be done.

"I didn't know I was coming. I'm supposed to be in LA, I guess, but it's just as easy to be here. I'd *rather* be here."

"What's wrong?"

Sighing, he unhanded her and headed to the armchair by the windows. He shooed her cat out of it and rubbed his eyes. "They didn't like it."

"They?" Everley sat on the loveseat nearby and gripped his knee.

Oh, hell.

Her makeup was half off. He must have interrupted

her midswipe during her pursuit of gray eyeshadow removal. She'd inadvertently gone semi-raccoon.

"Oh, love," he whispered, swiping the pad of his thumb beneath her eyes. She always dropped everything for him and he hadn't noticed.

"It's all right," she said, studying his stained thumb. "It always looks worse before it looks better. Tell me what happened."

"I get so caught up with…what I have to say that I don't stop to think that you might want to say something."

"It's all right. I'm used to waiting my turn."

"You should get to go first sometimes."

"I'll tell you when I need to."

Oh.

He never knew what to say when people surprised him, but he knew that people were supposed to say things. He'd had some of those things memorized once, but he'd stopped using them because they hadn't felt right.

"Thank you," he offered instead. He didn't know if it was right, but he genuinely meant it, at least, and she smiled upon hearing it.

"I sent my parents an early edit of the film. You know, the one about the band."

"You didn't tell me about that."

"Slipped my mind with all the back-and-forth I've been doing between here and LA."

He'd been in so many planes, going in so many directions, that he couldn't even say for sure what the date was or which time zone his brain thought he was in.

Her eyebrows raised. "And you said they didn't like it?"

"They don't."

"What about it didn't they like? I haven't seen it, so I don't know what you were doing. Was it like…you know…sex stuff?"

"Oh, *God*, no." He laughed. If there had been, his parents probably wouldn't have survived even an insinuation of it. "There was a bit that was filmed just before Nan died. We were talking about what the doctor had said."

"Your nan's doctor?"

"No. Mine. Nan always said not to tell anyone because it didn't change anything but I'm telling you because it's in the film and my parents are upset. Remember when I told you that they didn't want anyone to put a diagnosis on me?"

"I do. I didn't ask then, but what is it?"

"Better to ask what it isn't, probably. I've got disorders stacked on top of each other. At least three, but the doctor can't be really sure what's what because they blur together. Overlap. Not all one thing, but bits and pieces of several. My parents said it'd ruin my career if people found out. My brain's not wired right. They said for me to have them edit that stuff out, but I can't, can I?"

"Do you want to?"

"No. For what?"

Bruce didn't care, and maybe it was wrong of him not to care, but he didn't see how it could possibly make things worse.

Except with Everley. He couldn't predict how she'd react, and if she'd be like his parents. "Is that…off-putting to you?"

She flinched away at the question. "I have scoliosis and had to have my spine fused when I was a child. Does that disturb you?"

"You couldn't help that."

"All right, then." She stood and clapped her hands as though she was done with the topic and was ready to put it behind her.

"You telling me you don't care, Ev?"

"That's exactly what I'm telling you."

"Why not?"

She shrugged. "Maybe I don't find you all that unusual."

A surge of long-absent contentment pulsed through Bruce's chest, warming him from the inside out. It was that doesn't-matter sensation his nan had squeezed into him with every tight hug, every laugh with him, every odd gift she gave him.

He'd forgotten what it felt like—having all his foibles forgiven without ever having to ask.

Being liked for them.

"Most people do," he murmured, rubbing the warm place over his heart.

She didn't immediately respond. Bad things rarely came of her silence. She wasn't like others he'd tried to know.

"Most folks don't go to college with a bunch of guys who insisted that numbers made far more sense than people." Her brow creased and she stared at the dark red polish on her nails. "Most of the time, I agreed with them."

He must have done something right to have stumbled into her acquaintance, though for the life of him he couldn't guess what.

He edged closer to her, because she was too far away, and anyone in the doesn't-matter class wouldn't mind so much if he crowded them. He *hoped*.

"What would you do if you were me?"

There was no one whose opinion he valued more than hers. Since the day they'd met, she'd only given him patience and honesty. Those were qualities that rarely existed together in one person. Raleigh had been incredibly forthright, but he hadn't been patient.

Bruce hated that he still thought about him, and knew that he probably always would for as long as he had some attachment to Athena. Raleigh had been his idea of the gold standard, and even with what had transpired, his opinion hadn't changed.

Maybe it still can.

"I'm really not the best person to ask," she said quietly. "I can talk about ideal circumstances, but who am I to speak on them? I've got a job that I hate and that I'm afraid to leave because of what I fear *my* parents would say and do."

"I wish you'd tell me anyway."

"Okay. But remember, it means nothing coming from me." She wagged a finger at him and sidled back over at his gesturing. "If I were you, I'd say to hell with it and let the world know, because why not? Stigmas thrive because of ignorance and isolation, and I think some of them are long overdue to be starved. You could help that."

"I'm not going to be anyone's role model, love," Bruce said with a chuckle, pulling her into the vee of his open legs.

"You don't have to be a role model. You just have to be Bruce. I happen to adore Bruce."

"Why?"

She laughed and pushed his mop of hair behind both ears. "Give me some time to chew on that one. I happen to like chocolate, too, but I don't know if I'd be able to explain why. I just know that when I see it, it makes me happy. Chocolate has never disappointed me."

"I think I would like to be chocolate, then. The kind with some sort of sticky filling."

Everley snorted and gave him a kiss on the top of the head as she pulled away. "Smart. I always have to take my time with the filled kind. You've got to savor all the layers of flavor."

He liked that idea. He wanted to last with her.

Heading toward her bedroom, she called over her shoulder, "I hurried home from work to do a six o'clock conference call. I didn't want to be in the office at eight o'clock and have to worry about getting home in the dark."

"You're busy, then?" He sprang to his feet automatically because even if he knew she hadn't intended them that way, those sorts of words were used to dismiss.

"No, no, it's okay. It's not a terribly critical call, just that people take note of who's putting in the effort and who's not. I try not to be conspicuously absent whenever I can help it. I don't want anyone to think I'm getting special treatment, beyond the obvious sort. Can't do anything about that, though." Her voice was solemn and he was sad because he didn't know what to say. His response to his parents' meddling had been avoidance in recent years, and she couldn't very well do that. At least, he didn't think she could. She had her head screwed on right. He was counting on her to figure something out eventually, and for his own selfish reasons. He liked her when she wasn't stressed, because she helped him bounce all of his own pressure away.

She probably didn't even know.

"If you can occupy yourself for a bit," she called out, "we can do something later. I mean…if you want to? I don't know if you want to. Don't feel obligated to—"

"Corduroy is doing a gig uptown," he blurted before she could change her mind. Of *course* he wanted to spend every doesn't-matter moment he could with her. He had years of them to make up. "Sold out, but I could probably get us backstage. Don't know if that's your thing."

Water trickled in the bathroom. Floorboards creaked. He heard a murmured "Corduroy?"

He cringed.

Maybe not Corduroy, then. Stupid. So fucking stupid.

They weren't most people's thing, but he hadn't been raised like most people. The band had been good at reminding him of that as often as they could when they were still together. Bruce's nan had controlled the stereo in his earliest years, so he couldn't help who his influences were. Sometimes he channeled Billy Joel, Mick Jagger, or Springsteen. Other times, he channeled a group of geezers with harmonicas and accordions and the occasional bagpipe. Those windbags could really jam when they got enough whiskey in them.

"Where the hell are they playing?" Everley asked with a laugh. She emerged from the bathroom fresh faced and in sweats. He liked her sweats. They didn't match, but they had that lived-in look about them and proved that she didn't just pretend at relaxing. He envied her ability to do it. He'd never really learned how, in spite of his nan's best efforts. There always seemed to be too much to do, too much to learn, too many conversations to have.

"I can't imagine what venue uptown would draw a crowd for them," Everley continued.

"They're at Minnow's. It's an old dinner theater."

"Shit. I just undressed," she groaned. "I can't wear this at a place like that."

"You mean, you want to go?"

"Of course! I think it'd be fun."

Huh. He dragged hand down his face and stared at her with awe. The best he could tell, she'd meant it.

She was probably the only person he knew who'd think that.

Certainly, she can't be that perfect. Could she be?

He kept waiting to be disappointed. Everyone disappointed him eventually.

She poured herself a glass of water and settled in front of her computer. "I'm going to have to put this call on speaker. I think the cat dragged my headphones into some sort of unreachable nether region. I haven't seen them in two weeks."

"I'll be quiet."

"You're lovely, you know that?"

"Well, that's a new one. I'll take it."

She arched a wry brow and joined the call.

Bruce drifted around her apartment. Having crashed at her place several times in recent weeks, he'd already seen everything in it, the exception being the underside of her sheets. That was unusual for him, not feeling compelled to skip straight to the bedroom athletics, because there were so many other things he wanted to do with her and not enough hours to do them in.

He wasn't entirely certain what to make of the situation, but was content with letting things stand as they were. His relationship with Ev was the single most functional connection he'd forged in recent memory. Maybe she wouldn't agree, but he thought he was a better person for having had it.

"Why don't we just dismantle the program if no one ever wants to take it on each year?" came a strident voice from Ev's call. Bruce didn't recognize the speaker, but whomever he was, he was certainly impassioned.

"We can't dismantle it." Bruce knew that voice. It was that guy Joey. He'd been reaching out to Bruce's manager about book shit, saying something about promotional deadlines. Bruce hadn't gotten around to calling back. Or maybe he didn't want to.

Probably, he didn't want to.

"Charities count on our yearly donations," Joey continued. "The program has been in place for so long that it's practically become a line item in their yearly budgets."

"It's a lot of work," a woman said with a groan. "At the risk of sounding childish in the presence of the two human resources officers on this call, I gotta say that we've got enough to do during the holiday season without doing extra work for free."

"Especially here in the publicity hallway."

Ah.

Bruce's back teeth snapped together and ground upon registering the voice.

He turned away from the precariously tilting potted pineapple plant he'd been poking at right as Everley began to drum the end of her pencil against her notepad with agitation.

Apparently, that particular bitter baritone had a similar effect on both of them. He was all ears, though, hungrily lusting after every word because that dangerous obsession hadn't yet waned. He needed more, even if he didn't particularly want to have it.

"Cora's right, though," Raleigh continued. "If charity is important to Athena, Athena needs to incorporate the annual campaigns into someone's job and pay them for it. Athena is a for-profit business and shouldn't expect staff to do extra work for free."

"It's always so funny that you sound exactly like your father and yet say things that would never come out of his mouth," Joey said.

Some other man chuckled. "He'd be appalled at the insinuation that unpaid overtime isn't an honor, wouldn't he, Raleigh?"

Raleigh didn't respond, and Bruce squashed his compulsion to shout, "Well, say something, then." He'd behave.

Everley had stopped drumming her pencil, though, and was leaning toward the screen, massaging the bridge of her nose. "Let's try to stay on track," she said in a voice that gave away not even the smallest hint of the nervousness her red cheeks hinted at. "It's Friday night, and I'm sure we all have things we want to do."

"I just can't do it this year, guys," a woman said. "The daycare is already giving me flak about picking my kid up five minutes late every day. I can't take on one more thing."

Silence.

Bruce bit down hard on his tongue. He wanted Raleigh to volunteer for whatever it was, because at least that would prove he was kind sometimes, even if not to Bruce.

And then, from Ev, "So, what are our options? I can't see where this is a job we can pass on to junior staff. They don't have the clout."

"Or the pay grade," Raleigh murmured.

"I…agree. Senior execs are in and out of the office too much. The point of contact has to be someone who can actually be reached."

"I'm aware of that, Ms. *Shannon*."

Ev rolled her eyes.

"Why the fuck is he like that?" Bruce murmured.

Everley waved off the query, though he could tell she wasn't at ease with the circumstances. She'd started rubbing her temples.

"The job was mine last year," Raleigh said. "And the year before. And…the year before, I believe."

Ev's jaw hinges tightened and lips pressed into a flat line.

She didn't deserve the snark. He wrapped his arms around Ev's neck and gave her an encouraging squeeze. It seemed like the sort of thing she would do for him. "Don't let him rile you up," he said into her ear. "He doesn't deserve your energy."

The squeeze she gave his wrist was probably meant to be conceding.

"Can you not just do it again, Raleigh?" someone asked. "After all, you won't have a learning curve. You already know how the campaign works."

"Yes, and I happen to know how many hours it takes. I logged them last year and informed HR precisely what the duties were so that everyone involved could understand how it's impossible to put the task on one person without either forcing them to do unpaid labor or to undermine their efficiency in their usual job."

"How about if you split it, then?" Ev asked on a sigh.

"*Me?*" Raleigh asked with incredulity.

"Wait, wait," Joey said. "That might be a solution. If we can't find one person with enough flexibility in their schedule to spearhead the event then we could put a team on it."

"Don't do it, Joey," Raleigh warned.

"We'll take it on. Yeah. Publicity will handle it this year if maybe editorial can commit to next year."

"Fine with me," a man said.

"Of course it's fine with you," Raleigh sniped. "You have the largest department."

"Not our fault."

As the cacophony of jeers rose up, Ev put her forehead against her desk and tapped it a few times against the wood.

"It's all right," Bruce whispered. "Don't feel like you have to volunteer to prove anything to anyone."

"But I have to," Ev whispered back. "They know I can afford it."

He couldn't argue with that, even if he wanted to. She was probably right that they'd think that, and he hated that she was put into that situation—that she couldn't say no.

She took a breath and gave Bruce's arm another squeeze. "Listen," she told the haggling Athena senior staff on the call. "This is getting needlessly complicated, I think. We're all busy right now, but I don't think the solution is to spread even more people thinner. I'll organize the campaign this year with the caveat that HR or admin have someone in their departments absorb the duty next year."

The call went quiet.

Ev turned to Bruce with brow furrowed and lips turned downward. "Did I sound too bossy?" she whispered. "That'd be the last thing I need right now when they all hate me already."

"You did fine," he insisted. If the fuckers at Athena thought otherwise, Bruce could suggest some deep breathing exercises they could try. Or else prescribe some eight-inch dildos. They always had a way of making Bruce relax.

"Awesome," someone on the call finally said. "I know the major charity loves it when we show up in person at their holiday gala with the big check. You might want to go ahead and clear your calendar for that day."

"What all am I getting myself into?" Ev asked, thumping her forehead again.

"Get up with Raleigh," Joey said in the spirited tone of a man off the hook. "He'll hand off the baton to you, in a matter of speaking."

The staff of Athena all bounced off the call with few further pleasantries and the conference web page automatically logged her out.

"They didn't even volunteer to help you," Bruce said with a doleful shake of his head. "Why are they like that?"

"It's *fine*, honey," Ev said wearily. "It is what it is. I'm not expecting any pats on the back, but hopefully they'll all think a little more charitably of me."

"Even Raleigh?" Bruce drummed his fingertips with agitation against the sides of his arms. He couldn't trust Raleigh to think charitably of any of his perceived enemies, and he hated him for making Everley one. She didn't deserve it.

Ev stared at her computer screen. The machine was pinging, again and again, as emails streamed in—each with a series of attachments.

They were all from McKean, Raleigh C.

"Hot potato," Ev murmured. "I guess I lose."

She fired off a message to him when the pinging finally stopped.

Should we have a meeting to chat about this?

Raleigh's response: I think that's unnecessary, but if you need clarification on anything I can make the time.

Everley: I'll read what you sent and will let you know by Monday.

Raleigh: Fine.

Raleigh signed his message with a dash and a simple R.

"So fucking rude. He should sign his whole name."

"It's fine." Ev put her head back and laid a kiss on the underside of Bruce's chin.

"It's not fine. It's cold."

"Maybe, but you shouldn't worry about it. I'm not."

Ev retreated to her bedroom, ostensibly to finish getting ready. Bruce pressed his palms flat against the desktop and glowered at that dash and that R. Ev deserved better.

Bruce deserved better.

Ev had said, though—*it is what it is.*

It didn't have to be that way, though.

In his idea of a perfect world, everyone would understand everyone else and they'd forgive each other for what they couldn't say.

Real life didn't work that way, though.

In real life, second chances meant the giver was a sucker and the recipient was a user, and so the default was to not have them.

But he'd be fine. Ev wasn't a surrogate of the connection he'd desired with Raleigh. She was far more than that. She was his lesson that affection was supposed to be *easy*—both the giving of it and the receiving.

"I'm going to buy you a Purple Park Place, Ev," he called out. "I'd buy you the sun if you wanted it, but a cocktail sounds all right for the time being."

Staring at that screen, he couldn't help himself. The impulsive little creatures that lived in his nervous system had him moving the cursor to the Reply button and his fingers dancing across the laptop's keyboard.

"What the hell is a Purple Park Place?" she responded with a laugh. He loved her laugh.

"A god-awful drink the dinner theater serves. Comes with a cheese tray appetizer. Positively horrid but it's something of a rite of passage there."

You should be kinder to her. You won't always be able to be like that. You'll die lonely. Mark my words.

He clicked Send and closed the laptop lid.

Ev stepped out in a gray cardigan, a long black skirt, and black boots.

He assessed the masterpiece, framing the image of her with his hands. "Perfect."

"You're full of it." She grabbed her purse and keys and marched toward the door. "But keep that up, anyway. Sometimes a girl needs to hear it."

Mark my words.

"She must have finally gone off her rocker." Raleigh stared at the message in his work inbox, perplexed.

He was still reeling from it as he carried a stack of

hardcopy files to Everley's office and dropped them on the corner of her desk. Up until that moment, Everley's messages had always been professional, even if somewhat meddling.

"Maybe she decided it didn't matter anyway. She can do what she wants."

Joey, still at work at almost eight on a Friday, poked his head out of his office. "What's that, Ral?"

Raleigh opened his mouth to explain, but suddenly decided better of it. He didn't need Joey to intercede on his behalf. Raleigh had been advocating for himself since he was a teenager.

"Ignore me. Being in the windowless center of a building is getting to me. Everything seems more claustrophobic with them having installed the holiday decorations earlier this year."

"Yeah. Early as shit. They're trying to get their money's worth, I guess. Just try to ignore it until December first."

"I'll try."

Joey suddenly perked up. "Hey! Since you're here, I'm working on—"

"Joey," Raleigh warned. He knew that lead-up tone. It always preceded some major project being dumped on his lap.

Joey put up his hands and retreated into his hidey-hole. "Had to try. That's what managers do."

"You're only my manager because of a merger." Raleigh couldn't even remember which one anymore. Athena had been acquired, divested, and merged so many times in ten years that he could no longer remember who all had been there when he started.

"Okay, Mr. Lone Wolf. Don't rub it in. If you feel

any mercy at all for the guy who approves your time off requests for HR, though, you know where I'll be."

"Noted."

Raleigh went into his office to fetch his coat and bag. He took one last glance at the open message before closing the computer.

The wording wasn't right, or the point of view, maybe.

Either Everley was trolling him—which he, in spite of his wariness about the woman in general, doubted—or someone else had gotten into her email.

Know what that's like.

Grimacing, he stabbed the elevator call button with his index finger. He supposed he had to think charitably of her, for the moment.

He could worry about who the hell had gotten into her inbox later.

It wouldn't have been the first time Athena's email server had gotten hacked. Their IT department was basically an extern, a can of compressed air, and a roll of duct tape.

Sometimes, though, even spam massages cut to the quick.

He was going to die lonely.

That was probably true.

Chapter Fourteen

"Christ, you're harder to catch than Usain Bolt chasing a gold medal."

Bruce invited his manager into his hotel room, mulling over Kit's odd metaphor. It took him a moment to remember who Usain Bolt was.

"You've got to stop doing that, you know?" Kit laid in before Bruce even had a chance to turn back to him. "You can't just go off the fucking grid when people are trying to reach you."

"What are you trying to reach me for?" Bruce edged past him in the narrow corridor and retreated to the pile of papers on the desk that he'd been trying to make heads or tails of all morning. Investments he hadn't made, but had been made for him. His father had chosen everything since Bruce wouldn't. He'd been looking up some of the funds and ventures and hadn't yet had a good feeling about a single one of them. They were profitable, but antithetical to Bruce's evolving sense of world citizenship. He didn't want to make money at the expense of some less fortunate person's health or life. He had more money than he could ever spend. He didn't need more of it.

Uninvited, Kit had a seat on the sofa and immediately started riffling through a leather portfolio. "I've got interest from about ten magazines who want to do features on you—"

"No."

"—and it'd be good promo for the...what do you mean, *no*?"

Bruce shrugged. "Don't want to."

"Why the hell not? Do you understand how fame works?"

"Contrary to what you might think, I'm not a fucking idiot, Kit."

Kit stared, agape.

Bruce didn't hold his gaze. If he did, he'd change his mind even though he hadn't done anything wrong. People he'd worked with had gotten so good at getting him to change his mind. Time and distance from them had rendered Bruce highly sensitive to the attempts, and he wasn't going to let them railroad him anymore.

"Then let's put this another way and see if that makes a difference," Kit said flatly after a minute. "Do you understand that if you're not making money, I'm not either?"

Bruce felt bad about that for the few seconds he took to remember that he'd already known Kit would use that defense. His nan had taught him that in that business, almost everything came down to money and he had to assume that was people's first interest. Bruce was just a product.

"I can let you off the hook, if you want." He shuffled through the papers again, resorting them into piles by priority. He wasn't certain how to detach himself from those investments but it seemed increasingly vital to his mental health that he do so. His brother might know how. Arnold stayed on top of that shit. He was in South Africa all the time handling business.

"So, what, you're not going to make music anymore?" Kit emitted one of those snorts Bruce tended to hear from people who had habits of underestimating the willpower of the people they engaged with.

Bruce may have gone along with the program before, but his recent company had taught him that there was no program.

Not for him, anyway, and that was okay. Ev had reminded him that was okay.

"I'm done with that now," Bruce said.

"And when the hell did you decide that?"

"Dunno." Bruce shrugged. "Maybe it's been a long time coming."

"You're ridiculous. You know that? I've invested all this time and energy into making you into something and you turn around and say, nah, I'm done?" He scoffed. "Nah. Doesn't work that way. You owe me. Do you understand? You *owe* me."

Do I?

Bruce was wavering, and he knew it, but he hadn't considered that before.

Kit had been on Bruce's team for ten years. He'd paved Bruce's way in America and helped turn him into a household name.

Bruce had gotten to play his music for people.

He should have been happy.

It didn't seem like the right kind of happy, though. Or perhaps it was incomplete and it had taken Bruce a decade to figure out why. They'd packaged him into something he wasn't. He wasn't a rock star. He was a wildling from rural Scotland who held a tune all right.

I don't owe him. I don't owe him a thing.

That realization cleared out a bit of murk in the corner of his brain so the truth buried there could climb out.

"Your...contract is up, isn't it?" Bruce smoothed down the corner of a fund transfer form and then bent it once more. "Never got around to renewing it."

Kit didn't say anything.

Neither did Bruce. Not saying anything was always hard, but silence was the only way he could say what he needed to.

He wasn't a rock star. Just a musician. He could have his music and tell his stories without all the glamour. Without the spotlights and the unwanted jet setting.

In Bruce's periphery, Kit got up, snatched his bag, and stormed toward the door.

"Do what you want. You won't be successful. You can't even talk to people."

"I'm talking to you, aren't I?" Bruce did meet his gaze, then, because Kit needed to understand. They all needed to understand. "That's the problem with you. You think I only get it—whatever *it* is—if it's the thing you want. But you didn't stop to think that I didn't want it."

"Corrine said that—"

"*Don't* drag my nan into this," Bruce shouted.

Bruce wasn't a shouter, and that was likely why Kit nearly leaped out of his skin.

He recovered quickly, though, straightening his cufflinks and turning that haughty stare to Bruce.

"She's dead and gone," Bruce said in a forced, quiet volume. "I'm still here. And if she were here, she'd be helping to get what I want next, whatever it may be."

"And what is that, Bruce? Huh? What the hell do you want?"

Bruce went silent again and turned back to his papers.

"See, you don't even know. Whatever. You're going to fail without me. You're going to fail without the band. I thought you'd come to your senses and hook back up with them, but I guess you're not hurting enough, huh? You don't care about anyone except yourself. All those people counting on the money. They've got to pay their mortgages and their kids' school tuitions. You care about that? You don't even—"

Kit said a lot of words but Bruce stared at his moving mouth without listening.

I'm not important unless they're important.

Seemed like the start of a new song for that musical Ev said he should write. Sardonically upbeat. Bright instrumentation, perhaps with lots of flutes and bells. A slow transition to minor key. Ominous timpani.

Measures upon measures of anguished balladry and screaming pipe organ to wrap it all up.

It could be the big song right before the show went to intermission and the lead would walk off the stage with his head down and the spotlight trailing a few feet behind him.

But in act two, he'd get better.

He'd sort things out because he'd found someone to tell him that he could use his talents in different ways and that he could trust his abilities, even if he was anxious about the gaps in his knowledge. Even if he was certain he'd mess up many times before he landed successfully.

Everley had taught him that, perhaps without even meaning to.

The door slammed behind Kit.

Bruce stared at it for a minute, maybe more.

Then he picked up the phone and dialed his mother. He didn't have a choice but to make her understand that he needed change. That meant getting rid of the things that he'd never wanted in the first place. He needed to put his life on course. He wanted to establish his own routines and set goals that made sense for Bruce at thirty-three and that he could grow further at forty.

Essentially, he was going to have to turn himself inside out and rid himself of all the shit that didn't fit. Then, he could be creative again.

He'd spent his whole life waiting for other people to tell him they were proud and had wondered why he hadn't felt satisfied when they did. It was because he wasn't concerned enough with whether or not he was proud of *himself.*

"I...have to tell you something." The following week, Bruce drew Ev down to his lap and sighed as her body received his shaft.

His breath fell out in a reflexive gust and his arms tightened around her waist.

She was so warm, so accommodating.

She put her head back on his shoulder and groaned through clenched teeth. She placed her hand on her clit and started to rock. "Now?"

He was aching from navel to toenails, needing her so badly, body straining for her. "No," he rasped.

The connection was more important. Touching her was more important for the time being. He'd been so starved for it and he'd decided that only her skin would satisfy.

He satisfied his oral fixation with a tug of her earlobe with his lips. That made her crane her neck around so her mouth found his. Their tongues chased as she rocked up and down, squeezing him tightly in her heat. Setting fire to the short fuse in him. He couldn't last with her. He was too impatient and wanted her so much.

Too much, maybe.

"God, I love you."

She stilled, her ragged breathing suddenly halting altogether.

The words had tumbled out of his mouth without thought like so many other things, but he'd never blurted those before. He'd been thinking them so much, though, because he'd gotten attached because she made him comfortable and he didn't have to try so hard to be understood. She read him in a way few others could.

Most didn't want to try. Too much effort and they were busy.

Busy busy busy.

"Bruce—"

"Hush." He laid a hand over her mouth and put his lips on her neck again. She tasted of salt and smelled like cherry blossoms. He'd gotten so he'd become aroused by the scent even when she wasn't nearby. It was her signature—a dab behind each ear and beneath each wrist.

He imagined that heaven smelled like cherry blossoms.

"I need you. Okay?"

She nodded and gripped the wrist of the arm he held around her waist. She hooked her feet behind his calves and chased her pleasure on him. Up down, breathing chaotic and staggering again, body tensing with anticipation.

His burned as his toes curled into the plush carpet of her living room.

He closed his eyes and tried to linger at that place of pleasure, but he couldn't hold on. Not when she needed him so much for this thing he didn't have to think too hard about.

Feels good. Do it.

That was all.

He had to hurry her along, so he found that magic button, gathered up some wetness from the place they joined, and slicked it on her. He massaged her and prayed her intention hadn't been to outlast him. Rock star stamina was a myth as far as he was concerned.

She got into the race, lowering herself on him faster and churning out moan after moan.

"Come on, darlin', you know I can't keep up with you."

He kept strumming until she screamed and he'd never been more pleased to be ambidextrous. He held her tight against him until he stopped spilling and then collapsed back against her sofa cushions, taking her along with him and not bothering to unsheathe.

"You're leaving me, aren't you?" she said after their breathing had normalized and his legs had stopped twitching. "You had something you needed to say, but I don't think it was the confession of love."

He did love her, and as much more than a friend, but that's where they were for the time being. He couldn't make new attachments until he'd sloughed off some old ones. Maybe she wouldn't even like him when he was done.

Sighing, Ev scraped the hair back from her forehead and leaned slowly on her forearms. "So, this really is goodbye."

"I have to go away. I don't know when I'll be back."

"Why?" Her voice was so small and lacked its usual thrum of fortitude.

He'd done that to her and it broke his heart. He'd fix everything, though, if she gave him the time.

"It's all the attachments. The business stuff. The property and all the various investments. I tried to get my parents to help me sort it out last week but they didn't take me seriously. I think they assume I hadn't thought about it before now and that I've made a rash decision. I didn't. They don't get it."

They didn't get *him*.

"It's a fucking mess. I've got to unwind things in South Africa. The way things are set up, I have to present myself in person and for some, remain nearby for periods of one to two weeks before I'm allowed to terminate or cash out any of the properties or investments. Imagine that times five or ten. They're all seated in different places. I suppose my grandfather thought if it was too easy to unload that people could take it from us. He was probably too arrogant to think that one of us might not have wanted it in the first place."

If Ev had an opinion on the matter, her face didn't indicate what it was. In fact, he would have thought she'd completely tuned out if not for the fact that she was fondling a bit of his hair.

"I'm a grown man," he continued, just to get the words out. "I have to do some things for myself and not wait for someone to tell me I have to. Setting my family straight, for one. We're long overdue for some hard truths to come out between us all. I'm tired of feeling like I'm in the wrong and that they never meet me halfway. It's just hanging over my head and I always wonder when it's going to fall, you know?"

"Oh," she whispered. She picked up the pendant hanging from one of the gold chains around his neck. Too girly. Too ornate with all that filigree and those flower engravings. His granddad had given it to his nan when she was seventeen and she'd given it to Bruce when he was twenty because he couldn't help but to lift it for another look whenever it caught his eye.

Ev let it fall gently against his chest and gave it an attentive pat before withdrawing her hand. She hadn't asked about the jewelry, but knowing Ev, she might have figured out on her own that the pendant was important to him.

"I understand," she said. "You have to confront it all, for better or worse."

"I feel like I'd be able to make decisions if I could. I might be wrong."

"I think you're right. I think we both need to have conversations with our families that we don't want to. Or in my case, shouting matches. It's just... I don't know what to *do* anymore." With each word, her voice got softer, less resolute. "My father thinks that I can stay in my current situation and that in a few years' time, I'll become complacent enough to grow into it. I want more than that. I want to build something I can be excited about."

"Of course you should. Misery shouldn't be anyone's birthright."

"But here I am with this obscene amount of privilege and I have the audacity to be unhappy. I have the audacity to consider going without a salary for how-ever long and helping my friend get her business off the ground. That would make me happy, knowing that she has something, and that she's taken care of and suc-cessful. I feel like I can make a difference, but I have to disappoint people to do it."

They were in a similar boat, him and Ev, and they couldn't bail each other out. They each had to throw themselves overboard and make their way toward whichever mass of land could sustain them. That meant they wouldn't necessarily be going in the same direc-tion, but they could reunite once they'd found their moorings again.

"I'm never happy when I'm pretending to be some-one else," he said. "You helped me realize that."

After a few moments, she nodded against his shoul-der. "I'm smart sometimes. I should take my own ad-vice."

"Do. *Please* do, love."

"If your dealings with your family go badly, you're going to hate me, aren't you?"

"You know I won't." In fact, Bruce already antici-pated the confrontation going badly. They were going to talk over him in that quiet, but insistent, way they always did, and he'd get confused. He'd talk himself in circles. He'd forget his point. They would triumph over his "coming 'round to reality" and offer him tea.

He'd written it all down, though. Every single point, and he was going to stay until he'd made every single one of them, even if he had to camp out on their front steps. Even if he had to make himself a spectacle, he wasn't going to let them win.

Some of that shit was going to come out in the film

or the book, anyway. He may as well stop avoiding the truth.

"If all goes according to plan, my portfolio will be far lighter this time next month," he said cheerfully. "Do you think you'd still like me if I didn't have my diamond mines and sketchy ore investments? I plan on donating them all to charity in my sister's name as a wedding gift. That ought to cause a very polite riot in the Engle townhouse."

Ev laughed, pulling her face away and wiping away a few errant tears. "You should call that song you sent me that. 'Polite Riot.' It was lovely, by the way."

"It was a joke."

"No. It wasn't. It was amazing."

Oh.

Her opinion meant more than anyone's to him.

"It doesn't sound like much of anything without the band," he demurred.

"No, it just doesn't sound like what you'd gotten used to. It's funny how people lose their voices when they become overly concerned with other people's ideas of success. You've just forgotten what yours sounds like."

He mulled that over as she dressed. He helped. He liked smoothing her seams and tucking her in. Like having his hands on her and how patient she was when she didn't really need the help.

"Will you...see anyone?" he asked when her clothes had been completely righted. "I can't promise I'll be able to stay in touch. You don't have to answer. If I were your boyfriend, I suppose I could demand an answer, but we never got there, did we?"

He'd take her with him, if he could. Hold her hand throughout and let her more direct logic guide him through the mess, but he needed to try to navigate the bullshit on his own. He couldn't demand that she prop him up while she was so busy trying to stay afloat herself.

When he returned, he'd be better for it, and they could be more than friends. *Legitimately* more.

If not, he'd leave her alone because she deserved to have someone with discipline and a plan.

"I don't know," she whispered, carefully turning his pendant over in her palm. "But don't let me stand in the way of your perfect someone if you stumble across them. Don't let opportunities slip away, Bruce. I'll be fine."

She was his opportunity, and he doubted anyone else would understand him the way she did, but he nodded, anyway, because he couldn't be selfish. "Aye. You do the same."

Chapter Fifteen

Everley had spent so many weeks in a fog of anxiety that she hadn't even realized that Christmas was barreling down on them and the entire publishing company was in a state of constant hyperproductivity. She was essentially on autopilot, somehow managing to get last-minute promotional coverage for books she couldn't even remember having read.

Somehow managing to get the charity donation drive sorted and promoted, basically by robotically performing the items in Raleigh's careful outline of tasks.

She'd been like that since about a week after Bruce left. She hadn't heard much from him. The couple of emails he'd sent from Johannesburg had been scant on details and he hadn't responded to her follow-ups.

He was in the weeds. She understood that. And she understood that in his prioritization scheme, she had to be lower than certain things. His family. His unwanted financial entanglements. His music.

She'd just never been with someone she'd simply *liked* so much before and was feeling far too vulnerable that their connection hadn't been permanent. She could go out and try to find someone who was just like him, at least on paper, but he wouldn't be the same. The replacement wouldn't have the same energy.

And they certainly wouldn't insist on holding her hand when they crossed the street because *"Christ, you could get plowed over."* She'd been crossing streets alone since she was eight, but she'd been so touched by Bruce's concern—or at the very notion that her survival meant something to someone she wasn't related to.

"All right, let's get this over with for the day, shall we? You're last in the department."

Raleigh's flat delivery from her office doorway made her slowly raise her head from the gift basket catalog she'd been staring at without seeing for who knew how long.

He leaned in her doorway holding a green Sharpie and a square piece of cardboard. Somehow, the snowflake graphic on the back of the card was familiar, but she couldn't quite recall why, especially not with her brain far too focused on the holder's sweater.

There were ugly holiday sweaters, and then there were designer-ugly ones. Raleigh's was the latter. The festive red monstrosity featured a reclining Mrs. Claus draped over a chaise like Marilyn Monroe in *There's No Business Like Show Business*. Instead of crooning "Lazy" like the chanteuse, a speech bubble pointed toward her mouth read "Hazy." Snow was falling heavily outside the window behind her and Rudolph's flashing nose flashed in five-second bursts.

The man was wearing a battery-powered sweater.

Her brain couldn't make sense of it.

Raleigh knocked. "I see you, but I can't tell if you're in here."

"Sorry," she said in a rasp of vocal disuse and cleared

her throat. She hadn't been talking much in the past few days. "What did you need?"

He held up the card. "I'm doing the Athena bingo."

"Bingo?" she whispered weakly, thinking of Bruce's Nan.

She'd learned a lot about the old lady—that she was buried in her favorite slippers, for one thing. And that she fancied black coffee and had her hair dyed to match.

Raleigh's brow creased. "Haven't you seen it? HR droned on about it for fifteen minutes during yesterday's all-hands meeting. You know. Right after congratulating you for getting that charity campaign finished on time."

"Oh." She might have zoned out then. Her brain had been a swamp of ideas ranging from December holidays at her parents' place in Oyster Bay to the dearth of food in her refrigerator. She hadn't felt like grocery shopping. Takeout was easy, even if she was just picking at it. "Well, the charity thing turned out to be simple thanks to all the notes you left in the margins. You've got a knack for that kind of thing."

That may have been something of an understatement. Raleigh didn't simply have a knack for charitable giving organizing, but he had strong opinions about how donations should be earmarked. He'd put schemes into place with the charities they partnered with. It didn't cost Athena anything extra to donate books to needy schools, but cash was a whole other animal. Raleigh had always insisted that Athena's donations be distributed via a fund named for the company so that the charity execs couldn't skim off so much of it. If they complained, Raleigh looked for a different charity. Fortunately, Everley had been able to ride on his coattails and piggyback on his prior year's work.

He was brilliant. She'd known that, though, from her first day at the office. She'd been awed by how creative he was. Her math-inclined brain was rigid as concrete in comparison.

"How does it work?" She rooted through the scattering of papers on her desk until she found her stack of cards. There were five—one for each day of the work-week.

"The prize is for an extra day of paid time off," he said. "I had to offload all my accumulated PTO before the merger and I need that extra day for the holidays."

"Plans?" she murmured, still on autopilot, still squinting at the cards. It seemed the natural thing to ask.

"Heading down to Richmond," he said after a few uncomfortable beats of silence. "New tradition at Stacia's."

"Not your parents'?"

She didn't think he was going to answer, and she wouldn't have blamed him. They weren't friends, though not for lack of trying on her part. The question was far too personal.

But then, just after the heat vent kicked on and mussed his shiny red hair a bit, he intoned with an acid snap, "No. I don't do holidays with my parents."

"Must be nice," came her reflexive whisper.

She took a bracing breath and read the instructions on the top card twice. The intricacies weren't quite landing right in her brain so she gave up. "What do you need me to do?"

"I've got my card for today ninety percent completed. I still need to find someone who's broken a bone, someone who'd been suspended from school at least once, and someone who's a natural blond. With the way the card's arranged, one of those has to be you. The rows are sorted by department."

"I suppose I'm the natural blond."

"You...*suppose*?" His eyebrows shot up.

"Dye."

"Why?"

"Because in my head, I'm a brunette. Plus I got tired of guys treating me like a ditz in my college math classes." She twined her fingers together and peered at the card again, wondering which of those items on line five might have referenced him. "Where did they get these trivia items?"

"We all sent a list two weeks ago."

"I don't remember doing that."

He shrugged and straightened up from the doorway. "Maybe your father sent them in."

He left before Everley could think of a response.

That sounded like something her father would do, though.

She groaned.

The next day, Raleigh's sweater was somewhat milder, at least in hue. It was black with silver tinsel woven into the neckline and speckled with crystal stars. It was the kind of sweater Everley's mother might have worn, but somehow, Raleigh managed to pull off the blue-blooded-housewife look.

"Ballet or Roller Derby," he asked her.

She shook her head. "Neither."

"What?" He glowered at the card, muttered, "Shit," and vanished.

He returned ten minutes later. "All right. Nickerson got her wires crossed. That means you must be the Beanie Baby collector."

Everley could feel every ounce of blood drain from her face. "I... I was *ten!*" she stammered, searching for her fucking card. She should have looked, because apparently her father was trying to shame her into irrelevance. Seeing as how that was the opposite of his master plan, she didn't understand why.

Raleigh clucked his tongue—whether from scorn or pity, she didn't know—made a note on his card, and left.

On Wednesday, Everley had actually looked at the day's card before Raleigh appeared in her doorway. She wondered if perhaps she should have been more motivated to get that PTO. It was too late for her to do anything about it, though. She'd missed the previous two days' cards.

"Named after a grandparent," Everley said.

Raleigh wrote it down.

"Which are you?" She tapped her card with the end of her candy cane. She wasn't fond of hard candy as a general rule, but she'd been using them to stir her coffee. There was a bowl of the damned things at the end of every hall. Joey had joked that they were there to offset the company's collective Seasonal Affective Disorder.

"Failed out of karate class."

"How is that even possible? Don't they just keep you at the same level until you master it?"

"Yes, until the studio owner realizes that he can use you to pass messages to your father."

"Why would anyone want to do that?"

"Do you know who my father is?"

"Yes?" She didn't know anyone who didn't.

"Then you're not getting it." He dragged a hand down

his face and let out a breath. "Randolph McKean. Senior senator from Ohio. Judiciary committee member. Arguably one of the most powerful string-pullers in government?"

Oh.

She scuffed the heel of her boot against the plastic carpet protector under her rolling chair with frustration. She hated feeling so slow on the uptake, especially knowing full well that she wasn't. Anxiety was a cruel beast. It messed up head wiring and confused longstanding logic. She just wanted to feel good again, but couldn't. Not until she acted, but she couldn't act.

That was another funny thing about anxiety. It stopped people who knew exactly what they needed from having the faith to implement the changes they needed to thrive.

"I…suppose people will go to extremes for access," she said. "So, the karate teacher wouldn't test you?"

"Unless my father got back to him. To this day, my father thinks I got tossed out of the studio because I'm an uncoordinated ne'er-do-well, and I didn't see fit to correct him."

Raleigh left.

Everley stared at the empty doorway for a minute, unmoored.

Randolph McKean was absolutely a big deal. He sat on important committees. He was brash and unapologetic when he was wrong. People either loved him or loved to hate him, and Everley hadn't ever thought how Raleigh's upbringing and worldview might have been affected by the relationship. She'd known about their public feuds, which was part of the reason she'd been curious about him in the first place. He was someone who could understand what it meant to be a family's black sheep.

But no one had ever tried to use her as a bargaining chip to get to her father.

"Damn," she whispered, adding a second candy cane to her mug. "Explains why he doesn't do family holidays, I guess."

She wished she could go to Stacia's, too.

Anywhere but "home," really, because at home, her parents were going to finish plotting the course of her life without knowing how far off-track Everley already was.

I'm...so done.

She let out a panicked titter and stared unseeing at the Outward Reaction full-size Bruce Engle cardboard cutout Joey had decided to store in her office.

If Bruce had been there, he might have said, "Let's both mess things up, love," but he wasn't there. He was in South Africa being brave and adult and probably moving on with his life, and she was in her office wondering how to fail gently.

Wondering how not to make a scene, because that was how women were trained to be.

She wished it were easier to just not give a shit.

She wished she were more like Raleigh.

She barely managed to suppress the panicked laughter bubbling in her chest as she opened her desk drawer and located her employment contract. "I can wish, or I can do. I don't need to fail gently. Clean breaks heal faster, don't they?"

She sounded more convinced than she felt, but there was no cure for that.

Page seven, paragraph four.

There was nothing stopping her.

She could just go, and nowhere in that document did it say that her father had to know she'd put in notice.

In fact, no one needed to know except the head of HR.

"I could just go."

She could do her two weeks. Pack her things. Disappear from the Shannon dynasty.

She didn't feel brave, but she didn't *have* to be.

It was okay to be scared. Fear meant change, and she desperately needed it. Bruce was chasing his change. So could she.

"Tomorrow, then." She cracked a tired smile and slid the contract into her bag. It seemed as good a day as any. Her therapist would be so proud.

On Thursday, Everley had her back to the door when Raleigh arrived. Being so startled by the sound of his voice, she nearly dropped the glass figurine she'd lifted from the top of her file cabinet.

"I'm not even going to try to guess," he said.

She hadn't looked at the card. She'd stepped into her office that morning and decided that her tchotchkes would look better in her living room. It was a slow day at the company, anyway. They wouldn't start cranking again until holidays had passed and most editors and agents were back in their offices.

She peered at day four's facts and rolled her eyes again.

Why her father was intent on embarrassing her, she didn't know.

"I'm guessing the 'enjoys charity work' one is supposed to be me, though he certainly wouldn't know anything about it. My mother probably helped him with that one. His idea of charity is writing a check to his golf club."

Raleigh blinked at her.

She groaned. "Sorry. I'm rambling and I know it's more information than you want or need. I'm just... getting twitchy about holidays. Have to do the usual command performance for the family. In all the years since I moved out of their house, I've never come up with a convincing excuse to just not be there."

"Tell the truth."

"The truth isn't tactful."

"No one said it had to be."

"You don't understand."

"No, I understand perfectly. It's easier to complain."

"That's not fair."

He shrugged. "Maybe not." He left.

Everley didn't know if Raleigh arrived or not the next day. She'd been out of her office for most of her work hours, dealing with human resources, explaining that she couldn't be talked out of it.

Explaining that it was time.

Explaining that it didn't really matter, anyway, because *none* of them wanted her there.

She promised them two weeks, which was long enough to train whoever would take over her roster. They'd promised not to publicize the opening, if they needed to, until after she left. For the sake of a quiet transition, they'd promised not to announce her departure from the company yet.

She didn't know what she was doing, but it didn't matter. What she did know was that in four days, only one person—a surprising one, at that—had come by her office to ask about those damned cards filled with facts meant to make her sound cute and interesting because she was going to be their boss one day.

She didn't want to be their boss, and she was going to prove it and try not to be ashamed that she'd refused such a "gift."

Some gifts weren't worth their costs.

She'd left her phone somewhere. There was something conducive to phone gazing about waiting on a subway platform, and Everley didn't have hers.

It must have been on her desk. She'd been in such a hurry to leave the office after finishing her round of meetings that she must have forgotten. At the very least, she'd have three or four minutes to wrestle her thoughts. The trains never ran on time. She knew better. Ten minutes, probably. She'd stand there near the edge in pinching shoes for ten minutes with people bumping her shoulders without saying excuse me and having the busker playing increasingly louder because no one was providing patronage. Her shoulders hurt and that drummer had added two new buckets to his makeshift kit since the last time she'd seen him.

She shifted all her weight to her left foot and closed her eyes. What choice did she have but to think? The problem wasn't going to resolve on its own.

She'd quit because she had to, and *when* she'd had to, but her plans for the interim were specious. Obviously, she'd do what she could for Lisa, but "best friend with cash" wasn't a job title. When her parents asked her why she'd thrown away her promise, she wouldn't be able to explain well that it hadn't been her promise in the first place.

She'd never before let herself think that she'd be allowed a "next," so she didn't have the right words to defend herself for finally breaking free enough to take a deep breath.

"Shit. First you try to poach my authors. Now you're poaching my style?"

She forced heavy eyelids open and tried to make sense of the voice because it didn't belong in that place.

Raleigh stood in a heavy black wool coat with his workbag slung across his body. The small sliver of his sweater she could see hinted that it was the most garish of reds, much like her own. She'd grabbed it off the mannequin in her favorite Euro-style store thinking it'd cheer her up, but all it'd managed to do was make her think about where she was supposed to be on Christmas day and why she didn't want to be there. They just wouldn't get it. Publishing wasn't her dream, and dreams were what made human beings reach for new heights.

Her tears hit the concrete and spread into uneven circles. She watched, detached, without quite understanding that she was the one leaking and not the station's roof for a change.

Raleigh tilted her chin up and muttered the rudest of swears, but it didn't quite seem directed to her. Just the situation in general.

"Christ," he said. "The last woman I made cry was my mother, but she was faking it to get me to cooperate with my father."

She swiped away the newest tears, sniffed hard, and put her back to him. "Allergies. Rodent population down here swells this time of year."

"Sure. I was teasing about the sweater, Everley. I'm sorry if the joke didn't land."

"You wear it better, anyway. I look like I'm trying too hard."

And maybe she was.

Trying to make herself feel better.

Trying to get people who disliked her for all the wrong reasons to at least tolerate her existence.

Trying to get people to understand.

She was exhausted.

He edged around her. Their toes met. Her stylish stilettos. His polished brogues.

"I may have been unkind about the other part, too," he said.

"I don't want your authors. I just wanted to help."

"Why?"

"I know it looks bad," she admitted. "I know it looks like… I'm trying to put my thumbprint into something you've made. I realize now how it comes across, and…" She forced her gaze upward, feeling every muscle in her stiff neck coil and pop as she angled her head. She couldn't remember ever standing so close to him before. Close as lovers, even. His open coat had wrapped around back of her leg. Once, she'd wanted that. She'd wanted *him*, but then there was Bruce who was loving and kind and he'd wanted her back.

He was gone, though, and it didn't matter what she wanted.

Nothing mattered until she could pick her head up and march on her own path.

She just needed a little time.

Chapter Sixteen

She was a million miles away. If she'd noticed she hadn't completed her thought, she didn't seem particularly motivated to follow up on it.

He was good at making people talk, though. He had a handful of authors on his roster who couldn't string words together except on paper and he always managed to get some decent-sounding syllables out of them, too.

"I'm feeling generous today," he said. "I won that PTO plus a gift basket full of Athena swag because I'm the only one who got the bonus square right."

"Bonus square?" she asked in a nearly inaudible voice. "What was it?"

"It asked what's on the art print next to the door in your office."

She scrunched her nose. "I...don't even know what that is. It came with the office."

"Doesn't matter. I got it right." He rubbed his gloved hands together. "So, because you're indirectly responsible for my good fortune, I insist that you let me buy you lunch after we're both back in the office after the holiday."

Perhaps Christmas miracles were multiplying because the train showed up. It was stuffed to the gills with people in big coats carrying far too many bags, but Raleigh pushed her in anyway because the Express wasn't running and there wasn't a better option. That was why he was on that platform in the first place. He usually preferred to go straight home rather than the long way around, but that was better than walking thirty blocks.

Everley grabbed the pole, seemingly oblivious of her surroundings—a second after the train lurched to a start. That sort of distractedness couldn't be faked. Everley Shannon was no wilting flower. She was the epitome of forward practicality, but at that moment, she hadn't remembered that trains moved.

Something was wrong.

Stacia had been right about the weariness on Everley's face, but now there was nothing behind her eyes at all except more moisture.

Perhaps it was her family. He'd been too brutal in suggesting that she suck it up and speak her mind. Generally, he had little patience for people who skirted inevitable interpersonal conflicts.

But it was different for her. She didn't have older brothers go to bat, even if begrudgingly, for her. And maybe she didn't have those same aggressive self-protective instincts for when to cut people off who were no longer deserving of her energy.

He felt sorry for her, if she didn't.

"Anywhere except the restaurant downstairs," he nudged, hoping to normalize her energy level. The city was a dangerous place for people who weren't paying attention. "There's only so much egg drop soup I can eat."

"Uh. Dinner," she said.

"Hmm?"

She closed her eyes and gave her head a hard shake.

She was quiet for so long that he had to assume she'd retreated into her own brain again. He didn't know her well enough, but if she were anything at all like he'd been at twenty, or even thirty, that space wasn't always a good place to be.

He reached for her cuff, intending to stir her from her silence, but the train's speakers relayed the stop and roused her before he could.

"Dinner instead. I…my schedule at work. It's weird lately, so…maybe dinner tonight." Her lips twitched at one corner. Perhaps that was meant to be a smile, but it wouldn't have convinced anyone. "I'm a cheap date. Easily amused."

"I wouldn't have pegged you for it."

"Because of my last name?"

"If we're going to be honest, yes."

She let out a long gust of breath full of weariness and probably frustration, and tilted her gaze toward the overhead advertising.

"Unlike my father," he murmured, "lying doesn't come easily for me. Would you have me lie?"

"I prefer the honesty."

"And yet you're dating Bruce?"

Her posture righted then, and her suddenly steely gaze leveled on him. "I'm not…*dating* anyone right now. And what the hell is that supposed to mean?"

He turned his head just enough to hide his grimace from her. Of course, she didn't know about him and Bruce. Flawed character though he was, Bruce likely wasn't the sort who'd kiss and tell. Raleigh couldn't explain his insights without revealing his own imperfections. His only option, curious as he was about what had transpired in their evidently fleeting relationship, was to back off of the subject.

"Bruce has a certain reputation for…inconstancy, is all."

Her features softened after a moment and she expended another of those labored breaths. "In some ways, I suppose."

"What ways?"

"I'd still like the dinner."

That was a "mind your business" deflection. Stacia used them all the time, and so he knew not to press the issue. It wouldn't only be bad manners, but cruel.

"Just tell me where," he said. "I suppose the cash spends the same no matter what time of day it is."

Everley lifted her head at a stop around ten blocks down the line and angled her way through the throng.

He followed, deciding that he could probably switch trains there for a more direct trip, anyway. And he wanted to make sure she got home without issues.

She climbed up to street level, paused at the sidewalk as if to get her bearings, and scurried across the intersection before the light could change.

He was hot on her heels, thinking he might actually break a sweat for the first time in months.

Approaching a bored-looking hot dog vendor she pointed to a typical Coney Island dog and shoved her hands into her coat pockets.

He realized then that street meat was her idea of dinner.

"Seriously?" Raleigh asked. "When you said cheap date, I assumed you meant you want to eat at someplace with walls and a door."

"It's comfort food. I wasn't allowed to have them when I was a kid."

"Why not?" He ordered two of the same.

"My mother thinks the eating of them looks rude." She snorted and said in an undertone, "If only she knew what other sorts of things I've had in my mouth."

Then she seemed to realize what she'd said. She turned on her heel toward him, wide eyed. "I…"

He waved off the concern. "When I was twenty and in college, my mother decided to do a surprise visit to me on campus. I'd naively left my door unlocked, because I had a private room and no one ever barged in."

The vendor held out his bag and a couple of drinks.

Raleigh paid him and got out of the way of the next hungry New Yorker. "Caught me on my knees. Wasn't my most shining moment."

"On your knees…you were…"

"At that moment, I was pondering whether it was better to receive than to give, to be honest." If Everley thought he'd be ashamed to make such a confession, she obviously hadn't read many gossip blogs in the last decade. They'd all portrayed him as some kind of raging pansexual nymphomaniac, which was only partially true. "And why aren't you wearing gloves? It's like fifteen degrees with the wind chill."

Furrowing her brow, she looked down at her bare hands. "I must have left them in my office. I thought I had them this morning."

"Are they not in your pockets?"

"No. Just my keys."

"You ought to keep them in your pockets when you're not wearing them."

"I'll keep that in mind."

They walked in silence until the next corner. Then she stopped, holding her uneaten hot dog against her chest. "I live down that way. You don't have to walk the rest. I'm sure you want to get home before it's pitch black out."

"How far?"

She pointed to the building across the street in the middle. "Just there."

He nodded. "Good location."

"Good real estate agent."

"Enjoy your dinner, then. I'll see you in the new year, ready to tackle whole new projects, hmm?"

She grimaced but slowly salvaged expression into a quavering smile. "Yeah. None of yours, though. I promise."

He laughed. He believed her.

Waiting, he watched her cross the street and greet the doorman as she approached her building. Then he hurried back to the subway, eager to get back into the subterranean warmth.

The warmth didn't last long, though, because he hated walking away from things he'd left undone. He didn't want to care about Everley Shannon any more than necessary, but Stacia was right that there was something off about her smile. It didn't cost him anything to ask if she was okay. Sometimes that was all people needed. He'd certainly had his fair share of asks.

Everley was waiting in front of the elevators when he arrived in the lobby. He gestured to the guard at the desk, indicating whom he sought.

She started at the sight of him beside her.

"You're not okay, are you?" he asked.

"I…"

The doors opened. After a moment's hesitation, she stepped into the elevator and he followed at her beckoning.

"Miss Shannon?" the guard called out, standing.

"It's fine," she told him. "I know him."

He nodded.

After pressing the button for forty, she watched the floor counter tick up, up, up, and Raleigh let her have her silence. They were passing fourteen before she said anything. "Work is stressful, Raleigh."

"I agree, but for me, it tends to be good stress."

She managed to put on a crooked grin. "Unless I'm involved, right?"

"Do you want to talk some more about that?"

"No."

The car stopped at her floor. She went out and right, reaching into the coat pocket that jangled.

"Quiet building," he said.

"Yeah. People pay a lot for quiet. I thought that was what I wanted."

"It's not?"

She slid a key into the lock of 4022 and shook her head. "I think that's why I adored Bruce so much. He came with sound."

Past tense. Adored. Came.

Raleigh held his tongue on what he really wanted to say about certain rock stars and their noises and their irresistible passion, and instead asked, "What did he want from you?"

She popped the sticking door open with her hip and turned on the light.

"Well, he wanted company," she said, gesturing him in.

He stepped over the threshold and closed the door. "Wanted?"

"He had to go and so we let things come to a natural end."

"Go where? Back to LA? I'm certain he'll be around plenty around the time the band's film launches at the festivals."

"No. Overseas. He…had some business things to deal with that would require him to put down stakes in South Africa for a while. Also, he's been semi-estranged from his family for a long time and he was either going to fix it or make it worse. He wasn't quite sure. I think he was tired of being neither here nor there with them."

"Fascinating," Raleigh murmured. He didn't know much about Bruce's nonpublic life, and since the Athena deal had been purposefully avoiding any discussion of it. He didn't *want* to care, but he was too curious a creature not to. "So, you didn't talk about books or anything?"

She flicked off her heels and shrugged as she peeled back the paper on her hot dog. "I counseled him that his prose is weak and that he was far more powerful as a songwriter. I didn't want to hurt his feelings, but I didn't understand why he would want to shift gears when he was so obviously brilliant in what he was doing before. He didn't think people were listening to what he was saying, though. I suppose I can understand that. People only hear what they want to sometimes."

It was Raleigh's turn to grimace. He knew he was guilty of that, too.

"Well," he said, as gently as he could. "I'm sorry you broke up. Rebound sex usually improves my outlook."

"Are you offering it?"

"No."

He couldn't tell if she'd been joking with the question or if he'd been by offering the suggestion in the first place.

Both, maybe.

She evidently didn't feel any embarrassment over the exchange, and he respected that because he certainly didn't, either. She continued down the hall and turned on another light at the end of it. "Do you want a plate, Raleigh?"

"If you don't mind."

She handed him a dish in the kitchen.

He set the sloppy dogs on it and planned a consumption strategy. "I really shouldn't eat them. Red sauce doesn't play nice with my teeth whitening treatments."

"Ah, that explains it. The editorial staff is always murmuring about your teeth."

"Amongst other things, I'm sure."

She didn't take the bait.

Smart girl.

He laughed. "I splurged. It became an obsession."

"Kind of like eyebrow threading. You have to maintain the look."

"It's the era of Instagram. You've always got to be selfie ready. People like to see faces, not that they see much of mine lately. I had to lock down my account to keep the political spies out of my business, such that it is."

"I'm sorry you have to do that. I don't even know the password to my personal account anymore. I've been so busy comanaging the Athena one that I don't bother to update my own."

"Social media blasphemy."

She put up her hands and breathed out a strained laugh. "When I have a life beyond the walls of Athena, I'll post some pictures of it."

"You can't seriously tell me that you never do anything outside of work. Vacations?"

"My friend can't take time off to go with me."

"Day trips?"

"Same."

"Hobbies?"

"Mine aren't Instagrammable."

"What are they?"

"What are *yours*?" she returned.

"I'm pretty sure this interrogation was supposed to be focused on you."

"Can't stand the heat?"

He laughed. He hadn't realized how much he missed verbally sparring with people since Stacia had retreated into her Valliere love cave. "Sweetheart, I'm an open book."

Everley snorted—a precise, practiced sound suggestive of the private school nuisance she must have been. Just like him. "Then tell me."

"Travel," he confessed.

"Alone?"

"Usually. Also, DIY."

"Of?"

"Furniture and things of that sort. I get impatient with searching. If I can't find what I want in a store, I customize." Stacia always teased him about his predilection for elevating junky antiques when West Elm was *right there* for him to walk into. Everley didn't laugh, though. She made a little "hmm" sound and nodded in a gesture of familiarity. He shouldn't have been surprised.

Her building may have been modern, but beyond her new-looking sofas, nothing about her apartment hinted at catalogue chic. "One day, I'll have a garage to confine all that wood dust and the sandpaper bits to."

"What else? Obviously not politics."

It was his turn to snort. "Living is political and having opinions is healthy. I'm more of an advocate than an activist, however. I don't have my father's aspirations or want of power."

"Neither do I."

Raleigh pressed his lips together tightly the way his mother had taught him when he was nine. Back then, he'd lacked the tact to allow people to lie in peace. *"That's not true,"* would tumble out of his mouth, much to his parents' shame, and his father would tell him in very precise terms what Raleigh had ruined by speaking.

He wasn't in the mood to press on the issue. They were having a productive conversation, and he wasn't especially eager to end it just yet. Perhaps like Everley, he was in want of noise, and hers was pleasant.

"I don't do much." Everley nudged toppings back on her hot dog. "I read, sometimes."

"Oh?"

"Mostly magazines. The big glossy ones about organization and living your best life. It's competency porn, I suppose. Right now, there really isn't much else, except for Stacia's books because I trust her endings won't be shit. I don't have the concentration for anything else."

Brave of her to admit that.

Perhaps that was one thing she didn't feel compelled to inflate or impress with. That was what human beings did. They made their interests seem grander than the mundane boringness they really were. They made themselves sound like connoisseurs when at best they were dilettantes and dabblers. No one ever admitted they didn't have the capacity to master a hobby.

Her honesty moved her up a few ticks higher on his mental scale of regard—to just below the "We could be friends, *but*," level. Most people didn't make it that far.

"Has it always been like that?" he asked. "The shitty concentration, I mean."

"No." She gave up on the hot dog. A bit more than half remained on the paper wrapping. She stared at it.

He said nothing. He wasn't going to hector her about her consumptive habits. And besides, the things were massive. Maybe finishing an oversize meal was something else she didn't feel the need to perform.

"I used to quilt. I know it…sounds odd and old-fashioned, but it appealed to the numbers part of my brain. The counting. The orderly repetition. I liked devising new patterns and figuring out how much fabric I needed to buy and how many pieces I needed to cut. My friend Lisa used to complain that my serger replaced my need for socialization, but she adapted." Everley let out a dry laugh. "She has a key to this place. I gave it to her in case of emergency, but she used to come over when I'd go into my fabric cave for too long and she'd stand right next to my work desk, pour me a glass of wine, and then unload on me all the crap she'd endured during the week. Usually, she'd bring her own project. We'd sit there, sometimes quiet for hours, working out craft problems. It wasn't glamorous, but I miss it." She shrugged. "She's too busy, anyway. She's renovating an old summer camp upstate and trying to turn it into a viable business."

"A new camp?"

"No. It's hard to explain. I'm sure she'd love to tell you all about it if you can get her to slow down."

"I see." He was actually hungry, so he finished what was left of his dinner and disposed of the wrappers. The craft addiction cranked her up a little higher on the scale. She knew how to make things. He liked makers.

Everley cowered in the doorway between kitchen and living room, looking at him but not. Out of it again.

Whatever was eating away at her was heavy and chilidogs were only going to preoccupy her for so long.

He washed his hands and scoured his brain for something provocative to say. If she were like him, she'd probably feel better when she was arguing. "You know, I wouldn't have sex with you, anyway."

Her gaze snapped into focus.

A-ha.

Somehow, he managed to keep his expression still. "Intimacy with coworkers almost always leads to that unfortunate scenario of excrement meeting fan blades. The one notable exception I can think of," he said, tapping his chin, "is Steve Martinelli and Eugenia Fisher."

Everley's slow headshake indicated she didn't follow, but he imagined she wouldn't. Their story had happened before Tom Shannon had shouldered Everley into Publicity Row. "Those people who write those cozy mysteries set in Florida?"

"Yes, the ones with the reptile puns as titles. They weren't always cowriters. They were muddling along in their respective solo careers until they met at a conference. The details are scant, as you might understand, but apparently the two were so exhausted after a long day of events that Eugenia had followed Steve to his room. They'd both undressed, got into bed, said good-night, and went to sleep thinking nothing of it. Apparently, they'd both recently been through breakups of long-term relationships."

"Ah. I'm sure we've all done embarrassing things while in breakup fog."

"I certainly have. Perhaps one day, I'll tell you about what I did when I was thirty." He needed to look up the statutes of limitations on a couple of petty crimes first. "Anyhow, you can imagine how startled they were in the morning when they got their wits back about them."

"Apparently not so startled if they're writing books together."

"They can't keep their hands off each other." Raleigh gave his upper lip an exaggerated curl. "It's disgusting."

"You're such a villain. You know that?" Her laughter pealed down the hall as she disappeared from view.

"I'm aware, dear," he murmured, straining to catch the last of her throaty chuckles as they tapered off.

Her laugh was the closest thing he'd ever heard that could qualify as what his very evangelical grandmothers would have called a "joyful noise." It was bold and a little brash, but honest.

Real.

The scale clicked upward to a hair beneath "but," and the rush he got from hearing her laugh made him edge farther into the apartment, seeking her out.

"There's no danger of us writing books together," Everley said from some tucked away place. "I don't think you're creative enough."

"Ex*cuse* me?"

"You are almost certainly the type of man who

starches his underwear. You'd get boxed in. I need room to play."

He found her at the very back of the apartment in her bedroom. At the dresser by the door, she rolled up the hose she'd evidently just removed.

That should have been his cue to leave, but he also should have went straight back to the subway after seeing her home and he hadn't done that, either. She'd morphed from a project to an item of intrigue, and there were still so many of her layers to peel back.

"I don't iron my underwear, much less starch it."

Her resulting expression was a purest impersonation of a "Sure thing, Jan" meme that he'd ever seen in real life.

"Then you probably hire someone to do it for you." She bumped the drawer closed with her hip.

"On my salary?" He scoffed. "But I suppose the salary doesn't matter to you."

He couldn't help himself. He'd freed the truth dragon from its cave, and dragons rarely returned to confinement once they were out. "You probably don't even notice the infusion of funds into your checking account, do you? You're not there for the check. You're there for the bigger prize."

"Why do you insist on making assumptions about me?" She'd taken on that lifeless tone again. There was no laughter in it.

No anger, either.

He wondered what that meant.

I shouldn't wonder. Wondering is a waste of time.

Dragging a hand down his face, he took a deep breath and let it out. "I haven't made a single assumption. I'm merely relaying what your own father has told

the company on several occasions. He's very unambig-
uous about the fact that there *will* be another Shannon
at the top of the heap within the next few years. Didn't
you read his last Letter from the VP?"

"No," she snapped, anger finally pervading her voice.
Good. Defend yourself.

"I don't believe that," he said. "I can't."

"Believe whatever the hell you want. Go home and
take a selfie in your ugly sweater or something."

"You're wearing the exact same one," he said neu-
trally, suspecting his lack of passion on the subject
would spark real talk—not bullshit. "How unfortunate."

"Yes. Very unfortunate for me because who the fuck
can wear a sweater that garish and make it look like it's
intentional except you?" Incensed, she threw up her
hands. When she laughed, it wasn't the same as before.
It was choked and spastic. Titters of incredulity, and he
didn't think they were solely due to his sweater.

Say what you need to say, Everley.

"The colorway may be garish, but the cut is exceedingly flattering on me."

"And you just know that, don't you?" she snapped.
"You look at these ugly pieces of shit on the hangers
and think, 'hur hur, this'll make me look super athletic
and the color will bring out my vampiric pallor to its
best advantage, hur hur.'"

It wasn't her words in and of themselves that Raleigh
found wounding, but the robotic arm motions she made
while over articulating them. Under different circumstances, Raleigh might have found the exchange funny,
but she was obviously hurting, and Raleigh had been
living on the edge of hurt since third grade. At times,
humor required trust, and he could rarely offer it.

"I'm a ginger," he said flatly. "Being a vampire would be so very much easier given planetary warming and all that. I'll be one of the first to fry."

She huffed. "And you have an answer for everything. Go home, beauty king. Leave this mere mortal to her boring life and mock me from afar. At least at work, I can't hear the gears of your brain ticking. Standing right here, though, it's obvious I'll never, ever win in a conversation with you."

"I wasn't aware it was a contest."

"See. You're doing it again."

"Why do you concern yourself with winning? One day, you'll be a decision maker, and I'll be a peon wondering if you'll wake and think that you hate my sweaters so much that my name would be added to the next round of layoffs."

"Christ, would you shut up?"

He had no problem zipping his lips. He was a master of the quiet riot. All he had to do was stare with an eloquent squint and purse his lips ever so slightly.

"You. Are. *Insufferable*," she spat.

Her fists were twisting his cashmere and her weight was on her toes.

And somehow, his lips were on hers or perhaps the other way around.

He didn't really understand how they'd gotten to that place. Perhaps it was exhaustion. There was something to the Martinelli and Fisher phenomenon. People stopped thinking at the end of long days. Inhibitions were lower. Pride was quieter.

He vaguely registered that his hands were inching down the back of her sweater and that when his fingers found the hem they crept it up. When she moaned into his mouth, he clawed out yet another layer of fabric from the waistband of her skirt.

Soft, smooth skin, and so much warmer than the air. He decided all of a sudden that he was cold and needed her against him. That made the angle of their warring kiss exceedingly awkward but it continued anyway, just as her hands continued down to his fly and his brain continued to broadcast signals to his body that *"This is fine."*

He was heeling off his brogues and having his coat yanked off and sweater tugged over his head.

Hers went sailing after his to the floor. Two bright, garish, Instagrammable sweaters owned by people who shouldn't have ever been in the same room together.

And yet they were stumbling toward the bed. They didn't fall gracefully on it. One tugged the other down. Raleigh had already forgotten who'd done what because there was a woman straddling his waist and trying to get his undershirt off. She was down to her bra and had her pencil skirt tugged up to her waist so she could get her legs spread wide over him.

He didn't know what roused him out of the stupor he was in. Maybe it was the transparency of her underwear and the fact that him seeing straight through them meant the probability that he'd be welcomed inside had shot up astronomically. Or maybe it was the way she whispered "Off. Off. Off," as she tugged at his clothes. Either way, he sat up with alarm, holding her wrists together. "Everley."

"In the drawer," she said. "Over there." She canted her heard to the nightstand.

It dawned on him that she was referring to protective measures, but he was thinking about another one entirely—him getting the hell out of there.

"What are we doing?" he asked her.

"You offered me rebound sex."

Rebounding because she'd been with Bruce, and Bruce hadn't been a keeper. Under different circumstances, Raleigh might have laughed about them having such a perverted thing in common.

"No," he said in a careful tone. "I didn't."

Tugging her hands free, she climbed off of him and unzipped her skirt in the back.

"Then it's hate sex. I won't ever bring it up after the fact, and I'm sure you won't even think about it past tonight." She unfastened her bra and, because he wasn't a decent human being, he didn't look away.

He'd been imagining what her nipples might have looked like since the night of that disturbing company party when she'd worn that slinky dress. He wasn't sure that knowing was better. Instead of having his imagination preoccupied with amorphous nudity, he'd have her body in his mind in living color. Every little dip and pucker. Every striation of flesh. Every curve.

The lipstick weakened him the most. It wasn't fair for her to have that body for him to worship and also to have the audacity to have bold lips.

She didn't cover herself or shy away when he didn't immediately move.

She sat on her shins with palms pressed to the bed for balance, head slightly lowered, meeting his gaze with impunity.

He snorted. "Is that a dare?"

"If you can't handle it, beauty king, go home."

"You think taunts will work?"

She nodded toward his midsection, or more likely, to the indiscreet bulge in his pants. "Oh, you're dying to put me in my place. I'm inviting you to try."

I shouldn't, he thought, yet he was on his feet and yanking off his undershirt.

A warming shudder pulsed through him at her little laugh of satisfaction. After stowing his slacks over the back of a wooden chair and nudging off his socks, he opened that drawer.

He pushed aside thoughts that Bruce had probably been in that drawer and didn't think about what they might have used or which of them had initiated. Her business was hers and Raleigh would have his own as well.

She started to wriggle out of the skirt but he didn't let her. He had her on her ass and tugged her to the bed's edge. Wrapping one trembling leg and then the other around his waist, he put on a condom.

"This is going to be extremely impersonal." He hooked a thumb into the crotch of her panties and another into his mouth.

"Great." She laced her fingers behind her head and cleared her throat. "I'll close my eyes and pretend I don't know your name."

"And I'll pretend to miss the target two or three times so you can think I'm truly that excited." He slid his moistened thumb down her slit and teased her open.

Her eyes weren't closed. They were open wide and her expression, despite her words, was far from impassive.

"Shall we keep talking?" he asked her, sliding out his thumb and replacing it with two fingers. Then three. "Do we need the verbal volleys or can two masters such as us convey our meanness in silence?" He turned his hand and spread his fingers apart inside her heat.

"Silence," she hissed.

Her lower back arched off the bed, searching for the fingers he'd withdrawn.

She couldn't have them back because he had more in store for her. He angled himself in past the head and gripped her hips to keep her greed in check.

"You don't get to rush me," he warned.

She murmured something low and incomprehensible under her breath and stilled the clenching of her inner muscles.

"That's better. I promised you silence. I won't speak again."

She nodded.

He proceeded.

He hadn't truly expected that she would let him have his way. In fact, he'd expected she'd resist. She may have asked for a hard, emotionless fuck, but evidently her intention had never been to be passive about it.

As he rammed into her hard enough to make the headboard knock against the wall, she gripped his forearms, renewing her consent with a squeeze every time he slowed. Arching toward or away from him when his angle didn't suit her. Keeping her gaze pinned on his.

She wasn't floating away. She wasn't going to close her eyes and endure, and she certainly wasn't going to forget who was there fucking her.

Oddly, he found himself awash in satisfaction over that. Perhaps he thought she'd owed it to him for pushing every single one of his buttons in five years and continuously seeking to seek out new ones to jab. Or perhaps it all meant nothing and he simply wouldn't refuse an opportunity to screw a woman so sensual and intriguing, even if for years, he hadn't been able to stand the thought of her.

She was a usurper. Privileged. Undeserving.

And he was territorial.

He despised the idea that he shared a flaw with so many ordinary men, but the encounter had been made intensely personal by the fact they'd shared an attraction to the same person.

Maybe they weren't so different, except for the fact that they let people use them in different ways. He suspected that at the moment, as his mouth crushed hers and he swallowed her moans as he plunged deeper, that she was using him to some end.

He didn't care, because when he was done, he was going to put on his clothes, catch a train, go home, and pack for Christmas. Nothing else was going to change except their respective body counts.

"Raleigh…" she whispered, and he thought that was it and he withdrew a bit.

Her mouth shaped a silent word—something she couldn't quite express. She gave her head a shake. Swallowed. Slid her hands down to his forearms and looked away.

In all that time, she hadn't looked away.

"Never mind. Wasn't important."

He'd promised not to speak, but he hadn't made any agreements that he wouldn't respond.

Gritting his teeth at the awkward angle of their bodies as he moved her, he got her in line with the bed so her head was atop the pillow.

The panties were annoying him so he got rid of them. *That's better.*

The view was far more personal and too intimate a sight for a coworker to be kneeling in front of. He certainly shouldn't have acknowledged that he was even paying attention to it, but there he was, licking her fingers and guiding them down to her clit.

He didn't know how long he sat like that watching her play and squirm, only that it wasn't enough for her and she guided him back.

The tension in her body fled as his weight settled on hers. He'd been trying to hold it back, but her arms around his torso precluded distance.

She wanted him closer and he didn't see where he had a choice. He wasn't going to say no. He wanted to be closer to her lips, not farther away. Close enough to smooth down her hair at the sides and to track his thumbs across her flushed cheekbones.

Then she was struggling to keep her eyes open just as he was finding increasing difficulty and keeping the fire in him low. With each slow thrust, she blinked too long. Moaned even longer. And then her eyes stayed closed and she turned her face into the open hand he had beside her cheek, startlingly nuzzling against it.

He didn't understand why she would want that from him, but he didn't refuse her.

He got down lower, so he could play at one ear with his lips while stroking the other side of her face with his hand.

It'd been too long since he'd concerned himself with the softer things. No one really expected them of him and he rarely thought anyone deserved them. Especially him.

He wasn't sure if Everley deserved them, either, but the fact that she'd wanted them was enough to convince him that he may have been wrong about some things.

She'd wanted him. With any other person, he would have read the signs. He would have read their attraction and proceeded accordingly.

There hadn't been anything different about the way Everley had responded.

The only broken thing had been him. He hadn't wanted her attention.

Perhaps he still shouldn't, but for that moment, he reveled in the ownership because he liked winning. If he put aside her nepotistic career ambitions, she was certainly a prize. One he couldn't keep due to the changing nature of their association, but a prize all the same.

He may have ignored her attraction, but he couldn't ignore the change in her body as she reached her tipping point. She couldn't stop squeezing him and couldn't keep breathing. She was holding everything in until finally, she let it all out. Grinding against him, gritting her teeth, and groaning as she gathered the longer hair at the top of his head into her fist.

He chuckled and whispered, "I like it, too."

He couldn't hold on any more. That little gasp undid him.

She didn't move.

Neither did he.

They lay there atop her bedclothes with her fingers still clenched around his hair and his hand against the side of her face.

The radiator clicked on.

Way down below on the street, someone leaned on their car horn.

Somewhere in the apartment, a phone rang.

His, hers, he couldn't guess.

Neither seemed to care.

The stillness was nice.

Not having to say anything was nice.

It didn't really matter what they said, anyway, because they were certainly going to pretend none of it had happened.

shifted his weight and put the phone into his brother's hand. "I think that's why she and Mum didn't get on. Nan would never explain anything. She'd just say that she knew and that was that. Mum needed facts. *Logic.*"

"And I'm completely lacking in those things."

"No, that isn't it at all. You don't just say things. You have a tendency to make them stories, and I think some people get impatient. It's too much information or not enough of the right information and sometimes we can't fill in the missing bits on our own. We're not on the same wavelength, as the saying goes."

"Why are you telling me this?"

Arnold and Bruce had never really had the "communication conversation." Bruce had always assumed that they'd just do their own things and wouldn't interact, and that was that. He'd come to terms with it mostly, but there Arnold was, trying to understand, and Bruce was suddenly the one who didn't understand.

"I'll be straight with you. Went home last night after dinner and my girlfriend reamed me out. She said the whole lot of us are awful, miserable people."

Bruce gaped with delayed mortification. "*All* of us? I barely spent twenty minutes with the woman. I didn't tell her any of my stories, did I?"

"No, not you, Bruce. All of us except you. She thought we were ganging up on you and felt like she couldn't say anything because she wasn't blood and we've only been together for a year, you know? Doesn't want to start earning imaginary strikes from Mum and Dad yet. So, I'm trying to figure this thing out. I'm trying to see it from an outsider's perspective, but it's hard."

"You'll have to let me know if you're asking for pity."

Chapter Seventeen

"I need your phone. Give me your phone. I don't know where mine is."

Arnold notched his glasses up his nose and sniffed. "Do you understand the security risk there is in losing every bloody phone you buy?"

"I don't buy them," Bruce rejoined. "My manager does. Or...*did*. Fired him."

Arnold's skin went white as a sheet and eyes seemed to enlarge to owl-like roundness. "You *fired* your manager? In all this time you've been here, you haven't said anything about that."

"It doesn't matter."

"It absolutely *does* matter that the person who coordinated your whereabouts and arranged for you to have staff is no longer on your payroll."

"He didn't give a damn about me."

"I—" Growling, Arnold threw up his hands, then shoved them into his thick black hair. "Christ, he's going to give me a stroke."

"And they say I'm the dramatic one," Bruce murmured. He wished he could throw one good tantrum just to burn off some of the anxiety that had been clinging

to him like creosote since he'd started his trip of un-
desirable errands. Somehow, he'd lost the knack for it.

Arnold paced in front of the overturned chairs in
their parents' back garden. They had a sheen of frost
on them, and the moisture in the air warned that London might be about to get a dusting of snow. Bruce was
barely feeling the cold. His heart was beating too fast
and all that suffusing blood certainly had his body tem-
perature at a spike.

"Did your manager…wipe your phone contents remotely every time you tell him you lost track of the
things?" Arnold asked through clenched teeth.

"I don't know."

Arnold lifted his glasses back up so he could drag a
hand down his weary face. "Going to have to call the
phone company, whoever it is, and sort that out. For
God's sake, Bruce."

Obviously, he was tired of interacting with his older
brother, and the feeling was growing more and more
mutual by the moment.

Bruce hadn't asked his brother to follow him out to
the garden, though. Arnold had done that on his own
volition. Bruce had wanted a bit of air, even if it *was*
cold London air. It was better than that tea-scented smog
inside his parents' ancient townhouse.

They'd been throwing around phrases like "power of
attorney" and "guardianship" because Bruce had said
he was done with it all.

They'd thought he'd lost his mind and had been nat-
tering about it for the whole week since he'd flown in
from South Africa.

Only Arnold had gotten worn down enough to accept
that perhaps Bruce wasn't being unreasonable so much

as just overwhelmed. Arnold was trying his hardest, for
whatever reason, but he didn't really understand Bruce
and Bruce didn't know how to fix that.

Bruce took a breath and let the chill soothe his lungs.
He didn't know if he could explain, but he always tried.
"Listen. I keep track of the things that are important to
me. Okay? I understand that in this day and age, I have
to have a phone, but I don't *want* one."

"I suppose that's fair, even if it's ridiculous." Arnold
handed his phone over with tentative consent, pulling
it back to ask, "You won't lose mine?"

"I'm not moving from here for the next few minutes,
and even I have never managed to lose something while
standing still. That'd be quite a fuckin' feat, wouldn't
it?"

"Who are you calling?"

"My girlfriend." Bruce grimaced. "Well, not my girlfriend. I didn't ask her to be. Maybe I should have but
we were both coming and going and I didn't know if
that was how things are done."

Arnold raised a brow.

"I imagine that shit's easy for you. Always makes
sense what you need to say and do and when you should
do it."

"It's not that. You've just never said anything about
a girlfriend before. I didn't think you were the type to
commit."

"What's that mean?"

Arnold put up his hands. "No offense meant, mate.
We can just never tell where your head is at."

"You mean without my translator here."

"Well. Nan did have a certain knack for it. She was
intuitive in a way none of the rest of us are." Arnold

Chapter Seventeen

"I need your phone. Give me your phone. I don't know where mine is."

Arnold notched his glasses up his nose and sniffed. "Do you understand the security risk there is in losing every bloody phone you buy?"

"I don't buy them," Bruce rejoined. "My manager does. Or...*did*. Fired him."

Arnold's skin went white as a sheet and eyes seemed to enlarge to owl-like roundness. "You *fired* your manager? In all this time you've been here, you haven't said anything about that."

"It doesn't matter."

"It absolutely *does* matter that the person who coordinated your whereabouts and arranged for you to have staff is no longer on your payroll."

"He didn't give a damn about me."

"I—" Growling, Arnold threw up his hands, then shoved them into his thick black hair. "Christ, he's going to give me a stroke."

"And they say I'm the dramatic one," Bruce murmured. He wished he could throw one good tantrum just to burn off some of the anxiety that had been clinging

to him like creosote since he'd started his trip of un-
desirable errands. Somehow, he'd lost the knack for it.

Arnold paced in front of the overturned chairs in
their parents' back garden. They had a sheen of frost
on them, and the moisture in the air warned that London might be about to get a dusting of snow. Bruce was
barely feeling the cold. His heart was beating too fast
and all that suffusing blood certainly had his body tem-
perature at a spike.

"Did your manager…wipe your phone contents remotely every time you tell him you lost track of the
things?" Arnold asked through clenched teeth.

"I don't know."

Arnold lifted his glasses back up so he could drag a
hand down his weary face. "Going to have to call the
phone company, whoever it is, and sort that out. For
God's sake, Bruce."

Obviously, he was tired of interacting with his older
brother, and the feeling was growing more and more
mutual by the moment.

Bruce hadn't asked his brother to follow him out to
the garden, though. Arnold had done that on his own
volition. Bruce had wanted a bit of air, even if it *was*
cold London air. It was better than that tea-scented smog
inside his parents' ancient townhouse.

They'd been throwing around phrases like "power of
attorney" and "guardianship" because Bruce had said
he was done with it all.

They'd thought he'd lost his mind and had been nat-
tering about it for the whole week since he'd flown in
from South Africa.

Only Arnold had gotten worn down enough to accept
that perhaps Bruce wasn't being unreasonable so much

as just overwhelmed. Arnold was trying his hardest, for whatever reason, but he didn't really understand Bruce and Bruce didn't know how to fix that.

Bruce took a breath and let the chill soothe his lungs. He didn't know if he could explain, but he always tried. "Listen. I keep track of the things that are important to me. Okay? I understand that in this day and age, I have to have a phone, but I don't *want* one."

"I suppose that's fair, even if it's ridiculous." Arnold handed his phone over with tentative consent, pulling it back to ask, "You won't lose mine?"

"I'm not moving from here for the next few minutes, and even I have never managed to lose something while standing still. That'd be quite a fuckin' feat, wouldn't it?"

"Who are you calling?"

"My girlfriend." Bruce grimaced. "Well, not my girlfriend. I didn't ask her to be. Maybe I should have but we were both coming and going and I didn't know if that was how things are done."

Arnold raised a brow.

"I imagine that shit's easy for you. Always makes sense what you need to say and do and when you should do it."

"It's not that. You've just never said anything about a girlfriend before. I didn't think you were the type to commit."

"What's that mean?"

Arnold put up his hands. "No offense meant, mate. We can just never tell where your head is at."

"You mean without my translator here."

"Well. Nan did have a certain knack for it. She was intuitive in a way none of the rest of us are." Arnold shifted his weight and put the phone into his brother's hand. "I think that's why she and Mum didn't get on. Nan would never explain anything. She'd just say that she knew and that was that. Mum needed facts. *Logic.*"

"And I'm completely lacking in those things."

"No, that isn't it at all. You don't just say things. You have a tendency to make them stories, and I think some people get impatient. It's too much information or not enough of the right information and sometimes we can't fill in the missing bits on our own. We're not on the same wavelength, as the saying goes."

"Why are you telling me this?"

Arnold and Bruce had never really had the "communication conversation." Bruce had always assumed that they'd just do their own things and wouldn't interact, and that was that. He'd come to terms with it mostly, but there Arnold was, trying to understand, and Bruce was suddenly the one who didn't understand.

"I'll be straight with you. Went home last night after dinner and my girlfriend reamed me out. She said the whole lot of us are awful, miserable people."

Bruce gaped with delayed mortification. "*All* of us? I barely spent twenty minutes with the woman. I didn't tell her any of my stories, did I?"

"No, not you, Bruce. All of us except you. She thought we were ganging up on you and felt like she couldn't say anything because she wasn't blood and we've only been together for a year, you know? Doesn't want to start earning imaginary strikes from Mum and Dad yet. So, I'm trying to figure this thing out. I'm trying to see it from an outsider's perspective, but it's hard."

"You'll have to let me know if you're asking for pity."

Arnold sighed and pushed his unkempt hair out of his eyes. He always had that frazzled professor vibe about him. "You don't owe me any pity. I just want you to get that I'm making an effort. I don't want you to think that it's all of us against you by yourself, but you have to understand that none of us understand your decision-making process. You're impulsive."

"I'm *not*. At least, not the way I was when I was younger. Now, I fixate on every decision even when I speak it quickly. I don't just do shit willy-nilly and then expect people to pick up the pieces."

"Like quitting the band?"

"I quit the fuckin' band, Arnold, because—" Bruce was shouting.

Shouting was unproductive.

Shouting wouldn't make his arguments any stronger. It would only include the neighbors in Bruce's personal business.

He took a breath, walked in a circle, shook out the tension he'd been holding in his hands, and returned to face his brother. In a more modulated tone, he said, "I quit the band because it was all fake, okay? They never considered themselves to be anything but babysitters for me because that was what the label told them I needed. They were paid excellently for it, I assure you. I don't need to be babysat. I'm a grown man and I decided that either people are going to get me or not. I have choices and I'm exercising them."

That was what Ev had told him. He had choices. *So* many choices.

"What do you mean? What are you doing? You didn't say anything about it."

"When could I have? All any of you have wanted to

talk about since I've arrived are assets and investments, and the trail of havoc you think I've spun across South Africa in recent weeks. When could I have brought it up?"

"Well, I'm asking you now. What's your plan?"

"I think it's pretty simple. I'm just not going to record anymore."

"*What*?" Arnold's voice very nearly hit a C5 with that pinched shout.

Nodding, Bruce rocked back on his heels and clucked his tongue. He wasn't going to get distracted by defensiveness. "You see. I've got a plan that takes me elsewhere. Ev helped."

"Ev?"

"Everley." Bruce waved off the distraction. Knowing Arnold, he was going to start probing, and Bruce had too much he needed to say before he got distracted. He'd sing the virtues of Everley Shannon all day if left up to his own devices. "I haven't thrown a tantrum and decided that if I can't have things my way then I'm going to quit. I'm just making some tweaks. Some adjustments."

Everley had taught him that. He'd watched how she worked. She made small compromises until she could get something she could be satisfied with, even if it wasn't quite what she'd envisioned at the start. The pay-off would be the same in the end.

"I thought you loved recording."

"No. I love being a *musician*. I can do that without the rigmarole. Did you know that in medieval—"

Arnold groaned.

Bruce grimaced. He'd done it again. "Sorry."

"No, I'm sorry. It's a reflex. We always wonder why

you don't get to the point, but you are making a point, or more than one, and…" He let out one of his patented self-deprecating laughs. "We can't keep up."

Bruce couldn't have been more stunned if someone had poked him with a taser. Engles didn't admit that they were lacking in capacity. *Ever.*

Overcome with relief, Bruce decided that he'd spare his brother the history lecture. Just that once.

"Nan wanted me to make my own money, okay? Money that wasn't attached to the mines or the oil or goddamned sweatshops. That's how I ended up with a label. That was the best path she could think of. But I know more now. I can work behind the scenes. I can produce. I can write scores. I can write entire fuckin' musicals if I get the itch. Maybe I'll take up one of those offers I've been getting for years to guest star in a limited production. More people on Broadway march to their own beat. I fit right in there."

And he'd be closer to Everley. LA had its charms, and London was all right, but he was ready to make major changes. That was why he wanted to call. He wanted to let her know before he boarded a plane headed west what he had in mind. He hoped she'd like the idea.

"Just tell me your plan," Arnold said wearily. "I'll digest it and relay it to the rest of them. I'll try to smooth it over, if you want. I'm stunned you even care, to be quite honest. Anyone else would have given up on their family by now."

"I plan on making a new one." He realized seconds too late that the statement was rude, but it was honest so Bruce decided not to recant or walk it back. Found family would plug in all the gaps left by his natural one. Affection? He'd learned he could find that. Support?

Yes. He simply needed to ask the right people. Reality checks? Those, too.

And some things, he could learn to lean more on himself for. He could do anything he wanted as long as the framework was right.

Arnold grimaced, but nodded. "You'll have enough money to live on after you're done divesting?"

"My math says yes, but I would appreciate you looking over it. There's always a risk I've forgotten something important. Helps that I plan on selling the LA house. Hate it there. Housekeepers are mean and the Uber drivers are mercenary."

"Don't you have a driver?"

"Fired him, too. I don't have to pay people who don't want to talk to me."

"You should have told me."

"Told you what? That people are assholes, even if you sign their paychecks? I shouldn't have to tell you that."

"I'm just shocked you're not more assertive about it."

Bruce shrugged. "Not in my constitution."

That was what Nan used to tell him when he'd wished he was better at assertively defending himself. He just couldn't. It was easier to walk away and hope that karma did its job, but karma evidently had a massive backlog.

"You need to pay someone who is, then," Arnold insisted. "What did you have a manager for if he wasn't doing some of those things?"

"He was too busy on the music end." Bruce rocked back on his heels again. He found the movement meditative. "The contract had lapsed, but still, I sent him a formal termination letter right before I landed in Johannesburg. I managed to get that letter down to only five hundred words. Everley would be so proud of me. I'm getting better at self-editing."

"So, you have no staff."

"Just the cleaners, and naturally they'll go away when I sell the house."

"Christ," Arnold groaned.

"Did you know that in the Bible, blasphemers were hanged or stoned?"

"Yes, actually I did know that. I was an altar boy when you were in Scotland."

Bruce hadn't known that. His shock must have been evident because Arnold sighed and walked away, muttering under his breath about brothers not knowing anything about the other and pondering whose fault it was.

Bruce didn't know the answer to that, either.

When Arnold returned to his former position, clear eyed, he said, "All right. Let's go in. Write this all out for me. Show me your plan and I'll keep the folks off your back."

"I'll hardly be indigent, Arnold. I have various trusts that are staggered to mature every two years or so."

"Where'd those come from?"

"Set them up when I signed that first contract. I may have my head in the clouds, but I do think about the future on occasion. Perhaps I don't go about things as efficiently as some would like, but sometimes I get things right."

"I think you get a lot of things right, but no one's looking for the right things. They're too busy peering at the things that don't make sense, and those aren't even the important ones. I'm sorry, Bruce."

Bruce shrugged and clapped his brother on the back. "Plenty of hard feelings, but I'm sure I'll recover in time. I can only hold a grudge for so long. You just started the countdown timer on yours."

Arnold frowned. "How long's left on it?"

"About ten years, is the average, but do enough good deeds and maybe you can shrink that down to a manageable three."

Arnold sighed and pulled open the back door. "I suppose I deserve that. Anyone else you have long grudges with who aren't related to you or haven't gotten money because of you?"

"Of course. There's one motherfucker in particular I'd like to push into an oubliette and piss on. You'd probably like him. He wears brogues."

"Christ. What'd he do to you?"

"Broke my heart in less than twenty-four hours."

"Why?"

"Because I didn't do things right."

"What things, Bruce?"

"Just things. You wouldn't understand."

"Try me."

"Why? What do you know about passion, Arnold?"

"I'll try not to be offended by that," Arnold said, deadpan. "What happened?"

"Perhaps I wasn't totally upfront about who I actually was."

"So, you lied?"

"No!" He hated that l-word. It didn't allow for nuances or extenuations, and there were *always* extenuations. "He assumed I did. I didn't lie. I told him what I thought was important. That's what matters. Not my problem that he took it personally."

Bruce had told himself that countless times during his trip, as he navigated from one small township to the next, filing papers, waiting for approvals, arguing with bankers.

He'd almost convinced himself.

It was his problem, though, and if he could go back in time and edit that conversation at the concert, he might just do it, just to see what could have unfolded between them.

But it really didn't matter. Ev was the loveliest thing to ever happen to him and he wasn't going to squander that on what-ifs.

Yet again, Arnold dragged a hand down his face.

"Keep that up, and you're going to pull wrinkles," Bruce murmured. "I should look older than you, baby boy."

"Bruce. You can't *do* that. You're not a typical run-of-the-mill arsehole. You're a public figure. There are different rules. I don't rightly know what they all are, but I imagine nobody would want to feel duped by someone they perceive to have used them as a stepping stone toward something else."

"You think that's what he thinks?"

"I think that if he doesn't know you well and how your brain works—and God, who does?—he would have been extremely offended if he cared. The fact he was pissed meant he cared."

"I…honestly hadn't thought of it that way." Bruce had taken the exchange at face value, because that was what he always did. He couldn't second-guess every interaction in his life. Already, he spent too much time teetering on the edge of uncertainty.

Perhaps that one event had deserved more introspection beyond the pain of being rejected. But it was too late to matter.

"I suppose that's that. You can't do anything about it now, can you?" Arnold queried as though he'd been following the closed captioning of Bruce's thoughts. "You've already moved on with...what was the name?"

"Everley. Everley Shannon." Once more, Bruce shifted his weight. He felt heavier all of a sudden. Leaden. "They work together, actually."

"For God's sake, Bruce. Could you possibly make it more complicated?"

"It doesn't matter. I'm only seeing one of them."

"Because you replaced one with the other."

"No! It's not like that at all. I didn't even know who she was. She sort of just rescued me at the exact right moment. I'm not used to being rescued. Hard not to be fond of someone like that."

"I get it, I suppose," Arnold said solemnly, looking up at the gray sky. "You trusted her. Still, maybe you didn't mean to make her a replacement, but you did, knowing full well that if you had the opportunity, you'd go back." He met Bruce's gaze expectantly, but if he were waiting for validation, Bruce certainly couldn't give it.

"That's utter bullshit, Arnold. You can fuck right off with that. I wouldn't give up Everley. I'm going to tell her that." Bruce indicated the phone. Obviously, his brother had forgotten Bruce's intentions.

"But what if this other guy decides he's forgiven you?"

Bruce scoffed. "That's about as likely as the US figuring out how to balance its budget."

"All right. If you're sure."

"Quite sure."

Besides, Raleigh had been unkind to Ev, and they

had to stick together. As long as they were kind to each other, none of the rest of that shit mattered.

Bruce didn't owe him any brainpower…even if he had cared enough to care that Bruce hadn't been wholly honest.

Even if he had wanted him then.

Chapter Eighteen

"The debt may have already been repaid, but I brought you lunch just like I promised."

Raleigh set a pile of paper napkins on Everley's barren desk and set a greasy white bag atop it. "Not a hot dog, unfortunately. Just as good, though." His red eyebrows danced. "Better, actually."

Everley snapped out of the daze she was in from the sight of him and pulled the bag closer. She was surprised to see him. She really had assumed after he'd left her apartment the eventful night of the hot dogs that they'd revert back to their factory settings—that he'd avoid her like the plague and she'd bide her time until she'd served out her notice period.

But there he was.

And she was glad.

No one wanted to be so easily forgotten.

"What is it?" she asked.

"Pretzel burger. Probably has two thousand calories when fully loaded, but it's the new year. Make a resolution to take the stairs every now and then and you'll be all set."

No one at Athena had ever spontaneously bought her lunch before, except her father, and that certainly didn't count. He only did it on the rare occasion he was actually in the building, and she knew he had his motives for doing so. It had more to do with him wanting her to be seen with him than any sense of fatherly obligation.

She huffed.

Raleigh groaned. "You don't have to eat it."

"Oh, no. I'm sorry. That wasn't meant for you. I was…thinking about my father."

Raleigh leaned his forearms on her desk and whispered, "That is *not* what I want to hear from a woman when she's staring at me."

"My head is somewhere else today. Really. I appreciate the lunch. I'd lost track of time. Didn't even realize I was hungry."

"How were your holidays?"

"I…" She picked at a bit of lifting polish on her shellac manicure and gathered her words. She was used to doing the professional tap-dance routine and carefully tempering her words so she didn't sound too familiar, too complaining, too…*whatever*.

But she didn't see the point of that anymore. She had about a week left on her wind down. Come Friday, she'd be turning in her building badge and leaving publishing for good.

And Raleigh.

She could admit that she was going to miss seeing him strut past her open door every two hours or so. She was even going to miss the bickering.

"Can I be honest?" she whispered. "I need to be honest."

He moved around to the side of her desk and, nodding, crouched near her. "Honesty would be refreshing. I've grown used to the opposite."

"That's sad."

"It's what you get when you grow up in the household of a politician. You learn very early how people bend the truth and how manipulation is a slippery slope. They start by making small compromises to their ethics or relying too heavily on obfuscation. That changes. Outright lying is fine as long as it's for the so-called greater good and no one gets hurt, and then eventually, people become so dead inside that they don't care if people get hurt. They think it's the cost of doing business, but people's well-being isn't supposed to be a business."

"Not everyone is like that," she said breathily, reeling at the magnitude of what he'd said. It must have been miserable to go through life wondering when the people one had connected with would turn on him, use him.

He'd probably thought that about her from the day she'd started there, and how could he not have?

He nudged her hand away from the fleck of shellac and squeezed it gently until her compulsion to pick at polish died. "No," he murmured. "Not everyone is like that, but figuring out who the exceptions might be is hard as hell."

Somehow, she managed to suppress a grimace. It was hard not to take things he said personally. One night of intimacy didn't erase five years of war.

"I went to my parents' place after Hanukah," she murmured. "Of course, I got chewed out about that. The problem with being raised in a household with two religions is that you have to be on call more often than you have the heart to be. It was important to my father, though, and because I wasn't there, my mother was upset."

"Where were you?"

"In my apartment, doing nothing. Watching TV."

"You didn't call?"

She gave a jerky shrug. "It was easier to just not show up. How's that saying go? That's it's easier to beg for forgiveness than seek permission?"

"Yes."

"I did pack a bag and head to the island the day before Christmas Eve. They started screaming at me the moment I stepped through the door. Made my grandma cry, which always breaks my heart because she's eighty-nine and no one wants to be *that kid*. Everyone was there, Raleigh. Whole fucking family came out of the woodworks. Aunts. Uncles. Cousins I've never even met before."

He cringed. "Sounds like a typical McKean family gathering. There are scores of us."

"I felt like there were scores under that roof. I bailed out after Christmas dinner. Gave my grandma a kiss on the cheek and left while my father was outside having his cigar. Had a fantastic lecture from him last night."

"I'm sorry."

He sounded like he meant it, and somehow that pity made her feel even worse. She hated being such a chicken shit. She hated that she'd been groomed to be conciliatory and to avoid conflict and yet was expected to be some kind of flesh-eating shark the moment she stepped into the offices of Athena. The two things weren't complementary, and her father had to know that.

He probably just didn't care.

She could imagine what sort of lecture she'd be getting after Friday when he stumbled upon the news brief that Everley Shannon had left the company.

Pulling the burger bag horizontal, she raked out a few fries and shoved them into her mouth. She didn't want to say anything else, but wished she could. She'd bare her soul to him—scrape it out and start fresh. He could have been the astringent she needed, but she wouldn't burden him with her issues. Not when he'd stepped into that room voluntarily, finally. He had no bingo card to fill out, no motives that she could think of.

She didn't want him to go away.

"Anyhow," she said with a bit more sunshine in her voice.

Raleigh straightened up right when one of the foreign rights agents passed by the door. She didn't peek in, though. No one ever did because if they didn't make eye contact, they wouldn't have to speak to her.

"How was your visit to Richmond?" she asked.

"Wonderful. And quirky. Stacia's parents showed up. I'd never met them before and I guess she wasn't expecting them. They weren't there long, though. They'd booked a cruise out of Newark and were using Stacia's place as a lily pad for a couple of days before they were scheduled to embark. Two-week transatlantic. Stacia's brother and his fiancée are going along."

"Nice."

"Yeah. I wouldn't be caught dead on a boat with my family."

"Me neither."

Raleigh let out a little grunt, set the wrapped burger in front of her and left.

He had to have been thinking that it didn't matter if she liked her family or not. They were still going to give her the sort of future he would likely never be afforded. He wasn't going to flex his connections to get a job. He was too civilized for that.

So was she. She wanted to tell him. She wanted that pall of tension between them gone so she could find out if there was something between them besides anger and lust. They seemed like two loose ends that could possibly connect but they never would if they were going to keep approaching from the wrong angles.

But maybe those bad angles were important. Maybe the conflict mattered, because if they'd met under any other circumstances, she could have been forgettable. The raw truths of them would have never been peeled back.

That rawness was what she adored about Raleigh. No performance necessary, because to him, it didn't matter either way. He was going to call a spade a spade.

Telling him she wasn't meant to be that usurper wasn't going to work.

She'd have to show him. And then maybe, one day, they could try a new angle.

On Friday, Everley packed up the few remnants of personality from her office, turned off the light, and shut the door behind her. Fortunately, human resources had decided not to physically escort her out of the building, though they did promise to sue her into oblivion if they later learned she used privileged information from the company in future endeavors. There was no way that would become an issue because she had no desire to work anywhere near the realm of publishing ever again. It just wasn't her vibe.

She turned in her badge and had made it all the way down to street level before anyone else noticed.

"Flats today?" Raleigh asked. He caught her bag's slipping strap and set it back on her shoulder.

"Flats?"

He pointed to her shoes.

"Oh." She looked down at the boring brown things. She'd woken up a bundle of nerves at it being her last day at the company, but was in a reasonable enough frame of mind to know that people didn't make great escapes in high heels. "Figured I'd give my arches a break."

"Is that something women do?"

"I can't speak for all women." They crossed over to the northbound subway. "Are you going the right way?" she asked him.

He grimaced. "No. I usually head two blocks east but that station is shut down again. Flooded and I think they're going to do something about that big fissure in the platform, too."

"Gotta love New York."

"That's what I said before I moved here. The gleam is sort of wearing off, but I don't think there's anywhere else I'd rather be right now."

"Oh." She wanted to be anywhere *but* there, and was seriously considering pulling a Bruce—falling off the grid and reemerging better than before.

She hoped he was better, anyway. She hadn't heard from him. Apparently she hadn't meant as much to him as she'd thought. She was trying not to beat herself up about it. He hadn't promised her anything, nor her him.

Raleigh hooked her elbow as they descended the stairs into the station. A kind gesture—a *surprising* one, too. She didn't know what it meant that she'd stopped expecting decency from people.

"When I first moved to New York," he said over the din of two people arguing from opposite sides of a busted subway turnstile, "I moved into an apartment sight unseen with three roommates I hadn't met before. I literally got off the plane and hopped on a train to Harlem carrying a trunk, a suitcase, a duffel bag, and backpack."

Alarmed, Everley sucked in some air. "How crowded was that train?"

"Not very. It was three in the morning. Inbound flight kept getting delayed. Still, it was quite an adventure. I must have looked like a feral raccoon trying to watch over all my shit, you know? I knew there was no way I could go home and get more of it. I moved when my parents were out of town. They had no idea."

The train was just approaching the platform as they stepped off the staircase. Good timing, because the station was loud and she wanted to hear the rest of his story without straining.

Being rush hour, there were no seats, but they managed to squeeze through the crowd and found a couple of standing places that weren't too questionably hygienic. Also, they'd be able to get out without shoving people black-and-blue.

The train lurched to a start. "Why'd you do that?" she asked him. "Move out that way, I mean."

"Because my father was about to start campaigning again and I wanted to be gone before he did. I was twenty-three. Had been out of college for a year, but took some time to consider my options. Economy was shit. My parents left me alone for the most part as long as I was doing *something*. I got out of my mother's hair every day by volunteering at a school. She thought it was my old school, and I didn't correct her on that. They had money. They didn't need extra hands. So, I hung out at one that was perpetually understaffed and underfunded. Did a little of everything. Directing traffic in the carpool line in the mornings. Helping with field days. Following up on truant students and driving them in. Troubleshooting why computers wouldn't turn on. Cleaning up the occasional puddle of vomit."

"Jack of all trades?" The thought of Raleigh toting a mop and a box of absorbent granules put a massive grin on her face.

"Faked it a lot, but they didn't care. When the school year ended, I knew I was going to have to make some hard decisions."

"So you decided to leave."

"Yes. Basically, I flipped a coin. Heads, New York. Tails, Chicago. New York won, so I tapped into my college's alumni network to see who had a room and who had job leads."

"What'd you do?"

"The very first job I got in publishing was in fact-checking."

If Everley had the room to clutch her pearls, she would have. Fact-checking to publicity wasn't exactly a logical progression. Fact-checking to proofreading and copyediting, maybe, if he had a strong grasp on language mechanics.

He laughed and she suspected that her confusion was playing clearly on her face.

"I have a degree in history. I worked for a small imprint that only did nonfiction."

"Ah. Did you plan to stay?"

"Honestly, I didn't have a plan beyond the first couple of years. I was going to give some additional thought to law school, but as much as I liked the idea of studying law, I didn't like the idea of practicing it. Especially not given my family affiliations."

"I could see where that would be messy." She was shocked that at twenty-three he'd demonstrated such intuition about what would happen, and he'd been successful in his scheme. He was essentially hiding in plain sight. His job may have been to amplify voices, but he kept his muted. He was behind the scenes and he seemed to like it. Meanwhile, she hadn't been able to predict that telling her father "Yes" would cause a revolt. She'd worked for years in quiet hostilities, hoping things would change and that people would give her a chance, but she knew that would never happen as long as she was on that upward trajectory. No one liked that "friend today, boss tomorrow" dynamic, and they'd all steered clear of her.

She would have done the same.

"How did you get into publicity?" she asked.

"Imprint I was at was closing, and I had two choices. I was offered a content editing job at a different imprint, but at the same time, I saw that Athena was hiring a junior publicist. The pay was about the same, but I suspected I'd eventually earn more in a different department. I didn't like the idea of jumping to a different company, but staying at the old one meant I'd have to edit books I was categorically opposed to. They acquired books by a lot of televangelists and nationalists, and I honestly didn't want my name attached to content written by people who questioned my right to have basic liberties like being left the fuck alone. Higher-ups didn't understand why I didn't want the job, and I had to ask them point-blank if they knew I was queer. You should have seen the looks on their faces."

It likely would have mirrored Everley's on the day Raleigh had mentioned being caught on his knees, though her surprise was likely for an entirely different reason. She'd been shocked by his candor, and perhaps her imagination had started churning a bit too fast. She still couldn't picture Raleigh submitting to anyone, no matter how hard she tried, and she'd *definitely* been trying. The thought of Raleigh *in flagrante delicto* was one of her favorite things.

Or perhaps the thought of Raleigh just…*existing*.

She wished she didn't like him so much. She would probably be happier if she didn't. She might never see him again, and she would always wonder "What if?"

Would they have eventually been friends if she stayed?

Or more?

Maybe all she needed was time, but she never had time.

Bruce had left when she'd fallen for him, too.

She really knew how to pick 'em.

"That's your stop," Raleigh said.

She hadn't even noticed that the train doors had opened. It was a busy spot and people were pouring out of the car. She held tight to the grip bar, though, and tracked her gaze up to his.

"Doors are going to close. You'll have to catch the train back in the other direction."

She gripped it tighter. "I…don't want to go home." It was too quiet there.

He set his lips in a grim line and turned to watch the doors.

The train shuddered to a start again. For a long while, he stared out the window, and she stared at him. She was going to own her neediness. She was tired of pretending she was fine when the truth was that she needed people around her.

Twenty minutes later, he grabbed her elbow again and eased her through the crush.

They started walking east and she wondered which sweater he'd wear on Monday. For years, she'd played a guessing game with herself and see if she was right when he walked past her office door each day. Her favorite was a teal green one that played so well with his coloring. He didn't wear it as much as the blacks and grays, though. She could certainly understand that. She did the same.

"Are you hungry?" he asked.

"No."

"Did you have lunch?"

"I think I did."

"You *think*?"

"Today was busy. I had a sandwich from the corner store. I remember now." A cold sandwich, stale chips, and also a slice of birthday cake she'd gotten from the break room. It was the first piece of celebration cake she'd allowed herself since her first year at Athena. The cold reception she'd received from her peers had informed her that the cake wasn't for her and that she didn't deserve it. She'd abstained, but on her last day, she figured she was owed a little sugar.

"I see. Charlie was going in and out of your office a lot. I didn't ask him why."

Raleigh's assistant would be replacing her. He hadn't told Raleigh yet. He'd simply been adding more to his workload while trying to line up an applicant pool for whomever would be replacing him. It wasn't an ideal circumstance. Raleigh would certainly be pissed, come Monday, at the disruption to his routine, but he was called the "Hardest Working Person at Athena" for a reason. He always got shit done whether he had support or not.

"Charlie's curious about the authors on my roster. They're not like yours," was all she could say.

And his apartment building wasn't like hers. Where hers was newer construction and fully modernized, Raleigh's had probably been erected sometime around Hamilton's fateful night in Weehawken. Perhaps not that old, but the elevator was ancient and the stairs had actual tilework and not just industrial carpet.

"Go on ahead of me," he said, indicating the staircase. "The steps are pretty steep. This way, if you fall backwards, I'll break your landing."

"And who'll break yours?"

"I've got a hard head. I'll be fine." He smirked.

She'd never found smirks sexy before him.

She suppressed a sigh.

Girl, you are pitiful.

"How many flights?" she asked, bracing herself.

"All of them."

"Ugh."

"Too cheap to leave."

"I get it."

Somehow, she managed to get to the fifth floor without stopping to catch her breath or massage her cramping calves. "Is the elevator really so untrustworthy?"

"You tell me." He gestured her into the apartment and engaged all the locks once she was in. "I've lived here for ten years and I've been stuck in it twenty-three times. I kept the maintenance slips for all the reports I put in."

She set her heavy bag down by the door and took the place in. What she could see of it, anyway. They were in a corridor that extended both ways. The left route was short, ending at a door. Across from them was a set of glass double doors and through it was a dining room. She imagined that down the hall to the right was a kitchen and bathroom.

"How many bedrooms?"

He laughed. "People always ask me that. What is it with New Yorkers?"

"I guess we just want to know if all the stairs are worth it."

"Two beds, sitting room, dining room. Gonna ask me my rent, too?"

"No. I'm curious, but not that gauche."

The place had a decidedly 1920s feel to it with all of the ornate molding and detail work, but hadn't been allowed to go into disrepair. And of course, what she could see of the apartment was as immaculate as the man who lived in it. Understated colors. Art precisely hung in tasteful frames. Interesting rugs.

"Bottle of water?" he asked. "You don't want to drink what comes out of the pipes here."

"Sure. Thanks."

He vanished to the right after hanging his coat on the rack by the door.

She did the same.

She liked that he owned practical furniture.

In fact, she was beginning to like nearly everything about him. She wished that wasn't a problem.

He returned carrying water bottles and a bag of left-over candy cane chocolates. "I've got a freezer full of these. Stole them from Stacia."

"Does she know?"

He scoffed and nudged her toward the left. "No. Barely made a dent in her stash, if that tells you anything."

Everley took the bag. She deserved candy.

"I have a friend like that." She sank into his slipcovered sofa, clutching the candy bag and water bottle for dear life. "Lets me raid her fridge and sometimes puts things in it that only I eat. She doesn't live in the city, though. I don't see her enough."

"How'd you meet?"

"College."

"I'm surprised all your friends aren't in publishing."

"None of my friends are in publishing, though not for lack of trying."

"You had to expect that."

"Honestly, I didn't." She made a halfhearted dismissive gesture. "I assumed people would give me the benefit of the doubt."

He leaned his rear end against the credenza and fidgeted with his water bottle cap. "Maybe we could have if Athena was a small family-owned business. We'd expect it. Your situation is different, and nobody likes the reek of nepotism."

"Sometimes I think about where I might be instead if I'd never walked into that building."

"And?"

"And I stop quickly because it's depressing to think you've wasted part of your life doing something you were expected to do but hadn't planned to do. I wish I could have been more like you."

"What, avoiding your family at every turn and copy and pasting the same Q&A statement into reply emails whenever journalists contact you about something your father did?"

"No. Brave."

"I'm not brave. I'm cynical. Also, I'm stubborn, just like my father, but I tend to manage how much suffering other people endure as a result of it. I'd prefer not to be so cynical. I don't particularly enjoy expecting the worst of people. I shouldn't be surprised when people turn out to be decent."

"I was just thinking that earlier."

He lifted his water bottle in a toast, which she returned. "Write your own story, Everley. Keep your eyes on your own paper. Ignore what other people are shouting at you to copy down, or you're going to be miserable."

"I know."

She wanted to tell him that she'd already come to that conclusion on her own, but she couldn't. He'd see. He'd have his proof. He'd learn on Monday that she'd decided to do the decent thing—not just for her, but for everyone struggling to succeed in a hard business.

And she'd just...go away.

He settled on the sofa beside her and scrolled through his phone's contents. "I haven't been to a movie theater in ages. Hate going alone. Want to see something?"

"*Me?*"

It was a silly question, and she knew it. There was no one else in the room but her, but certainly he didn't mean *her*.

"Would you rather just fuck? That might be easier than coming to a consensus about a movie." He tapped his chin contemplatively. "We'd probably talk more in the movie, ironically enough."

She stood and reached for her purse. "I'd like to see a movie with you."

"Was the sex that bad?"

"No. I just…like the talking more. I can pretend I have a boyfriend that way."

She was joking, but not.

It wasn't really the worst idea she'd ever had.

They could get along, once they figured out they could trust each other.

He didn't respond, and she suspected that was a good thing.

Grabbing her by the arm, he draped her coat over her shoulders and took his own off the rack as he passed.

"We can cab it. It isn't far."

Chapter Nineteen

Less than one hundred words. Short sentences. He made sense when he used short sentences.

Bruce clicked Send and sat back against the rock hard sofa cushion. It needed replacing. Everything in that apartment did. It'd been decorated with fashion and trends in mind, and Bruce had paid for it all because he supposed that was what wealthy people did. He didn't like it, though. Any of it. He should have been better on top of it, but he was so rarely in New York that it was easier for him to just stay in a hotel when he was there than to have the apartment opened up.

What was there would suffice for the time being, though.

Feeling a sudden, belated surge of trepidation, he fished the message out of the sent box and reread it.

Ev.
Tried calling. Maybe something wrong with my brother's phone?
Back in the States. Getting settled in city. Have a landline. Here's the number. Call please. Want to see you.

Seemed all right. He'd waffled over the nuances

between "want" and "need," and decided that "want" sounded less petulant. He did need to see her, though. They'd already had a head start. She knew all the gristly bits about him and didn't seem to mind, so he was ready to take a leap. He was ready for definitions and labels. He just wanted to have her.

A new message appeared in his inbox. He quickly clicked over to it, excited, only for his enthusiasm to quickly pivot to confusion.

SUBJECT: Out of office response

The employee you have emailed no longer has access this account.

This mailbox is unmonitored. Please send queries relating to publicity of Athena books to...

"No...longer has access?"

What did that mean? She couldn't get fired. Everyone at Athena thought she was on deck to be the next head honcho.

He set the computer down and fetched the phone from the kitchen. He called Everley's cell again, but calls were going straight to voicemail after a single ring.

"Call me, will you? This number's okay," he left on his third attempt.

And then it suddenly dawned on him that perhaps she didn't want his contacts. Perhaps he'd dodged a hit by the clue stick when he'd really needed it. She wasn't answering her phone and hadn't responded to the last couple of messages he'd sent to her personal address. Granted, he hadn't given her much to work with. All she could have responded to what he'd sent was "Okay," but at least he'd feel less like a fool if she had.

He squished the rubber bumper of the handset beneath his thumb and thought.

Shit.

He'd had everything all figured out, he'd thought. Everley was supposed to be his first order of business after getting settled in, and he was already off track.

"No no no." He shook his head and stood so he could move. Idleness led to fixating on shit he couldn't fix. Movement kept his brain cycling.

He still had calls to make. People to see. A list to go down. He could pencil Everley in to a later spot just to follow up.

If she told him to fuck off, he could handle that.

He just needed to hear *something*. He needed to know if he was a fool for feeling the way he did.

He probably was.

As soon as Raleigh had dropped off his coat and gym bag in his office on Monday morning, he headed to Everley's. He had a fist raised to knock on her doorframe before entering, but the door was already open.

Music played at low volume and there came a murmur of frustration right before a metal file cabinet drawer slammed shut.

Everley wasn't a grunge band lover. The music coming out of her office had always been either show tunes, Motown classics, or yacht rock.

And Everley wasn't a man of around five-eight who tended to forget to brush his hair in the back or tuck in his shirt all around.

"Charlie, what the hell are you doing in here?"

Charlie spun on the heel of his loafer, blue eyes round and open wide.

Supposedly, Charlie was many years past the threshold of adulthood. Twenty-four. Twenty-five. He sure as shit didn't look it, though.

"Oh...kay, well, you see—"

A sigh came from the corner behind the door.

Raleigh looked behind it and found Joey seated atop a low stool. His fingers were tented. Eyes dead with malaise or fury or something. One could never really tell with Joey.

"She's gone," Joey said.

Immediately, Raleigh's teeth went into perfect alignment for gritting and hands clenched at his sides.

She'd moved upstairs.

One of the global strategy specialists had announced she'd be leaving for good before having her baby. Everley had probably showed up bright and early to move in and find new necks to walk on.

By the end of Friday night, she'd convinced herself that she wasn't capable—that like him, she was just a kid trying to make the most of a shitty situation a parent had created. She'd spent half the movie with her head on his shoulder and keeping her hands warm in his coat pocket, and he'd let himself think, "This is nice."

If that was what being her boyfriend was, he was exactly cut out for it.

But evidently it wasn't.

She'd known all along it wasn't going to happen because they would no longer be equals in the organization.

"I've been in this business for twenty-five years and

I've never seen anything like this before," Joey muttered.

"They said I couldn't say anything," Charlie said. "Obviously, I wasn't going to blab and lose a promotion."

"So, you *knew* she was going?" Raleigh demanded.

Charlie shrugged. "Since before the holidays, and that was only because HR forced her to loop me in close to the end. She was going to have to get me up to speed on what she was working on. She couldn't just drop it in someone's lap and go."

"But now my workload has gone up thirty percent and no one saw fit to tell me in advance." Raleigh was practically shaking with anger.

Yet again, he'd been used. People's strategies at manipulating him were becoming far more sophisticated. If he weren't so pissed, he might even want to congratulate her.

"I'll help you out in the interim," Joey said flatly. "HR made the job posting for Charlie's old position live this morning. We'll start interviews in two weeks or so. Unfortunately, you're going to have to absorb a couple of Everley's authors as well—just the ones who do solo appearances. Charlie's not ready to coordinate that stuff yet."

"So that makes my workload, what, *fifty* percent larger?"

"For now," Joey conceded. "Sorry, Ral. At least you're not working on the rock star book. Know who is?"

"Who?" Raleigh snarled.

Joey hooked both thumbs toward himself. "Me. Remember? Thanks a lot to you assholes for not showing up for meetings. I should have known something was up when Everley evaded it. Nothing was getting done and the nonfic team doesn't know their heads from their assholes."

"You really mean to tell me you didn't know she was moving upstairs? She reported directly to you."

Joey's brow creased. "That *who* was moving upstairs?"

"Everley. She took Natasha's job, didn't she?"

Joey leaned away from Raleigh as though he were suddenly looking at an alien and was trying to figure out which part of him was the head. "What? *No.* Natasha's job is still vacant. They're trying to poach someone away from another house so they haven't advertised it. Everley is *gone.*"

"Gone?"

"Yeah, like *Gone Girl,* gone."

"She peaced out," Charlie said. He held up double deuces.

Raleigh wanted to throttle him. The only thing holding him back was the knowledge that if he did, his workload would get even larger.

"She coordinated it with HR before we went on holiday break." Joey stood and released another of those weary sighs. "All they told me was that someone in publicity was leaving and that they'd have details coming soon. I'd assumed it was one of the interns or even Charlie, because he'd been avoiding his cubicle a lot. I've never seen a situation where someone's direct supervisor didn't know they were exiting the company."

"She's...*gone,*" Raleigh repeated, because it didn't make sense.

She hadn't said anything and she'd known for weeks that she was leaving.

If she'd told him, so much could have been different.

He realized then that perhaps that was *why* she hadn't told him—because it mattered to him. Because he hadn't been able to trust her words. Because he'd assumed that her motives were anything but pure.

Gone.

If Joey hadn't been in the way, Raleigh would have plopped with agitation on that stool. Instead, he gripped the doorframe and tried to remind himself that he wasn't allowed to take it personally.

After the way he'd treated her, he didn't have the right to.

"Gals in HR informed me that she probably didn't tell her father, either," Joey said, "but I'm sure he'll be on the warpath soon enough. If I were you, I'd keep my office door closed and avoid any calls coming from his extension."

"Shit," Raleigh whispered.

"Yeah." Joey clasped his shoulder on the way past. "You're too busy to care though, huh? You've got all that cross-promo stuff to work on for Stacia's television show tie-ins. You'll probably be in the weeds for weeks just with that."

"I can handle it," Raleigh said hoarsely.

He couldn't remember the last time he'd had the rug pulled out from under him like that.

She'd surprised him. Not in a bad way or a good one. Just in a big way. He wasn't certain how to digest the shock except to go directly to the source for answers. He needed to know she was okay, because she hadn't seemed like she was. But of course she wasn't. She'd known what was coming.

She'd done exactly what he had when he was twenty-three, and left before anyone could tell her she couldn't. He could respect that, even if he wished she hadn't had to do it.

He owed her so many apologies.

He retreated to his office, scrolled through the last incarnation of the employee directory, and dialed the number marked, *Shannon, Everley (c)*.

"The number you have dialed is no longer in service."

Chapter Twenty

"You'll get used to the smell," Lisa said with a laugh. She sifted more manure out of the straw scattered about the stables at the Burnout Bungalows and flicked it toward an established pile with unenviable precision.

"Not sure I want to," Everley muttered.

She'd gotten a late start to the day, at least late by Lisa's standards. Lisa had been up with the sun, pouring what must have been gallons of coffee down her throat and whistling jaunty tunes near the guest bedroom door that had either been meant to cheer or annoy.

Everley had pulled her pillow over her head and gone back to sleep. She just hadn't been ready to face the day yet. Avoidance was probably the most difficult job she'd ever accepted.

"I can't believe this is your life," Everley said. "Nubs for fingernails. Dry skin. Burrs in your hair."

Lisa pointed to her in warning. "Watch where you're going with this."

"I'm just saying." Everley laid her head atop the stable door and closed her eyes. "I guess I could see the appeal, though. The busyness. The uncomplicated relationships."

"The busyness I like. I could do with less quiet,

though, Ev. I need to get more people into this place or I'll be paying my property tax bill with an IOU come summer."

"You know I'll help you out."

"I know you would, but I won't let you. You're not exactly employed right now, at least by anyone who isn't me, and I know what I pay you."

"I have money."

"Yeah. So do I. A dwindling inheritance. When my grandmother moved up north, all she had was two pennies to rub together. I sank everything she left me into this place. If it doesn't take off, she's going to rise up out of her grave down in Rocky Mount and drift all the way here to fuss at me."

"I'll *help* you."

"With the ghost?" Lisa scrunched her nose. "You got some talents you didn't tell me about?"

"No." Everley grabbed a mangled towel off the hook nearby and lobbed it at her friend. "With the *place*. I told you. I can't promise you miracles, but figuring out some sort of marketing plan for you is the least I can do to repay you for being my rock for so many years."

Her father would never think to look for her there, if he cared enough to go looking at all. She didn't think he'd ever been farther west in the state than Staten Island.

She'd tried to do the responsible thing so no one raised any panic alarms. She'd sent notes to both parents saying she was going to be off the grid for a while and that she'd forward her new number whenever she had it. She'd been at Lisa's for a week. She suspected her inbox was overflowing, but other than to pay a few bills that couldn't be ignored, she'd been avoiding the Internet.

The truth was that she was half afraid that no one really cared that she'd left. She didn't want to scroll through her inbox and be pelted with the evidence. The worst mistake she'd ever made was to mold her life around the desires of people who cared more about their happiness than hers. She was through with doing that.

"I'd appreciate any help you can give," Lisa said warmly. "I've racked my brain over it, but I think I'm just too rigid a thinker. Maybe you can come up with something outside the box."

"Like your business?" It was a hideaway for burnt-out professionals. Kind of like Everley was at the moment.

"Yeah. I guess just like the business." Lisa set her pitchfork aside and pointed to the building that contained the property's office as well as Lisa's on-site apartment. "We can chat it out over lunch. You've got that look on your face like you've already got ideas churning."

Everley laughed. "I guess I do. It's amazing how much freer the ideas come when you're doing something you want to."

"It'd be great if you could get that guy Raleigh to help. Didn't you once tell me that he was the most agile thinker you'd ever encountered in a publicity position?"

There was no chance at all that Lisa didn't see Everley's graceless stumble over her own feet or her flinch, because she stopped on the path, hands on hips, and pointed a scolding stare at her.

"What was that?" Lisa asked.

"What was what?"

"I said his name and you got a look on your face like you just realized you'd sat on a wet subway seat."

"Just startled me, is all. I don't expect to hear names from work outside of work, especially since I no longer work there."

"Nuh-uh." Lisa shook her head and got Everley moving again. "It was more than that. I know you had a hard time with the staff at Athena, but I don't know if it's normal for you to have a tiny panic attack at the mention of a coworker's name. Did he antagonize you?"

"*No*," Everley drawled out. She cleaned her soles on the mat outside the office and crossed the threshold before Lisa could study her face again.

"So he was no different than any of the others, is what you're telling me? No special animus?"

"Stop using SAT words." Everley knelt in front of Margo, the ancient basset hound Everley's cat had been antagonizing for days, and scratched her between the ears. "And no," came her strained reply.

Lisa knelt right beside her. "You're full of shit. You never figured out how to lie. I've been trying to teach you how to look like less of a babe-in-the-woods since college. Have you learned nothing?"

"Apparently not."

"Is it embarrassing? The thing you're not telling me."

"No, I wouldn't exactly call it that. More like… confusing. Emotionally shredding."

Lisa cocked a brow. "You had a thing?"

Everley grimaced. "Yeah, I guess so. At the end. I liked him a lot, but… I couldn't…*we* couldn't do that. After so many years of hostility from him because of what he thought I wanted, I knew I couldn't really pursue anything. I didn't say anything to him about leaving. I knew I had to do a complete break from the place until things settle down a bit, and it's just…*awful*, because

I got five or six years being generally disinterested in the men I've gone out with, and then I get two in a row who I adored but couldn't keep. Why even try?"

"Two in a row in a just a few months' span is pretty damn good odds."

"Only you would think that."

"Maybe so, but my dating prospects out here in the wilderness of New York all tend to be pretty scant. Did I tell you that around Thanksgiving, I relented and went out on a date with the mayor's son?"

"No!" Everley gasped.

Like Everley, Lisa didn't date much, though for entirely different reasons. The lady was inordinately picky and her tastes tended to be ephemeral.

Lisa shrugged. "It was awful. He kept talking about bass fishing and tax rates, and the degeneration of the institution of marriage."

"Ew." She got a sneaking suspicion that was a button of Lisa's that guy wouldn't ever press again.

Lisa shook a few kibble bits out of the treat bag for Margo. "I told him that I, personally, didn't ever plan to marry. I was just going to collect lovers and swap them out as my moods changed. Then I asked him for his sister's number. I was joking, of course, but unbeknownst to me, we were actually at the lady's restaurant at the time." She scoffed. "That cheap bastard was counting on her to comp the meals. Anyway, we were sitting near enough to the kitchen door that she heard me. She came out in an apron all covered in marinara sauce and slapped a sticky note on my purse with her number on it."

Shaking her head in awe, Everley stared speechlessly at her friend.

"He got up and stormed out." Lisa shrugged. "I haven't called. That'd be weird, right?"

"There are so many parts of what you just said that were weird."

Yet again, Lisa shrugged. "Small town life for you. I'm trying not to be a scandal here. No reason you can't put yourself out there, though. If you like either of those guys, there's no reason you shouldn't pursue them when you're done with this woman-in-the-woods phase of your life, which I'm completely certain will only last for about three weeks, by the way."

"I don't appreciate the insinuation that I can't hack it away from the city."

"I'm not insinuating that. I'm saying that you're a smart lady and you won't need long to figure out what your path forward is. It's not here. I mean, I'd love to have you here as my full-time partner-in-crime, but this is my dream. I don't want to turn you into a supporting player in it when you have to be the leading lady in your own epic story."

"That sounds like something Bruce would say," Everley said on a self-pitying groan. "He has the loveliest way with words."

"Well, it's true. Stop hiding behind your own self and figure shit out fast. You've already wasted enough time being miserable."

"And that sounds like something Raleigh would say."

"Well, shit, just keep them both, and maybe between the two, they can talk some sense into you."

Everley laughed so loud that Margo scrambled up on her arthritic legs and bayed at the ceiling. "Sorry, doggy. Your mommy is super silly. I think all the horse shit fumes have gone to her head."

"You laugh now," Lisa said, "but guys do that shit all the time. They keep a side chick on the hook until they're *sure* their main chick will be their future chick. Trust me. I was a dude's side chick for three years."

Everley did that math. Lisa hadn't had many long-term relationships, so that could have only been one person. "Dwight?"

Lisa's eyebrows raised ominously.

"But he was living with you."

"Because his other girlfriend was still living with her parents. But we're talking about you, so let's not dive into that right now, okay?"

Everley put up her hands in defeat. She had no idea what she'd say, anyway. The fact Lisa had kept the betrayal such a closely held secret meant she didn't want the situation dissected, even by her best friend. Everley could certainly understand the motive of not wanting to be harshly judged.

"You know I'm not really suggesting that you rock the boat like that," Lisa said, "but don't assume that you have to throw either away yet."

The possibilities swarmed in Everley's mind. Having two men wouldn't be the worst thing ever, especially given their considerable differences. Bruce's companionship was all about touch and words and feeling better. Raleigh's was more about movement and primality and, in an odd way, motivation. She learned so much from both. Adored them both, and realized the two of them should never, ever be put in the same room together. They'd get on like water on a grease fire and yet there she was, bridging the two of them. If she could keep them from arguing themselves into states of asphyxiation, she'd certainly have a damned good romp in bed.

And she'd probably laugh a lot, too. It was all pointless without the laughing.

On a needier level, there were worse things than being the focus of two men's attention when she'd gone for so long pretending that she didn't need anyone. It would probably take two just to get her back to a state of equilibrium. She certainly wouldn't consider her role in the middle to be such a hardship. In fact, she'd never believed love was such a rigid thing that it would break rather than stretch to accommodate needs.

But it wouldn't happen. Bruce was in the wind and Raleigh didn't trust him, anyway. There was no way in hell they'd share.

"You've got that ideas face on again," Lisa said.

Everley smoothed her features and went to the sink to wash her hands. "Bad ideas this time, and it's all your fault. All right. Give me your computer. I want to see how you've been marketing this place."

Chapter Twenty-One

A few weeks later, Raleigh was sitting at his desk squinting at a book tour itinerary when his desk phone rang. Technically, it was his lunch hour and no one would fault him for ignoring it, but he glanced at the display screen, anyway.

The call was coming from the reception desk.

Instinctively, he lifted the handset. If there was something he could quickly resolve rather than keeping it simmering on the back burner, he wanted to get it done. He'd made a New Year's resolution to get the hell out of the office every day by five.

Plus, it was Friday, and he had someplace to be.

Everley's defection had seriously jarred him, and he'd had to do some serious meditation on why that was. He hadn't wanted to like her. Attraction was fine. Fucking her was fine. But feeling like there was another layer of compatibility he'd ignored truly bothered him. Connecting was hard for him because trusting was. She was a woman who'd keep his secrets and he'd keep hers. They both understood what it was like to have to be so cautious.

That was a rare find.

"This is Raleigh," he told the receptionist.

"Hiya. There's a gentleman here who wanted to see you. Didn't know if you had anything scheduled with it being lunchtime. He insisted on seeing you, though."

"Who is it?"

He heard the muffling of a mic and then her query of, "Tell me your name again?"

Raleigh couldn't hear the speaker, but the receptionist came back on and said, "He says his name is Theo."

Theo.

Theo was Bruce.

Raleigh muffled the phone mic with his thumb and spat, "Fuck."

He didn't want to see Bruce.

Only in the past week had he finally gotten to the point where he didn't grind his teeth every time he passed the life-size cardboard band member mockups at the end of the hall. He'd managed to shove that piece of the past into the "educational mistakes" part of his brain.

Seeing him would drag all the bad faith back to the surface.

But he also didn't want Bruce to make a scene.

After lifting his thumb from the receiver, through gritted teeth, he said, "I'll come get him."

"Thanks!"

By the time Raleigh had made it to the waiting room, he'd shaken the fists out of his hands and more or less flattened his scowl.

He managed to greet the receptionist without baring his teeth and nodded at the visitor.

"Theo" was wearing head-to-toe black with the exception of the chunky fuchsia scarf tied around his neck and up to his chin. In spite of the dimness of the florescent lights in the building, he still had his sunglasses on and his wool cap pulled down low on his brow. A few bits of dark hair escaped from the bottom.

Once again, he was that irrepressible enigma Raleigh had been so captivated by back at the Hollywood Bowl. The star who'd been hiding in plain sight and yet had managed to enthrall all the same.

Bruce picked up his bag and his battered guitar case and trod to Raleigh.

Raleigh didn't say a word until they were halfway down the main hall and past all the open conference room doors. By then, he was sure he could speak without yelling. "Where the fuck is your coat? It's twenty degrees out."

"Lost it somewhere. Coffee shop, maybe. Shouldn't have taken it off there. Was already carrying too much stuff. Did you know that one of the most expensive coffees is sourced from beans scavenged from civet shit? I haven't tried it, but—"

Raleigh pushed him into his office and closed the door. "What do you want?"

If Bruce got started with all that diverting trivia, Raleigh was going to forget why he couldn't stand the sight of him. He was just going to stand there and stare like an asshole while marveling over how he hadn't recognized those famous lips the first time they met.

"Everley." Bruce shifted his weight nervously and took off his sunglasses. There were dark circles under his eyes and a certain gauntness about him that hadn't been there before. With all the film promotion amping up, he'd probably been burning the candle at both ends. Raleigh certainly understood the feeling. "Where's Everley? They said she's not here."

"That's why you came to see me? To ask about Everley?"

"I don't know where she is. I was in South Africa dealing with bureaucrats for a month and then London and she said she wanted to see me when I got back, but…" Without completing the thought, Bruce dropped his gear on the chair on the other side of Raleigh's desk and drifted to the wilting poinsettia atop the low bookcase. He gave it a few curious pokes.

"Bruce," Raleigh snapped.

Bruce spun on his boot heel, eyes wide with something like surprise. It was as though he'd *forgotten* whose office he was in.

"You've got to come to my thing. I'm supposed to… do a thing. Everley's not here."

"If it's a book thing, call Joey or send him an email."

"No, it's a preview thing. Supposed to be there in two hours. I made some songs for a show. I just need a second head."

"And you've just spontaneously decided that in absence of Everley, I should volunteer? Maybe I need a second head, too."

"I don't have anyone else to ask."

Ah.

Raleigh let out a dry laugh. He hated being the person people called on as a last resort.

"Don't you have a manager?" he asked wearily.

"I set it up. I can do it. It's just, this first time, I wanted to make sure I wasn't missing anything. I don't want to get so focused on one part of it that I miss something that might bite me in the arse later."

"I don't know anything about the music business, Bruce." A copout, perhaps, but still honest.

"It's not the music industry. It's a stage production. I'm working on the score. Kinda in a hurry. The last guy quit halfway through. Money issues. I don't have those. *Please.*" Bruce's words sped incrementally with each passing syllable, and there was particular panic in that last word, spoken in a rasp.

Please.

It was such a dangerous little word. It was a word that insinuated that the hearer had some power, and Raleigh didn't want any.

Not over Bruce.

"I don't have anyone else," Bruce continued in a cadence of hesitance—a cadence of *please.* "People don't always tell me the truth."

That raw admission hit Raleigh in the chest like a sharpened brick, and the voice in the back of his mind screamed at the irony. "I have that same problem," he found himself saying. He braced himself against the edge of his desk and stared at his calendar.

And sometimes people told the truth but omitted so much that their honesty felt like lies.

He understood why Everley had done what she had. He was just angry that it had to be that way. She'd been afraid of rocking the boat.

Perhaps she was still afraid. He'd find out.

He'd found her and that was why he needed to get out of that office on time. There was a lot of road construction between the city and upstate. He had hours of traffic ahead of him.

If nothing else, he'd make sure she was well, but he was also sticking his neck out. She'd joked that she wanted a boyfriend, and he thought he could be far more successful in that role than in the one he'd played as her coworker.

"I understand you're put off by me," Bruce said. "I'm sorry I put you in a bad place. It was rude of me. That didn't mean that all the stuff that happened before wasn't honest."

Raleigh wasn't in the mood to wrestle with other people's ideas of honesty. His had always been so clear cut, and he had little mercy for people who changed rules as they went along. "I don't want to have this conversation right now."

Bruce put up his hands. "Okay. That's fair. I just needed to say it. Really. If there were anyone else around who I thought had the right kind of gumption for this, I'd ask them. I'll pay you in signed guitar picks, if you'd like. I hear those sell pretty well on eBay."

"Save the picks for Joey. He might be able to do something with them."

"So, you're going?"

Raleigh shook his head, even as his mouth started to shape the word *yes*.

He considered going just to get Bruce out of his office.

He considered going because he was an imperfect, vain creature who didn't hate the idea of walking beside a man that beautiful.

And if he were being truly honest with himself, he'd admit he would go because he couldn't trust anyone else to do what needed to be done.

He didn't like Bruce for what he'd done, but he'd done what Raleigh never could and asked for help. Bruce was extending trust to him even after everything, and Raleigh realized that Bruce could be so vulnerable in a way that Raleigh simply couldn't be anymore.

Vulnerable people got used up.

Perhaps he'll learn one day.

Bruce tracked a hand through the untied half of his hair and stared pensively at the window.

He walked around like that, completely oblivious to his appearance, or perhaps aware and uncaring. There was a certain appeal of that sort of comfort with one's own body. It was a kind of bravery Raleigh didn't possess. He put on a good front most of the time that other people's opinions didn't sway him, but they did. Every single one since his father had decided that he wanted to be a policymaker. Everyone around him had become more critical of him after that.

He edged around the desk and slid his index finger into Bruce's loose hair elastic.

"It's driving me to distraction," he said when Bruce gave him a curious sideways look. Bruce's hair was enviously thick and required rougher handling, but Raleigh managed to get it all scraped together at his nape and tidily bound. "Cut it if you're not going to do anything with it."

"Keeps me warm if I forget my hat." Bruce's brow creased as he smoothed a hand back from his hairline. "And no one cuts it right. They just do what they want."

"You have to be descriptive."

Bruce made a face.

Yeah.

Raleigh felt that way about a lot of things. Like vulnerability.

Fuck.

He picked up his phone and tapped in Joey's extension. "Hey. I never do this, but I'm heading out early today. Need to get something done across town." He assumed they were going across town, anyway, and hoped Bruce wouldn't make him a liar.

"Everything all right?" Joey asked dispassionately.

He'd been sounding like that for a few days. He was swamped and disenchanted. As always, he'd come around whenever they were fully staffed again. Everley's value became increasingly clear with each passing day she wasn't there. She'd been an incredibly productive employee, and even her most introverted authors had been at ease with her.

"Fine," Raleigh said to Joey, and he watched Bruce watch him with rapt curiosity, golden eyes intensely, brazenly fixed on him. "Just hard to get stuff done during daylight hours when you work seven to seven."

"Yeah. You should see the accusing looks my dog gives me when I get home."

"Sorry, Joe." Raleigh disconnected before Joey could launch into one of his spiels about the unreliability of his dog walking service.

He stuffed some work into his bag, and grabbed his keys and coat before he could change his mind. "Let's go."

"But you said no."

"I did. I had a change of heart."

"Why?"

So you don't become as broken and cynical as me.

"Where's the thing?" Raleigh deflected. "Earlier's better than late." If they got started earlier, Raleigh could get the hell out of the city earlier and maybe even see Everley before obscene o'clock.

"Oh!" Bruce grabbed his guitar. "Not far. Just up Forty-Second. You going?"

"Just to get you out of my office."

"Oh."

Bruce had an extraordinary range of motion in his expressions, so his instant shift from hopefulness to despair was evident and shattering. Contrary to what many people might have thought, Raleigh didn't actually enjoy hurting people's feelings. Caustic words had simply become his primary defense mechanism, and he didn't always intend to deploy them. His reflexes were broken.

He murmured an apology as they walked.

Bruce waved it off and said "Used to it" under his breath.

There went that sharpened brick again.

"I'm out for the day," Raleigh told the receptionist as they passed.

He called the elevator. It was empty when it arrived. Bruce stared solemnly at the crease between the doors as it descended and fidgeted the end of his guitar case.

Raleigh gathered his messy, scattered thoughts of vanity and vulnerability and savage honesty and swept them away for the moment. Bruce had been looking for Everley. She'd thought he was gone for good, but there he was looking for her.

She probably didn't ever make him think he should beg.

"What is it that you like about Everley?" Raleigh murmured. "What makes you trust her?"

The questions hung in the air for a long moment before it dawned on Raleigh that the words had come out of his mouth.

Someone joined the elevator on the fifth floor. The men parted toward their respective sides of the car to make room and said nothing further until they'd reached the lobby.

"She listens first," Bruce said.

"First?"

"She doesn't say what's what until she's heard the whole thing, and then not for a while after that, either."

Raleigh was about to hail a cab and had just stepped to the curb, but Bruce grabbed his wrist. "Hold on. I have a service for when I'm in the city. Prepaid. Might as well get my money's worth. You can call it. I don't have my phone."

Of course you don't.

If nothing else, Bruce stayed true to character.

Raleigh had to respect that.

He let Bruce put in the number and handled the rest of the request for him. Five minutes, they'd quoted.

They could wait inside the building, where the temperatures weren't indicative of Demeter's wrath and where a certain coatless rock star wouldn't be at risk of hypothermia.

But Bruce seemed content with being outside. Bright eyed. Looking about with curiosity, staring up at tall buildings. Attention snatched by people leaning rudely on car horns and the scathing opinions of city-hardened pedestrians.

It was hard to think uncharitable thoughts about Bruce when he was like that—when his attention was captured and his curiosity working in overdrive.

He'd looked at Raleigh that way, months ago. He hadn't known to be flattered then, but he thought he was.

When the car arrived, Raleigh helped him stow his guitar in the trunk and crowded into the back seat with him.

Bruce ferreted a crumpled piece of paper out of his pocket and handed it to the driver. "Actually wrote it down this time," he said to Raleigh as the car edged into traffic. "I usually try to remember but when I've got too much going on I forget things."

"How do you function? I can't live the way you do. I need to carry details with me."

"Yes, because you're a proper, rational human being who thrives on structure, whereas I'm wired to pick up my spear at the slightest provocation and run off on a hunt." Bruce tried to angle himself more ergonomically in the tight space, putting his left foot on the hump at the center. "That's what my nan said. She said everyone's a way for a reason. Sometimes there are advantages. Sometimes, they have to…make accommodations to fit in. We weren't so good at figuring those out at first, and I admit that too soon I started leaning on Ev because she's so bloody *everything*, you know? I'm going to do better." He pointed a warning finger at Raleigh. "I'm *not* turning Ev into my keeper. I swear I'm not. I just want her."

Of course you do.

Unfortunately, that made two of them.

Suspecting that he was going to wake up with yet another sore jaw, Raleigh gritted his teeth, anyway. That mysterious email he'd gotten from Everley's account suddenly returned to haunt him—that he was going to die lonely. He refused to believe that was true.

"I've got a therapist for that," Bruce said. "She's a right bitch at the moment, but I can't blame her. Here I am, thirty-three fucking years old, rich as Croesus, and I've never stayed still long enough to get into a routine. I'm sure she and my doctor are having wonderfully sigh-filled conference calls as they try to sort out what's what. You see, I have a grab bag of issues playing off each other."

Enemy. Competitor. It didn't matter. When Bruce talked, Raleigh absorbed the words. Devoured them, really. "Does that frighten you?"

"What? Knowing the names they put on that shit?"

"Yes."

Bruce shrugged. "Doesn't really change anything, does it? Brioche is still white bread, even if you don't know the fancy name for it."

Raleigh envied that sort of logic. It was a different sort of practicality than he possessed. It was part of that seductive rawness, Raleigh supposed—that urgency that made him so aware that he was made of flesh and flesh craved touch.

"Doesn't it frighten *you*?" Bruce asked.

"What do you mean?"

"Some people act like it's contagious. It doesn't rub off, you know. None of it. Not the ADHD, not the Asperger's, not my mood disorder."

"I didn't know you had any of those things. Hadn't suspected them, and hadn't thought that I should." They were in one of the most diverse places in the world, and rarely was his immediate thought to attach a diagnosis to someone's unpredictable behavior. If he started doing that, he couldn't be surprised if others started doing the same to him. "I'm not frightened of you. Not for that, anyway."

"Then why?"

Raleigh didn't respond because he couldn't lie.

He couldn't say that he terrified him. Bruce had become the living embodiment of Raleigh not being able to get what he wanted.

Or *who*, rather.

First "Theo," and Everley could possibly be next.

Bruce didn't push. Pushing never got anyone anywhere with Raleigh, anyway.

"That's in the film, you know," Bruce said after a minute.

"No, I didn't know."

"Band didn't want anyone to find out. I don't care if they do. I can't be the only one like this. People shouldn't have to be afraid to admit it. People punish them for being honest."

"I agree. They do. Nothing I say can fix that, but I hear you."

"That's all I want sometimes."

It didn't seem like much to Raleigh.

When they arrived at the small theater and Bruce had overtipped the driver and fetched his guitar from the trunk, he held his head up with confidence until they got into the lobby. Then he turned to Raleigh in a panic.

Before he could get a word out, Raleigh said, "I'll listen. That's what you wanted, right? An extra head."

"Right. Just for a bit." Bruce notched his teeth into his lower lip and turned his gaze toward the open auditorium doors.

"I won't say anything," Raleigh said. "I'll sit where you want and I'll keep my mouth shut unless something smells off."

"So you're just going to let me blather unfettered? Thanks a lot."

"Yes."

"You hate me that much?"

"I don't hate you, Bruce."

"You don't?"

Raleigh shoved his fingers through the last vestiges of styling product in the back of his hair and tugged as he forced out some air.

God, that earnest fucking face.

Just standing there looking at him was driving that brick further into his chest.

"I'll be honest," Raleigh said. "After what happened, I found it incredibly difficult to be anywhere near you. I felt like you'd manipulated me, and I've been trying to cut people like that out of my life for nearly twenty years."

"What about now? You don't want to be around me now?"

I'm here, aren't I?

"You know," Raleigh hedged, "you have a very intense personality."

"Is that a bad thing?"

"Depends on who you need to impress, usually."

"I don't impress you?"

Raleigh put a hand to Bruce's back and got him walking toward the auditorium doors. He hoped that whomever he needed to see was already inside and that they could escalate the appointment.

"I won't forget I asked you," Bruce whispered. They paused in the doorway, letting their eyesight adjust to the darker room.

Raleigh spotted a cluster of musicians down in the pit and a couple of people who looked like decision makers studying piles of paper at the stage edge.

"I want an answer," Bruce said as they started down the carpeted aisle.

"Why does it matter if you impress me or not?" Raleigh whispered.

"Because I want to know if you think my personality is bad."

Fuck.

Had he implied that? He certainly hadn't intended to.

Raleigh dragged a hand down his weary face and placed a firm grip on Bruce's arm. He was too busy watching Raleigh that he wasn't watching the floor.

"I don't think your personality is bad. You just frustrate me."

"I know all about frustration. It lives in me. It's a constant companion and feeds my social ails. It tangles up my thoughts and makes my words come out all wrong or too late."

"Well, you hide it well. Mostly, your face is an open book, but every so often, you have a way of looking like you don't actually give a shit about anything."

"Like right now?"

"Yes."

Bruce's expression was as dead as a mannequin's.

"That's interesting because I give a shit about you and I'm looking at you right now."

Bruce looked forward before Raleigh could think of anything else to say. It was just in time to catch the hand of one of the ladies who'd climbed out of the pit.

"I give a shit about you," Bruce had said. If it was a lie, it was a well-sharpened one that could slice clean through to the bone, but Bruce couldn't possibly know how badly Raleigh needed to hear it.

"Yay, you're early. I'm so glad. If you've got bits of

score for me to photocopy, we'll jump right in and see if we can make the sounds meld with what we've already got. I'm Karen Settle, by the way."

Bruce's features opened up once more. "Yes, yes. Took me a moment to recognize you. Glasses aren't right. You got new ones?"

"My...*glasses*? I—" Gaping, she put a hand against her heart, but quickly regained her composure. "I got bored with the cat-eye frames. After thirty years, my optician convinced me to move on. No one else noticed that."

"That was what my memory filed you under. Cat eyes." To Raleigh, he said, "Director and a fantastic musician in her own right. Played harp with the philharmonic for years and then hid in the pit at the NYC Ballet for a while. Can't miss her if you know her style, though. Her percussion instincts are impeccable."

"Hey!" she grinned. "I love it when people know I didn't come fully formed out of a giant seashell and decided to show up here to make shows. I put in my years."

"Oh, I could go on for hours talking about that modernized piano accompaniment you wrote into Johnny Gallagher's new rendition of 'Sleigh Ride.'"

She groaned with her head back. "Christ, no one bought that record."

"Obviously, *he* did," Raleigh murmured, eying him with some of the curiosity and wonder Bruce must have felt for the things that caught his attention. He wouldn't put it past Bruce to buy *every* record and to know a little bit about all the major players.

"Of course I bought it," Bruce told him. "Nan loved Johnny. Had the hugest crush on him since she was a little girl. She'd be tickled pink to hear that ancient motherfucker is still recording."

"Cute." Raleigh chuckled.

Or maybe Bruce was cute when he talked about his grandmother. Or because he was lively and passionate. And he was just a good time if he could be kept up with. Sometimes, Raleigh forgot what that felt like.

Karen tried, and failed, to suppress a snort of laughter with a hand over her nose. "So, who's this?" she squeaked out. She tilted her head toward Raleigh.

"Raleigh McKean," Bruce said, handing her a sheath of loose music from his bag. "He's the—"

As dread pooled in his gut, Raleigh turned his head, prepared for the undesired appellation and the aftermath. That he was a senior publicist at Athena. That he was the son of a controversial senator.

But instead of completing the statement, Bruce took a breath.

"He's...the *guy*," he stated.

Bewildered by the abstract appellation, Raleigh faced forward in time to see Karen's brows knit. "The guy?"

Bruce shrugged. "Sometimes you've got to bring along a guy, and this one's mine."

Raleigh knew there was no way in hell that ill-defined statement was going to fly.

"Oh!" Karen said, perking up. "I used to have a guy."

Raleigh let out the quietest of guffaws. *Are you kidding me?* Only in Bruce's world would such an exchange be accepted and perhaps even expected.

"Carried my coat sometimes and told me I was pretty after I got bad haircuts," Karen said in a wistful tone. "He got poached away by a competitor who could pay him a little more."

"Do you want me to tell you you're pretty, Bruce?" Raleigh asked, deadpan.

"You think my haircut's that bad?"

"I swear, you leapfrog to outlandish conclusions like no one else."

Bruce smirked. "So, you like it, then."

He was fishing for a compliment. Raleigh realized he did that a lot.

He also realized that he probably needed them more than most.

"I like it," Raleigh confessed. Liked everything about Bruce's dangerous panther look, really, even if it was chaotic.

Karen bounded away, waving the music in the air and shouting at a production assistant.

Grinning, Bruce loosened his scarf and draped it over the back of the chair in the front row. "You think I'm pretty."

"I shouldn't dignify that question with a response, but yes." Raleigh settled into a chair in the next row back. "Don't let it go to your head."

"Oh, I'm gonna be on cloud fuckin' nine all day." He popped the latches on his guitar case and smiled ruefully. "And I'm going to remind you that you told me immediately after this meeting."

"And I thought I was petty."

"Petty and Pretty." Bruce rubbed the scruff on his chin. "Can you sing? We can be an act."

"You don't ever want to hear me sing, Bruce. I can't hold a tune."

Bruce darted in close before Raleigh could think to lean away. His mouth was at his ear, breath tinged with quiet laughter. "Sound pretty good when you moan," he whispered. "That talent usually conveys."

Raleigh forced down a labored swallowing and bobbed his knee to keep his cock from agitating.

"Should I have said that?" Bruce whispered.

"No."

"I kind of knew."

"And yet you said it anyway."

"Are you uncomfortable?"

"Yes."

"I'm going to go play music now."

"Good. Get the hell away from me."

"You gonna watch? Like you said?"

"I suppose," Raleigh grumbled dramatically. "If I must."

"And then I'll remind you that you said I'm pretty. I wish there was someone I could brag to about that. It feels like a coup."

"You are a bonafide mess, Bruce Engle."

"Ev says that so much more nicely and she puts her hands on my cheeks when she tells me. Medicine's easier to take when the person giving it is straddling your lap."

"You're an asshole," Raleigh said, grateful for the dark so he could discreetly adjust the tent in his slacks.

"You were mean to me. You deserve it." With a wink, Bruce walked away.

He had no way of knowing just how much Raleigh deserved it.

And he didn't really deserve either of them, but there he was, pondering possibilities and weighing options.

He put his foot up on the armrest in front of him and

let out a dry laugh as Bruce shook hands of the musicians in the pit.

It was ridiculous. He was imagining opportunities that months ago, he would have found insulting.

But the odds of any of them coming to fruition were low. He was going to see Everley and let her know why he'd been a dick and offer her whatever she wanted.

Bruce was probably better for her. Any fool could see that, but Raleigh was long overdue for some good luck. Maybe his time had come.

Chapter Twenty-Two

"That was all right, wasn't it? Felt good. Can't remember the last time I could say that about something related to work. Maybe because it didn't feel like work." Bruce pulled his guitar case in tight against his body so he and Raleigh could squeeze through the theater's exit simultaneously.

With a hand already raised to flag a taxi, Raleigh grunted.

"Oh, hell. What'd I do wrong?" A vicious gust of wind snapped between the buildings and drove right through Bruce's body. He shuddered. He needed to keep moving or he was going to freeze to death before the producers could even make him an offer.

"You didn't do anything wrong."

Three taxis in a row sped past, flooring it through the yellow light.

Raleigh swore under his breath and took a deep breath. He found his phone in his briefcase and started fiddling with apps. Peering over his shoulder, Bruce observed that they were ride apps.

"I could call my service. You know that, right?"

"I'll call it for you when I'm done. I've got to head home and I doubt you live anywhere near me."

"You in a hurry? I think I left my coat around here. I figured we could go get it."

"I did have somewhere I needed to be." Raleigh grimaced. "Shit. Where are all the cars tonight? Any other time, they'd be swarming around here." He closed the apps and glanced at the clock on his screensaver. "We were in the theater for nearly three hours."

"I didn't think it would take that long. Are you angry with me?"

"No. I don't think you could have known."

Yet another cab approached without stopping.

Raleigh spewed out another stream of profane frustration and spun around to Bruce. "All right. If you want me to help you find your coat, let's go. What's it look like?"

Bruce got his bearings and planted his foot toward the shop. Two blocks, if he was remembering correctly. "It's plaid. It's—"

"*God*, not the coat you had on in LA."

"Is that what I was wearing?"

"Do you have more than one plaid coat?"

"No. Why do you sound like my jacket perturbs you?" Bruce asked with a laugh. "It didn't do anything to you."

They wove through a slow-moving throng of tourists and rejoined on the other side.

"It's…" Raleigh grimaced. "A bit threadbare."

"It's comfortable."

"Out of fashion."

"I don't think it was ever in fashion. That's what my nan told my granddad, anyway."

"It was your grandfather's coat?"

"Yep. He thought it made him look dapper, but he

was a shepherd, you know? That's in the book, I think.
I put that in there—that he was a shepherd and Nan
was a seamstress, and aside from my school uniform,
all my clothes were homemade until I was ten. I didn't
know any better."

"You've lost your *grandfather's* coat, then."

"I don't like to think of it like that. I lose a lot of
things, usually not for good, though, except the phones.
I'd be gutted if that coat didn't turn up."

"We'll find it. You should probably stop wearing it
after we do."

Raleigh made the rediscovery sound inevitable rather
than speculative.

And he didn't make him feel foolish for having lost
the damned thing, again, in the first place. Bruce was
used to that—the gentle scolds, the clucking tongues,
the shaking heads.

Raleigh was a man who had his shit together and who
should have scorned Bruce for his lack of organization,
but he seemed oblivious to it. Or perhaps he was just
so together that he was used to being everyone else's
brain as well as his own.

"In here," Bruce said when they'd reached the coffee-
house door. "I'd stopped in for a bit to check my emails.
I'd sent Ev a bunch before but she didn't write back."

Raleigh held the door open for him and gestured toward the inside. "Did you wonder why?"

"I could only guess. One moment." Bruce scanned
the shop, standing on his toes to see over all the people
and the crowded tables. His coat wasn't at the table he'd
sat at or anywhere nearby. He doubted anyone would
steal it. It wasn't worth anything to anyone except him,
and as Raleigh had stated, it wasn't fashionable. He

waved at a barista and breathed and swallowed before speaking so his words didn't all come out on top of each other. "Hello. I was here earlier today and I may have left my coat. Long plaid?"

"Yes, yes! Hold on." She disappeared into an adjoining room and returned seconds later with his coat, completely unharmed.

Overwhelmed with gratitude and relief, he clasped a hand over his heart and mouthed, "Thank you."

Raleigh pulled the coat over the counter and draped it around Bruce's shoulders. "Order something and tip the lady heavily," he whispered as he straightened the collar.

Oh.

"Could I have a tea, please? Earl Grey. To go." Turning to Raleigh, he asked, "You want anything?"

"Mm. Black coffee. It's going to be a long night."

"Why's that?"

"Got to do some driving."

"To where?"

Raleigh leaned past Bruce and said to the barista, "Is there something happening around here tonight? There's a cab shortage all of a sudden. I've never seen anything like it."

"Two things. One is there's a big awards show," she said cheerily as she ripped off the top of a tea packet. "Everyone's swarming over there. Second is that I heard some rumbles there might be a strike starting in the next twenty-four hours. Something about a law regarding idling in a traffic lane to pick up fares." With the teabag half-paused on the way to the cup, she yanked her head up and gaped. "Wait. You—"

Before panic could completely settle, Raleigh interjected with, "Awards show? Oh, is that tonight? I totally forgot. He doesn't go to them anymore."

"So, he...*is*? You know." Her gaze flitted rapidly between Bruce and Raleigh as though she were afraid to say his name.

"Don't feel bad. I didn't recognize him the first time I met him, either."

"Wow," she breathed. "You'd think I'd be used to seeing musicians come in here, but I never do. Every single time, my brain goes..." She made a fizzling sound and finished depositing the bag into the cup. "I was scrolling through the red carpet feed before you came in. Your band was there. You weren't with them."

"He couldn't very well be two places at once, could he?" Raleigh asked.

"But why isn't he there?"

"Probably because he's recovering from the flu. Not contagious anymore, but he certainly doesn't have the endurance to sit through four hours of speeches."

"Ugh, I missed a week of work last month to flu. It's so bad this year. I'm trying to pick up extra hours at my other job to get back on my feet."

When she turned her back to pour Raleigh's coffee, Bruce stuffed a couple of twenties into the tip jar. And then one more, because certainly his coat was worth at least that.

After paying for their drinks and having Raleigh snap a picture of Bruce with the giddy barista, Bruce thanked her again for rescuing his coat and followed Raleigh back to the sidewalk.

"Thank you for that," Bruce said as Raleigh stepped toward the curb and looked both ways. "I know you don't like lying."

"Amazing how good I am at it when I try, hmm? Not a habit I want to get into."

"You did it to protect me. Didn't you?"

"She's going to talk. All of the staff are. You'd much rather have people think you've been ill than have them speculate that you're avoiding events because of something dramatic going on with the band. They'll find out soon enough. Relish your peace while you have it."

"You could have thrown me to the wolves."

"No, I couldn't have," Raleigh murmured.

Bruce fully intended to follow up on that enigmatic statement, but a cab stopped at that exact moment and Raleigh climbed in.

He'd dropped his newspaper on the curb. Bruce bent to fetch it for him, but stopped short at the picture on the thin periodical's front page.

It took him a moment to register. She was at the side edge of the photo, but her name was clearly listed—though misspelled—at the bottom. *"Lisa Cartwright, owner, discusses need for rejuvenation facility as assistant Evelyn Shane looks on."* She was in snow boots, shapeless jeans, a slouchy beanie hat, and a flannel shirt. She didn't look like herself, but Bruce would have recognized her anywhere. Obviously, Raleigh had as well.

That was his Ev in some place the paper called the *Carvel Courier* reported about.

He snapped the paper open to read the publication's location as the cabbie yelled out, "You gettin' in bud?" and Raleigh said from the far side of the back seat, "Get in."

Bruce did, shoving his guitar in first and slamming

the door. "Paper's dated three days ago. You didn't say a damned word to me."

"No. I didn't." Raleigh leaned forward and gave the driver an address.

"Why not?"

"She's not returning your calls or responding to your emails."

"Is she responding to yours?"

Raleigh didn't respond.

Bruce let out a dry laugh. "Oh, I see. Well. Looks like we're taking a little field trip, then, hmm? Don't you fucking dare tell me I'm not invited. I'm going to see Ev. She told me to come see her when I got back."

Raleigh folded his arms over his chest and stared out his window. Apparently, he had nothing to say for himself.

"I can't believe that I thought even for one minute that you were trying to help me out of the goodness of your heart," Bruce said acidly. "I won't make that mistake again. Trust me."

"If only I could."

"That was fun. I don't think I've ever been on a road trip before. Why are you leaning so close to the steering wheel?" Bruce unfastened his seatbelt and turned to Raleigh.

He'd put his car in Park at the front lot of The Burnout Bungalows' front office, and for a minute had stared at the parking lot, just gripping the steering wheel.

Bruce scanned the office's windows hoping to get a glimpse of Ev, but they were dark and likely covered. If anyone was in there, they probably hadn't seen Raleigh's headlights.

"In case I didn't make that perfectly clear hours ago when I got into your car," Bruce said, "I do intend to fucking brutalize you as soon as I've seen Everley. You were coming and weren't going to say anything."

"I was coming to make sure she's fine."

"Because she quit on you."

Raleigh's nod came slowly.

"I see. So you're doing this out of pure concern?" Bruce just couldn't buy that. Pure concern didn't generally come cloaked in subterfuge.

"Anyone would be concerned about a person who walks away from the prospect of a guaranteed six-figure job without even telling her family she's leaving."

"So, when you've decided she's fine, then what? You gonna go back to the city and forget she's here?"

Raleigh didn't respond.

Apparently, Bruce had pie-in-the-sky ideals and he'd gotten played again, just like he had the day he met him.

No matter what he did, he was never going to make Raleigh bend.

He got out of the car and marched to the door. His fist was poised to knock, but the inner door flew open before his hand could make contact with the frame.

A statuesque woman with dreadlocks gathered into a ribboned ponytail and who wore brown shimmer eyeshadow leaned in the doorway.

"I have that eyeshadow," Bruce blurted and immediately mentally berated himself. He was there for one reason and one reason only, yet the non sequitur had tumbled out. It was his nervous trigger.

She blinked at him.

Fuck. He shifted his weight. "I can tell by the glitter color. Ethereal Blends, innit?"

She sighed, letting down her guard, it seemed. "It's on backorder again. Trying to make it last. Tonight's a special occasion."

"You can have mine. Undertone's not right for me. Makes me look like I have glitter on top of a shiner."

"You can go ahead and mail it here, care of Lisa Cartwright. Thanks."

"My pleasure."

"Good! So, what do you want?"

"I'm Bruce."

"Yes, you are."

"And you said something about a special occasion? Is it Ev?" He was rambling, but he didn't care. Lisa was playing gatekeeper and he wasn't going to get past her until she allowed it.

She blinked at him again.

"I want to see Ev. She's here, isn't she? I promise I won't bother her, if that's what you're worried about. If she wants to tell me to go away—"

"Let them in, Lisa," came a weary-sounding voice farther inside the office.

"Oh, good." Lisa straightened up spryly and got out of the doorway. "Cold as my bed out there. I knew you weren't going to hold out for long." She called over her shoulder to Bruce, "We saw you on the security camera."

"I see." He was about to shut the door and lock it but Raleigh got his foot in the gap before he could and levered it open.

"Fucker," he said in an undertone.

"Feeling's mutual, lover. I meant what I said." He gave Raleigh a hard elbow to the side. "And I believe you still have something to tell me. Now you'll have to tell me twice just for pissing me off."

Raleigh rolled his eyes and passed Bruce, looking around the room. Mismatched furniture had been artfully arranged to create seating areas around the massive space. There were rustic tables made out of what appeared to be fallen logs, kitschy artwork featuring nineteenth-century hunting scenes, and a lot of faded hand-tied rugs on the floor. Everything didn't match, per se, but somehow, it all went together. It was cozy.

Ev was seated by the fireplace, laptop on thighs, short hair held back from her eyes with one of those thin elastic bands athletes favored. He was wearing more makeup than she was at the moment, which was to say she was wearing literally none and he had a full slap.

After all, he had an image to maintain, and he didn't think he looked like much of anything without contouring.

Her eyes were wide with emotion when Raleigh knelt in front of her. Bruce was about to walk between them so she wouldn't have to look at Raleigh if she didn't want to, but she said, "I had a hunch someone would find me when I planted that news item, but I sure as shit didn't think it'd be you."

"You thought you could disappear without anyone caring?"

"My father cares." She tapped her laptop lid. "Want to read my emails?"

"If you want me to. I can pass along the important bits."

It sounded like a joke to Bruce, but surprisingly, Ev passed Raleigh the machine.

He tucked it under his arm.

"I guess I mistakenly believed he'd get over it in a week or so," she said. "He's taking it personally."

"He's embarrassed. You left him hanging. He made everyone think you were going to be something you had no intention of being, and now he has to save face. I've been there. It'll blow over. Maybe not soon, but he'll back off. Maybe he'll even stop mentioning your name to friends and staff, and his associates will know not to ask about you."

"Are you sure?"

"It'll be fine. Just skip the next couple of major holidays." Raleigh grinned, and much to Bruce's surprise, it seemed to be genuine. Apparently, something had transpired when Bruce had been away and the two had shaved down some of their hostility for each other.

Or perhaps all of it.

Of course he'd come here. Of course he'd look.

She took one of Raleigh's hands in both of hers and, sighing, squeezed it.

"You'll feel better tomorrow," Raleigh said. "You just needed someone who's been through it to tell you."

"I'm…sorry I had to leave like—"

"Don't worry about it. I get it." He stood and adjusted the machine beneath his arm. "I wanted to see you were okay."

"I'm fine." She chuckled quietly and studied her filed-down nails. "Busy. Busy's good, though. Trying to make something happen with this place. It's a challenge. A *good* challenge."

Raleigh nodded.

Worried he'd been mistaken about whatever impact he'd had on her life before he'd left, Bruce angled into her view.

"Hi," she said softly.

"You weren't there when I got back."

She smiled again. "You weren't there when I left."

"You angry with me for that?"

She shrugged. Grimaced.

He sat next to her.

Immediately, she put her head on his shoulder and he took her hands. "I haven't held anyone's hand in weeks."

"Somehow, that's my fault."

"Yes. I believe so."

In his periphery, he caught the edge of Raleigh as he walked out of view. He closed his eyes and memorized Everley's scent. "I got everything sorted, I think. Took some doing just because the way my grandfather set things up. I wanted to come back and tell you that, but you weren't there."

"I couldn't be."

"Are you here now?"

The question didn't make sense, and he realized it immediately after speaking it. Of course she was *there*, but that wasn't what he meant.

"Do you want me to be?" she asked in a warble.

"Oh, love, you know I do. You make things make sense for me. And I love the way you make me feel like I have a shot in hell even when I'm chaotic."

"Leave it to the lady with the math degree to manage chaos," Lisa said from across the room.

Bruce had already forgotten that they had an audience, but he didn't really care about that, either. He was used to being watched.

"You should know, though," Everley said, "that I'm staying here, at least through next fall. Probably longer. I'm not going to be in the city. Does that matter?"

Bruce stared into the fireplace and tried to do the impossible—count flames. That was easier than conceptualizing what she'd just told him—that she wouldn't be there. She wouldn't be close, and that was the entire point. What good was having a person if he couldn't hold a hand, smell their hair, put his lips against that place on the jaw that always elicited sighs?

"Think about it if you want to," Everley said. "Take your time. There's no hurry. I'm not exactly surfing Tinder out here."

"There's no one on Tinder out here," Lisa sniped.

He didn't want to think about her Tindering or whatever it was. He just wanted to make sense of the moment. He needed to hold her tighter and remind his body that she was real again, and when that made sense, he'd somehow try to chunk the rest into portions he could manage.

The idea of her never going back scared him.

Chapter Twenty-Three

It was too late for Raleigh to drive back into the city, so Lisa found him an open room. Bruce had stepped outside to make a call on Lisa's cell. Reception was miserable in the woods.

Lisa sidled behind Everley on the sofa and chuckled.

"It's not funny."

"From where I stand, it's extremely funny. I bet if only one of them had showed up, doesn't even matter which, you'd be in bed with him right now."

"Shut up. I would not." That was the last thing she'd thought when they'd arrived. The first had been *Oh, shit.* The second had been *They're both here?* She'd convinced herself that neither would give chase when they could literally have anyone in the world they wanted.

But there they were.

"Anyway, they didn't kill each other during the drive up," Everley mused. "At least one good thing has come out of this."

"Why would they kill each other?" Lisa asked.

"Because Raleigh intensely dislikes Bruce and Bruce gives him an extremely wide berth."

"You mean that Bruce?" She crooked her thumb toward the window at the back of the lodge. It faced the bungalow she'd sent Raleigh to—the only one with a made bed. She'd told Bruce he'd have to make do with the sleeper sofa in the office. There were no other clean sheets because Everley had the only other set at the moment.

Raleigh was standing in the doorway in a white shirt and boxer briefs, looking aggrieved. Bruce thrust the phone at him.

Raleigh looked at it consideringly, then took it, put it to his ear, and disappeared into the room.

Bruce followed and closed the door.

Lisa lifted her eyebrows and smirked. "Hmm?"

"Maybe it's work. Bruce's band has a book coming out with Athena." It didn't seem like something Raleigh would do, but he'd never been able to watch train wrecks occur on the business end. He always stepped in and fixed things before disaster could strike.

"And you think Raleigh would have anything to do with that shit on a Friday night out in the middle of Bumfuck, New York?"

"Absolutely not."

"And certainly not in his underwear."

"Why would he open the door in his underwear?" Everley asked. "There's a peephole in that door. He knew it was Bruce."

"Like I said," Lisa trilled. "They don't hate each other or even actively dislike each other. I bet they're friends outside of work."

Everley guffawed at that line of patent ridiculousness and scrambled to her feet to get to the window. "No. They're not friends." She couldn't see anything through the windows of the cabin. The windows were too dark. "If he's got Raleigh talking to people for him, they're not just friends."

"You think they're fucking?"

"No, but I think they *fucked*. That would explain everything, wouldn't it? Why Raleigh didn't want to work with him. Why they've been so snarly with each other in public. And why Raleigh seemed so disgusted when he knew I was seeing Bruce. It makes sense."

"This is deranged. Now they're both trying to gain an advantage with you."

"No they're not."

"They are. Nobody forced them to come here. Raleigh may have backed off when Bruce swooped in because that seems to be his style, but he didn't like it. Trust me, I was watching. I think he only backed off because that was what he thought you wanted."

"That sounds like him," Everley whispered, more to herself than to Lisa. Raleigh McKean was too dignified to put his personal business on blast that way, and that was what Everley was and why he was there. *She* was his personal business.

She'd wanted him to understand her, and maybe he did.

And of course, Bruce. She couldn't think his name without smiling. He'd shown up, too, sounding worried that she'd turn him away. She hadn't even wanted him to leave.

"You don't really think that...they're both interested in..."

"Yes. They both want you and you want both of them. Even I can do that math."

"Why does everything in my life have to be so complicated?"

"Probably born under a bad sign or something, but you'll figure it out." Lisa snapped her fingers and held out her hand. "Give them a few minutes to sort out their bullshit and then run me my phone. I don't play that finders' keepers shit here."

Raleigh handed the phone back to Bruce and retreated to the bed he'd barely had a chance to turn down the covers on. He hadn't driven to the sticks to make a fool of himself. He'd gone because he couldn't *not* go and see that she was fine. She was. And she had Bruce. Raleigh was extraneous. "All set. You can retreat now."

"No need to snipe at me. And thank you. I wanted to make sure I didn't miss anything."

"I don't think there were any booby traps in that conversation. That show is going to shoot straight from the hip with you because they're in such a time crunch. Take the money."

"Yeah?"

"They're giving you composer credits on the show, right?"

"That's what they say."

"Use it as your entry into that side of the business then. Keep in mind that I'm not a lawyer. Have yours look at the contract." Raleigh got under the covers and flicked off the lamp on the nightstand.

Darkness shrouded the room.

Floorboards creaked beneath Bruce shifting his weight.

"I'm sure Lisa would like to have her phone back," Raleigh said.

"Why are you rushing me away?"

"I'm not. I'm simply giving you the opportunity to

exit without further pleasantries. Call it reverse ghosting, if you'd like."

"I don't mind the pleasantries."

Truthfully, Raleigh didn't, either. Bruce was a rare exception to Raleigh's intolerance of idle conversation. He could count on one hand the number of people he enjoyed listening to speak.

Two were on that property.

And two were going to be together. That would have been obvious to anyone paying half a whit of attention.

"Rushing me away is the same as you running out the door," Bruce murmured.

The floorboards creaked again.

Raleigh didn't say anything. Bruce hadn't lied. It was exactly the same, even if the reasons for doing it were different.

"Why can't we talk?"

"Because—" Raleigh clamped his teeth on the truth and scrounged in his brain for anything that wasn't a true lie. Because talking wasn't enough, and he couldn't want things he wasn't ever going to get. He wasn't going to let Bruce flirt and then flirt back knowing full well that the moment Everley crossed the threshold, Raleigh wouldn't be the one being chosen.

He supposed that in time, he might be able to be happy for them.

A long time.

Bruce turned on the flashlight app on the phone and pointed it squarely into Raleigh's face.

Raleigh hurled a pillow at the offending device, and it must have made contact because Bruce emitted an oomph and the light disappeared. The pillow was hard as slate. He'd have to quietly take Lisa aside and inform her that if she really wanted to get that place filled up, she needed to invest in pillows that hadn't been stuffed with bricks. People who were burned out by their day jobs wanted comfort, not punishment.

"If you're not going to return Lisa's phone, then go to bed. It's late. You can go sleep with Everley. That's why you're here, right?"

"You're going to sleep now, then?"

"Yes." *No.*

When Bruce left, Raleigh had emails to send. Favors to call in. He'd told himself years ago that he'd never flex whatever unearned clout to get what he wanted, but for once, he'd make an exception. He could have full character reports on everyone involved in the show Bruce was attaching himself to by morning. In the end, it'd be up to Bruce to decide if the venture was worth attaching his musicianship to, but Raleigh wanted him to know the whole truth. Time was just as expensive as talent, and he didn't want Bruce getting burned.

"You know damn well you've got the only bed in the place," Bruce said after a minute.

Raleigh could only see the outline of him, but that was enough. His mind could fill in all the blanks. Where his lips were. What his hands were probably doing.

He closed his eyes, anyway. The outline was a tease. "Sofa's long enough."

"Sofa's hard as bricks. You know, I like the Raleigh who's nice to me better."

Raleigh liked the way being that Raleigh felt, until he stopped to think.

"What would you have me treat you like, Bruce? Hmm?" Raleigh asked with a tinge of frustration. "Like a friend? Like the lover you're not? A business partner?

A peer? Tell me what you want, and I'll try to accommodate you."

The floorboards creaked again. Raleigh opened his eyes and watched the long, lean outline cut slowly from one end of the footboard to the other, and then back. "You can't be kind without being...any of those things?"

"No. I tend to need to know which way I'll end up being used so I'm not surprised when it happens."

"I don't intend to use you. I don't have people, lots of people, who I'd want to interfere. But you're good at it. And classy."

Raleigh snorted. "I suppose I do a good job of pretending. I don't mind helping you. It's just..."

Tell him the truth and send him to bed.

Raleigh wanted out of the misery. He wanted the anticipation squashed, because there wasn't going to *be* anything for him. He wasn't going to be Everley's boyfriend and Bruce certainly wouldn't need him if he had her.

He has her...

He expelled a dry laugh and thumped the heel of his palm against his forehead.

The tone and style in Everley's unusual email from weeks ago suddenly made sense. Those words were from an angry Bruce, not some random hacker. He'd been rushing in to Everley's defense because he'd figured out long before Raleigh had that she was worth it.

"Well," Raleigh said through what felt like a throat full of gravel. "This afternoon when you came into my office, I didn't anticipate that I'd be delivering you into the arms of the woman I was intending to pursue. But here we are. You standing here is like torture for me. Do you understand that?"

Torture in so many ways.

With the lights off, Raleigh couldn't tell if Bruce's silence was due to shock or distraction, and he didn't really want to know, either. He needed to care less what Bruce thought and what Everley felt, because it didn't matter. In the morning, he'd be back in Manhattan and as much as possible, he'd pretend the two of them didn't exist, much less with each other.

The floorboards creaked again, but the sound approached Raleigh rather than being confined at the foot of the bed.

"Pur*sue* her?" Bruce asked tentatively.

"You really thought I drove up here because I was that concerned about a coworker who'd quit?"

"That's something a decent person might do."

"And I might have grown up to be a decent person if I hadn't had to throw up barriers at every turn."

"You wanted to take her from me?"

"Bruce, you left her."

"No, I was coming *back*, don't you understand? When I was done. I said I was going to be gone for an age because—fuck, she thinks I didn't want to hold on to her? That I'd just move on to the next person and forget?"

"Did you ask her for a commitment?"

"No. I just assumed—"

"Right, you assumed, and assumption is quite a murky swamp, isn't it? It's a dangerous place filled with traps you needlessly walk straight into. You assumed, but I was there, Bruce. You were gone. I was there."

"You were...*with* her?"

"We started something."

"And it's not done?" Bruce asked in a panic that

would have splintered Raleigh's heart in two if there'd been anything left of it. "Is that what you're telling me? Is that why you *helped* me? Because you knew I was due for a major fucking disappointment?"

He had it all twisted up.

Raleigh scrubbed his eyes with his fists and forced out some pent-up air. "I'm leaving tomorrow, Bruce. You and Everley can do what you want. I'm not going to fight with you about her. I can tell she's very important to you and I know she adores you. Be well. I won't interfere. You'll have to find your own ride back, though."

Interminable silence stretched between them. Raleigh kept his lips pressed tightly together because there was nothing left to say that would further the discussion. He risked hurting rather than harming, and Bruce didn't deserve it.

The right end corner of the bed sank, and then bounced with the telltale rhythm of a knee being nervously bounced.

Raleigh found himself sitting up and turning on the light because he needed to see Bruce's face.

He needed to see if he'd hurt him, anyway, even with the silence.

Bruce sat with forearms leaned on his knees, fingers twined, lush lips tilted downward into a scowl.

"You just...fucking yanked the rug out from beneath me. You knew I was with her."

"You left, and when you leave things unresolved, oftentimes, someone else will enter a person's life to lend the support they need. That's all. She was down and someone needed to prop her up."

Bruce cut a sideways glower to Raleigh and let out

a dry huff of humorless laughter. "Like Everley did for me after you walked away?"

"That's hardly the same thing," Raleigh said in an incredulous rush of words. "I didn't walk away from you. I left the situation because I could see where it was going."

"But it wasn't going to go there, was it?"

"We have no way of knowing."

"Yes we *do*!" Bruce snapped. "You know. I know. I wanted you to stay because I was so fucking tired of being lonely. You expected me to do a hard sell on you. Thought I was going to use you for access—thought I was going to use my *body* to influence you."

"You'd be surprised at how many times that has happened."

"How many?"

"I stopped counting by the time I turned twenty-two. I can spot a political operative at ten paces now, by the way. Not a trick I ever expected to have in my skill set. I was once in a committed relationship with a woman I thought cared about me, but in the end, she cared more about her career aspirations. She exploited my private calendars and pictures and databases for personal gain. And then after all that, she told me that she wished things could have been different. She told me that she did truly like me, you see, but she hadn't expected things to go that far. She didn't expect to keep a toothbrush at my place or spare clothes to change into after spending the night."

There was no inflection in Raleigh's voice. He didn't really *feel* anything about the situation anymore, except shame for being so fucking gullible in the first place.

If it weren't for what she'd done, she would have been utterly forgettable.

She wasn't like Bruce.

She wasn't like Everley.

"What did she do?" Bruce asked. Worry creased his brow. He'd evidently forgotten just that quickly that he was the wounded party.

"The same as so many others. Tried to turn me into a package of harm to be used either against my father or for him. Trust me, there are plenty who would put me up on some kind of twisted pedestal to say that things are better some other way, but they dehumanize me in the process. I'm not a person. I'm a pawn that becomes evidence when convenient."

They sat in silence for a minute. Maybe two.

Raleigh had nothing left to say. Bruce didn't seem to want to go, and Raleigh evidently couldn't make him.

"I'm...offended that you'd put me into that category," Bruce finally said. "I am. I'm not going to lie."

"I'm sorry you're offended."

"But you can't be sorry you did it."

"No. I can't be sorry for doing what I have to do to keep myself from becoming someone's fool again."

"I see. Then are you a fool for helping me now?"

"No. That's different. Helping you in ways that don't require me to leverage my position or my family attachments is just...normal human cooperation."

"So, you'll willingly cooperate with me *and* pursue my woman?"

"We're going in circles on this."

"Because the logic is tenuous."

"It isn't for me. You don't get to call dibs and then drift away. If only life were that easy. You could hold someone aside until you've made up your mind or gotten your wild urges out of your system and then come back to decide if they're worth the effort."

"Of *course* she's worth the effort. I wish we could call *dibs*, as you put it. Maybe you'd have slapped a 'maybe' sticker on me and came back 'round, hmm? After you had a chance to think about it and decide I wasn't a complete fuckin' punter."

"I probably would have."

Bruce's spine snapped straight and head whipped around toward Raleigh. He opened his mouth, but before he could get a word out, there was a cautious rapping on the door.

Thank you, whoever you are.

He'd said too much. Way too much, and he couldn't take it back because that would be lying.

He *would* have kept him, and it was too late to fix the fact that he couldn't.

They both sat in silence, staring at the source of the sound.

The knock came again, followed by the feminine clearing of a throat.

"Um," Everley called out. "Lisa needs her phone. Could you maybe hand it out to me?"

Bruce hurried to the door with the cell and undid the locks. "Sorry! Sorry." He gave her the phone, clasping both of her hands inside of his, and stared at her.

Raleigh wondered what was going through his head, or if anything was at all. He may have just been looking. Raleigh could certainly understand the compulsion. Everley in bright lipstick and slicked-back dominatrix hair was irresistible, but the scrubbed-clean Everley who had visible freckles and bags under her eyes was beautiful, too. And different. It was nearly impossible not to stare at things that were different. *Nearly*, as Raleigh had managed not to for years at his own personal expense.

She was someone else he wouldn't have turned away from if he'd known better—if he'd been able to trust sooner.

"I'll just take this to her," she said.

"I'll walk you over," Bruce said. "I should thank Lisa. Actually, will you hand it back, please? I'll give it to her."

"Of course."

Bruce hustled toward the main building with his usual reserve of energy.

Everley watched him through the open doorway until he was no longer visible, and then turned to Raleigh.

Saying nothing, she tugged her bottom lip between her teeth and gave him one of those platonic little waves.

He waved back. Waving was easy. Emotions were hard.

So he tamped his down as far as he could.

"So…" she said softly. There was a question in the word, or many, but if she wanted answers, she'd need to be direct.

"Yeah."

"Was I easy to find?" Her volume tapered off so quickly that by the end of the sentence, he was leaning forward, straining to hear, fearing the words would drop.

"You shouldn't have to ask," he said. "Part of my job is searching bad spellings of author names on the Internet to see what people are saying about them."

"Well. Here I am."

"Yes. You look well," Raleigh said at the same time Everley said, "I'm glad you came."

Apparently, neither of them knew what to do with those words because all they could do was stare.

He wasn't used to staring at her. In the past, he'd made it his business to evacuate her presence in the most expeditious means possible. But back then, he'd had a grudge, and probably, so had she. They were adrift from those old connections, and yet ensnared by other ones.

She had Bruce, and Raleigh…

Raleigh had Athena.

"Do you…have anything for me to read in your car?" she asked haltingly. Gone was the forthright woman who would walk up to bestsellers, actors, and dignitaries and boldly introduce herself as a publicist at Athena, and in her place was the impersonator who sometimes forgot to hold on to subway poles. Perhaps they were aspects of the same person, and she wore whatever face she had to stay afloat. He hated that he'd contributed to her being that way, and wished he could turn every slight, every snub back on himself if she'd be better off for it.

"I left my e-reader in the city," she said. "Can't fall asleep without reading something."

"There might be a couple of reptile mysteries in the trunk along with Stacia's books."

"I haven't read those. The reptile books, I mean."

"They're an acquired taste."

"Will they make me laugh?"

"Groan, more like. The humor is unsophisticated, but I suppose people need that sometimes."

"Good enough." The words drifted in the quiet, spoken almost like an afterthought. She wasn't even looking at him anymore.

He wondered what was in her head.

Wondered if he was allowed to ask.

But what came out of his mouth instead was, "I think the doors are unlocked. You can look around. See what's in there."

"Should I lock up when I'm done?"

"Yeah. Thanks."

"Do you—"

He'd sat up and leaned into the oncoming words, but they'd vanished and her mouth had closed.

She did that wave again and backed to the door. "Okay. Thanks."

She was gone, and Raleigh couldn't help but feel like someone hadn't said enough.

He simply wasn't sure whom.

Chapter Twenty-Four

"Well, that's it," Lisa said with a mournful sigh. "The only other reservation I had for today just called to cancel. They can't get in. I guess you can have their bungalow, Bruce. Hope you weren't supposed to be anywhere important this morning."

Bruce, standing near the coffee bar, barefooted in too-short sweatpants he'd borrowed from Lisa and an Ithaca is Gorges T-shirt, looked over with sudden interest. He pulled out the earbuds Everley hadn't noticed he was wearing. "What's that?"

"The snow." Everley crooked her thumb toward the front windows and the nasty weather beyond it. "I hadn't looked at the forecast for days because I hadn't planned on going anywhere. I didn't know there was a big storm on the way in."

"So, we can't get out? Is that what you're saying?"

"We could probably get into town if we tried really hard," Lisa said. "The road has been plowed, but I guarantee that visibility is going to be poor and nothing interesting is going to be open, anyway."

"I've never been snowed in before," Bruce mused and turned back to the coffee.

Lisa cut Everley a "Well?" look.

Everley shrugged. She didn't know what to tell her. Just before bed the previous night, Lisa had tried to wheedle some details from her about Everley's feelings about Raleigh and Bruce's unannounced visit. Everley had deflected the conversation. She didn't want to hear her friend's judgment about how Everley hadn't known what to say to Raleigh when she'd had the chance and the privacy to talk to him. Suddenly, the man she'd worked with for half a decade, and who she'd even slept with once, had become a stranger. Circumstances were different, and perhaps, so were they.

She cleared her throat and called over to Bruce, "What are you listening to?"

"Show tunes. Stuff I want to tinker with as soon as I'm in front of a piano again."

"I have a piano." Lisa gestured to the bulky upright unit obscured by several layers of dust and drop cloths. "Hasn't been tuned since I bought the place, and probably not for many years before that, but feel free to plonk away on it."

"I will. Thank you."

"Of course."

Lisa stuffed her feet into her boots and shuffled to the door, eying Everley discourteously as she went. "I'm going to trudge down to the road and see if I can find the newspapers. Call search and rescue if I'm not back in five minutes."

"You assume we won't look for you ourselves?" Bruce asked.

"I like you Bruce."

He grinned. "I like being liked."

Lisa cut Everley another look and then left, chilling the lodge with a subarctic gust before the door shut.

Everley knew Lisa, and she also had been in that little town enough weeks to know that Lisa never bothered to bring in the papers unless she was hoping there were pizza coupons inside. No one was delivering pizza in that snow.

Everley got the jig, though. She was trying to give Everley space to get a reading on Bruce. She couldn't help but to wonder what was going on with him and Raleigh. As she'd read herself to sleep, she had checked in with herself and pondered how she would feel if the two men really did have a past.

She'd tried to froth up some emotion about it, but couldn't.

She was just curious about the circumstances and why the affair might have petered out.

She needed to know.

"Bruce."

While sipping his coffee, he lifted a corner of drop cloth covering the piano. "Hmm?"

"I want to ask you something rather personal."

He laughed. "Can we possibly get any more personal than we already have? If so, I'm willing to try. I live for new experiences."

"I might have to hold you to that," she said in an undertone. At his raised brow, she shook her head and, smiling, said gently, "I want to ask you about your past lovers."

He dropped the cloth and slowly set the coffee atop the piano's shelf.

Perhaps she hadn't been quite as gentle as she thought.

"Is this…about something you read in the book? I didn't take part in any questionably legal trysts with those guys as witnesses. Whatever they said, it wasn't about me."

"The book?" Everley could feel her nose scrunching in the way that always made her mother warn her about the plastic surgery she'd need one day to fix all the wrinkles she was making. She made a concerted effort to smooth her features, not because she cared so much about a few creases, but because she didn't want Bruce to think she hadn't been following along. She never wanted him to think she wasn't listening.

"The Outward Reaction book."

"Oh." Relieved, she scoffed. "I have no idea what's in that book. I steered clear of it when I was at Athena."

"Thank God. Nothing could be as bad as all that, then."

"Well. We'll see." Everley patted the space on the sofa beside her and warily beckoned him over. They were about to either prove or disprove his assertion. "Come here. It's kind of awkward having this conversation from the other side of a room."

Bruce twined the earbud cord around his fingers and tucked the mass of wire into a sweatpants pocket. He plopped beside her and immediately slung an arm around her shoulders.

Her body's immediate response was to go soft and to melt into his side. She'd missed that when he was gone. "I could get used to this," she whispered as his fingers cupped her chin and stroked along her jaw.

"To me?"

"Yes."

"Then get as used to it as you'd like."

"I plan to. But…maybe I should ask you this before we make any promises to each other we might regret."

"Oh, hell." Bruce put his back against the sofa's arm-rest and folded his arms over his chest. "I know that voice. That's the let-down voice."

That made her laugh outright. It was the same voice *he'd* used when he'd informed her he'd be engaging in weeks-long bureaucratic adventures across South Africa. "Not at all. It's a curiosity voice, and a *worry* voice, because I have to ask but don't know how and don't want to offend you."

"I'm the master of offending people without trying."

"But you're also sensitive and I'm respectful of that." And she loved him. Just...*loved* him, and that meant everything required carefulness, because new love was fragile and emotional, and she was already those things without the added layer of worry that came with belong-ing to someone. She took a deep breath and let it out. "I'm just going to ask and I hope you understand I'm not asking from a place of disdain."

He gave her a go-ahead nod.

"Have you...and Raleigh..."

"Have we *what*?"

"Were you lovers?" she spat and immediately looked away out of embarrassment because in a million years, she would have never have imagined she'd be in such a situation. There was no rulebook for asking a boy-friend if he'd slept with another boyfriend candidate, and certainly not when she was more than willing to entertain them both simultaneously.

And why not? I deserve it.

She was sick of not having anything or anyone, es-pecially knowing that her fail was a self-inflicted one.

When Bruce didn't immediately respond, Everley looked at him. He was dragging his tongue along the edges of his top teeth. She could practically see the gears turning in his head. He was thinking up an excuse— something to keep him out of hot water.

Oh, Bruce. You don't need to, honey.

"If you're going to say yes," she said, "Say yes. Not yes *but*. If I want to know more, I'll tell you. If I want excuses, I'll tell you that, too."

"Yes," he said quietly.

"Lisa was right, then."

"Lisa?"

"She has a radar for it, I guess. She can tell when people have hooked up."

"You're angry with me."

"No." She gave her head a hard shake, because who was she to judge someone for *needing* someone? "Why would you think that?"

"It was...not too long before I'd met you. My brother Arnold said you were a rebound, but you *weren't*. I wanted you anyway. Do you believe me?"

"Of *course* I do, but help me understand. Why are you two so angry at each other?"

Bruce twined his fingers and peered at the door as it swung open. Lisa marched in, stomping snow off her boots. She tossed the papers on the welcome mat and groaned. "It's coming down even harder. I'm going to check the weather report again."

"Can I do anything to help?" Bruce asked.

"Maybe? I've got to make sure the animals around here are warm enough and have food. Give me a few minutes, though. Let me see how big this thing is." She disappeared into the bedroom.

Everley gave his hand an affectionate squeeze. "Thank you."

His brow creased. "For what?"

"Just offering."

"Sometimes I have to offer because people aren't bold enough to ask."

She pondered that and pondered *him* as he stared back in that hyperfocused Bruce way of his.

"So, it's over between the two of you?" she asked.

"Yes."

"Do you want it to be?"

She would never know what response would have accompanied that panicked expression on his face, because at that precise moment, Raleigh stomped in through the back door, jangling his keys.

"Fuck. A foot in an hour? I don't think I'm going to be able to get out of here."

Foiled, Everley springed to her feet. "You were leaving? You can't leave yet."

They had things to talk about.

Or she did.

Or him and Bruce.

Someone, any of them. They needed to figure things out before Raleigh slipped out of reach.

He tugged at the knot of his cashmere scarf and looked from her to Bruce and back. Try as she might, there was nothing to glean from his expression, except the typical haughtiness that always lived there. She'd come to learn that was just Raleigh, though. The arrogance was an intricate veneer he painted on to keep people from getting in, but it wasn't going to stop her. She'd broken through it once. She knew all the secrets and he couldn't take them back.

"I didn't see any reason to stay," he said. "I've seen what I need to."

"I don't think you have," she whispered.

"Well!" Lisa said in a voice dripping with annoyance. "Looks like this storm is going to take a squat on top of us for the better part of two days. Sorry, Bruce, I'm fresh out of sweatpants for you to borrow."

Bruce didn't appear to be listening. He was looking at Raleigh, who was looking at Lisa.

It wasn't an I-hate-you look, or even a this-is-weird look, but a longing one. An awed one.

Everley understood. She felt the same way.

"I'm going to go check on the horses," Lisa said.

He'd heard that, apparently. He got to his feet and found his boots near the fireplace. "Put me to work, love."

"We'll try to get through it as quickly as possible. I hate snow."

Bruce went with her, but not before tossing a querying gaze over his shoulder that Everley could only meet with worry.

She didn't know what she was doing or what he must have been thinking. She knew what she wanted, though, which was a rare feeling for her.

She wasn't going to run it away or tamp it down. She was going to ride the wave and see where it took her.

Maybe it wouldn't crash.

"Do you hear that?" Lisa asked.

She and Bruce were halfway back to the lodge with snow shovels leaned on their shoulders. His heart had been thrashing in his ears so bombastically from worry that he hadn't heard what she was referencing. He stopped and took a breath. Ev was going to be exactly where he'd left her, but with Raleigh there with her, her opinion of Bruce might change for the worse. He needed to get in there and do damage control.

He heard what Lisa must have been referencing then—the wet, whirring sound of spinning tires atop packed snow. "Someone's here?"

"Yeah, and that's not Raleigh trying to get out." She gestured toward the lodge's window, through which they could clearly see Ev idling by the coffee table and Raleigh moving toward the door.

"Are you sure you weren't due any guests?" Bruce asked.

"Sweetie, I wouldn't forget if I had paying customers on the way. *Trust* me."

A door slammed up front.

Bruce hurried to stow his shovel, and Lisa's.

There came the hollow thud of a heavy-fisted knock against the thick front door.

Bruce caught a glimpse of Ev shooing Raleigh away and opening the door herself, just before he caught Lisa's spit of "Shit," and her tug of his arm with a "Get out of the window!" warning.

Memory caught up—prior images of the man who'd darkened the doorway.

He'd joked about Bruce's novel in front of a full ballroom.

Bruce had played along then as a defense mechanism, and he regretted that he had. He didn't have time to chase old regrets, though. Somehow, Ev's father was there, and Lisa's harried pacing by the woodpile was a major hint that she found some flaw in the visit.

"*Fuck*," she whispered.

"I'm going in. I'm not going to just leave her in there."

"You can't go in there, Bruce. It's bad enough that Raleigh's in there because he works for Athena."

"And?"

"*And* I hope Raleigh's a damn good liar on the fly because whatever the truth is, it's none of Shannon's business."

"And what truth are you referencing?"

"Whatever the truth is about you two dudes and my friend."

"Ev's my girl."

"Super. And what about him?"

Bruce gritted his teeth. He'd thought he liked Lisa. He wasn't certain anymore. "What about him?"

"Whose boy is he? Because it seems to me like he belongs to someone."

Bruce must have been as obvious as a lit-up lighthouse. Maybe it was apparent to everyone that he was hung up on Raleigh and shouldn't have been.

Maybe it'd been obvious to Ev, too, and that was why she'd asked him what she had. She didn't think Bruce could want her, but that wasn't true. He wanted her more than anything, *loved* her more than anything, but that didn't make the ache in his chest go away when Raleigh was in a room. That didn't make the yearning stop or the desire to put the man in a "Saving for Later" compartment in his brain, because of course he'd need Raleigh again. He'd *want* him again, even if he already had more than his fair share of companionship with Ev, and there was no damn way to make sense of why that was.

Lisa leaned toward the window and immediately grimaced.

That lit a fire under Bruce. He wasn't going to stand out in the cold in too-short pants waiting for disaster to sort itself out. He had the back door open and his stare laser-focused on Ev's stricken expression.

He was heading toward her, heedless of the fact Raleigh had drawn her in close to him and was holding her about the waist.

Heedless of the fact that Shannon was yelling and that Lisa had called out some kind of greeting.

Whatever she'd said silenced Shannon and made him turn to her.

Raleigh leaned into Bruce's gaze and gave his head a terse warning shake. The crease in his brow deepened as he pressed a finger to his lips.

Ev's cheeks were red as rosebuds and eyes a bit wet, but even she mouthed *"Wait. Please."*

Only because she'd asked, he would.

"Damn. I knew Everley had to turn up somewhere," Shannon bellowed. "I should have checked here first."

Lisa's smile was big and undoubtedly disingenuous. "I had no idea you kept up with my whereabouts. I'm flattered."

"I get the alumni magazine."

The grin fell off. "That so?"

"It is." He turned and glowered at Everley.

She'd dried her eyes, but the hurt was still there and Raleigh was in the way. Stroking her arm. Standing far too close.

"What's wrong with your phone? Had my assistant call ten times or more but there's something wrong with it. Your mother is worried sick."

Bruce would have spoken, had he been the one on the receiving end of Shannon's furious stare. His nerves would have tumbled out of his mouth and further ensnared him in the other man's anger. She was silent and still, barely blinking as she returned the look.

Her eyes may have been glassy, but she was fierce, his Ev.

He hated that she had to be.

And he hated he couldn't take the brunt on her behalf.

"I want to know what the *hell* is going on here," Shannon shouted and Bruce's whole body stiffened into its familiar fight-or-flight stance.

He knew damned well he wasn't running anywhere—not without Ev.

Fight it is, then.

Shannon clipped Bruce in his gaze as he spun back around, and as though he'd finally realized who Bruce was, he turned back and jabbed a finger in his direction. "The hell are you doing here? You're supposed to be in the city promoting your book."

"Fuck the book." Full of impatience and irritation, Bruce snarled, "I'm getting my gi—"

"My first high-profile client!" Lisa interjected in a high-pitched, syrupy voice that could have made his nuts shrivel.

He was so stunned by her interference that when she looped an arm around his and guided him within a collegial distance of Shannon, he didn't stop her.

"Bruce is doing me a tremendous favor," she said cheerily. "He's going to do a bit of word-of-mouth advertising and help get the right kind of clientele in here for me."

"Did you know Everley was here?"

The question was directed at Bruce.

That time, Raleigh intervened with, "Evidently, you have nothing to be concerned about. Everley is fine."

Bruce's indignation flared at being talked over yet again and this time by people he'd thought cared for him. But it flopped.

It was different.

They weren't trying to silence him. They were trying to protect all of them and silence *Shannon*. Bruce simply wasn't used to that sort of teamwork. He was, apparently, in a team. The idea made him smile, but only briefly because Shannon had turned his ill temper back to Everley.

"Who says she's fine? Doesn't look it."

"Says me?" Everley quipped in a shaky voice. "Perhaps you and Connor can head back into the city before you get stuck out here. I don't know if you've been watching the weather, but it's going to get worse. You... you *don't* need to be here."

"You're slumming."

"Excuse the hell out of me?" Lisa snapped.

"Stop," Raleigh said in an authoritative tone that actually made Shannon back up a bit. "Just stop. You don't want to believe her. I get it. You can't understand why she would choose to do anything beyond what you prescribed for her, but perhaps you should have listened. And perhaps now, you should consider that the clues were there all along but no one listened. She was unhappy. Would you truly demand that she remain that way?"

"You're walking on a knife's edge right now, McKean," Shannon said, stabbing a finger in Raleigh's direction. "You helped her with this? Why are you here?"

"I thought it would be very obvious by now that we're in love."

Shannon may not have caught the brief widening of Ev's eyes before Raleigh hid her against his chest, but Bruce certainly did. And in that moment, he wasn't certain which of them he envied more.

He was even more confused as to what that meant.

"You're...*what*?" the man bellowed.

"I'd chase her to the ends of the earth," Raleigh said in a tone nearly as syrupy as the one Lisa had earlier utilized. Even Bruce almost bought it. "That's why I'm here."

"You're dating my daughter?"

"I am."

"Since when?"

"If you're asking if I thought I could sleep my way up the Athena food chain, I take full offense. And obviously, that is no longer an issue. I'm there because I choose to be."

"And... I'm *not* for the same reason," Ev said, finding her voice again.

Good for you, love.

She squared her shoulders and faced her father, and Bruce couldn't have been prouder of her than he was at that moment. "You really should go, Daddy. Seriously. Get the hell out of here before the plows stop running and whatever road you took in becomes a parking lot. The fact you got here at all is a miracle."

"Are you going to be at work on Monday?"

Ev pointed to herself. "Me?"

"Yes, you. I invested a lot in you, little girl. You're not going to embarrass me. You got to be grateful for the opportunities you've been given, and you haven't been. Not once, have you?"

Bruce whistled low and made everyone in the room turn toward him.

His mistake, but he wasn't going to pretend he wasn't there. If there was a chance he could take some of the heat off Ev, he was going to try. They were a team. He could pull his weight. "Here I was, thinking my family reunions were awkward. When I was in London recently, my father offered me my choice of small islands if I'd do an advance retraction of some things I said in the tour documentary. Unfortunately for him, I'm not as mercenary as all that."

"And neither am I," Ev said, "though no one's ever offered me an island." To her father, she said, "Just *listen* to me, Daddy. I'm done. I should have been out years ago and given someone with passion a shot at the job. Athena's authors deserve to have teams filled with people who are not only enthusiastic about the products they put out, but also about their place in the company. It's done. *I'm* done, and I'll appreciate you keeping your unkind sentiments to yourself about what I'm choosing to do now. I'm going to be happy. It doesn't matter to me anymore if my idea of happy looks right to you. It's right for me. I love you, Daddy, but if you can't accept my choice, then perhaps this should be the last conversation we have for a while."

Shannon stared. Nostrils flaring, lips tight and pale, skin going blotchy.

And then he sniffed, tugged his coat lapels tight together, and gave Lisa an "As you were" nod.

She didn't nod back.

There wasn't a sound anywhere in the lodge except

for the crackling of wood in the fireplace until long after whatever vehicle Shannon had arrived in had trudged back to the road and the sound of the motor abated.

Lisa shut and locked the front door and put her back against it.

Ev stood, staring at nothing in particular and wringing her hands.

"It feels bad," Raleigh said softly, smoothing back her hair. "It feels like shit when you have to do it, but when they don't see you as adults, they're always stunned when you make a stand."

"I hate to admit that he's right." With Shannon gone, Bruce could pull Ev against him and hold her until her shaking stopped.

He felt better that he could help. He felt better that she molded against him, hiding her face in his borrowed shirt and gripping the waistband of his pants for dear life.

"It's all right," he whispered. "Will you let me help you feel better?"

He would feel better, too. *Wanted.*

"Yes," she whispered. "Please do. For as long as you want."

"That might be for a very long time."

"Perfect. That's *perfect.*"

He truly believed that until Raleigh walked away, jangling his keys and heading back to his lonesome bungalow.

She watched him leave and Bruce was annoyed until he'd realized he was going to do the exact same thing.

"Whose boy is he?" Lisa had asked.

Raleigh wasn't anyone's.

And somehow, that seemed wrong.

It seemed wrong that he was the most honest one of them all. The one who fixed things. The magician who could speak a few words and make pressure disappear.

Someone should have him. If not Bruce or Ev, then…

"I love you to death, Bruce, but…there's something we need to sort out."

All too often, Bruce experienced the surge of elation and then the crash moments later when the totality of a statement settled into his brain. Ev had given him the words he'd desperately needed to hear—"I love you"—only to snatch him back down with "but."

Some caveat. Some "but."

He swallowed thickly and closed his eyes. Too many sensations to process all at once. "What is it?"

"Come." She took his hand in hers and led him past Lisa and out toward the bungalows. "It's not what, but *who*."

Chapter Twenty-Five

Raleigh had just taken off his soggy-hemmed pants and draped them over the radiator when the door rattled.

God, what now?

If there were an inventor nearby looking for test subject volunteers to try out a new teleportation device, he would have been first to throw his hand up. Although he wasn't foolish enough to follow Shannon out on those icy roads, Raleigh wanted off that property, and away from the continual letdowns. Bruce was there, taunting with his mere proximity, wanting to talk, wanting to create, wanting attention for it. Getting Raleigh out of his own head and making him freewheel in a chasm of ideas and energy, but he wasn't for him. It was too late. And Everley was there, as tender and demanding of comfort as ever, and he wanted to provide it. But there was someone better at that---more *natural* at that—and she'd figured that out.

She'd made her choice.

They'd be happy, her and Bruce. They knew how to visit each other's wavelengths for a while, and all that mattered was that they wanted to keep trying to.

Good for them.

He couldn't bring himself to hating, either. He didn't know how to anymore.

"What?" he shouted at the door.

"Can we come in? It's *so* cold out here."

"Everley?" he murmured.

Elation surged. There she was—coming to *him*—but there went annoyance, too.

"We" she'd said, and he didn't think her entourage was Lisa.

He yanked the tragically cold pants off the heater. If he was going to get tortured, he was going to endure it fully dressed.

He'd barely gotten his fly fastened and the door unlocked before it crashed open, letting in the bitter cold and his last two lovers.

Everything he wanted in one small place.

Everley stomped snow off her boots and turned up the heat. "You left so fast. I had things I wanted to say. This morning has jarred me in unexpected ways."

Bruce was giving Raleigh an inscrutable stare, but there was an obvious tinge of annoyance about it. Or inconvenience, perhaps.

Rolling his eyes, Raleigh plopped on the bed.

Of course Bruce was inconvenienced. He probably wanted to be rolling around in a warm bed with Everley watching snow fall instead of doing what he was.

Raleigh wasn't actually sure what that was, but he hoped it was quick.

"I'm not going to beat around the bush," Everley said. "We have some things in common that I didn't know about before, and I just want to get a reality check about what's possible and what's just ridiculous."

"What are those things?" Raleigh asked warily.

She pointed to both men at once and then each other. "I don't follow."

"Nor do I," Bruce said.

"Because we didn't get to finish our conversation earlier, either. But here's what it is. You've been with each other."

Raleigh started toward the door to invite both to leave. He didn't particularly wish to have his laundry aired with such candor, but Everley got in his way. "This isn't Athena," she said. "You can't shut me out of your office and close the door here. I get to talk. Okay?"

He put up his hands in a conciliatory gesture, although he was feeling anything but. He was glad, though, that she'd put away her forgets-to-hold-on persona for the moment. In fact, he was wondering if *he* should get a grip somewhere.

"You're not going to deny it?" she asked.

"Let me know if you're accusing me of something and I'll decide if I need to edit my history."

"I'm not accusing you of anything. When Bruce confessed it, I was just stunned that the two of you would have some intimacy in your history. You've never seemed to like each other very much and I'm honestly taken aback that you were attracted to each other."

"No need to be cruel, princess." Raleigh rolled his eyes.

"Oh! No no no." She clapped her hands over her face and let out a choked-sounding laugh. "Shit, that didn't come out right. You're both attractive. I'd probably do a better job at this thinking thing if I didn't think you both were."

"I think I get it." Bruce rubbed the scruff on his chin and stared in the general direction of Raleigh's wet cuffs. "Why would a hard-living rocker be at all interested in a man who wears dress socks? And a *ginger* at that." His lip curled.

Oh, I see how it is, then.

"And what could I possibly see in a man who uses bar soap instead of shampoo and who has to baby powder his pants to get out of them?" Raleigh asked drolly.

"You weren't so distraught by the fit of my pants when you were jerking me off."

"And I don't recall you complaining about my socks when my cock was in your mouth."

"Oh, boy," Everley said.

"Sorry," both men said at once.

Certainly, Everley knew the full extent of Raleigh's pettiness, but he didn't want that to be one of her last memories of him.

"I happen to like tight pants *and* socks that go with really nice shoes, so I'm probably the worst person to referee this exchange," she said.

"No need to referee," Raleigh said. "I really don't want to argue. I'm leaving as soon as the sun comes up and the roads warm a little. We're done talking."

Bruce scoffed. "No, we bloody aren't. Apparently, we're having a fight over a woman, so let's fight it out. You can keep your clothes on if you'd like. I've tussled both ways."

"I bet you have. That lifestyle of yours leaves something to be desired."

"Not particularly. I have Ev now."

"Yesterday, I was relatively certain you wanted *me*."

"Fuck you, Raleigh."

Raleigh ground his teeth. He deserved the aspersion, and he knew it. He shouldn't have said that thing, and certainly not in front of Ev, but when he felt caged, he lashed out. At the moment, he was feeling extremely caged in with the two of them.

"I believe the want of that is what got us into this mess in the first place," he mumbled.

"You said yes."

"Because I thought you were hot and I was curious."

"And you're not anymore?"

"When did I say I wasn't?" Of course Raleigh was still curious, even after everything. Still far too open and willing to be used a little, if that was what Bruce wanted. Bruce was everything new and interesting— a work in progress who would never go stagnant. The opposite of Raleigh, maybe. He had almost everything Raleigh needed.

But so did Everley.

He'd never before felt such an acute urge to take care of someone, and all along, he'd thought she was the one person who didn't deserve it.

He didn't deserve *her*.

"Wait." Everley darted a hand into the air like a ref calling a bad play. "Hold the hell up. Fighting over *me*, you mean?"

"You're worth fighting over, Ev." The words may have been directed at Everley, but Bruce's gaze was on Raleigh. "Told you that you could keep me. You said you would. Said you loved me."

"Did she?" Raleigh mouthed, daring him to gloat. Hating him but not.

"She did," Bruce whispered. "What do you know about that?"

Enough to be jealous.

"I...haven't...changed my mind about that." Toward the end of Everley's statement, her voice had deteriorated to a nearly incomprehensible puff of air that sounded like the precursor to strangulation. And then she made that choking sound again. But the next sound was longer, fuller, and had her doubling her at the waist. Uproarious laughter. "Oh. My. God."

Bruce turned to him for counsel as her laughter intensified, and he shrugged. Whatever the joke was, Raleigh wasn't in on it.

"Perhaps you could let me in on the joke," Raleigh said.

It wasn't a joke, though. Not really, even if Lisa had made it sound like one.

On paper, the arrangement could work. The men were argumentative, but that was all bluster and them picking at old wounds. She could tell because she knew what hurting looked like. She'd been facing it in the mirror for the better part of her adult life.

They didn't have to be that way. There was no scarcity of affection in that room. There was plenty to go around if they were willing to trust.

She moved at a snail's pace into the room and twined her fingers in front of her belly. As she sat on the foot of the bed, she met Raleigh's gaze. "I'm sorry for laughing. It was a visceral thing. Reflex, you know, because I don't really know how to propose this. But it makes sense to me."

"I'm not following you."

"Oh." Bruce made a noise of revelation and put his head back. "Yeah. I guess so."

"Or it could be the worst idea ever," she conceded.

"Would be better than fighting."

"*What* would be better than fighting?" Raleigh demanded.

Bruce leaned over and knocked on Raleigh's forehead as though it were wood. "Anything alive in there? There's a massive eureka moment happening and you're evidently sleeping through it with your eyes open."

Raleigh grabbed the wrist of Bruce's retreating arm and rolled his eyes, but otherwise didn't respond with hostility. "Perhaps I need to be on a different plane of reality to make sense of it. Elucidate me."

"Gladly." Bruce maneuvered Raleigh nearer to Everley. He made her take one of Raleigh's hands. He took the other. They stared at each other in silence with their hands chained and Raleigh looking like he still hadn't ascended to that different plane yet.

Bruce swung their arms. "See?"

"No."

Bruce pulled them in closer to Everley. "How about now?"

"The last time I stood in a configuration like this, I was on the stage at one of my father's reelection night events and as he waited for his opponent to concede, he pulled my mother and I into a prayer triangle."

Everley was reasonably certain there was nothing prayerful about what she wanted to happen. There may have been a few obscure Bible passages about partner sharing that may have been relevant, but whoever had penned them likely hadn't envisioned the vagaries of modern times. Everley's desire of the two men had nothing to do with ensuring the survival of her genes. It had more to do with her own survival. Happiness wasn't a luxury. It was a necessary vitamin that offset some of the bullshit people hurled at her.

"I like the idea, Ev," Bruce said. "Like it a lot. I could have a guy."

The way he drawled "guy" while looking contemplatively toward the ceiling hinted at some obscure meaning that flew right over her head.

"Guy?" she whispered, needing to be sure they were all playing in the same key.

"My bullshit translator. My second head. He's good at that. Not that you aren't, but because he's such a naturally regimented bastard, I don't feel as ashamed when I ask him do it."

"You shouldn't feel ashamed, anyway," Raleigh said quietly.

"Most people act like I should."

"I think you already know how I feel about most people."

Never taking his gaze from Raleigh, Bruce gave a slow nod. "I do. Can't trust a single bloody one of them, can you?"

"Maybe a select few," Raleigh said as he notched Bruce's messy hair behind his ears. It immediately fell right back where it was, so Everley helped untangle the elastic barely holding on to the ponytail. Between the two of them, they could probably smooth it all out.

"Everyone would get more of what they need this way," she said.

"Are...you talking about..." Raleigh was still wearing that news anchor frown—that expression of privileged naivety that usually accompanied talking heads on fake news shows.

"We're talking about this." Bruce, with his hair half bound, sat Raleigh on the bed beside Everley, grabbed the sides of his face, and crushed his mouth against the other man's.

Raleigh exhibited several stages of struggle in seconds. The shock with the ineffectual push. The groan of reluctance that came with him gripping the front of Bruce's wrinkled shirt. Then his hand finding purchase in Bruce's hair and pulling Bruce's head back with it. His scolding stare.

And then the capitulation.

He pulled Bruce closer and exhibited the depth of their familiarity. They'd been through the song before and had evidently learned all the opening strains.

"And now you kiss her," Bruce said on a gasp as he pulled away from Raleigh. "You see. We take turns."

Everley turned her knees toward Raleigh.

Raleigh being Raleigh, he was low to show his concession. His jaw was tense. Expression grim.

"If you don't want to..." she whispered, trying not to be sad. Of course she wanted enthusiasm, but she also knew who Raleigh was. She couldn't expect him to behave the same way as Bruce, even if he wanted the same thing.

She tried to wait patiently and let him assess her with that critical hazel gaze, but she was tired of waiting for her life to sort itself out. She'd have to put some things into motion on her own. So she leaned in and laid a gentle kiss on his lips. Fortunately, his mouth was yielding. When she leaned for a second press, his lips parted. The tip of his tongue probed delicately against hers, or perhaps tentatively.

He didn't need to be tentative with her.

"Stop tiptoeing around me, Raleigh," she whispered

as she eased onto his lap. "You came up here for me. I assumed that meant you gave a damn."

"I do."

"Then act like it."

He put his forehead against hers and made a sound of pure exasperation. "What do you want from me? What could you possibly want from me that you couldn't get from him?"

"Don't frame it like that. It's not about what Bruce can't give me or what you can't give me that he can. It's about spreading out the effort." Everley fidgeted the collar of his undershirt, pleased to be able to assist even in some small way. "Some people need people more than others. I think we all know how hard it is to connect to people when their natural instinct is to expect the worst of you. Or to prejudge you on who you're connected to or where you've been seen rather than on your heart."

"Are you entirely certain I have a heart?"

Bruce plopped on the bed behind them and lounged with the side of his face propped atop his fist. "It's all right, lover. You don't need to tell anyone else. It can be our little secret, just the three of us."

Everley laughed because she was certain Raleigh had a heart. People who forged friendships as deep and nuanced as the one he had with Stacia couldn't be completely devoid of empathy and emotion. People who'd squeezed every possible spare coin out of staffs of malaise-stricken white-collar professionals to donate to literacy charities had passion.

And people who would choose to take Everley to the movies and sit with her through not one, but *two*, rom-coms, couldn't be at all bad...even if the movies were.

"You have a heart," Everley said. "And I think that you might even like me enough to give me a piece of it."

"I get the rest," Bruce said.

"You're fighting over scraps," Raleigh murmured, seemingly absently. He was toying with the sides of her hair, fondling the elastic band holding it all back from her face. A rare fidget on his part, perhaps. He'd done it to Bruce, now her.

"We're not fighting at all," she said, pressing her cheek against his roving hand. "See? We get along just fine if we let ourselves."

"Do we want to?"

"I think the question should be do *you* want to?" Bruce returned. "I'm not so hung up on traditionalism. I won't feel any particular angst about there being two of you, trust me."

"And as we all saw earlier, I'm through with letting other people's expectations shape my life," Everley said. "Why can't I be with you both, if you want me?"

"Wanting you isn't in question," Raleigh said, his lips to the side of her neck, tenderly skimming along her pulse point.

"So say yes," Bruce said. "That way we don't have to fight."

He didn't want to fight, but Raleigh didn't say yes, either. At least not with words.

They'd talked too much already. For a little while, they could simply react and feel.

He nudged her jacket over her shoulders. She didn't look back at the thud it made as it hit the floor, or when her shirt followed.

He undressed her efficiently, but carefully. Unbuttoning. Unzipping. Easing fabric down her legs. Unclasping her bra at the back and smoothing his hands around her ribs to cradle her breasts before the straps tangled on her arms.

"Fewer seams and gouges today, hmm?" Bruce asked her. He was sitting up, then, watching Raleigh undress her with rapt attention.

"No shapewear. Don't need it out here."

"Don't really need it back in the city, either."

She shrugged again and let Raleigh turn her to face him. "Sometimes I don't mind. It's a kind of armor. It's one way of presenting myself. Sometimes I like to look cinched. Other times, I don't care."

"I see."

Raleigh tipped her chin up to him. "Are we going to talk?"

She laughed. "Bruce likes to talk. You'll have to cope."

Seeming to realize what they were talking about on a delay, Bruce gasped with mock indignation. "The more I talk, the less sore you'll be tomorrow. You should want me distracted."

Raleigh chuckled. "I don't care if you talk. I'm just wondering if you need me to antagonize you to get wet."

"No, but you can tease me if you want to." She slid her hand into his briefs and looped her fingers around the hard length of him. "Just know that sometimes, I tease back."

She smiled at his hiss and moaned at the dig of his fingertips into her biceps.

"Not to be crass," Bruce said, standing, "but who's doing who? Because I think I'm owed."

Raleigh raised a brow. "Are you?"

Out of the corners of her eyes, Everley could see Bruce wrestling off his sweatshirt. "You abandoned me."

"*I* did?" Raleigh's gaze sank rapidly, so Everley turned to see directly what the point of interest was.

Bruce wasn't wearing underwear.

"Of course he isn't," she murmured to herself. It seemed so Bruce.

"You left me in my basement," Bruce said, raising his chin in defiance. "You left me and you weren't done with me."

"Or the other way around, perhaps?" Raleigh asked.

"Well, that's obvious."

Raleigh looked down at Everley.

Grinning, she put up her hands and eased away to let Bruce in. "I can wait my turn."

Already, she was getting so much more than she'd expected. If she'd ever thought it was possible that either of the men would have shown up, she would have left a trail of breadcrumbs for them to follow. Sometimes, people who went missing wanted to be found, but not by just anyone.

She pulled a rough afghan from the back of the hard wooden chair by the door and wrapped herself in it. Making a mental note to inform Lisa of the scratchiness of the blanket, she watched the men. She'd been expecting to see a struggle for dominance between the two of them because their personalities were each so large, so expressive. But there wasn't any true dominant in the room. Not really. Raleigh's hands may have been roving along Bruce's skin, but only because Bruce had put them there.

She couldn't hear what he was whispering in Raleigh's ear or what Raleigh whispered back, but she could see that there was no tension between the two of them. Raleigh's shoulders had relaxed and that tic of tension he always wore in his jaw had abated.

When his fingertips disappeared into Bruce's mouth only to be replaced by Bruce's tongue, Everley had to look away because the exchange was rapidly heating. The wet fingers had slid to a lower orifice, and of course she knew that was something that was *done*, and something she'd had done to her more times than she could count. She simply wasn't used to people being so overt about their needs, and apparently they needed each other.

"You don't get to sit this one out," Bruce scolded.

A few seconds elapsed before she realized he was talking to *her.* "What?"

"I thought you publicity types were supposed to be innovative thinkers, but apparently, it's only obvious to me that I have a cock that's being ignored."

Like so often with Bruce, she couldn't tell if she was supposed to laugh or hop to attention, so she did both. "What would you like me to do with it?"

He groaned and put his head back on Raleigh's shoulder. "I don't know. Who's conducting this thing, anyway?"

"Seemed like you were," Raleigh said. Tugging his briefs down, he sat on the edge of the bed and pulled Bruce along with him. "Here we are, all naked, more or less, and thoroughly unprepared."

"I'm a so-called rock star. I'm never unprepared to fuck," Bruce said, squirming atop Raleigh's lap. "There are condoms in my wallet and lube in my guitar case."

"Your guitar case is in my car," Raleigh said drolly.

"So it is."

Springing to his feet, Bruce snatched the keys off the

dresser and gently unwound the afghan from around Everley. He wrapped it around his waist and ran into the storm.

Jarred, and more than a little unmoored, she met Raleigh's gaze.

Tell me this is all right. Please.

He raised both eyebrows as though her thoughts had been conveyed from her brain to his via psychic megaphone.

"Thank you for helping with my father, by the way."

"I'd do it again and again if you need me to, Everley. Let me be the villain. I don't care."

"I hope I can be more like you one day."

"You don't need to be like me if you have me. Do you?"

"Yes. I do."

It's all right.

Had things been different and if she hadn't been brought up to suppress her enthusiasm, she might have bounced to him. Grabbed him. Kissed him too much, like Bruce might have.

But maybe one day she'd shake that off just like the career she hadn't wanted. She could be a hundred percent honest in words and acts, and she'd be so glad.

Raleigh's SUV bleated its keyless entry beep.

He expelled a scoff laced with disbelief. "I'm apparently in love with someone who stores personal lubricant in his guitar case," he murmured.

"Yeah. Same."

And I love you, too, she thought, too afraid to say the words because love wasn't supposed to work that way. People assumed there was a finite amount, but that wasn't true. It was multipliable and indivisible.

The heart made room.

"Must be interesting getting that through TSA screening," he mused.

"I doubt he'd care if they found it."

"Probably doesn't. I bet he'd be a heap of fun to travel with."

"Well, the trip certainly wouldn't be boring. He'll never be boring."

"And that's what you want?" Raleigh leaned back on his forearms, unabashedly nude, gaze soft.

"I want a lot of things, Raleigh." She could read between the lines. "I want too many things."

"Is that so?"

"Offer still stands if you want to be my boyfriend." She tilted her head toward the door Bruce had sprinted out of. "I won't mind if you already have one. I'm a cheap date. I like hot dogs and will eat dodgy chicken lo mein."

"Just so you understand where I'm coming from, I can't compete against him, Everley. He's always going to be more interesting, more exciting."

"He's exciting. I'll grant him that, and I love that about him, but he wasn't first. He wasn't the one I wanted to pay attention to me for so many years. He wasn't the one I sought validation from."

Raleigh pointed to himself, scowling. "Validation from *me*?"

"Of course."

"What the hell for?"

"Because you knew what you wanted to do and you were doing it. Do you know how sexy that is?"

He looked thoroughly taken aback. "Apparently not."

"Well, it is."

"You're ridiculous. You know that?"

Everley gestured to herself, sitting naked on a cold, hard chair by a semi-ajar cabin door, and nodded fervently. "I so am, but I'm owning it."

"We'll get along just fine then."

"Even if you love him more?"

"Who said that I did?"

Before she could kick her trembling brain back into service and respond, Bruce lumbered in with his guitar case, closed the door, and locked it.

"Couldn't decide," he said. "Too many options. Not sure if I'm in the mood for the kind that warms with friction or the super slippery kind."

"How much lube do you carry around with you?" Raleigh asked, obviously appalled.

"Just four tubes. Been in there for ages. Don't worry. I haven't been slutting myself all over the place or anything. I can't get hard for just anyone, you know?" He opened the case and tossed a little bottle to Raleigh. "That one. I decided."

Raleigh held the purple tube up to Everley. "It's called 'Bone Straight.'"

Everley pressed her lips together tightly and shook her head. She wouldn't touch that one with a ten-foot pole.

A condom was applied. Ridiculously named lubricant slipped on. Bruce settled slowly on Raleigh, face to the ceiling, eyes closed. "Fuck."

"Tell me what you want," Raleigh said.

"E-everley. Closer."

Everley peeled herself off the chair and reclaimed the scratchy afghan. She draped it around her shoulders as she approached the edge of the bed.

"Hand right there. This won't take long. So strung out."

She gripped his shaft the way he guided her to and massaged up and down, trying to stay out of the way, but that was difficult. Between two pairs of legs that were twitching from excess energy and pleasure.

She closed her eyes and devoured the sounds they made—Raleigh's grunts of effort as he thrust upward. Bruce's whines of pleasure as he received Raleigh's cock.

Bruce tightened her fingers around him and had her squeeze tighter and tug faster, but then there was another hand shooing hers away.

She opened her eyes as they shifted, Raleigh with some effort, pulling out. Pressing a condom into Everley's hand.

Oh.

Bruce's legs were shaking even faster as Everley rolled down the latex on him and Raleigh removed his own. "Christ, don't fuckin' edge me like that. Don't like it."

"Noted." Raleigh laid a kiss on his cheek and guided him to his back, half laying on Raleigh's thigh. "I'll remember next time. Can't leave Everley out."

"I know. Come here, Ev." Bruce gestured for her to join them, or join with him. It didn't matter which. She was going to do it.

She'd never been fond of having an audience before, but with those two, she didn't really mind.

"There you go, love," he whispered as she straddled his thighs. "Right on down."

She usually closed her eyes after she'd climbed on because the sensations overwhelmed, but she wanted to sear the view into her memory. Bruce's look of indolent satisfaction as his hands steered her hips. Raleigh's knowing smirk as he threaded his fingers through Bruce's thick hair and watched the place where she and Bruce connected.

She could get used to that view of two.

Finally, she did close her eyes because Bruce had found a pocket of energy to tap into. He met every one of her punishing squeezes with a thrust—a sort of erotic call and response made fortissimo by the injection of Raleigh's hand. His fingertips skated around her distended nipples, pinched and tugged until she crested with a shout.

"Thank fuck," Bruce muttered. He slammed her down on him as far as she could go. Once. Twice. Again, and then he lifted her. A reflex, perhaps. He held her hovering over his cock.

Her arms strained to hold her weight over him, and she wondered why she even bothered.

She collapsed on him and Raleigh, by extension, and they lay there, breathing, recovering, touching.

"That's how it should be," Bruce said several drowsy minutes later. "That's how it should always be."

Everley couldn't have agreed more.

Epilogue

"You drive like my nan." Bruce didn't care if he looked petulant. He folded his arms over his chest and tapped his foot against Stacia's porch floor with impatience.

Raleigh gave him a bored look and reached for the storm door handle. "Your nan drove through the night at seventy-five miles per hour on one of the busiest roads in the country?"

Stacia's front door was evidently unlocked. Raleigh pushed it in and guided Bruce inside.

"I take it back," Bruce said. "Nan would have driven faster, but she would have needed to avail herself of the facilities every forty-five minutes or so. Tiny bladder. Could never get anywhere on time."

"Coming from a man who hasn't driven a mile since he's left Scotland, I hardly feel the urge to change my habits."

"I *could* drive here."

Stacia walked past the front door, handed coffee to both of them, and retreated back from where she'd come, snickering.

Bruce had gotten used to it. For whatever reason, Stacia's insults rarely landed very harshly.

"So do it," Raleigh said.

"I will," Bruce murmured with his lips against his coffee mug.

"No you won't."

Bruce shrugged and headed toward the kitchen. He'd only been to Stacia's house once before—the weekend of a book release back in late winter—but he thought he remembered the layout.

And he was following the guidance his nose gave him. He smelled sausage and eggs. He'd been too wired to eat for a day, so he needed hot food to immediately get in his belly.

Plus, Everley's voice was in there. He'd follow that voice anywhere.

"You're right, I won't. All that lane changing and merging into traffic stresses me out." Bruce crossed the threshold, did a rapid scan of the room, and found Everley at the stove stirring something in a big pot.

"I was wondering when you two would show up."

Somehow, he managed to enfold her into a crushing hug without spilling his coffee. His Ev. He'd missed her. He didn't like how she was always gone, but there was nothing to do for it. Things would sort out eventually. "Raleigh couldn't leave the office until eight, and then he hadn't packed anything. Took him two hours."

Raleigh sidled up to the stove, assessed the knots Bruce and Everley had wound themselves into, and opted to just put his arms around both.

That suited Bruce fine, anyway.

"Your father is a raging jackass," Raleigh said. He planted a kiss on the top of Everley's head, looked in the pot, shrugged, and then turned to the room. "Hey, Adrien. Hey, Dara."

Oh.

Sheepishly, Bruce turned and waved to the couple. He'd known there were bodies in the room beyond Stacia's, but his mind had been on a singular track and he'd been craving Everley.

She spent most of her week working with Lisa and went into the city for long weekends, or else Raleigh and Bruce would go to her. It wasn't enough, but after being miserable for so long, they all thought it was crucial that Everley like her work.

She did.

They'd manage.

According to Raleigh, there wasn't anything unusual about her commuting situation, but usually it was men doing all the back-and-forth.

"What did my father do?" Everley asked, groaning. She resumed her stirring.

Bruce couldn't discern what was in the pot. It looked like some kind of porridge, but he wasn't usually up in time for breakfast unless he had a meeting. Raleigh shook him out of bed for those.

"You shouldn't have told him we were still dating."

"I had to. That was the only way I could get him off my ass. True love would be the only reason he'd accept for me leaving the company. Even he knows how sketchy our relationship would look if I were still there."

"Yes, well, now he's holding out hope that you'll return some day. He keeps inviting me to lunch. I keep refusing."

"Isn't that risky?" Dara asked, but immediately waved off the query. "Oh. Never mind. I forgot for a moment that you were attached to Stacia. No one in their right mind would disrupt that partnership."

"I'm a model employee." Raleigh took a slow sip of

hot coffee. "Everyone knows it. I'm not getting myself tangled up with her father any more than I have to. Part of the reason I got out of the office so late last night was because Joey called an all-hands PR meeting about the Outward Reaction book. Needed to get promo kits out. I was up to my elbows in packing peanuts and signed swag, and in rolls Shannon. Because I'm an asshole of the same par, I made eye contact with him. I guess he took that as a challenge."

Everley groaned and lifted the pot off the burner. "Please don't have a pissing contest with my father."

"Too late."

"Raleigh."

"He started it." Unchastened, Raleigh took another sip. "He said your mother was expecting you home for Easter."

Everley's brows darted up and she scoffed loudly. "*What*? My mother doesn't do Easter at home. She goes to her cousins' and I imagine that's where she is now."

"Yes, sweetheart, I know that, and suffice it to say that he now knows that I know that. I was perfectly calm until he said something about you living beneath yourself. I can't be responsible for what I said after that."

"Oh, hell," Stacia murmured. "What'd you say?"

"When I say I can't be responsible, I mean I can't remember. I kept on taping up a box as though he hadn't just subtly offended me. Whatever I said in response must have been rather acid because I looked up to see his face turning red and him storming off. Then Joey trundled over to lecture the shit out of me about respectability and all that bullshit, as though he really cares."

"He has to go through the motions," Adrien said.

"Exactly. He didn't want to be there any more than I did, but there we were. Being team players and such."

"I'm sure the band will make it up to you once the book starts hitting lists," Bruce said. He did feel a little bad about Raleigh getting roped into the project, but at the same time, he was pleased they could commiserate about it. Reviewers had already gotten their hands on it and there were extracts flying about with details of Bruce's retelling of how Outward Reaction originated. Bruce was getting lots of nasty feedback from the band, as they hadn't seen those sections before the book went to print. They hadn't seen the full documentary, either, until the recent screening. They hadn't liked that, either.

In spite of how uncomfortable the attention made him, Bruce was glad the mystery had been defused and he did his small part in breaking the stigma of atypicality. Even his parents had accepted that it was for the best.

Arnold thought that Bruce could very well turn out to be some kid's hero one day, and Bruce thought that was all right.

"Last money they'll get out of you, right?" Adrien asked.

"If I have my say, yes. Thank you for having your agent send over that referral, by the way. I hate having to interview people."

"Hey. I get it. I hope your new management is a better fit for you, though. I learned that lesson early on—the first person to offer isn't always the best person to represent you, or the one who'll grow the best with you."

"My last one very nearly talked me into giving him a second chance. I thought he was sounding reasonable.

However, Raleigh has ears like a wolfhound, took the phone from me, and hung up on him."

Stacia grinned. "He hangs up on people for me, too."

"If I ever decide to leave book publicity behind, I'm glad to know I'll have a fallback job as a call ender," Raleigh said. "I refined my skills hanging up on my father. That's why I still have a landline phone—so I can have the satisfaction of hearing the plastic slam."

"We envy you and Adrien for your families," Everley said on a dramatic sigh to Stacia. "They're so lovely."

"And the rest of us do the best we can," Dara said softly. "We make our own sort of families. I don't feel sorry for myself anymore."

Bruce certainly didn't, either. He didn't expect an overnight miracle with his relatives and would probably always hold some grudges, but at least they were trying in small ways, and they understood he couldn't be fixed and that he didn't actually need to be.

"What's in the pot?" Raleigh asked Everley.

She had a big ladle and a smile on her face. "Grits."

Raleigh scrunched his nose. "What?"

"Grits. Stacia said you once stated you either needed a husband, a wife, or a decent bowl of grits. As luck would have it, you're probably not going to get either of those first two things, but I can offer you silky grits."

"You told her that?" There might have been annoyance laced through Raleigh's tone, but the telltale start of a grin twitched at the corner of his mouth.

Stacia shrugged. "If you'd gotten here sooner, maybe I wouldn't have. Expect me to entertain your guests and I'm going to run my mouth."

"Fair." He took the bowl Everley offered and a spoon and dug in.

Bruce had no idea what a grit was or why anyone would want to eat something so unfortunately named, but he took a bowl of whatever they were, too, and sat next to Raleigh at the island.

He looked around, pleased at the people he'd collected, who he could count on to listen even if they didn't understand. He hadn't understood how gratifying that was until he'd gotten it back.

Everley squeezed in between the two of them and draped her arms around their necks. "So?"

"Not a single lump," Raleigh said brightly.

"Good. Maybe I can add cook to my list of titles at the Burnout."

"So that means you'll never go home?" Bruce asked, glumly.

"I'm just kidding." She gave him a hearty squeeze and a kiss on the cheek before abandoning him for her pot. "Lisa won some kind of local business development grant that'll infuse a heap of cash into the venture. Has to be used on local hires, though. By the end of the summer, she'll have her staffing situation sorted out and I'll be able to work remotely. I'll be back in the city full time."

"Am I awful for being impatient?"

"No," Dara said. "If you love people and they make you feel safe, you want them around you. I don't think that's unreasonable."

"That's right. I find it incredibly flattering that someone loves me that much," Everley said.

"You're easy to love, Ev." Bruce loved watching her blush.

Raleigh was focusing on his grits, smiling gently,

adding nothing to the brew of conversation even as they picked up elsewhere in the room.

Bruce gave his foot a gentle tap with his own. He was always demanding attention, but Raleigh was used to that. "Compliment me so I won't feel awful for being needy," he whispered.

Raleigh set down his spoon, twined his fingers together atop the counter, and stared in the general direction of the backsplash.

"I don't have a compliment for you right now," Raleigh said. "I'm too tired. Brain's not cooperating."

"Oh."

"But I love you, maybe because you are demanding and you picked me."

"Maybe my supposed genius in music carries over every now and then to other things. I mean, look." Bruce gestured to Everley who was in the midst of what appeared to be a heated discussion with the Vallieres about sugar in grits. He couldn't tell which side of the debate she was on, but he loved seeing her happy, talking, *arguing* even. Being included. Just like him.

"We'll do, right? Tell me we will, because I'm happy for the first time in a decade and I don't want that to stop."

"We'll *do*." Raleigh dragged Bruce's stool closer so they were shoulder to shoulder. A bit of touch always helped, because Raleigh's touches were always promises. When Everley tried to track past toward parts unknown, Raleigh grabbed her by the hand and pulled her back. "Won't we do, Everley?"

"Who said we wouldn't?"

"Bruce needed a reminder."

"I get it." Everley grabbed his face and kissed him

fiercely until he couldn't think, couldn't fret. "Sometimes, I worry, too," she said against his lips when they pulled away to breathe. "You're not used to having what you need, and so it feels like a fleeting thing when you finally get it. But I'm not going anywhere. Neither is Raleigh. This is for us, too. Of course we'll do."

"I believe you."

And he meant it.

And he didn't feel bad that he'd probably need more reminding, because it always came with kisses.

* * * * *

Reviews are an invaluable tool when it comes to spreading the word about great reads. Please consider leaving an honest review for this or any of Carina Press's other titles that you've read on your favorite retailer or review site.

To find out about other books by Holley Trent or to sign up for her newsletter, visit her at www.holleytrent.com.

About the Author

Holley Trent is an award-winning and bestselling author of contemporary and paranormal romance. As a lifelong people watcher, she loves to create story worlds that mirror real world conflicts but have guaranteed happily-ever-afters. Her favorite question is "What if?" followed closely by "Well, why not?"

She was born in New York City, raised in the sticks of North Carolina, and now resides on the Colorado Front Range with her husband, two kids, and two elderly cats.

She's an avid gardener, a competent knitter, and a frustrated high-elevation baker.

She's been known to write a book on a dare. (Not this one, though.)

Connect with her online at www.holleytrent.com, where you can subscribe to her newsletters, and also on Twitter at www.twitter.com/holleytrent, Facebook at www.facebook.com/writerholleytrent, or Instagram at www.instagram.com/holleysees.

Chapter One

Stacia Leonard pulled her lips into a tight smile. She nudged the signed hardcover copy of her book across the electric-blue tablecloth printed with her publisher's insignia. Athena Publishing was big on branding. They probably would have tried to put a brand mark on *her* if her contract allowed it.

"I hope your aunt enjoys it," she said to the fan whose eyes were a bit too open and grin a mite too manic.

"Oh, she will," he said. "I'll make sure of it."

"That so?" Stacia gave her publicist's foot a discreet kick under the table, and Raleigh immediately stood and gestured to the bookstore employee who was supposed to be managing the line. Apparently, she'd gotten distracted by a display full of kitschy, funny bookmarks and hadn't noticed that the guy in front of Stacia had already overstayed his welcome by about three minutes.

The line was winding down and Stacia needed to decompress. She'd become a writer because she was antisocial. That had backfired epically. Apparently, being a successful author meant she wasn't allowed to hide from the public. She was expected to *engage* and shit like that.

The employee finally got her head out of her ass

and whisked the fan with the stack of books to the gift-wrap table.

"Just two books left," Raleigh whispered. "Bet the manager has egg on his face now. He didn't want to stock your books before. He said woman-penned mysteries don't sell."

Stacia simply bobbed her eyebrows and then smiled at the young woman who passed one of the remaining books over to her. "Hi. Would you like me to personalize this for you?"

The lady clucked her tongue and shook her head. "Nah. It'll be worth more without my name in it, I think."

Stacia scribbled her signature on the title page and blew a little air across the slow-drying ink. "I think you overestimate my collectability."

"I don't think so. I know you don't do many appearances, so there aren't many of these signed books floating around. Ooh!" The lady snatched the last book just as the store manager entered the line with one hand extended toward the final volume. "That one, too. Just in case."

Stacia chuckled and signed that one as well. "There you go."

"Awesome. My book club friends aren't going to believe I saw you." She furrowed her brow and ignored the manager looming beside her, clearing his throat. "You know, you're smaller than I imagined."

Stacia shrugged. "I get that a lot. According to my genetic genealogy test I'm half leprechaun. I'm not going to be breaking any backboards in this lifetime. I'm really good at getting under a limbo pole, though."

The lady snickered as she walked toward the line

exit. "Ah, that's why I love you. You got a way with words."

"Just think, my eleventh grade English teacher said sarcasm was a mental illness," Stacia said to Raleigh. "Sometimes, I think she was right."

Raleigh plucked some invisible lint off his necktie and smiled like the cat that got into the cream. "Sarcasm is your brand, and your brand sells pretty nice, doesn't it?" He cut his hazel gaze to the store manager, who rocked on his heels with his hands jammed into the pockets of his pleated khakis.

"So I stand corrected," the manager said in an undertone. "Any chance you'll still be in town in four days? I put in an order for the other eight books in the series. I hoped you'd sign a few for us to shelve."

Stacia opened her mouth, but before she could get a word out, Raleigh said, "No way of knowing. If we're lucky, Stacia will be home in four days working on book ten. If the studio guys want to quibble over creative license, we may be here longer."

"When's the TV show supposed to debut?"

"In the spring if the schedule doesn't get botched."

"Maybe we could do the launch party here."

"Maybe," Raleigh demurred, drawing out the "a" in the word for a few seconds too long. He turned to Stacia and pointed to the phone in his hand. "Gonna go see if the driver's nearby."

"Okay. I'll wait outside." She bent to grab her tote from under the table.

"No need to rush away," the manager said. "I thought maybe we could set up some events before you left."

"Raleigh will take care of that." She slung the strap of her bag over her shoulder and put a smile on her face before she stood. "And I really need to go outside. The air conditioning in here is going to trigger a fit of narcolepsy."

"Yeah, it is a little bit aggressive. I keep meaning to get that fixed."

"Uh-huh." Stacia pulled up the hood of her cashmere sweater and pushed her sunglasses onto her ears as she stepped outside into the bright Los Angeles evening.

She leaned against the pergola support and rooted her phone out of her bag. No messages, but she hadn't expected any. Her friends knew she never responded. They went months without speaking and then they'd catch up with hours-long phone calls that would fill up her social well for the rest of the year. There were eighty-seven Twitter mentions, which she'd let her assistant deal with, and a bunch of buzz on her Facebook fan page. She ignored that. Last, she scrolled through the bunch of notifications from an Instagram picture Raleigh had posted of her early in the signing. Most comments were permutations of "Wish I was in LA!" Her perusing of her direct messages, however, brought her up short. There was an unexpected and familiar name mixed in with the handles of so many strangers.

ADRIENVALL: you're in LA?

It wasn't the message that took her off guard. After all, the words weren't so different from all the rest. What made her heart stutter was the name and the familiar headshot in the avatar.

Adrien Valliere was the face of the fictional potential love interest in her book series. The leading man, Detective Pierce Holloway, was introduced in book one as a background player. He became a powerful secondary character in book four and a coprotagonist in book five.

On the cover of book five, for the first time, Adrien had appeared with the model portraying the plucky heroine, Jennifer Daughtry. Fans had nearly rioted when early art was leaked and they saw that he wasn't on the cover of book six. The publishing house's design team had to go on a frenzied, last-minute quest for Adrien Valliere stock art and had managed to dig up one more image that hadn't already been used on a bazillion book covers. The cover had been *beautiful*, which was an odd thing to say about a guy photoshopped to hold a bloody hand mirror.

At that time, no one knew his name or how to find him for a custom photoshoot for the next books. He may as well have been a ghost. The photographer holding the copyrights to the images hadn't responded to queries. The team had to do a hard pivot with the art direction, but the timing had worked out well. Cover looks were trending toward more abstract feels. No people, just a lot of stylistic blood splatter and some props. By then, it didn't matter if Adrien was on the cover or not. When people thought about Pierce Holloway, they thought of him with Adrien's face.

Him finally connecting with Stacia on social media after book seven hit the shelves, though, had apparently ignited an afternoon of mayhem at Athena's art department. He looked even more like Pierce than he had when he'd posed for those stock photos eight years prior.

"Oh, *shit*," Stacia whispered.

She'd never actually had a conversation with the guy. She followed him back because that was easier than stalking his account every day for new candids—the guy was amazingly pretty. She imagined that he'd followed her in the first place because he was in the image business, and she had a little name recognition.

She dragged her tongue across suddenly dry lips and tapped the reply field to activate it.

Mostly, she didn't respond or she'd let her assistant answer any reasonable questions. Ignoring the guy whose face had probably launched her books to the *New York Times* bestseller list for twenty weeks straight seemed extraordinarily snobbish.

"Oh, shit," she repeated, then input a response.

For a few days.

Seemed friendly, in her opinion, but not *too* friendly.

She hit the post button, then scrolled through all the new pictures from fellow author friends. Mostly pictures of their cats.

One new picture of Adrien. Ultra-close-up of a brand new ring of sickly looking blue and black bruising around his bright gray eye.

Stacia gasped and clutched her chest as she read the caption.

wife is playing with special fx makeup. how does it look?

"Dammit." She let out the breath she'd been holding and closed the app.

She wasn't sure what it was about him that was so unmooring for her. Every single time he appeared on her screen, her heart rate kicked up. She felt as though she needed to perform, somehow, and like she needed to for-real brush her hair and wear a grown-up bra. Maybe her feeling of discomfiting was because he was attached to a figment of her imagination. He wasn't supposed to be real. There she was, being so very ordinary, and yet writing about people who were too perfect to exist in real life. Her ex had groaned about that all the time. *You don't think this guy is a little bit unbelievable, Stacia? Is that how you think men should be? I'd tone it down if I were you. Make it realer.*

She hadn't, and Oren wasn't around anymore to editorialize on what was desirable.

Her characters were superheroes, really, and one had just slid into her DMs.

Another DM notification alert lit up as Raleigh stepped outside holding his phone to his ear.

She was glad for the distraction. If that was Adrien responding, she couldn't imagine what he might want and was afraid it was something mercenary. There were so many damned con artists in the business and she'd been propositioned by nearly every sort.

"Driver is a few blocks from here," Raleigh said. "Hit a bottleneck, but he'll be here in a jiffy."

"Cool. Hope you don't mind if I forego dinner and go straight to the hotel. It's six here but nine on the east coast. I'm ready to fall over."

"If that's what you want." He muttered, "Party pooper."

"True." Stacia tapped her phone screen for the message. It *was* from Adrien.

"Oh, shit," she whispered yet again.

wife says to ask-do you have free time? photo opp.

"Ah."

That query wasn't weird or scammy. Bold, maybe, but being in his business, he probably had to be.

"What, *ah*?" Raleigh asked.

"This would totally make Oren flip his lid if he ever sees it. Remember how he used to disparagingly call Adrien Valliere 'Mr. Faultless'?"

"Oren wouldn't know his mouth from his asshole, and he deserves a burial beneath a pyramid of rhino shit. But what is it that he might see that'd set him off?"

She wasn't going to argue with him about Oren. The two had immediately clashed at first meeting. She and Oren had broken up a year ago and she didn't want to set Raleigh off on another of his rants. At least, not in public. She fell into cyclical slumps about the things Oren had accused her of, however. She'd probably need to hear another of Raleigh's "fuck that dude" sermons sooner than later.

"Adrien wants a picture with me," she said. "Or me with him. Probably the latter."

"What's the difference?"

"Depends on who draws the eye. The guy with the perfect face gets my bet. I'd just be a prop." A five-foot-tall prop with dopey hipster glasses because she'd lost a contact lens somewhere in Richmond International and her backup lenses were in the suitcase that hadn't caught up to her yet. She'd left her assistant to get her luggage from baggage claim, and apparently there'd been a delay.

"Tell him 'fuck yeah,'" Raleigh said. "I'll take the pictures myself. The first one I send will be to that trollop who shares an office wall with me." He bared his teeth and stuffed his phone into his suede messenger bag. "That scheming bitch."

"What's wrong with her? And are you really worried? You're the one with all the high-profile authors."

"I just don't like her. I can feel it in my bones, she's got that upstart gene. The moment I turn my back, she's gonna start reaching out to my authors to ask if there's anything *else* they need while I'm busy with you."

"I think you're paranoid, Ral."

"The pot calls the kettle black. How rich."

Stacia shrugged and hovered her thumbs over her phone screen. "I'm upfront about my neuroses."

In fact, she was generally so paranoid about people's intentions, that if Adrien had been anyone else, she would have told him to shoot a message to her assistant. Adrien wasn't just another fan. He was part of the reason her mortgage had been paid off at the age of twenty-eight. That, and the fact she'd been writing two doorstopper novels per year since she got laid off from her first newspaper job right out of college.

She typed, Send me a text when you're free and tapped in her digits.

Ice dropped into her gut right after she hit Send.

She didn't give out her real number. Her parents had it. Her brother had it. Her closest friends had it. And of course, Athena had it, but only Raleigh ever called her.

She'd dropped her last number after Oren had moved on. She'd gotten tired of the You see, it's just that... texts from him.

He didn't need to explain in seventy different ways why he'd dumped her. One had been enough. He'd decided that he couldn't compete with her career and her "fake paper people."

It'd been a year since he'd left, but she didn't really try to connect with people anymore. Partly, she was busy. Partly, she worried that Oren was right that her priorities were upside-down. She wasn't an easy person to be with, and he certainly hadn't been the first to tell her that.

As the hired car pulled up to the curb, her phone vibrated from the incoming text message from a number she didn't recognize.

how about now? They'd included an embarrassed emoji. i keep weird hours. don't want to miss you.

"Adrien," she whispered. "Now?"

Raleigh was holding the back door open and gesturing for her to get in.

She scooted in and to the left door, and tapped in, Heading to hotel now.

can be downtown in thirty minutes. meet you somewhere?

She chewed on the inside of her cheek and pondered her options. If Raleigh were involved, the encounter would turn into a big to-do, and incredibly awkward, and Stacia was too tired for added awkwardness. Meeting at some darkish bar for drinks to loosen up her dorky ass and then a few quick selfies was just about her limit. She didn't really know how to be social outside of publisher events anymore, except with Raleigh, and he didn't count. He only pretended to be a people person when there was a paycheck involved, and he was very good at pretending.

Adrien texted, can drive you to hotel afterward if u want. won't keep you long.

Those were her magic words—the promise of brevity. He was making it hard for her to find a reason to say no, and, if she had to be honest with herself, she didn't want to say no. Beyond the fact that the opportunity was one that shouldn't have been ignored, she wanted to squash that nervous energy she felt every time she saw his picture.

Fictional character. Real person. Same face.

Tell me where, she sent.

He relayed a street address, which she quickly input into her map app. The location was about a ten-minute walk from the hotel.

She texted, Make it forty minutes in case there's a delay with hotel check-in.

She cut a side-eye to Raleigh to see if he was watching her.

He was busy looking out the window at a fender bender to their right and shouting into his own phone, probably at his assistant.

And I need to get rid of a headache, she added to the message.

c u in 40.

She tucked her phone into her tote and cleared her throat right as Raleigh disconnected his call.

"Do I have to do *everything* myself?" he groused. "Sheesh. Seems like I can't even leave the office."

"You know what?" she said. "Take a break tonight. I'll get out to the photo op on my own."

"No way."

"Yes way. I don't need to be babysat. I'm a grown woman who's been making her own way since seventeen. I can certainly get from the hotel to the restaurant and back."

Raleigh narrowed his eyes.

"What?"

"You're going to flake, aren't you? You're going to your room to…hmm, what was that last lie you told me?" He tapped his chin contemplatively, and then snapped his fingers. "Oh, yes. You're going to brush your teeth, and then I won't hear from you again until you're due at the next meeting tomorrow morning."

"I'm not going to flake."

"Don't piss in my pond, girlie. Meet and greets are my bailiwick."

"Yes, but your bailiwick is also making five-minute meetings turn into three-hour-long soirees. I don't have the endurance tonight."

If Raleigh narrowed his eyes any more, his upper and lower eyelashes would knit.

"I'll behave," she insisted.

"Writers make the best liars. I don't believe you."

"I'll send you the picture first thing."

"Smile in it or I'm coming there."

"Jeez." Had Raleigh been a reasonable person, she would have thought he was joking, but the scene was playing out in her head like a clip from an old silent film, and Raleigh was the overly flamboyant villain.

Minus the cape.

She shuddered, and spat, "Fine. Tiny smile. No teeth. Too late for teeth."

"Nine eastern is too late for teeth?"

"It is when you make a habit of going to bed at nine thirty."

Really, it was probably a good thing she was single. She'd become such a bore.

Don't miss
Writing Her In *by Holley Trent,*
Available now wherever
Carina Press ebooks are sold.
www.CarinaPress.com